QUEENSLAYER

THE SPELLSLINGER SERIES

SPELLSLINGER
SHADOWBLACK
CHARMCASTER
SOULBINDER
QUEENSLAYER

Look out for

CROWNBREAKER

Coming in October 2019

QUEENSLAYER

SEBASTIEN DE CASTELL

HOT
KEY
BOOKS

First published in Great Britain in 2019 by
HOT KEY BOOKS
80–81 Wimpole St, London W1G 9RE
www.hotkeybooks.com

A CIP catalogue record for this book is available from the British Library.

HARDBACK ISBN: 978-1-4714-0546-4
TRADE PAPERBACK ISBN: 978-1-4714-0817-5
also available as an ebook

1

Typeset by Palimpsest Book Production Ltd, Falkirk, Stirlingshire

Printed and bound by Clays Ltd, Elcograf S.p.A.

Hot Key Books is an imprint of Bonnier Books UK
www.bonnierbooks.co.uk

For Eric Torin,
Spellslinger's been a long and wonderful journey,
but I never would've had the courage to begin
had you not walked those first miles with me.

OUTLAW
OF
TEARS

The world's seen plenty of old hermits, but it's never seen an old outlaw. The hermit and the outlaw both forego the companionship of their fellow human beings, but only the outlaw lives with fear for a companion, the never-ending gnawing at the soul warning that someday a noose will find your neck. Makes no difference how careful you are, nor how clever. After too many cold nights away from the friendly hearth of civilisation, you get tired of being hunted by your own kind. You get mean. You get sloppy. And real soon after that?

You get dead.

1

Snow and Copper

Shush, shush, shush, whispered the silvery snow, as soothing as a man clamping his hand over your mouth as he sticks a knife in your back in the middle of a crowded street. There were seven of us in this particular crowd, shivering on the frigid plateau high up in the border mountains. Merrell of Betrian, the man I'd come to kill, cowered behind Arc'aeon, the war mage he'd hired to kill me first. A few yards away stood two bored Daroman marshals who'd graciously offered to oversee our duel (which is to say, threatened to arrest us unless we paid the overseeing fee). That just left the tall, graceful eagle that was Arc'aeon's familiar and the short, nasty squirrel cat who passed for mine. Oh, and me, of course.

'You're gonna get it now, Kellen!' Merrell hooted at me from across the fifty-yard stretch of snow-dusted ground separating us. 'Arc'aeon here's a proper ember mage. Ain't no fool, neither, so your spellslinger tricks ain't gonna work on him.'

'Yeah, you're right, Merrell,' I shouted back. 'My tricks only work on fools.'

Merrell swore, Arc'aeon smirked and the two marshals chuckled. Neither the bird nor the squirrel cat paid any attention. They were focused on each other. Me, I was thinking that maybe Merrell wasn't the biggest sucker shuffling about trying to keep his toes from freezing off.

I thought I'd been running him down, racing to keep him from crossing the border into the Zhuban territories where he knew I wouldn't follow. I thought I'd been chasing after a dumb, pug-ugly wife beater who'd tried to cheat me at cards. Turns out that was all wrong.

Merrell was a lot wealthier than he'd let on. He was also a lot better connected, because however much money he had, hiring a full-on war mage couldn't have been easy. My people usually shun contract work from repugnant borderland hicks.

Looking at Arc'aeon, on the other hand, was like staring into a distorted mirror of myself. I was a few days shy of my eighteenth birthday and unlikely to see twenty. Arc'aeon looked to be in his early thirties, already the head of a notable Jan'Tep house, with wealth, power and a long, glorious future in front of him. My hair is what's politely referred to as 'manure coloured'; his gleamed in the morning sunlight like it was spun from strands of platinum and gold. I was scrawny from hard living and a life on the run; he had the muscular build of a soldier.

'I like your armour,' I shouted across the swirling patch of snow that lay between us. Shining form-fitting plates linked by bands of silk thread protected his chest, arms and legs. 'It's very . . . golden. Matches your bird.'

'Shadea is an eagle, boy,' he corrected me, smiling up at the hunter flying in lazy circles through the air like a buzzard anticipating his next meal. 'A bird is something that flitters around before you shoot it for dinner. An eagle makes a meal of you.'

He pointed absently towards me. I didn't have any armour – just my leather coat and riding chaps to keep myself from getting scraped to bits every time I fell off my horse. 'I like your hat,' he said, nodding at the Daroman frontier hat I wore to keep the sun off the black marks that wound around my left eye. 'Those silver glyphs on the brim are . . . cute. Do they do anything?'

I shrugged. 'The man I stole the hat from said they'd bring me luck.'

Arc'aeon smiled again. 'Then he overcharged you. This fool has paid me rather a lot of money to end you, Kellen of the House of Ke, but I would have done it for free had I known you were shadowblack. I'm going to send a bolt of lightning straight through that filthy left eye of yours.'

The bird . . . *eagle*, rather, let out a caw for emphasis, as if it understood the conversation. 'You think the bird knows . . .' I began.

'Of course he knows what you're saying,' Reichis chittered in reply, then added, '*Idjit.*' The squirrel cat meant to say 'idiot', but we'd been travelling the borderlands for a few months, and he'd taken to talking like a gap-toothed sheep herder. 'The eagle's his familiar. Whatever that skinbag mage hears, the bird hears.'

I glanced down at Reichis. He looked a little ridiculous holding his paw just above his eyes to shield them from the harsh sunlight reflecting off the snow and ice so he could scowl at the mage's eagle. If you've never seen a squirrel cat before, imagine some drunken god had gifted a slightly tubby two-foot-tall cat with a big bushy tail and furry flaps that ran between its front and back legs, enabling it to glide down from treetops and sink its claws and teeth into its chosen prey – which is pretty much everything that moves. Oh, and then that same deity had given his creation the temperament of a thief. And a blackmailer. And probably on more than one occasion a murderer.

'I bet that guy's eagle doesn't call him "idjit",' I said.

Reichis looked up at me. 'Yeah, well, that's probably because I'm not your familiar, I'm your business partner. *Idjit.*'

'You think that's going to make a difference in about five minutes when the marshals tell us to draw and that eagle snatches you up and rips out your entrails?'

'Point,' Reichis said. He patted me on the leg. 'All right, so you're a genius, kid. Now blow this guy away so we can eat that ugly bird of his for supper. I call both eyeballs.'

I let my hands drift down to the powder holsters at my sides. It had cost a small fortune to convince a leather-smith to make them for me, but they let me pull powder faster than my old pouches, and when you're duelling a war mage, even a fraction of a second can mean the difference between life and death. Merrell nearly fell on his arse and the two marshals instantly had their crossbows trained on me in case I was about to cheat the duel, but Arc'aeon ignored the gesture entirely.

'He ain't afraid of you blasting him,' Reichis said. Well, he doesn't speak exactly – he makes squirrel cat noises – but the nature of our relationship is such that I hear them as words.

'Right,' I said. 'Intransigent charm shield?'

'Gotta be.'

I peered across the gap between us and the ember mage. I couldn't see anything on the ground. I'd picked this spot intentionally because it's pretty damned hard to keep a circle intact when the only thing to draw it in is ice and snow. I couldn't see markings, so that left only one logical possibility.

'Say, fellas? You all mind if we move just a few feet to the right? I've got the sun in my eyes here. Can't have an unfair duel, right?'

The older of the two marshals, Harrex I think his name was, shrugged his bony shoulders and nodded towards Arc'aeon. The mage just smiled back and shook his head. His eagle did a little dive towards us and turned up just a few feet away from my face.

'They got here early and laid down copper sigil wire under the snow, then poured water on it and waited for it to turn to ice,' I said to Reichis. 'Guess you were right that we should've camped out here last night.'

'Idjit.'

Harrex held up a miniature sundial. 'Well, gentlemen, I reckon we're just about there. In a minute it'll be mid-morning and Marshal Parsus here will start the countdown from seven. You both know the rules after that?'

'Kill the other guy?' I offered.

Reichis glared up at me. 'That your plan? Crack jokes until that mage can't blast us on account of he's laughing too hard to speak the incantations?'

'Might be our best shot. No way am I going to be able to blast through that shield.'

'So what do we do?'

I looked over at Arc'aeon and watched the smile on his face widen as he stood there, calm as could be, waiting for the duel to begin.

'Seven!' Marshal Parsus shouted out.

I looked down into Reichis's beady squirrel cat eyes. 'How about we switch dance partners?' I suggested.

'Six!'

'You're saying I get the mage?' Squirrel cats don't usually

9

smile, but Reichis had a big nasty grin on his fuzzy little face. He might be greedy, he might be a liar, a thief and a blackmailer, but the little bugger loves nothing more than a knock-down, drag-out fight. A few months ago he got himself the same shadowblack curse around his left eye that I have around mine. It hadn't improved his disposition any.

'Five!'

'Don't screw around, Reichis. You know what to do.'

'Four!'

Reichis gave a little shake. His fur changed colour from its usual mean-spirited brown with black stripes to pure white, making him almost invisible against the thick carpet of snow. I flipped up the metal clasps on my holsters to open the flaps.

'Three!'

Arc'aeon brought the fingers of both his hands together in a steeple shape. I knew the somatic form, even if I couldn't cast the spell myself. I winced at the thought of what it would do when it hit me.

'Two!'

Arc'aeon winked at me. The eagle pulled around from his last circle to get ready to dive after Reichis. The squirrel cat got down on all fours and pressed his back feet against the snow, digging in for leverage.

'One . . .' Parsus said, a little too much enthusiasm in his voice for my taste.

Observers of such things will note that there are usually only two ways to lose a duel: end up on your knees begging for mercy, or on your back waiting for the falling snow to cover your corpse.

'Begin!'

I was about to discover a third option that was even worse.

2

Fire and Lightning

The first tiny blue sparks of lightning materialised around Arc'aeon's fingers just as the eagle began a downward dive to kill Reichis. I could almost taste the ember magic in the air that preceded the bolt and I prayed that Arc'aeon was just arrogant enough to want to follow through with his earlier threat. I dropped to the ground, already jamming my hands into the holsters at my side, forefingers snatching a pinch of the red and black powders that awaited there. I watched the lighting bolt tear past where an instant ago it would've struck my left eye. This guy had good aim.

Reichis was kicking up a miniature snowstorm behind him as he raced towards Arc'aeon, screaming all the while, 'Die, you stupid pigeon!'

The eagle's talons were reaching for the squirrel cat's hide when I threw the powders up in the air in front of me as my right shoulder hit the ground. Inert and innocent as babes on their own, the two powders had a hatred for each other that created a monstrous explosion on contact. The magic's not in the blast, you see – that's just the effect of the powders themselves. The magic's in the hard part – guiding the explosion without blowing your hands and face off in the process.

My fingers formed the necessary somatic shape: bottom two pressed into the palm, the sign of restraint; fore and middle fingers pointed straight out, the sign of direction; and thumb pointing to the heavens, the sign of, well, somebody up there, help me.

'*Carath Toth*,' I said, uttering the two-word invocation. Only the first two syllables were needed, strictly speaking. Toth was the name of a particularly mean-spirited bounty hunter who'd tracked down Reichis and me a few weeks ago, declaring before an entire town that he'd be the one to finally put an end to me. Since my powder was now suffused with his blood, saying his name gave the spell a little extra kick.

A blast of red and black fire, the flames intertwined like snakes, followed the direction of my forefingers as they shot out at the eagle, leaving a haze of smoke in their wake. I missed the bird's heart, but got one of his wings. He went careening to the ground a few feet away from Reichis. The squirrel cat didn't stop to look though – just kept those little legs pounding towards his true target.

'Shadea!' the mage screamed, his hands unconsciously relinquishing the somatic shape for his next spell. *Hurts when your familiar gets hit, don't it?* I thought maliciously. I had nothing against the eagle, you understand, but he was trying to kill my business partner.

Arc'aeon aimed his second blast just as I was getting back to my feet, forcing me to drop again, this time flat on my stomach. I felt my hair stand up as the lightning passed just above my head. I wasn't going to be able to evade a third bolt.

Reichis bridged the gap between himself and the war mage. With a feral growl he leaped up into the air. Arc'aeon nearly fell back, despite the fact that there was no way the squirrel cat was going to be able to breach the shield. But the shield wasn't the target. The instant Reichis hit the ground he started digging ferociously, tearing through snow and ice to where the fragile circle of copper wire holding the spell must be buried.

Arc'aeon was just starting to figure it out when I fired another shot at his familiar.

'Carath Toth,' I murmured.

'No!' Arc'aeon screamed. He fired a different kind of spell this time, some kind of blessing or protection that enveloped the eagle and dissipated my blast into airy black smoke. *Nice trick*, I thought.

'Now!' Reichis growled at me.

I saw the crease in the snow where he'd been digging. That was my opening. But I wasn't in the right place to send a bolt through the hole in the shield.

'Damn it,' I said, as I got to my feet and ran towards Arc'aeon.

I saw him look down at the ground, his hands forming a new and ugly shape. His eyes went from the hole to Reichis before settling on me and aimed the spell at my chest. *Too soon, damn it, too soon.* I wasn't in line with the gap yet.

'Carath moron!' I shouted at the top of my lungs, aiming my fingers at Arc'aeon as if I'd really been casting the spell. The 'moron' part wasn't necessary, but when you're an outlaw with a price on your head, you take your fun wherever you can. Reflexively he changed the configuration of his fingers and formed a transient shield. A mistake, since I hadn't actually fired and his warding would only last a second without copper to anchor it. Arc'aeon's mouth went slack as he realised I'd tricked him. I was now in line with the gap in his shield.

13

With the opening in the shield now visible as a stuttering shimmer in the air, I whispered, '*Carath Toth*,' one last time. The powders slammed against each other before me. Aiming down the line of my fingers, I sent the explosion through the gap before Arc'aeon could get another warding spell up. The bolt took him in the dead centre of his belly and right through the decorative plating of his armour.

There was quiet then, as we waited for the last echoes of the explosion reverberating off the mountains to fade. For a few seconds the war mage remained standing, ignorant of the fact that his body now lacked the vital organs necessary for life. The blast had left a hole big enough for me to see right through him to where Merrell was cowering behind his champion. I walked towards him as the mage's body finally figured out what had happened and collapsed to the ground.

If that all sounds too easy, it wasn't.

Besides, we're still not at the part where I screwed everything up.

3

Blood and Silk

'Now, Kellen, don't you go doing somethin' we're both gonna wish you hadn't done . . .' Merrell pleaded. He turned to the two marshals, Harrex and Parsus. 'Don't let him get me!' he cried out. 'I'll pay you! I've got good money here, now that the mage is dead.'

The marshals gave Merrell stony looks. Trying to bribe the queen's marshals service? Not too bright. I suspect the only reason they didn't arrest him on the spot was because they knew I was about to make it a moot point.

'Don't you come no closer, Kellen!' Merrell had his hands clasped together in prayer, which was a waste of time. My people are too civilised to believe in gods. We worship our ancestors instead.

'Me?' I asked. 'I'm not planning on doing anything reckless, Merrell.'

I gave him just enough time to look relieved before I added, 'Now the squirrel cat, he's a mean little cuss, and I figure he's going to rip your face off while I eat me some breakfast.'

Ancestors. Now Reichis has me talking like a borderlands hillbilly.

'No! Wait! We can still make a deal. Everybody knows you're

lookin' for a cure for the shadowblack, right? Well, I got a guy.'

When it comes to snake oils and miracle cures, everybody's got a guy.

The snow crunched pleasantly under my boot heel as I took another step towards Merrell. I could still see the look on that girl's face when he . . . *No. Anger just makes you sloppy. Focus on the here and now.*

'I swear, Kellen! I got a guy! He can fix your shadowblack!'

Reichis was crouched down, ready to jump. He turned his puffed-up squirrel cat face towards me and I could already see what he thought of that idea. 'Don't fall for this crap again, idjit.'

The warning wasn't needed or wanted. I'd travelled two entire continents and spent every penny I could earn or steal searching for a remedy for the twisting black marks around my left eye. Only thing I ever got was constipation and a bad case of rose pimples that one time.

'What's this miracle worker's name?' I asked.

Merrell was either too smart to think I'd fall for his game or too stupid to come up with a fake name. It didn't matter though. He'd made me hesitate and that was enough. He reached behind his back and I caught a glimpse of steel just before he sent the knife whirling at me with an underhand throw. The blade took me square in the right shoulder and I went down like a sack of dirt. Reichis scrabbled up Merrell's body and went for his face, clawing a strip of flesh around his left eye socket that sent a trail of blood into the air. Then the squirrel cat went for his neck.

Merrell was screaming a good one as I got back to my feet, but then I saw him reach behind his back again.

16

'Reichis! He's got another knife!'

The squirrel cat ignored me. Bloodthirsty little monster.

I sprinted the few steps towards them, rubbing my fingertips together in hopes the feeling would come back so I could risk using the spell again. It was hopeless though – I'd used too much powder in my last shot and now my fingers were numb. If I tried again, I'd just blow my own hands off. I had a deck of razor-sharp steel throwing cards strapped to my right thigh, but those wouldn't do me any good with numb fingers and a knife stuck in my shoulder.

Merrell brought the blade around and tried to slash at Reichis, but the squirrel cat was savvy enough to drop off his chest and go after his leg. Merrell kicked him hard and the squirrel cat landed a few feet away. In a fit of rage, Merrell chased after him and brought his foot down like a hammer. Had Reichis not rolled away he'd've been crushed. Merrell was about to give it another try when I caught up with him. Whistling through my teeth as I presaged the pain, I ripped the knife out of my shoulder and used it to stab Merrell of Betrian through the neck. In the end, I think I screamed more than he did.

The two marshals waited patiently for Merrell to bleed out, then led their horses towards us. As part of the overseeing service, they always patch up the victor's wounds. The Daroman are civilised like that.

'You're bleeding pretty good there, fella,' Parsus said.

I looked at my shoulder and realised he was right. There was more blood than there should have been. The knife must've hit something important. Absently I grabbed the first cloth I saw from the side of the marshal's horse and pressed it against the wound to staunch the flow.

'Oh crap,' I heard Reichis mutter.

My gaze went from the squirrel cat to the two marshals. Parsus looked like he was about to go into shock. Harrex was pulling out his crossbow. That's when I realised what I'd just done.

I'd come a hundred and fifty miles to kill a man with no legal justification other than that he'd cheated me at cards. I'd killed a Jan'Tep mage in a duel, murdered his employer in cold blood and up until that exact moment . . . when I'd grabbed the red-and-white flag of Darome off that marshal's horse . . . I hadn't even committed a crime.

Funny thing about the empire: by their way of thinking, unless you're a foreign diplomat, the instant you cross into Daroman lands you become a *citavis teradi* – a territorial citizen. That dubious honour that comes with one or two minor legal protections and the sacred duty to defend the monarch. Unfortunately, I'd just soaked the queen's flag in blood, which was how you declared war against the Royal Family of Darome, the very definition of an act of treason. And I'd done it in front of two of the queen's own marshals.

I didn't have the strength for another spell, but I probably would've tried anyway if Parsus hadn't prudently hit me on the back of the head with his marshal's mace. As I went down the last thing I heard was Reichis's terrified, chittering voice.

'*Idjit.*'

4

Horses and Handcuffs

My first thought on waking up was that Reichis was dead. Well, that's a bit of a lie – my first thought was that someone must have vomited, because an acrid smell filled my nostrils. My second thought was that, since I could also taste it, the vomit had likely come from me. My third thought was that someone had strung me up over the side of a boat. But since the ocean below me appeared to be frozen, it was more likely I'd been tied to the side of my horse. The marshals had strapped me face down across the saddle and that's not a good position to be in when the thing under your stomach is trotting through the countryside. My fourth thought, I promise you, was that my partner was dead.

The marshals don't like wildcards and they don't take chances. Having seen Reichis go after the bird and then the mage, not to mention shredding Merrell's face, they'd have put him down rather than have him attack them when he realised I was being taken away. Poor little guy. I hoped he hadn't seen it coming.

Then I heard a noise that sounded like a grunt and the sound of laughing. *Ancestors*, I thought. *They're torturing him for kicks.*

'Bastards,' I said. At least he was still alive. Now I just had to find a way to free myself and rescue him. I twisted my neck uncomfortably to see what they were doing to the squirrel cat. I don't know quite what I was expecting to see, but it certainly wasn't the sight of the older man, Harrex, on his horse behind me, with Reichis lying with all four of his paws up as the marshal plopped bits of food into his mouth. The squirrel cat gave another little grunt, followed by a burp.

'Let me take him for a while,' Marshal Parsus called to his partner.

'You had him practically all the way from the border,' Harrex said. 'Besides, he's comfy as he is.' Then Harrex held another morsel of food a few inches from Reichis's muzzle. 'You're just a comfy fuzzy little bear, aren't ya?'

Reichis reached up with his little paws and plucked the food from Harrex's hand. This sent the marshal snorting with pleasure.

'Oh, you're a clever one, aren't ya, little fella?'

'Son of a bitch,' I muttered.

'What?' Reichis chittered. 'It's not like you'll feel any better if I'm on an empty stomach.'

This is probably a good time to mention that I'm fairly sure squirrel cats are a type of flying rat.

I tried to pull my hands free, intent on murder but not entirely sure who to start with. That's when I felt the Daroman handcuffs and realised – with the distant curiosity they say you experience just as the hangman drops the trap door below you – that I was screwed.

I don't know what it is about handcuffs that fascinates me. It's not the state of being bound, that's for sure. As a frequent, if involuntary, wearer, I promise you my experience is nothing like the erotic pictures you sometimes see decorating the walls of the second-floor stairs of full-service saloons.

The thing about handcuffs, though, is that they tell you a whole lot about the country you're in. Take the Zhuban, who live just north of where I'd been arrested. Now their handcuffs are really something: thick iron rings lined with sharp protrusions that provide steady, painful pressure against the nerves in your wrists. Anyone wearing the cuffs for more than a couple of hours experiences intense agony and frequently bleeds out from the cuts on their skin before they even meet their Zhuban advocate to prepare for trial. On the other hand, if you're smart, and you can handle a lot of pain, the blood from your wrists can be an effective lubricant in the process of escaping the cuffs.

That's the Zhuban people for you: they're cruel, fearless and not altogether bright. The instruments of torture that pass for Zhubanese handcuffs are what you get when you have a culture completely devoted to the idea that all of existence is governed by destiny. They figure that if you're in cuffs, whether guilty or not, you must've done something to annoy the universe and you deserve all the pain you get. On the other hand, anyone who breaks out of one of their jails is presumed to be innocent because, after all, it was their destiny to escape.

Now the Jan'Tep dislike using iron for anything. Magic is their game, or, I should technically say, *our* game, since I come from a Jan'Tep clan. Mages don't have much use for pure iron since it interferes with magic. Besides, they don't need anything as blunt as thick iron rings to keep a person bound. A pair of Jan'Tep binding loops are just thin copper wire inscribed with intricate little symbols. Binding loops have the insidious property of tightening the more you put pressure against them. So the more scared and frantic you get, the sooner you'll see your hands flop down to the floor, cut through by the sharp copper wire.

Nasty things. Unbreakable too, unless you happen to be a more powerful mage than the one who charmed the binding loops. Well, that's not entirely true – there is one trick that can get you out every time, but I'd rather keep that little secret to myself. Regardless, the Jan'Tep never bother asking the question: 'What if the person being bound is, in fact, a more powerful mage than the one who made the loops?' because, for the Jan'Tep, whoever is the better mage is almost certainly the better man, and thus if the prisoner escapes, he must not have deserved to be in cuffs in the first place. Which tells you pretty much everything you need to know about my people, my family and my life.

But the handcuffs that the marshals had put on me were Daroman in design. Daroman handcuffs are unlike those of the Zhuban or the Jan'Tep. Oh, don't get me wrong; they're strong like you wouldn't believe: a half-inch-thick band of Gitabrian steel connected by a chain you could waste a dozen serrated blacksmith's saws trying to cut through. But unlike the painful protrusions of the Zhubanese cuffs, or the wrist-cutting magic of the Jan'Tep, the inside of Daroman cuffs are thickly padded with silk. They're extremely comfortable. Soft as a courtier's winter glove, I swear.

This tells you a lot about the Daroman culture. For them, being an imperial people who over the past hundred years have come to dominate many of the smaller nations on the continent – including the Jan'Tep – the most important thing

22

is to be seen as trustworthy. The Daroman have a queer notion of justice compared to most people: they think you shouldn't be punished for a crime until you've been found guilty of committing it. It's a crazy way to think, but seems to have worked for them over the years.

By Daroman reckoning, if they do have to hold you in order to take you to trial, you should be, if not comfortable, then at least not in pain. Darome is nothing if not a civilised country. No wonder they've taken over half the continent and killed a good portion of the other half.

But the Daroman people are also incredibly practical: the silk padding inside the cuffs actually fits so tightly around your wrists that it makes escape impossible because it forms a perfect seal. Daroman cuffs, in addition to being the most comfortable shackles you'll ever encounter, are also the only ones that guarantee you'll never get out by yourself. That's why, when I say, I knew I was screwed the moment I felt the Daroman handcuffs around my wrists, I know what I'm talking about.

5

Unlucky Eights

'Y'need anything?' Marshal Parsus asked me, nudging his horse alongside mine.

'The key to these handcuffs would be nice.'

The slightly confused expression on his plain, freckled face was a testament both to his genial disposition and utter lack of any sense of humour. 'I was thinking more of some water or food,' he said.

Daroman marshals – they truly pride themselves on making sure their prisoners reach the gallows in perfect health. The thought of food, however, only brought on another wave of nausea. 'Just some water, thanks.'

He pulled out a leather flask and brought it to my lips. I had to turn my head sideways to catch the stream, giving the marshal a clear view of the shadowblack markings around my left eye.

'Those things hurt any?' he asked, tilting the flask a little closer to my mouth.

I swirled the water around a little before swallowing. 'They get cold when the sun shines on them. But other than that, not really.'

'Funny-looking thing.' He traced his finger in the air a few inches from my face. 'Kinda like three rings being eaten by vines.'

'I've heard worse descriptions.' Mostly having to do with parts of people's anatomy.

Parsus glanced back at Reichis, who was at that moment cooing – actually *cooing* like a damned pigeon – as he wheedled more treats out of Marshal Harrex. 'Your pet there's got the marks around his eye too. Are they . . . ?'

He let the question hang there. Six months ago, Reichis had gotten infected with the shadowblack thanks to a girl who thought she was doing me a favour. I guess she was, in a sense, because doing so had restored the bond between me and the squirrel cat. On the other hand, I was pretty sure that one day the little monster was going to become a full-on demon and kill half the population of the continent in a rampaging search for butter biscuits. 'It's just an unsightly birth mark,' I lied, then louder – so Reichis could hear me – added, 'It's because he was the runt of the litter.'

The squirrel cat seemed unconcerned with the slight. 'Says the guy who's the weakest mage in his whole clan.'

Parsus brought his finger a little closer to my face. 'Mind if I . . . ?'

'Kind of, yeah,' I said.

He stopped. 'You ever think about spendin' a little money and gettin' that seen to by a, well, a doctor or a whisper witch or some such person?'

Reichis snorted. 'Only every day of the last two years and every coin he ever earned.'

Parsus looked at me. 'What'd he say?'

I shrugged. 'How should I know? He's just a dumb animal. Probably saw a bird and got scared.'

'I'd say the dumb animal is the one tied to the horse,' Reichis observed.

The marshal peered in at me a little closer. 'You know, they're not so much black as, well, I can't rightly describe it. The queen's got some fine doctors in the capital. Saw one cure a man what had a skin condition even nastier than yours one time. Maybe he can help.'

I smiled. 'Does he cure the burn around a man's neck after the noose is done with it?'

'Oh, yeah, sorry.'

'Parsus, don't go rilin' the boy up,' Harrex shouted. 'Just give him his water and leave him alone.'

'Fine,' Parsus shouted back, then to me: 'Your hands look a little singed, fella. Want me to pour some water on 'em and clean 'em off a bit?'

'Don't bother,' I said, clenching my fists. I wasn't just being obstinate – I had a very good reason for not wanting my hands clean.

'Suit yourself,' Parsus said. He nodded to the long, dusty road ahead that cut through the mountain ranges on either side of us. 'But it's two more days to the capital.' Then he went back to arguing with Harrex about whose turn it was to play with the squirrel cat.

I tried flexing my shoulder where Merrell's knife had made a temporary home. The marshals had dressed it, but it still burned. The smell of vomit and my own bad breath assaulted my nostrils, and my ears were filled with the sounds of the world's most ornery creature making appreciative cooing noises.

'Squirrel cats don't even make that sound, you know,' I said.

'What?' Harrex asked.

'Nothing.'

I turned my head a bit and looked up at the sky. The sun was starting to sink towards the horizon. The marshals would want to make camp for the night, which was good since my escape plan relied on me not being completely nauseous. The plan wasn't brilliant and it depended on temporarily convincing them I was a much stronger mage than I appeared. It also meant burning the living hells out of my hands – never a good idea when the only magic you're actually good at requires your fingers to be fast and sure. Still though, I was fairly confident it would work, just so long as nothing—

'Raiders!' Parsus shouted.

I tried to spin my head around so fast I would've fallen off the horse if I wasn't tied to it.

'Damn it all,' Harrex said. 'How many and how far?'

I could see Parsus out of the corner of my eye. He was looking through a brass-banded long-glass up towards the border mountains. 'I count seven. At least half a mile out, I'd say.'

The older marshal let out a grunt. 'Damn, Parsus, you scared me for nothing.' He took the long-glass from Parsus and held it up to his eye. 'It'll take them a good three hours to get down that ridge on horseback.'

Harrex put the long-glass in his saddlebag. 'Damned Zhuban keep pushing further south every year.' He pulled his horse up to mine and reached over to make sure the ropes were tight. 'Sorry, kid, no supper tonight.'

'What do you mean?' I asked, my heart sinking deep enough into my stomach that it was a safe bet it was going to come right back up the next time I vomited.

The marshal looked down at me. 'We ain't going to mess

with no Zhubanese raiding party. We've spotted seven of them, and with just Parsus and me, well, I don't like those odds. No, we'll ride on through the night to the barracks at Castrum Tovus. There we can pick up a few more marshals to ensure we all make it nice and safe to the capital.'

As I contemplated the fact that there was no way I was ever going to be able to escape an entire squad of marshals, I felt Harrex's hand pat my back. 'Sorry, kid. Looks like you'll have a bit of a rough ride for the next few hours.'

He flipped open the small quiver of crossbow bolts attached to the front of his saddle and tapped a finger on each one, counting aloud. I found myself counting along with him. He had eight bolts, which, if the Zhuban raiders caught up with us and Harrex was the best shot in the world, would be one more than he needed. I ran through all the things he might use that last crossbow bolt for: shooting dinner, picking his teeth, killing me . . . When you're handcuffed and slung over the side of a horse you can't help but think about those things. That extra crossbow bolt was nagging at me though.

The marshal gave me a cockeyed look as he checked his saddle. 'You planning something, fella? Cos I don't think you're going to have much luck sneaking up on me while you're tied to that horse.'

My head snapped up. 'Marshal Harrex?' I said as quietly as I could.

'Yeah? What's the matter? Straps too tight?'

I shook my head. 'You ever hear of the Zhuban Wheel of Destiny?'

The old marshal shrugged. 'Sure, sorta. It's the symbol of their country, right? We got a big bronze one in one of the libraries in the royal palace.'

'More importantly, it's the symbol of their philosophy. They think fate turns like a wheel. You recall how many spokes there are on that wheel?'

He pursed his lips. 'Spokes. Right. Learned that in school. Eight, if I recall. Let's see . . . beginnings, endings, duty, joy . . . Can't remember the others.'

'How many provinces in the Zhuban territories?'

'Eight. What's this abou—'

'And how many times a day do the Zhuban meditate?'

'Eight. They like eights, all right? They're a very consistent people. Happy?'

I shook my head. 'How many raiders did you say you saw through the long-glass?'

'Seve— Oh hell. Parsus!' he shouted. 'Check for—'

A flash of red silk and brown leather filled my vision for an instant as a huge, muscular man came out of nowhere and slammed into Harrex, knocking him off his horse. Barely giving me a glance, the attacker thrust his right arm downwards and a short knife appeared in his hand. He flicked it underhand at Parsus and took him in the right shoulder. The younger marshal screamed, his body twisting back in agony and sending him too tumbling to the ground.

I tried frantically to twist myself out of the straps holding me to my horse, not that it would have done much good since I still had the handcuffs on.

The Zhuban warrior was well over six and a half feet tall and looked strong enough to toss me, my horse and half of Darome off the mountain. The tanned skin of his face was exposed, revealing eight tattooed stars on his brow. Four sinewy lines stretched out across each cheek like the whiskers on a wildcat. He was dressed head to toe in red cloth bound with

29

brown straps. A Crimson Elite. Why the hell would an Elite be part of a simple raiding party?

Harrex, still on the ground, swung his marshal's mace at the attacker's knee. The Elite skipped back gracefully, bringing his hands up in front of him in one of those Zhuban guard positions that make no sense to anyone else. He didn't even bother to pull out another knife. In Harrex's defence, the move did allow him to get to his feet, where he could square off against his opponent.

'Reichis,' I shouted. The little squirrel cat leaped to the back of my horse. 'Get these things off me.'

The squirrel cat looked at me like I was drunk. 'What am I supposed to do? Chew through your handcuffs?'

'Use the key, idiot.'

'Harrex has it,' he said. 'I saw him put it in his belt pouch.'

'Why didn't you steal it when he was feeding you?'

Reichis's snout went down towards his chest. 'I . . .'

'It didn't occur to you that it might be helpful if you stole the key? What kind of thief are you?'

'A hungry one?'

Marshal Harrex went down hard to the ground, his mace falling from his hand. The Zhuban kicked him in the stomach to make sure he wouldn't get back up. Then the big man turned his attention to me. A bundle of brown blur flew towards his face. He caught Reichis under the neck and held him just far enough away that the squirrel cat's claws couldn't reach him.

'You are fierce, little creature,' he said in broken Daroman, presumably for my benefit. 'But the Fourth Aspect of Duty is dominion over the animals and the earth.'

He threw Reichis a good thirty feet away and the squirrel cat landed with a painful-sounding thud.

'You're going to pay for that,' I said.

The Zhuban smiled. 'Would you like me to undo your bonds so that you can try?'

'No need.'

He nodded. 'Because, free or not, I would break you in an instant, yes?'

I shook my head. 'No, because you hit Marshal Parsus in the right shoulder and I get the feeling he's left-handed.'

The Elite's eyes widened as his stomach grew the tip of a crossbow bolt. He spun around, his back to me for a moment before he fell to the ground. Beyond him I saw Parsus, the knife still in his right shoulder, holding a shaky crossbow in his left hand. The freckle-faced young man looked as if he was about to say something. He didn't though. His eyes went glassy and he fell unconscious to the ground.

I turned my head to look at the others. Reichis, the Zhuban Elite and both marshals were now unconscious. That just left me, strapped to the side of a horse and wondering whether anyone would wake up before the rest of the raiding party arrived.

6

Cages and Crossbows

I was impressed that Marshal Harrex was the first to pull himself together. He'd taken some heavy hits from the Zhuban warrior but still managed to grunt and growl himself to his feet as he shook off the effects of the beating. The marshal surveyed the scene in front of him, and gave a wry chuckle at the sight of me tied up, Parsus passed out, Reichis stumbling around in a daze and the Zhuban Elite unconscious, hopefully dying from the arrow protruding from his belly.

Harrex's first move was to check on the Elite. He didn't kick or stab the other man – which most soldiers and guards I'd ever encountered would've done. But that's the marshals for you: they have a set of rules and they play by them every time, no matter what cards they're dealt. You have to admire the determined stupidity of it all. He placed a pair of handcuffs on the Zhuban's wrists. The solid click made the ones binding me feel tighter.

'It's too bad I can't untie you, kid,' he said to me as he went to work on Parsus's wound. 'I could use the help.'

'I could just give you my word that I wouldn't run. I suppose you wouldn't believe me?'

Harrex looked over at me and smiled. 'You know what,

kid? I probably would. But you'd never give me your word, would you?'

'I—'

Harrex pulled the knife from Parsus's shoulder, eliciting a sharp grunt that made me admire the younger marshal's grit. Then he poured a viscous substance from a copper flask onto the wound. The liquid had a colour that matched the flask and it sparked as it touched the gash in Parsus's shoulder.

'Is that really . . . ?'

Harrex nodded. '*Aquae sulfex*. More potent than *oleus regia* and twice as expensive.' He sighed as he walked over to the Zhuban Elite and poured some around his belly wound before pulling out the crossbow bolt.

'You're wasting it on that guy? He tried to kill you.'

The old man shrugged. 'He's my prisoner now, and Marshal Colfax would have my head if we didn't bring him back safely to the queen's court.'

Colfax was the legendary head of the marshals service. How legendary? Even *I'd* heard of him, and I'd never been to the Daroman capital. I doubted he cared much about a Zhuban raider though. 'They'll just hang your prisoner after the world's shortest trial,' I said.

'Yeah, probably. But that's not my problem. I'm a lawman, son. My job is to get this fella in front of a magistrate, safe and sound.'

I heard a shuffling sound coming from a few feet away and turned my head to see Reichis ambling towards us. 'Tell the marshal to take a walk, Kellen. I'll save him the trouble of a magistrate's fee.'

Harrex put the stopper back on the copper flask. He set it down and slowly pulled a knife from his belt. 'Your little friend is growling, son. Call him off so I don't have to hurt him.'

I heard a groan as Parsus pushed his way to his feet and started reloading his crossbow.

Reichis bared his teeth. 'I'll take 'em all.'

'Don't be stupid, Reichis,' I said. The little monster gets especially ornery when he loses a fight.

'Does he really understand you?' Parsus asked, stepping closer to us but keeping his crossbow pointed at Reichis. The time for tummy tickles and tasty treats was over now that they saw Reichis for what he really was: ten miles of monster stuffed into two feet of mangy fur.

Harrex rose and walked towards Parsus. 'Give me the crossbow and go get the rabbit trap from the supply horse.'

After a moment Parsus returned with a square metal cage barely big enough to hold Reichis. The young marshal set it on the ground with the snare door opened. Reichis growled. The shadowblack markings around his left eye were starting to twist and turn.

'Listen, Kellen,' Marshal Harrex said. 'There are two and only two ways this can go. You get your little friend to go in that cage and behave himself, and I swear no matter what else happens, I'll set him free when all this is done. I don't want to hurt him none, but I can't have him ripping my face off tonight neither. The second option is I eliminate the problem before it becomes one.'

'There's no gods-damned way I'm getting in that cage, Kellen,' Reichis chittered.

Harrex's finger was looking twitchy on the crossbow. 'I'm not fooling here, Kellen. He gets in the cage alive or dead, but one way or another he's going in.'

'Reichis,' I said slowly, 'listen, we've got to play this smart. You've got—'

The squirrel cat growled at me, and I wondered if maybe the shadowblack was getting to him – making him angry. Mean. 'Coward,' he snarled, his voice deeper than usual. 'Play it smart. Run. Hide. Make excuses. That's all you ever do. I should've never busted you out your parents' house that day they were counter-banding you, Kellen. You never really left anyway.'

'Reichis, he's going to shoot you!'

The beady little eyes twinkled, his fur going white and red to match the snow and blood around him. 'Maybe. Maybe not. He's old, and scared. I'll bet he's going to miss. I won't! I sure as hell won't be caged.'

'Marshal, please, let's figure something else out,' I begged.

Harrex shook his head. 'Sorry, kid.'

'Reichis, get in the damned cage! They're going to kill you!'

The little squirrel cat's eyes were fixated on Harrex and his lip curled, almost as if he was smiling.

Parsus took a step towards Harrex. 'I have an idea. Maybe we can make this work if we just—'

Reichis took three fast steps and then sprang in the air towards Harrex's face, the furry glider flaps between his front and rear legs catching the breeze just as the marshal squeezed the trigger on the crossbow. I watched as the bolt slammed into Reichis, the force momentarily suspending the momentum of his body before he fell to the ground.

7

Blood and Water

We rode half the night down the high mountain passes until snow and ice gave way to cobblestone roads that marked the end of the border region and the entry into Darome proper. Now that we were out of danger from the rest of the Zhuban raiding party, Harrex called a halt and got me down from the horse, before doing the same for the Elite. Parsus worked up a fire and gave us all dried meat and brown bread before setting a pot of water to boil for coffee.

We sat there, largely in silence. Harrex kept himself far enough away that if either the Elite or I tried to attack there would be more than enough time to pick up his reloaded crossbow and end us. The Zhuban didn't eat; he just alternated between meditating and glaring at each of us in turn. Harrex did a passable job of ignoring everyone else as he cleaned and checked his weapons. Parsus sat next to the cage that held Reichis's limp body, occasionally sticking a finger in the cage to lightly pet the squirrel cat's damp fur.

'You're going to lose that finger if that thing wakes up,' Harrex warned, his eyes still focused on his long knife. The marshal shook his head as if he'd found a nick. 'Stupidest thing I've ever heard of, using aquae sulfex on a damned animal.'

Parsus withdrew his finger. 'Wasn't the little fella's fault. He was just being brave, trying to protect his master.'

'Business partner,' I said reflexively.

'What?'

'Never mind.'

Harrex snorted. 'You two deserve each other.'

I watched the lump of fur lying in the cage. He was breathing. That was something. 'Thank you,' I said.

The fire crackled and my eyes went to the dried meat on a small metal plate in front of me. I was starving. The marshals had helpfully switched my cuffs so my hands were in front of me, but using my fingers to pick up the meat would mean losing the one ace I still had. There was just enough powder on them that if I could think of any way to get out of the handcuffs I might be able to get off one final shot.

'Jan'Tep,' the Zhuban Elite grunted to me, his voice low enough to be buried under the crackling of the fire.

'What?' I asked.

'You Jan'Tep?' He said the word as if it was an insult.

I nodded.

'*Naghram*, eh?' he said, grinning. That last one required no inflection to be understood as an insult. To be fair, it is true that, centuries ago, many Jan'Tep had been eunuchs. They believed that castration relieved the mind of the distractions inherent in the desire to mate, thus freeing them to better focus their minds on magic. Turned out it just relieved them of their testicles. Also, since there aren't a lot of Jan'Tep mages left, reproduction is kind of a big deal to my people.

The marshals had put the Zhuban in handcuffs like mine so I wasn't worried about him getting free and killing me, but I still found him daunting. He gazed at me the way the

Zhuban like to do – as if they can weigh and measure a person just by staring at them. Maybe he could. But so could I, though what I saw didn't make me very comfortable. His head was shaved, his sleeveless shirt revealed muscles that ensured I'd be no match for him in a fist fight. His arms bore the scars that marked a soldier, but they were tanned, like the rest of him, all the way to his wrists. His hands, however, were smooth and pale. Harrex had removed his gloves and burned them. The Crimson Elites wear gloves to protect them from having to touch those who are 'tainted', which is to say pretty much everyone who *isn't* Zhubanese.

The assassin's gaze shifted away from me to a point in the air straight in front of him. He curled his bound hands in front as if he were choking a man to death. He stayed like that for several minutes, until every part of him was sweating.

'*Dehbru habat*,' I whispered without meaning to. The Zhuban's eyes flickered to me before going back to his imaginary victim. I wondered if the marshals should be feeling anything yet. There are stories told that the Crimson Elites can crush an enemy's windpipe from a distance. I'd never witnessed it myself, never even seen it tried. Seemed like a lot of effort considering the marshals were right there; if he really wanted to take a chance then he could just as well leap at one of them and get a grip around his neck. Then I realised his hands were too close together and were low down. It wasn't a man's neck he was envisioning; it was a child's.

'Too far,' he said at last. 'The little bitch is too far away.'

'Who?' I asked.

He nodded towards the marshals. 'The presumptuous child they call a queen. We are too far away and my dehbru habat is too weak.'

38

'Oh, well, sorry to hear it. Don't suppose you could take out the marshals? Then we could get free and go our separate ways?'

He shook his head and held out his palms. They were marked with an intricate set of symbols. 'The dehbru habat is high magic, granted to us by the angels of the second constellation. The target's name is imprinted on our flesh by master astronomers. The death sentence I carry will only work on the girl.' Frustration played across his features. 'But I must be closer, much closer.'

Most cultures on the continent would consider belief in angels to be a form of religion, but the Zhuban argue that they don't worship gods and are thus atheists whose worldview is philosophically and scientifically pure. In fact they consider religion – that is, everything different from what they believe in – to be childish superstition. Should you ever encounter a Zhuban Crimson Elite, I recommend you not explain the flaw in their logic. 'I suppose you should have skipped trying to kill us and snuck into the capital instead,' I observed.

He shook his head. 'Stupid naghram. I would never get within a thousand steps of her. Not unless—'

'Not unless you were brought before her after being condemned to death by the magistrate.' I shook my head. 'You *wanted* to be captured . . .'

He smiled. 'Do you think these two imbeciles could have stopped me if I hadn't let them?'

'So then everything's going according to plan?'

'No. I was a fool. I thought he would try to sneak up on me and strike me with his mace. But he used the coward's way.' The big man's lips curled into a snarl as he looked down at the bandaged wound the crossbow bolt had left.

'But the aquae sulfex . . .'

39

He shook his head. 'Their medicine is strong, but something is broken inside me. I will come to my execution too weakened to perform the dehbru habat.'

'Guess you'll just have to strangle her the old-fashioned way,' I said.

He spat and held up his hands. 'I have no gloves,' he said. 'An Elite cannot touch the flesh of the profane, not even to kill her.'

'I'm sure if you ask nicely, someone will lend you their gloves. Or maybe just mittens. Can you strangle someone with mittens?'

'You mock me, naghram. The gloves we wear to slay the profane must be blessed by the Celestial Astronomer herself. The business of souls is not a matter for weavers.'

'Seems like a lot of work,' I said.

'The path of destiny is not easy, naghram. But when I die I will climb the hundred thousand steps and take my place upon the great wheel to sit alongside the angels of enlightenment. You? You will burn for a thousand years. You should turn to the path of reason while you still can.'

I pointed to the shadowblack around my left eye. 'I think my afterlife is already spoken for.'

The Zhuban leaned in to look at me more closely. 'Those markings, joined half-circles like the crescent moons, and twisting vines like angry snakes . . . are you a holy man of your people?'

I shook my head. 'Just the opposite. I'm . . .' How the hell do you explain the shadowblack to a Zhuban zealot? 'You might call me an apostate, though an unintentional one.'

He nodded. 'It is well then. You will kill the bitch-queen for me.'

'Why in the world would I do that?'

'They have captured you for some crime, yes? You killed someone, perhaps?'

I shook my head. 'I mistakenly wiped blood on the Daroman flag so, technically, I declared war on the empire.'

The Zhuban gave a small, churlish laugh. 'A vain and superstitious people, these Daroman. It will be their downfall.' He leaned towards me. 'Now listen to me, naghram. When they prepare you for death they will take you to her. They will expect you to plead for your life, which will be your instinct. Do not beg. It will make no difference to the outcome. Instead, set your eyes and your mind to finding an opportunity – an instant in which you can strike her down. Perhaps you keep a small blade hidden on your person? Or if that fails, simply use your hands to crush her throat.'

'So you want me to skip a quick death in favour of being tortured for days?'

He smiled even as he shook his head in disgust. 'Coward! I cannot imagine how you think. What does pain matter to one who acts in accordance with destiny?'

I shrugged. 'The only thing "destiny" ever gave me were these marks around my eye that've gotten me hunted by every man, woman and halfwit who has a clue what they are. Other than that, "destiny" hasn't had much to say to me.'

'It does now. The universe speaks to you through me, naghram. But if your soul is too tainted to hear its words, then know this: within the Daroman court there are those who await the performance of this deed. Strike down the queen and they will protect you. Think, naghram, of the rewards they will grant you!'

I considered his words. Serving some barbarian Zhubanese

41

philosopher's notion of fate wasn't my idea of a good time, but staying alive, however unpleasant, was something I'd grown accustomed to. And money? Money meant freedom. It meant more chances to find someone who could cure my shadow-black before my soul was completely eaten by a demon or one of my beloved clan members finally got a good clean shot at me. Money was something I needed badly.

Could I murder a queen? A child, no less. I looked over at Reichis. What would happen to the squirrel cat if they killed me? No matter how merciful the marshals tried to be, the little bugger would keep coming for them until he'd gotten revenge. Harrex would put another bolt in him and this time there'd be no aquae sulfex to save his life.

The Zhuban leaned his head back and looked up at the stars. 'The voice of destiny reaches inside you, naghram. It is well. You will be blessed in this life and the next.'

Then he took in a deep breath and suddenly let it out, hard, his stomach clenching as if it was caught in an iron vice. He took in another deep breath and did it again.

'What are you doing?' I asked.

He tensed his stomach again, even harder. Blood seeped through the dressing covering his wounds.

'I have fulfilled my service to the angels. You are my arrow now, guided by my hand to strike down our mutual enemy.'

He continued breathing in this way, tensing his stomach over and over.

Harrex and Parsus noticed the strange convulsions and got up.

'He's trying to kill himself,' Harrex said.

Parsus reached him first, trying in vain to get him to stop. 'We're out of aquae sulfex! There's nothing I can do.'

'Knock him out with your mace!' Harrex shouted.

Parsus unbuckled the mace from his belt, but it was too late. Blood was dripping through the bandages onto the ground in front of the Zhuban.

'I go to rest upon the wheel now, little naghram. Fulfil our mission and know that you do so with destiny's blessing . . . and with mine.' He leaned into me, and before I could pull away I felt his kiss on my cheek. His head slumped down against my shoulder as the life left his body.

8

The Queen's Game

Two days of travel, twelve hours in a holding cell and a twenty-minute trial in front of a bored and irritable old magistrate later, I was finally dragged into the queen's court of justice, duly convicted for my rather sloppy declaration of war against the Daroman empire. There was a certain irony to the fact that while my offences until now had been entirely accidental, there was a decent chance I was about to murder their queen.

A roomful of arrogant nobles gave me dirty looks as they arrayed themselves around the throne of their eleven-year-old ruler in eager anticipation of seeing me hang. It wasn't doing much to improve my outlook on Daroman society.

The queen's court of justice was beautiful in the way that only a lie – well told and delivered with the soft flick of a seductive tongue in your ear – can be. The whole place looked as if it had been carved from a single slab of polished marble. Ornate columns rose from the floor to a magnificently domed ceiling above without revealing seams or joints. Delicate gold and silver inlays entwined like lovers with cherry-wood engravings along the walls, telling the story of the Daroman people's journey from a loose collection of pastoral herders to the mightiest empire on the continent, all of it leading to where the world's youngest (or perhaps oldest, if you believed the stories) monarch sat waiting for me.

Her throne was made of oak, small and almost preposterously modest. The Daroman people fancied these touches of humility differentiated them from the more brutal empires of old. They were a sophisticated people, learned in philosophy, agriculture and, of course, warfare. These represented the Daroman way of doing business: first, try to convince your small country to join the empire, through well-intentioned and civilised debate on the benefits of territorial partnership; then bribe you with assurances of a better food supply than you've ever had before; if neither of those work, kick the crap out of you with the biggest and best-trained army the continent has ever seen.

But if the Daroman empire had absorbed the resources and citizenry of other nations, they had also absorbed a lot of their culture. Daily life in the Daroman capital looked nothing like that of those pastoral herders with their tall, brown horses and short, fierce tempers. Oh, some of those folk still existed – hundreds of thousands of them lived in the small towns that littered the countryside of Darome. But they were relics now. Cute anachronisms long abandoned by their great-great-great-grandchildren. Other than making the 'heartland pilgrimage' – a kind of rite of passage for Daroman teenagers – the average noble hadn't seen any of their coarser kin in generations. I suppose that's why the queen could be forgiven for asking the question she did.

'Are you one of our heart-folk?' Her voice was small but dignified, a pleasant, if not quite reassuring, contrast to the coarse hands of the marshals who forced me to my knees before the throne.

The queen was a lovely-looking girl. Darker skinned than most of her subjects, thanks to a bridal choice made several hundred years ago by her great-grandfather dozens of times removed that seems to have stuck. She wore a simple headdress over black hair that fell in tight ringlets around her young face. The first hints of cheekbones had emerged to complement a small, flat nose and an eleven-year-old's soft jawline. A gold lace dress with rose-coloured trim covered her from the tops of her feet to the base of her neck and back down again to her wrists. She wore no jewellery other than a simple silver circlet over her headdress with a single black gemstone at its centre.

'No, ma'am,' I replied. 'I'm nobody's "heart-folk".'

Someone slapped me across the head from behind. I suspected it was Marshal Harrex. He'd been friendly enough up until now, all things considered, but here in the queen's court I guess he had to show he wasn't soft on men headed for the noose. He leaned over and whispered in my ear. 'You'll call her "Majesty", or they'll make me gut you right here.'

'No, Your Majesty,' I amended.

'Forgive my assumption,' the queen said, tilting her head as she examined me, 'but you have a kind face, unlike those normally brought before me. I was . . . reminded of our heart-folk.'

I had to laugh at that. I suspect the marshal did too since he didn't hit me again. 'Pardon me, Your Majesty, but I don't think anyone's ever said that about my face.' I winked my left eye.

She leaned down a bit to see under the brim of my hat. 'Ah, of course, the black markings.' She had an oddly wistful tone to her voice. 'Like the flowing letters of a language we've all forgotten. They hold a kind of magic, do they not?'

'He's got the shadowblack, Your Majesty,' Marshal Harrex said.

Her Majesty leaned forward some more and peered at me even more closely. 'Yes,' she said, 'I do note it, and yet still I find you have a kind face, for all the devilishness of your tattoos.' Then she looked at my hat. 'And you wear a frontier hat, much like our beloved shepherds do!' she observed with delight.

Her apparent innocence was getting on my nerves. 'Keeps the sun out of my face, that's all.'

She nodded silently but kept her attention on the hat. 'Those symbols . . .'

'This is superstitious ignorance, Your Majesty,' came a voice from behind the throne.

I looked up at one of the women standing behind the queen. She had chestnut hair and wore long white robes with a rose-lace band across the top, covering her shoulders. A taller man and a blonde woman in similar garb stood next to her, he with a gold-lace band and she with a pale blue one.

'Forgive my tutor, Master Kellen,' the queen said, an odd mixture of remorse and anxiety in her voice.

I shook my head. '*Mister* Kellen,' I said, 'not Master.'

The queen's eyes narrowed. 'You're not a mage? But those symbols around your hat, and the tattoos around your forearms . . . I assumed you were Jan'Tep.'

'Disowned, Your Majesty. A minor disagreement with my father.'

'Might I inquire as to the nature of this disagreement?' There was a cough somewhere and the queen's eyes glanced quickly around the room, as if she knew what the dozens of

47

assembled nobles must be thinking: that this interview was supposed to only be a formality that preceded my beheading which preceded lunch.

'It was a small question of mystical theology, Your Majesty. We disagreed over whether I was, in fact, a demon child left by the shadowblacks in place of his true son.' That wasn't strictly speaking what had happened, but it was slightly less humiliating than the truth.

'Very well,' she said, ignoring what I thought was some fine gallows humour. 'Have you been informed, and do you fully understand why you are here, Mister Kellen?'

'Because I broke the law, Your Majesty. Oh, and because today is my eighteenth birthday, which makes me eligible for the death penalty here in your fine, civilised nation.'

She looked just a little bit surprised. 'You are rather young to be facing death for treason, if you don't mind me saying.'

'You're a little young to be sending me to my death, if you don't mind me saying,' I replied.

There was a smattering of laughter in the room and the queen's face twitched with uncertainty. She was wondering if I was making fun of her. Queen or not, she was an eleven-year-old girl in a roomful of adults – well, an eleven-year-old girl unless you buy all the Daroman claptrap about the monarch being the reincarnated soul of the entire line of previous rulers, which would make her somewhere around two thousand years old.

Harrex struck me in the back of the head again. 'Marshal,' I said without turning, 'if you keep stroking my hair like that, people are going to think you fancy me.'

I heard something sharp come out of its sheath.

'Marshal,' the queen warned, her voice calm and soft, 'would you draw a blade in front of your queen?' It was barely a question. She was re-establishing her primacy in the room without stamping her feet or raising her voice. A good tactic, I thought.

Whatever blade Harrex had pulled was quickly hidden away again. 'Forgive me, Your Majesty. I sought only to ensure your safety.'

A dozen logical replies hung in the air, ranging from, 'I know you only have my best interests at heart' to 'The guy's on his knees in unbreakable handcuffs surrounded by over a hundred people; are you thick?' The queen used none of these. In fact, she said nothing at all for a long while.

'Mister Kellen, we will proceed now,' she said finally. 'I ask again, have you been informed, and do you fully understand, why you are before me today?'

This was Daroman justice at work. They considered the death penalty so abhorrent and so demeaning of the general good that even once a magistrate's court had heard your case, even when that same magistrate, in conjunction with his esteemed Council of Nine has rendered judgment, the death penalty can't be administered until the queen herself has interviewed the defendant and validated the verdict. Again, like all things Daroman, it sounded very civilised until you figured out that these interviews took, on average, two minutes and no monarch had ever, not once in the last two hundred years, overturned the verdict of a magistrate.

'I have been informed, and I do understand,' I said, confounding expectations. The room went silent. Usually the defendant said he either hadn't been told, or didn't under-stand, the verdict. But that made no difference at all because all that would happen is one of the marshals would simply repeat the verdict and then you'd be killed anyway. My plan didn't have much better odds, but it did have the virtue of being original.

I figured they were going to kill me no matter what I said. The deed is done right there, in front of the queen (because of course the Daroman sense of justice requires that the eleven-year-old should have to witness the act when she has someone killed). I didn't have any weapons on me, and, of course they'd taken away my powder holsters. They'd been thorough in checking me over again once we arrived – too thorough for such a supposedly decent people, in my opinion. But apart from confirming I hadn't managed to sneak in a weapon, they hadn't checked my fingers, or under my nails. I'd spent the last three days in captivity, making sure I never touched anything with those fingers. Eating, drinking, defecating – these things are all a lot more complicated when you can't use your hands, trust me.

So now I reckoned there was a fifty–fifty chance I had enough powder left on my fingers and under my nails to get one shot in. When they asked me if I had any last requests I was going to request that my cuffs be removed so I could face death with some semblance of freedom. Again, not a given by any means, but they wouldn't be too worried; it's not like they'd let me get within two feet of the queen. But even with just a trace amount of the powders on my fingers I can fire the spell a good five yards. So the idea was to get them to take the cuffs off and then blast that lovely, delicate eleven-year-old child to a quick reunion with her ancestors. What possible good could that do, you may ask? Probably nothing. Probably some would-be hero would just kill me right there to make a name for themselves.

Here's the thing though: every ruler has enemies. There's always some Count of This or Baron of That who thinks they should be ruler instead of a snot-nosed little girl with pretensions of some mystical reincarnated lineage. So there was a chance – a small one, granted, but a chance nonetheless – that the Zhuban Elite hadn't been lying, and that if I killed the queen, some faction of the court would seize power before the two marshals behind me stuck a blade through the back of my head. After all, I might be the paid assassin of the next guy who was going to sit in that chair.

So, best-case scenario, someone comes along who feels just a little bit grateful that I knocked off the competition. Worst case, I'd have murdered a young girl who'd done nothing wrong. Well, nothing except condemn me to death.

Harrex hit me again – not hard, just enough to remind me he was still there. 'Her Majesty asked you a question, outlaw. Answer.'

I shook my head, trying to remember what she'd said. 'Forgive me, Your Majesty, my mind was elsewhere.'

There was laughter in the room again.

'I asked why you did what you did, Mister Kellen,' the queen said.

'Wiping blood on the flag?' I glanced down at the travel-stained ruins of my clothes. 'Didn't want to soil my best shirt. They're expensive, you know.'

'I'm talking about the man you killed.'

The tall chestnut-haired tutor stepped out from behind the throne. 'Your Majesty has many lessons this afternoon and should conclude this business quickly.' By all conventional standards she was a beautiful woman, until you caught the

51

expression she made when looking at me. Then she got real ugly, real fast.

'I still have questions for Mister Kellen,' the queen replied, somewhat tentatively.

The taller man, thinning grey hair belying a soldier's physique, put his hand on the back of the throne. 'Your Majesty knows that if we must start later the lessons are prone to being more . . . arduous.' He had a genial smile on his face.

The queen's eyes flashed to mine. It was an odd, reflexive action, as if she was hoping for support. *Hey, don't look at me, kid. I don't care how hard they make you study arithmetic.*

She steeled herself. 'Nevertheless, Tutor Koresh, it is my royal duty and prerogative to ensure that the sentence of death meets the necessity of the defendant's crimes.'

The man took his hand off the throne and stepped back. He was still smiling, but he wasn't *really* smiling, if you know what I mean.

I coughed. 'To answer your question, Your Majesty, I did what I did because I believed it was the appropriate response.'

The queen stared at me now, eyes wide and disbelieving. 'You ended a man's life over a game of cards, Mister Kellen. I hardly think that an appropriate response to a game!'

'Ah,' I said simply.

'What?'

'Am I correct in assuming that, although you seem ably supplied with tutors, you have no tutor in cards?'

'You are correct, Mister Kellen. I do not have a tutor in cards. Is there a reason why I should have?'

'Only because cards aren't a game.'

'And what are they, if not a game?'

'They are a map of the world, Your Majesty. An augury of the future. A negotiation between warring states. And we all have to play the cards we're dealt.'

'Well, that does sound like important knowledge for a queen.'

Again that unsettled dance in her eyes, but only briefly. What I saw next was something else – something that I wouldn't expect to be in the expression of a young girl: the look of someone who's about to bluff the other player. She turned to Koresh and the two women behind the throne. 'Learned tutors, is there one among you who teaches cards?'

Chestnut lady replied this time. 'Your Majesty, we are tutors of the royal house. We do not play with dolls, we do not recite fairy tales and we do not amuse ourselves with cards.'

'Your Majesty should consider her lessons,' the blonde tutor said. She was a little younger than the others and, unlike her colleagues, spoke as if she was genuinely concerned for the queen.

'Your tutors speak boldly,' I said. 'I'm surprised you don't have them whipped, Your Majesty.'

'They are not half so bold as you, it seems, master card player.'

I shrugged. 'The dead need no manners. But if Your Majesty so desires, I would be happy to administer a whipping to any of your subjects who you deem deserving. Why, I could even recommend that we start with my friend Marshal Harrex here. Of course, if you'd rather I whip your tutors first, then that would be fine as well.'

'Kill this fool,' the grey-haired tutor, Koresh, shouted at the marshals behind me.

'Ah,' the queen said, a soft and calm counterpoint to the

tutor's anger, 'I see that you do not fully know our ways, Mister Kellen.'

'That I don't, Your Majesty. Why, to an uneducated outlaw like me it sounds like your tutor there just tried to countermand his monarch. That would be treason most places I've been.'

'Yes, I do understand your confusion,' the queen said. 'You are unaware that the royal tutors are not subject to any punishment from our imperial person.'

I looked at her to see if she was joking. My former Argosi mentor, Ferius Parfax, had told me something about this before, back when she was teaching me the ways of the world, but I'd always assumed this was just the same kind of Daroman crap about justice and good governance that masks the fact that rulers generally do whatever they want.

'I see you are suspicious, Mister Kellen. But I assure you, it is true. After all, how can the royal tutors educate a young monarch if they must fear retribution over assigning lessons or criticising poor work?'

'So those three behind you are beyond the law?'

The queen shook her head. 'No, no citizen is beyond the law. Once I reach the age of thirteen, or if a four-fifths majority of the nobles in my court so rule, a tutor may be dismissed. At which point they lose their special protections.'

I looked at the three tutors standing behind the queen. They didn't appear particularly worried about that possibility. 'Forgive me, Your Majesty, but I have a hard time imagining four-fifths of any group of people can agree on whether the sun is shining.'

Koresh stepped forward, his hand once again on the back of the throne like he owned it. 'It is to ensure the proper education of a young monarch, you ignorant borderlands fool. Can you imagine a nation governed by an ill-informed and undisciplined child?'

'I thought Her Majesty was over two thousand years old.'

The queen spoke before anyone else could. 'My soul is that of the first Daroman kings and queens, it is true,' she said. 'But my body, and – some would argue – my mind, are yet those of a young girl. For this reason I must have tutors, and they must have certain . . . discretionary powers.'

She rubbed briefly at the edge of her sleeve. For an instant, a small fraction of her left arm was exposed. Beneath the rose-coloured lace I saw what looked a lot like a mark. A burn mark. 'We must all – how did you put it? – "play the cards we are dealt"?'

I nodded casually, as if I hadn't seen anything amiss. 'I understand, and I appreciate Your Majesty's gracious time considering my case and therefore delaying her lessons. Might I ask only that the marshals remove my handcuffs prior to removing my head?'

She gave a quizzical smile. 'You seem eager to have your life ended, Mister Kellen. Am I keeping you from something important?'

Laughter again in the court, followed by a sort of collective sigh of frustration. This must have been a record for one of these royal interviews and we were, after all, keeping them from their lunch. I was about to reply when the queen suddenly asked, 'Will you play a game of cards with me, Mister Kellen?'

'Your Majesty . . .' the chestnut-haired tutor warned.

'Be silent, Tutor Arrasia,' the queen snapped. 'Am I yet queen of Darome?'

No reply.

'I asked you a question, Tutor Arrasia – am I yet queen of this nation?'

Arrasia waited the longest possible time before finally acquiescing. 'Of course. No one questions that Your Majesty is our monarch.'

'Then I shall investigate every possible means to be the best ruler I can be,' the queen said. 'Now, Mister Kellen, you have made card playing out to be something significantly more important than I had assumed. Apparently worth a man's life and perhaps more than that if you are to be believed. Therefore I wish to understand this phenomenon. So I ask again, Mister Kellen, will you play cards with me?'

My mind was racing as I tried to figure out what she was up to. Was this some kind of trick? How could it be? Among the most important lessons I learned from Ferius was *arta precis*, the Argosi talent for perception. Right now that particular talent was telling me to play along. Thing is, I've always been better at *arta valar* – or what Ferius calls 'swagger' – so I decided to press my luck a little.

'Your Majesty, I fear I cannot in good faith accede to your request.'

'Why not?' she asked.

'Because one cannot play cards without a stake.'

'And what is a "stake"?'

'A bet, Your Majesty. Each of us must have something to win, or to lose. Otherwise the cards become meaningless.'

The queen nodded thoughtfully. 'Ah, I see. What would be an appropriate bet in this case, Mister Kellen?'

'Well, I suppose if I win you could grant me my life,' I said.

Arrasia scoffed. Koresh's expression was more than a little concerned. The blonde tutor just looked confused.

'I see,' said the queen again. 'And if I win, what do I get?'

I shrugged helplessly. 'I fear I have nothing to offer, since my life is already in your hands.'

The queen thought about that for a moment. 'It is true,' she said. 'I do have the power to determine whether you live or if you die, but I am content to have your life as my stake. If you win, you live; if you lose, your life is mine.'

I shook my head sadly. 'Alas, Your Majesty, that doesn't really work. You see, since losing doesn't make me any more dead than refusing the game, I will be prone to playing recklessly. If I had something genuinely at stake, it would affect my choices.'

'Very well. If I lose, you will be free to go. If I win, your life is forfeit and there will be no last request for you. It is a small thing, I know, to be deprived of a sip of wine or a last statement, but perhaps it is enough to keep you from playing too recklessly.'

I felt my eyes go wide. This was a problem. If I lost now – as hard as that was to imagine, given that my opponent was an eleven-year-old girl who didn't even know what a stake was – I wouldn't be able to request that they take the handcuffs off before my execution. If I won, would the queen really set me free? She'd lose the respect of the whole court.

The queen discretely scratched at the lace near her neck, revealing a trace of yellowish skin around a darker patch. There was a bruise there, I was sure of it. What was she up to? What was her endgame? And why, ancestors, hadn't I been paying more attention when Ferius had tried to teach me arta precis?

57

I kept hoping the shadowblack rings around my eye would begin to turn like the dials on a lock and reveal the truth to me through a vision. Back at the Ebony Abbey, the other shadowblacks had called this ability *enigmatism*. An awfully impressive name for something that mostly gave me headaches and never granted me answers unless I happened upon the exact right question. *What is she up to?* I asked tentatively.

Nothing. No tell-tale pinching of the skin around my eye, no mystical insights into secret motivations. I was going to have to play this hand on my own. I'd become a pretty damned good card player over the last couple of years, so if I couldn't beat an eleven-year-old girl on her first game, she might as well have my head. 'I agree to your terms,' I said.

'Enough!' Koresh shouted, apparently no longer able to contain his disdain for me or the queen. 'Magistrate Chapreck, will you please advise Her Majesty on decorum? Or must I do it myself?'

The magistrate who'd accompanied us into the court – the same old man who'd passed sentence on me earlier that day – stepped forward. Rarely have I ever seen a man so much in want of an obscurement spell to make himself disappear.

'Your Majesty,' he said a little warily, 'it is your prerogative to interview the defendant as you see fit, and to render judgement, be it life, or be it death, by whatever means you see fit.'

Koresh was giving Chapreck a dangerous look.

'However,' the magistrate went on, 'think of the consequences of this action. If you should lose to this man, this gambler, it would . . . embarrass the court insofar as—'

'I see,' said the queen, her voice as soft as ever but somehow making the room a little colder. 'Do you mean to say, honoured magistrate, that you believe that the two-thousand-year-old monarch of the Daroman dynasty will be beaten in a test of wits by an inveterate card sharp?'

Odd . . . Most people didn't know what a card sharp was – especially those who never gambled themselves. The queen knew more about my profession than she'd previously let on. For his part, Magistrate Chapreck looked like a man who'd just discovered he was waist deep in quicksand. 'I . . . No, of course not, but—'

'Or would you rather say to this court that – as I am nothing but a foolish eleven-year-old child – I will certainly lose a simple game of cards?'

'I . . . Your Majesty, this is—'

'Kindly answer the question put before you by your queen, honoured magistrate.'

Chapreck found himself boxed into an unpleasant dilemma. If he truly believed the queen was a two-thousand-year-old soul, he had no basis to doubt her ability to win a hand of cards. If he pressed the possibility of her defeat, he was as much as declaring that Darome's monarch was nothing more than an eleven-year-old girl. You had to give Her Majesty this much: she knew how to bluff.

The magistrate shuffled backwards into the crowd. 'Of course, Your Majesty, forgive my insolence.'

'Good then. Mister Kellen and I will play a hand and we shall see whose wits are the sharpest. Now, does anyone actually *have* a deck of cards?'

There was silence in the room as the nobles shuffled around and looked at each other. After a minute or so there was a cough from behind me.

'I, uh, I might have a deck right here, Your Majesty,' the gruff voice said.

59

The queen raised an eyebrow. 'Marshal Harrex, am I to understand that you keep a deck of cards upon your person?'

'Oh no, Your Majesty. I mean, yes, I do have . . . I mean, I must have confiscated them from someone and forgotten to dispose of them.'

Ignoring the minor scandal, the queen said, 'Then that's good fortune for us. Someone bring us a table, and a chair for Mister Kellen. And for goodness sake, someone remove his handcuffs. It's not as if he is likely to try to assassinate me with all of you here to protect me, is he?'

Murmurs and grumbling rose from the audience, but a servant nonetheless brought out a small, simple table and chair while Harrex undid my cuffs. I sat in the chair and looked down at the deck of cards sitting between myself and the queen and wondered what to do next. The problem was the cards. If I started shuffling them, the powder would come off my hands and all my efforts to preserve enough grains on my fingers to fuel my spell would have been wasted.

Games of chance turn on probabilities. Unfortunately for both the queen and me, statistically my best move now was to fry her and hope someone liked me for it. But the prospect of outwitting the supposedly two-thousand-year-old ruler of the Daroman – to walk out of here as a free man and thumb my nose at the most powerful empire in the world – that was more than a little tempting. I'd always been on the losing side of power. Always. The only thing that had kept me alive this long was taking a gamble now and then.

'What game are we playing, Your Majesty?' I asked casually.

'Excuse me?'

'What game? County Roundup? Straights and Aces? Royal Court? Uneven Steps?'

'Wait,' the queen said. 'That one, what was it? "Royal Court"? Tell me about that one.'

I smiled and picked up the cards with my right hand and started shuffling them, feeling them to see if Harrex had a trick deck or the occasional bent card to help him cheat. It was a Daroman deck, which I wasn't used to. Ferius had taught me dozens of games of chance and strategy, but we'd rarely played with a sixty-five card deck: four suits, each with an ace, nine numbered cards, five court cards, supplemented by five coloured jokers, which in a Daroman deck were called, appropriately enough, outlaws.

'Well, Your Majesty, it's interesting that you'd choose Royal Court –'

'Because I am royalty?'

'No, though that would make sense too, I suppose. But the reason it's interesting to me is that most players believe that Royal Court used to be a much older game called Four-Card Borderlands.'

'Why is that relevant?'

'Well, Your Majesty, Four-Card Borderlands was a game that came from the old continent, on the plains of a little place called that used to be called *Daromis*, many, many centuries ago, before her people crossed the sea.'

A murmur rose from the assembled nobles. Even the tutors seemed curious.

'Hey, that's right,' Harrex said from behind me. 'I think I heard that too.'

I dealt the cards. Four each, with another four face down at the edge of the table.

'The four corner cards are the "court",' I said. 'The game is simple. The more of one kind of card you have, the better.

61

We take turns drawing one card each from the deck. Every time you draw a card, you have to discard one face up from your hand onto one of the four corners of the court. No corner can have more than four cards, so the game ends when each of the corners is filled and there are four cards left in each of our hands. You can choose to play your hand, take one of the corners, or do both. But if you take both then you have to turn it into two separate hands and both of them have to beat my hands. You have first claim on the corners nearest you, I have first on the corners nearest me.'

The essence of Royal Court was those four corners: you watched the other player to see how they reacted to what was in each one, and tried to use those observations to guess the contents of your opponent's hand.

The queen examined her cards as she fanned them out. 'Ah, I see. So if the cards in the corner complement the ones in my hand, I might be able to make two stronger hands than if I just used a single set of cards?'

I nodded. 'Right, but you can just as easily get stuck with one great hand and one terrible hand, which means you're likely to lose. So there are a couple of different strategies. You can play it simple, or you can stack a corner with cards you'll want later, but then you risk me taking control of that corner by stacking it with bad cards.'

'Ah, so it's just like in real life. If I were to "stack", as you say, one part of my court with too much influence, I'd risk someone else taking control of it by "stacking" it with some of their own people.'

I bit my lip. 'You learn fast, Your Majesty.'

The queen smiled, seemingly pleased with my praise. 'Thank

you, master card player. I believe I shall take a card now.' She picked a card up from the deck.

'Now you'll want to take some time to—'

She immediately pulled one of the middle cards from her hand and threw it face up against the corner closer to me and to my right.

'Or, I suppose you could just do that.'

I looked at the card she'd thrown. It was the knight of chariots.

'That's a pretty high value card to be throwing away,' I remarked.

The queen said nothing but looked at me placidly.

I picked up a card from the deck. I'm not going to tell you my hand because, well, that's a bad habit to get into. Suffice it to say things were looking all right for me. I discarded to my left corner.

'My turn again?' the queen asked.

I nodded.

She picked up a second card, then tossed another knight – this time the knight of arrows. She threw it on the same corner as before. A dangerous move unless she planned to pick up that corner. But it was on my side of the table, so I would have first rights to it. 'When you were playing cards with the man you fought and killed, were the stakes very high?' she asked, her tone betraying barely any interest at all.

'In truth it was a small matter, Your Majesty. A dispute over a mare.' I dropped my card, the three of blades, on the corner she was building up.

'And what was the nature of the dispute?' the queen asked, picking up another card.

'I felt that he was riding the mare too hard. Shame to waste a good horse. So I offered to buy her. He thought she was worth more, but we came to an agreement for either a much larger sum if I lost, or no cost at all if I won.'

The queen dropped her card, this time a king of trebuchets, on the corner near my left arm. She really didn't seem to be very good at this.

'I'm not sure you're fully understanding the rules of the game, Your Majesty. Would you like me to explain them again?'

'I believe I understand them well enough, thank you.'

I shrugged and picked up my next card. Two of chariots. Nothing special. I realised I should probably spend more time worrying about my own hand.

'And so,' the queen continued, 'when this man, Merrell of Betrian, tried to cheat you in a card game with nothing more at stake than the price of a mare you didn't really want, you killed him.'

'To be fair, Your Majesty, I did go to the trouble of goading him into a duel. He just wasn't very good at it.' I tossed the king of arrows on the corner to the queen's right. I doubted I'd be getting a lot of them, and thought it better to remove them from contention by spreading them around.

The queen looked at me. 'Is this what you would call "bluffing", Mister Kellen?'

The question surprised me. 'No, Your Majesty. You see by preventing the kings from accumulating, I—'

'No, no. I mean you lying to me about your game with Merrell of Betrian,' she said casually, picking up another card. 'It wasn't a mare that you fought over, was it?'

I thought about how to respond for a moment, but then I just answered. I really needed to focus on the cards, not the game. 'No, Your Majesty, it wasn't really a mare.'

'It was a woman.'

'Yes.'

'The man's wife, in fact.'

'Yes.'

'But you're still lying to me, aren't you, Mister Kellen?' the queen said.

'Respectfully, Your Majesty, I don't see how this—'

'She wasn't a woman either, was she?'

I put my cards face down on the table for a moment. I knew what I had in my hand, I knew what was sitting on the corners, and I was pretty sure I had a sense of what the queen was holding. She had played well – almost masterfully in fact. Better than an eleven-year-old girl who'd only just learned the rules had any right to, that's for sure. But not well enough. We were down to the last card each, and I knew I could take the game. 'No, Your Majesty. It might be more accurate to call her a girl.'

'She was twelve,' the queen said.

I nodded, wondering how she'd managed to find this out.

'A year older than I am now.'

'Yes.'

'You killed a man for cheating at cards because you knew he was going to continue . . . what was that charming euphemism you brought into my court? "Riding his mare too hard"?'

'How do you know any of this, Your Majesty?' I asked.

It was her turn to either play her hand or one of the corners or both. But she wasn't moving. 'And you didn't tell this to my magistrate because—'

'Because it wouldn't have made any difference.'

The queen nodded. 'Because the law is the law, and in

Darome twelve is old enough to be married if the parents consent, no matter how old and brutal the husband might be.'

'That's right.'

'Because going to the marshals wouldn't have stopped the abuse so you played the cards you were dealt. Since you knew the facts wouldn't help you in court, you decided to be clever instead.'

I shook my head, growing irritated at being peppered with questions by a child. 'No, I told you, that's—'

'You told them it was a dispute over a mare, because in the eyes of the law it didn't matter if it was a mare or a twelve-year-old girl. She was still his property.'

'I had to—'

'You . . . What's the term? You "folded".'

She wasn't letting me finish a sentence. 'Damn it. I checked the law books, there's no—'

'You don't trust anyone or anything except yourself, do you?'

'There's no one else to trust,' I said, shouted really.

'You just play the cards you're dealt.'

'That's all I can do!'

'That's all any of us can do, isn't it, Mister Kellen?' the queen said, her voice suddenly soft and quiet again. 'Now look at the table, and play . . . your . . . cards.'

Our gazes met, locked on each other. What was she doing? What was the point of all of this? The nobles were quiet as death. The tutors had murder in their eyes. I had started this whole thing with a simple, stupid, impossible plan and now I wasn't sure who was playing whom.

The queen closed her eyes for just a moment. 'We're out

66

of time, master card player. I am due for my lessons and cannot keep my tutors waiting much longer. Look at the table, and make your decision.'

I looked down at the cards. The queen had placed the rest of her hand on the table, face up. Three tens and a knight. A respectable hand, but not the right one. She could've taken the jacks and won right there, but she'd put them on my side, where I had first right to take them. Something about the layout of the cards bothered me. *The four corners*, I thought. *They don't make sense.*

The queen had put two jacks in the same corner on my side of the table – as far away from her as she could. A stupid move. I was closer to them and could take them first. She'd dropped the queen of trebuchets near herself. But she'd also placed low cards – a two and a seven – on top of it, weakening the corner. No power there. The jacks had all the power. I glanced at her for a second. She knew I was holding the outlaw of blades. She had to, since it hadn't appeared anywhere else. In some games outlaws were wild, but not in Royal Court. The three kings on the table were distributed across three different corners. Nothing to play there. All I had to do was take the corner with the other jacks and I'd win. It didn't make sense. She clearly knew the game – a lot better than she'd let on – but she was playing a master's strategy and then leaving it open for me at the end. I'd have to be a fool not to win. Was she letting me win? Why? What possible reason could she have?

I looked up from the table and into the queen's eyes and, like clouds coming out to block the blinding sun, the tears I saw hidden there made the whole table visible to me for the first time. That, and the fact that I'd just remembered something Ferius had once told me on one of her drunken benders, that the jacks in a Daroman deck represent hidden knowledge and scholarly pursuits, which is why they used to go by another name.

Tutors.

For all the seeming casualness of this procedural interview, the queen knew who I was – had known it the whole time in fact: an outcast spellslinger with a bad reputation and a long list of enemies. Dead if I walked into Berabesq, under a spell warrant from the Jan'Tep, unwelcome in Gitabria and unworthy of the notice of the Daroman empire until I made the mistake of going after a man who wouldn't stop battering his twelve-year-old wife. My day-to-day survival was contingent on a few tricks, a propensity for dirty fighting and a willingness to gamble on the foolishness of people smarter and more powerful than me. This eleven-year-old queen had just tricked me into a game of cards that was nothing more than a way for her to show me what was really happening in the Daroman court.

Did this two-thousand-year-old monarch hold the wisdom of eighty generations of rulers? I couldn't say. But right then? At that precise moment? She was a terrified eleven-year-old who was getting beaten and burned by her tutors and knew she didn't have long before they did something worse. She was surrounded by weak men. Twos and sevens who either wouldn't or couldn't do anything to protect her. The strong ones – the jacks – had no intention of letting the queen reach her thirteenth birthday, when she'd be free to rule as she saw fit.

'It's time, Mister Kellen. You must make your choice now.'

She'd set me up to win, no question there. It was as if she

68

was trying to show me that I could trust her. But then where would that leave her? Was she really asking me to give up a winning hand – give up my chance at life and freedom – to trust her back? I had come here to kill this girl on the off-chance it might save my own hide. My life was already in her hands, but now she wanted me to put it there willingly. I looked down at the corner with the jacks. They were the tutors. Pick them up, and I'm siding with them. She wanted me to pick up the corner with the lonesome queen.

Damn, I thought, reaching for the corner cards, *Ferius warned me about the dangers of gambling with anything other than your coin purse.*

'The queen wins!' Marshal Harrex declared when I tossed my combined hand on the table. Nothing there worth anything except a lonesome queen and an even lonelier outlaw of blades.

The crowd cheered. Loudly. Their young queen had just played her first hand of cards and had beaten someone who gambled every day of his life. The nobles were so proud of themselves they could've pissed themselves and still would've walked around with smiles on their faces. The queen didn't waste any time basking in their goodwill. 'Well, this has been most diverting,' she said, standing. 'I have decided that, while Mister Kellen was clearly wrong about the importance of cards, they are nonetheless a fine way to pass the time. I would hereby ask my united court to approve him as my tutor of cards.'

There was some laughter and a few cheers from the nobility. Arrasia wasn't amused. 'No! This is an insult to the royal tutors.'

'Oh, give it a rest,' someone shouted.

'Your Majesty,' Koresh said, icicles hanging off his words, 'the court has the right to debate and test any tutor and vote on their suitability.'

The queen played her biggest bluff of the day. She turned around and looked at the crowd with a theatrically weary expression. 'Royal Tutor Koresh is correct. If the assembled court wishes, it may indeed delay our lunch a while longer to debate the relative merits of appointing Mister Kellen to teach me cards. Or, if the four-fifths majority agrees, we may bypass debate, appoint Mister Kellen as tutor of cards, and the court shall be free to leave for their repast.'

There was a surprisingly resounding chorus of 'Aye!' in the room.

Arrasia started to say something but the queen interrupted. 'Magistrate Chapreck, in your learned opinion, would you say the "ayes" constitute four-fifths of the court?'

Chapreck stepped forward, miserable but resigned. 'I would say they do indeed, Your Majesty.'

'Then it is decided,' the queen said, her voice no longer the soft, calm breeze I'd been listening to for the past half-hour. Now it was strong, strident and victorious. 'Mister Kellen is hereby appointed tutor of cards to the Daroman court, with all the rights, privileges and protections afforded his station.'

She turned to me and in a quieter voice said, 'Though I do believe I would grow weary of those markings around your left eye, Mister Kellen. If your service to me continues to be as diverting as it was today, I may choose to use some of my considerable resources to seeking to have this "shadowblack" of yours removed . . . That is, if you would find such an alteration acceptable.'

70

I tried to read her eyes but they were flat as still water. *Your Majesty, you're either really two thousand years old or else you're the craftiest eleven-year-old the world's ever seen.* 'I believe I could learn to live with such an outcome,' I said.

She smiled and gave a slight nod. A contract of sorts had just been made between us, but only one of us knew the exact terms. The queen turned on her heels and walked towards a passageway in the eastern side of the room, attendants in tow. The royal tutors stayed behind.

'I wouldn't start celebrating any time soon,' Koresh said to me, quiet enough so the audience, who were milling out of the room as quickly as their legs could carry their hungry stomachs, wouldn't hear.

'You won't last here long, "tutor of cards",' Arrasia mocked. 'You have no friends at court, no base of power. You'll be back on your knees in a week, and the queen's lessons will resume with especial fervour.'

Koresh was looming over me, waiting for me to cower. For a moment I was fifteen again, strapped to a workbench in a darkened study, my father standing over me, dipping his needles into molten metals as he burned counter-glyphs into the bands around my forearms, forever denying me the chance to be a true mage. There had been a self-righteous fire in his eyes that night, not so different from the one I saw in Koresh.

Ferius says that the most dangerous moment in a person's life is when they've just escaped death; the rush of beating the odds overcomes you and makes you reckless. I suppose that's the only excuse I have for what happened next. I looked briefly at the blonde woman, who'd spoken little during the entire affair. 'Do you have anything to add?' I asked.

71

She looked up only briefly before her eyes retreated back to the marble floor. 'I . . . I serve at Her Majesty's pleasure.'

'And who are you?' I asked.

'I am Karanetta, Mister Kellen. I teach the queen mathematics and astronomy.'

'Hmm.' I nodded. 'The queen ever get bruised or burned in her mathematics and astronomy lessons?'

The woman looked up, a little horrified by the accusation. 'No, no. Her Majesty is a most able student. A remarkable mind. She—'

I raised a hand. 'That's fine,' I said. 'You can stay.'

Koresh pushed my shoulder with his hand and I took an involuntary step back. He was a big man who could probably take me in a fair fight. As if I'd ever let that happen. 'What do you mean, "You can stay"?' he asked.

I gave a little laugh and shook my head. 'Don't you get it? I thought you were supposed to be the smart ones around here.'

'Play games with us, boy, and you'll soon regret it.'

That made me laugh more. 'Really? You still haven't figured it out? You moron. Didn't you hear me before? I don't play games. I don't have time to play games. You think the queen wants me to teach her how to play cards? You dumb, ignorant thugs. The eleven-year-old girl you beat and burn every day just gave me all the protections of a royal tutor. Right there, in front of the whole court. I can't be brought up on charges for anything. The only way they can get rid of me is if they can get four-fifths of the court to dismiss me. How likely you think it is that anyone's going to get that to happen anytime soon?'

'A royal tutor who turns up dead can't benefit from any royal protections,' Arrasia said, smiling.

72

'You got that right, you dumb bitch.' Ferius would've scolded me for using that word, but I was pretty sure she'd've found something even worse for Arrasia. 'The queen played the outlaw of blades for a reason, lady. So if you and your half-witted friend here aren't long gone by the time everyone goes to bed tonight, I'm going to kill you in your sleep.'

'You'll never—'

'No? How do you think I've stayed alive all this time? A disowned Jan'Tep with next to no magic, a spell warrant on my head and shadowblack marks on my face? I'm a spellslinger, lady. I rely on magic that's got half a chance of blowing my hands off every time I use it. And I'm still here. You think I don't know how to get around whatever guards or friends or wards you have protecting you? You think I won't come a-knocking tonight? Ask yourself one question: do you really want to gamble with the only cards you're holding?'

Arrasia started to say something but then stopped herself, turned and left by one of the corner passageways. Koresh followed her. I breathed in and out several times in quick succession, unable to stop my heart racing now that I wasn't in immediate danger.

Karanetta had tears in her eyes. I had paid little attention to her up until now. She seemed neither a threat nor an ally, and so didn't figure much into my thinking. 'I'm so . . . I'm so sorry,' she said. 'I knew they . . . but I'm not like Koresh or Arrasia. I really am just a mathematics tutor. I have no power other than my knowledge, no friends or influence at court. I just—'

I wanted to say, 'Then what good are you?' but I had just narrowly avoided being killed on my eighteenth birthday by gambling that an eleven-year-old girl was smarter than all the political forces of the Daroman court. I was feeling merciful. 'Just go. Teach the queen some astronomy or something. I'm told she missed most of her lessons today.'

Karanetta paused for a moment, as if she was going to apologise again or start telling me her secrets. Instead she nodded once and walked away, her eyes full of tears and heartache.

Her departure left me entirely alone in the queen's court of justice. Only then did the unbelievable stupidity of my actions occur to me. I was exhausted, bruised and battered, in unfamiliar territory with no allies and no plan, and I'd just declared my intent to murder two people who up until a few minutes ago had been powerful enough to control the queen of Darome. And Reichis wasn't even here to appreciate it.

I looked down at the table we'd scuffed up in our card game. Someone had left my handcuffs there. A reminder? A threat? Well, it wasn't the first and wouldn't be the last. I picked them up and put them in the pocket of my coat. Maybe I could find someone who could sever the chain and use them as bracelets. They were, as it turned out, surprisingly comfortable.

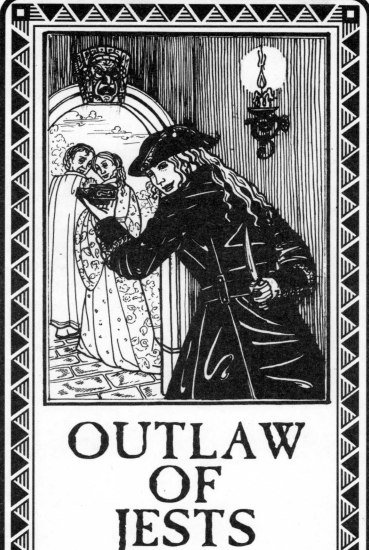

OUTLAW
OF
JESTS

There's one way an outlaw can survive beyond those first few years on the run: go straight. It's not that hard; there's always some desperate town or wealthy patron willing to pay for the services of someone who can perform dirty deeds, quick and quiet-like. After a while though, all those little things about civilisation you got used to living without start to make you itch. It's just a matter of time before you do something stupid – something that reminds people why they don't like outlaws in the first place.

9

Uncommon Comforts

They gave me a pleasant room on the same floor as the queen's own chambers, a courtesy which, I assume, came by custom rather than by anyone actually wanting me there. Harrex and Parsus were waiting outside for me. My powder holsters, deck of throwing cards, castradazi coins – even the pair of long knives I'd taken off old Merrel of Betrian – were conspicuously in their care. I motioned for the powders with a slight grin on my face.

'Now, see here, Kellen, I mean, tutor of cards—' Harrex began.

'You can just stick with Kellen,' I said, 'seeing as how we're old friends.'

'Come on now, we didn't have no choice. We had to bring you in and –'

I took the holsters and attached them to the sides of my belt. He and Parsus took an involuntary step back.

'Relax, gentlemen,' I said. 'We're square.'

'Really?'

'You could've done a lot worse to me if you'd wanted. I know you had to show off how tough you were back there. But you played things straight on the road and you treated the squirrel cat right, all things considered. As long as he

79

hasn't been hurt since the last time I saw him, we're good.'
I turned the handle and started opening the door.

'Wait!' Harrex shouted.

Something small and furry slammed into me with the force of a tornado tearing up a dead tree. I fell backwards, reaching hopelessly for the powders at my side. My head hit the stone floor and I saw stars.

'Kellen!'

I opened my eyes to behold teeth, fur and beady little eyes.

'Damn it, Reichis, whose side are you on?'

The little bastard gave me a sheepish, lopsided smile. It's the closest thing you get to an apology with him. 'They had me locked in there. I was getting ready to escape.'

Harrex reached a hand down. 'Tried to warn you,' he said.

Reichis nearly bit his hand off.

'Hey now, little fella, didn't we treat you right? You didn't give us no choice about the crossbow. But we fixed you right up, fed you treats and such, didn't we?'

'Yeah,' Reichis chittered. 'Then you locked me up in a cage like I was some kind of pet rabbit, arsehole!'

'What's he sayin'?' Harrex asked.

I pushed Reichis off me and got back to my feet. 'He says he's sorry and he promises not to do it ag— Ow! Damn it, Reichis,' I swore, rubbing my own hand.

Harrex shook his head as he and Parsus headed back down the hall. 'Little guy sure has a temper on him.'

You have no idea.

'All right,' I said, my hand still smarting. 'How are the accommodations?'

Reichis hopped in ahead of me and gave me the tour.

'Two exits,' he said. 'The one we just came in and the

window. The window's not great – it's a long drop and hard to climb down if you're big, dumb and clumsy.'

'Thanks. I was thinking more about the bed.'

Looking inside the room they'd prepared for me was like drinking a very expensive bottle of wine much too quickly. Marble floors reflected traces of gold-leaf gilding from the painted ceilings. The furniture was all of a set – elaborately carved oak chairs, a sofa whose shape was remarkably feminine and a table carved with a battle scene from the Third Berabesq War (the one in which the Daroman were the victors.) It wasn't so much a large room as a small mansion. 'Guess tutors of the queen's court don't lack for the finer things in life,' I said aloud. Some enterprising servant had even managed to find an array of card decks and laid them out elegantly inside a display case next to the bed. But the opulence and elegance, like the taste and smell of an overpriced wine, left quickly, replaced by a single thought: *Don't fool yourself into thinking this is for you. Not for long anyway.*

Exhaustion overtook me and I found my way to the bed. My head hadn't even hit the pillow before Reichis crawled over and asked, 'What's the play?'

'Could you move down a bit?' I asked. 'You don't smell so good.'

He sniffed. 'You should talk.'

'Yeah, well, it's my bed.'

Reichis looked at me askance. 'For how long?'

I shrugged. 'Who knows? They made me a royal tutor, if you know what that is.'

'Really? A Daroman royal tutor?'

'Yep.'

'All rights, privileges, stationery . . . whatever and such?'

I lifted my head and opened my eyes. 'How do you know any of this stuff?'

'Heard them two morons through the door talking about it when they were waitin' for you.' He hopped up and down a couple of times excitedly. 'Damn, Kellen, you're practically untouchable in this place! Let's go steal something! They can't do hardly anything about it. No, wait, let's . . . yeah, let's go murder somebody, right in broad daylight!'

I stared at him just long enough to establish that he was dead serious. 'You really are becoming an evil little monster, aren't you?'

Ever since Reichis had gotten infected with the shadow-black, I'd been careful to keep an eye on any especially demonic new proclivities. This is hard to watch for in an animal that basically wants to kill anyone who irritates him – and in case you haven't noticed? *Everybody* irritates Reichis.

He offered up the squirrel cat equivalent of a shrug. 'It's an evil world. Let's have some fun while we can.'

'The queen, she . . . implied she might be able to remove the shadowblack, Reichis. If I do whatever the hells it is she wants done here. You and I could be rid of this once and for all. I could—'

Reichis snorted. 'What? You still think your daddy's going to welcome you back with open arms if you just get those marks off your face?'

I shook my head. 'No, but I'd settle for not having to spend every day of my life with a big black target on my face.'

He scampered off to stare at himself in a full-length mirror near one of the armoires. 'Well, I *like* how it makes me look. Fierce. Deadly.'

'Psychotic?' I offered.

'Psy-co-tic,' he repeated slowly, making it clear he had no idea what the word meant. 'Yeah, *psychotic*. Cool.'

Few people know much about the true nature of the shadowblack. I'd heard a half-dozen theories even before I'd found the Ebony Abbey and plenty more in the months since I'd left it in flames. Is it a demonic curse? Or just a different form of magic that no one's mastered yet? No one knows for sure, but there are no end of Jan'Tep hextrackers, Berabesq Faithful, and a host of other righteous folk ready to ritually sacrifice anyone who has the marks. I'd done my level best to kill as many of those upstanding citizens as I could, but there would always be others eager to try to murder me in my sleep. And yet, there was always some arsehole glibly telling me that there are worse problems to have than a few swirling black markings around my left eye and that I should quit whining. That arsehole usually happens to be Reichis.

'This is how all those other skinbags sucker you, Kellen. They spin you some story about a spell or a potion that'll rid you of the shadowblack and off you go, taking chances with our lives and, worse, spending all our money, just to find out you've been tricked again.'

I ignored him. It was an argument we'd had too many times already.

'Fine,' he growled. 'At least let's go explore the place and see what there is to steal.'

'Can't,' I said, and pulled my hat down over my eyes. 'Gotta get some sleep. We've got work to do tonight.'

The squirrel cat did his best impression of a sigh, which sounded a lot like someone blowing their nose. 'Great. No doubt something just slightly more boring than being trapped in a room with nothing to do and nobody to eat.'

'Oh, I wouldn't say that,' I said sleepily. 'Chances are it's going to involve killing some very uptight people.'

My eyes were closed but I was pretty sure Reichis was smiling.

10

The Langzier

I managed a few hours of sleep before the combined smells of Reichis and myself – along with the natural unease caused by sleeping in a place that I wasn't sure how to escape – dragged me unwillingly into consciousness. Reichis was already awake.

'Bath,' he chittered, kicking me with his back feet.

I made an appropriate grumbling noise and stumbled off the bed. 'I thought you wanted to kill somebody?'

'Bath first,' he said, wandering over to the window. 'Then murder.'

I pulled on my trousers and attached the powder holsters to my belt before peering out the window with him. 'Two hours until daylight,' I said.

He padded over to the door and stretched up on his hind legs to open the latch. 'Plenty of time.'

I quickly rummaged around the drawers in the room on the off chance that they'd brought clothes for me. I found a few shirts in varying degrees of embarrassingly shimmery fabrics and colours not remotely suited to blending into a crowd. I discarded them in favour of my own filthy shirt. I may as well get clean before dressing up like a comfort artisan.

We left the rooms expecting to spend some time finding the baths, but there was no need. A servant was waiting outside my door. The boy was young, barely into adolescence, with jaw-length brown hair atop an innocent face, and wearing a long, white Daroman servant's robe. He looked practically angelic when he asked, 'Tutor of cards, how might I serve you?'

Reichis sniffed him and snarled. The boy took a discrete step back.

'The baths,' I said. 'We're looking to get clean.'

'There's a bath in your rooms, sir. If you give me some time I can start a fire and heat water for you. It would take no more than an hour.'

Reichis gave a low growl.

'We were hoping for something a little faster,' I explained.

The boy looked down at the squirrel cat with a dubious look on his face. Reichis, despite his many feral proclivities, approves of the civilising quality of a good bath.

'There are the court baths, sir. They're connected to the hot springs that run beneath the palace, so they're always hot. But I'm afraid they aren't private.'

'Anyone likely to be having a bath right about now?'

The boy shook his head.

'Then those sound perfect.'

'But are you sure you wouldn't rather—'

Reichis opened his jaws and closed them again several times, clacking his fangs and saving me the trouble of repeating myself.

'Yes, sir,' the boy said, though I wasn't clear whether he was talking to me or the squirrel cat. 'I'll take you there now.'

* * *

The court baths were set in a vast marble room that contained all kinds of watery delights, from oval tubs set into the floor meant for a single person to more elaborately shaped pools clearly intended to house multiple guests and serve purposes other than just getting clean. Small green trees in clay pots stood throughout the room and small tables stocked with wine and dainty assortments of slightly soggy-looking biscuits stood like waiting servants next to each of the baths. Soon every part of me was submerged in the heated, slightly sulphuric water, except for my hands. Those I rested on towels on the rim of the bath. Wet hands are not a good idea for someone whose survival often depends on handling exploding powders.

'Well, this is just awful, isn't it?' I said.

Reichis's reply came in the form of a small grunt that was halfway to a groan of pleasure. We had found a small upholstered stool and – over the objections of the servant boy – placed it in one of the tubs so that the squirrel cat could bask in luxuriating warmth without drowning. He was lounging on his back with his snout out of the water, a biscuit held between his teeth that he was gradually nibbling his way through.

The boy coughed politely. 'Sir, if you've no more need for me, then perhaps I could return to my other duties?'

'Sure, you go ahead and—'

Reichis swallowed and then chittered, 'Biscuit.'

The sight of the squirrel cat, his face sticking out of the hot water with its mouth open, teeth revealed, made the boy look ill. 'Sir, does it want me to . . . ?'

I nodded. 'Just get him another biscuit and then you can be on your way.'

The servant picked up another one of the crumbly delicacies from the nearby table and held it up to me as if for inspection. I nodded. 'Just pop it in his mouth.'

The boy held one tiny edge of the biscuit between his fingers and stayed as far back as possible while reaching towards Reichis's mouth. The squirrel cat clacked his teeth together several times, nearly sending the servant falling backwards. After taking a moment to recover his wits, the boy half dropped, half threw the treat into the waiting maw before turning and scampering out the door.

'Moron,' Reichis mumbled as he chewed.

'You really aren't very respectful towards servants,' I said.

Reichis made a hissing sound. 'Anyone who allows themselves to be made a servant deserves whatever he gets.'

'It's not something people choose, Reichis.'

'I didn't see a collar around his neck. What? He doesn't know where the door to the palace is? He could be a free creature any time he wanted if he wasn't a coward.'

I let it go. Reichis has some strange ideas and we've known each other long enough to have accepted that we're not going to change each other's mind. We sat in silence for a few more minutes before he spoke again. 'Kellen?'

'Get your own damned biscuit. See? I'm a free creature. You should be proud of me.'

'No, the other stuff. Who are we killing?'

I proceeded to tell Reichis about what the tutors had been doing to the queen, and what I presumed she wanted me to do about them. When I started to describe Koresh and Arrasia, Reichis stopped me.

'I'm pretty sure I already know them,' he said.

'What? How?'

'When those two idiots, Harrex and Parsus, had me locked in the room, just a few minutes before you arrived, I heard them arguing with two people outside. I got a good smell through the gap at the bottom of the door. A skinbag male who stank of muscle and sweat even though he talked like some pissy manor-born noble, and a woman. Someone should tell her that perfuming your underarms is a crime against nature. Anyway, her voice was younger but twice as mean.'

That certainly sounded like the two tutors. 'What were they arguing with the marshals about?'

'They wanted to get into the room. Said they were supposed to make sure it was ready for you. They had something with them, but it was encased in metal so I couldn't smell what it was. The marshals were having none of it though.'

I wondered what they'd been trying to do to my rooms. My lack of experience with the Daroman nobility was going to be a problem sooner or later. No doubt Koresh and Arrasia had allies of various sorts and ranks. There had to be at least a few Jan'Tep here, either hired out to the Daroman court or on some diplomatic mission for the newly crowned mage sovereign. The fact that our illustrious leader happened to be my father reassured me not one bit.

'Kellen, if you're just going to sit there like a stump, you might as well get me another butter biscuit.'

'I'm thinking,' I said.

'Do it out loud then. While getting me a biscuit.'

'Fine. I'm thinking that if Koresh and Arrasia decide to eliminate me instead of running, I have no clue how they'll go about it.'

Reichis grunted. 'Probably should have thought of that before you threatened them.'

'I'll get you another butter biscuit if you promise to stop being an arsehole,' I said, rising out of the bath.

'Well, look at it this way: how would *we* go about killing *them?*'

I walked over to the table, careful not to slip on the marble floor. 'Well, I'd want to do it without witnesses, of course. Even if a tutor can't be prosecuted by the marshals, it's still not a good idea to advertise a murder.' I picked up one of the biscuits and tossed it at Reichis before taking another for myself. The squirrel cat's paws snapped up out of the water and snatched it in mid-air.

'That means you need to keep an eye on your victim. Make sure you know where they are at all times so you can find the perfect opportunity.'

I nodded, looking over one of the bottles of wine before taking a swig. 'So you need spies,' I said. 'People who can get close to the target without attracting suspicion . . . Ah, crap.'

'What?'

'Get out of the bath. We need to get away from here.'

Reichis hopped up onto his hind legs and shook himself. 'What's the problem?'

'The boy.'

'What about him?'

I grabbed a towel and started drying myself off. 'He said he needed to return to his duties.'

Reichis jumped out of the bath, sliding a bit on the smooth marble before coming to a stop. 'So what? He's a servant.'

'Yeah, but what duties? What was he doing before he brought us here?'

The squirrel cat shrugged. 'Sitting outside our door, waiting.

I guess every noble gets a servant waiting on them in case they need anything.'

'Did you see servants waiting outside any other rooms on our way here?'

Reichis growled as he worked it out. 'Damn it. I was really enjoying this bath.'

I pulled my trousers on and flipped open my powder holsters. 'He was keeping an eye on us for Koresh and Arrasia. Remember how he wanted us to stay in the room? Maybe they were planning an attack.'

'That quickly?' Reichis asked.

'I wouldn't have thought so, but now I'm not so sure.'

'So now the kid's gone and told them where we are.'

I looked around the room. 'This isn't a bad place to do a murder.'

Reichis and I split up, checking for hidden entrances. There were windows in the room, but they were over twelve feet up and looked to be locked tight, designed to let the light in, nothing more. In theory someone might have climbed up, but it was an unlikely route in. Other than that there was only the one door into the room.

'Kellen . . .'

I turned to see Reichis was stalking towards me, his belly practically on the ground. 'What is it?' I asked.

'Behind you.'

I turned to face the wall. It was about ten feet away and there wasn't much to see except the elaborate mosaic depicting happily bathing Daroman shepherds. The thing Reichis had warned me about moved so slowly that at first I mistook it for part of the decor.

A snake.

'Back away and let me get it,' Reichis said. I could hear both anticipation and trepidation in his voice. Squirrel cats have a thing about reptiles.

I shook my head. 'I'll hit it with the spell.'

The snake was working its way along the wall, inch by inch. It wasn't very big – just a foot and a half long, and no more than an inch thick. It had some kind of membrane folded against its back.

'Regular snakes don't look like that, Kellen. They don't crawl along walls, and they don't move that slowly.'

I pulled powder from my holsters and I was about to blast it when the thing shot out at me like an arrow. I barely dodged out of the way in time to avoid its fangs attaching themselves to my throat. I spun around to see Reichis try to leap up after it, but the snake held itself in the air as membranous folds of skin, green and glistening, waved gently from its sides like water lilies floating in a pool.

'What the hells is that?' I asked, already sounding out of breath from the speed at which my heart was racing, no doubt in an attempt to convince me to run out of there as fast as my legs would carry me.

'It's a gods-damned langzier,' Reichis growled.

A *langzier!* I'd never actually seen one before, but from the way Reichis talked about them, squirrel cats hated langziers even more than crocodiles. And squirrel cats *really* hate crocodiles. Rumour had it the tiny snakes had been a gift from the Shan people to the Jan'Tep, bred with a singular ability: the damned things can fly. Once given their target, the langzier lies in wait, almost catatonic, until the intended victim appears. From that moment on, the langzier will attack over and over until its venomous teeth have sunk into its prey.

92

It's doubtful any culture has ever devised a more perfect form of assassination. Now one of them was floating before me, eyeing me with calm certainty, knowing I wasn't fast enough to stop it.

'Kellen . . .' Reichis chittered nervously.

'I've got a plan.'

I really didn't.

The snake was going to come at me again. Outrunning it was impossible. So was trying to slice it with my throwing cards, which were on the other side of the room in any case. It's possible one of my castradazi coins might've been of some use, but those were also too far to reach. There was no way I'd be able to hit it with my usual blast spell, so instead of tossing the powders straight at each other, this time I flicked them from my fingers as I spun my hands in opposite directions, like a lady opening a fan. 'Cara'juru Toth,' I intoned as the powders collided.

I'd spent half my nights over the past several months working on the *juru* variation of the *carath* spell. It's not nearly as powerful as the basic form of incantation, but always relying on the same trick risked making me predictable. Besides, hard as it is to believe, there are times when the solution to my problems isn't blasting a hole through someone's torso. I leaped back as the spell took effect, the flames fanning into the air before me, becoming a kind of shield that would set anything that passed through it on fire.

In theory anyway.

The langzier flew through the explosion, missing me but dousing itself in the remnants of powder that glowed like burning embers. I watched as the snake swam through the air, shaking itself once, shedding the flames like dead skin.

Stick to the tried and true, I thought, reaching into my holsters to pull more powder. 'Carath Toth,' I shouted. The snake evaded the blast easily, and this time I felt its oily skin rub against my own as it flew by.

Reichis was chittering angrily. 'It's toying with you, Kellen, figuring out how you move before it strikes for real. With your pathetically frail constitution, that poison in its fangs is going to take you down faster than a farm boy at his first—'

'Cara'juru Toth,' I said, going back to the fire-fan spell but this time using more powder. The air in front of me filled with flame. The light seemed to confuse the snake and it swam around blindly in the air, trying to relocate me. The heat on my fingertips was starting to worry me though.

'Get it over to me,' Reichis said. He was climbing up one of the taller tables so that he'd be high enough to glide down on top of the snake.

'He's too small and too fast for me to hit, Reichis. Even if you grab him, he'll bite you before you get your teeth on him.'

'That's when you blast him! The langzier can't dance when it sings!'

The snake came at me again. This time I fire-fanned too much powder in the air and felt my fingertips really starting to burn. I was screwed now. If I tried again I'd blow my own hands off.

'Get over here, Kellen, you idjit!'

Not knowing what else to do, I raced over to the table where Reichis was standing. The langzier flew through the flames, setting itself on fire and once again snapping in the air to shed the burning layer. Its skin underneath was red now, matching the fury in its eyes. I looked around for anything to defend myself with. I picked up a wine bottle and smashed the end against the table.

Just as the langzier flew at my face, brown fur filled my vision. Reichis landed on the floor with the langzier in his mouth. The creature wriggled, its sinewy body whipping around too fast for me to catch it. Reichis was trying to snap its spine by shaking it, but the thing's head came around and bit him on the back.

'Reichis!'

'Now, idjit! Now!' he growled.

I was having trouble concentrating over the strange music that had suddenly appeared. A soft, melodic hiss came from the langzier's jaws even as its teeth buried themselves into Reichis's fur. The snake's body was almost completely still though. *The langzier can't dance when it sings!*

Problem was, the squirrel cat wasn't moving any more either.

The langzier delivers two different poisons: the first one temporarily paralyses and the second kills. At the spot where the creature's fangs were embedded into Reichis's back, his pelt began to change colour. A sickly green spread across the squirrel cat's fur like a swarm of locusts. I dropped to my knees and grabbed the snake's tail with one hand and jammed the broken end of the bottle into its hide with the other. The damned creature's skin was thicker than I'd expected. I raised the bottle and smashed it back down on the langzier again and again until I felt the glass shatter against the marble floor. Tiny shards flew up at me, stinging my cheek. My hand was bleeding, pieces of glass embedded into my palms. I now held half of the snake's body in my left hand. I'd severed the creature in two.

With a soft hiss, almost a sigh, the snake's jaws came free from Reichis's back. I slammed the remains against the floor until I heard the bones of the langzier's tiny skull splinter to dust.

'Reichis . . .'

He didn't respond at all. He was giving off a horrible noise, halfway between a snarl and a desperate wail. His body began to shudder uncontrollably. I put my hands on his sides to steady him but the squirrel cat growled at me, 'Don't touch . . .', green bile slithering out from between his teeth.

'Reichis, tell me what to do!'

'No . . . Nothing . . . Different for squirrel cats . . . We're tougher th—' He convulsed several times and vomited on the floor. 'Arsehole snakes,' he groaned.

I picked up a flask with water, poured some into a cup and put it near him. Reichis threw up again, much of it going into the cup. I tossed it away and reached for another one. He vomited once more, this time shitting himself as his little body tried to empty itself of everything it could.

I kept saying his name over and over again, but every time I reached out a hand to try to comfort him, he shrugged me off and crawled further away. 'Gods-damned snakes,' was all he kept saying. Finally the vomiting stopped and he collapsed in his own filth. I came to him on my hands and knees and picked him up off the ground. His fur was so cold. I'd never known him to be so cold. The stench of vomit and defecation was overpowering. I held Reichis against my chest, trying to keep him warm.

'Get your damned hands off me,' he rasped, still shaking uncontrollably. He couldn't get away though. He was too weak to do anything but lie limp in my arms. 'I'm not your damned familiar.' His teeth snapped at me feebly. 'We're not family. This is business; that's all it's ever been.'

'I know, Reichis,' I said, trails of sweat sliding down my cheeks. 'It's just business. That's all.'

We sat like that for nearly an hour, until the first tentative rays of light began to slither into the room from the windows above. The day would start soon, and someone would find us. Reichis had fallen unconscious, though his body still convulsed every few minutes. I rose carefully, still keeping him in my arms, and made my way back to our rooms.

I laid him down on the bed and found a towel and a jug of water and carefully cleaned his fur. I didn't want to disturb him so the work was slow. When I was finished I threw the towels out the window and folded my blankets over him. Then I washed and carefully dried my hands. The feeling in my fingertips hadn't returned yet, but I didn't care. I adjusted my powder holsters and took a chair to face the door. I didn't think Koresh and Arrasia would try a second time, not this morning, not now that the palace was awake. But my vigil gave me time to think, to consider strategies and to plan. I'd been an idiot to provoke them. They'd taken their shot and nearly killed Reichis. Now it was going to be my turn, and I wasn't going to miss.

Because that, too, was just business.

11

The Butler

In between bouts of checking on the squirrel cat and contemplating various ways to murder Koresh and Arrasia, I packed our things. What had happened to Reichis had been my fault. I'd gotten distracted. I hadn't come to the Daroman court for the money, and I sure as hells hadn't come because I wanted to try to save their queen. The marshals had arrested me. That was their job. Mine was to escape. I should've done so last night, but I'd gone and let my sympathy for an eleven-year-old girl get in the way.

So, fine. I was an idiot. Reichis could tell me all about it in a few hours when he was ready to travel and I'd gathered our things together. Farewell, Daroman empire – may you fade from the pages of history faster than spilled water on dry sand.

It didn't take long to pack our meagre belongings into our two leather saddlebags – along with a few items from the room that might fetch a decent price on our way out of the city. When I was done, I sat back down on the chair and let my hands rest inside my open holsters, my fingers close to the powders that wanted to burn almost as much as I did. I'm a coward by profession, but I longed for that door open, to see Koresh and Arrasia and whichever allies they could muster coming for us. I would use up every last grain of powder I had to blow a hole through the lot of them.

Despite my anger, exhaustion overtook me, and sometime later I fell asleep in my chair. When I awoke it was full light. I looked over to check on Reichis, but he wasn't under the covers. It took me a few minutes to find him asleep under the bed. Sometimes he does that, when he's hurt – finds somewhere to hide away and lick his wounds. I saw his eyes open when I spotted him, but he didn't say anything so I just left him alone.

Someone knocked at the door and I had to hold myself back from blasting a hole through it. I kept my hands near my holsters though. For all I knew, Koresh and Arrasia might have decided not to wait before taking another swing at me. Or maybe they'd fled and now it was the queen herself who'd sent assassins to my door. Even if, by getting rid of her old tutors, I'd eliminated all her problems, how likely was she to want to replace two abusive tyrants with an unknown quantity who might be just as bad? Maybe the smart money was on using me to get rid of them, then having me disappear without a trace shortly thereafter. No doubt officially the blame would fall on Koresh and Arrasia's supporters, but everyone would know that accepting the position of royal tutor had become a dangerous endeavour, and probably not worth the risk.

The second knock was louder than the first. Finally I took a few steps back from the door and said, 'Come in.'

The door opened slowly and a man entered. He looked to be about forty, with a thick, muscular build. He was taller than me, which isn't saying much, but he was taller than most Daroman folk too. If you needed someone to beat your enemy to death, this was the sort of guy you'd send to do the job. 'I'm Arex Nerren, the queen's social secretary. You're her so-called tutor of cards?' he asked in what would've been a pleasant baritone if he didn't sound quite so self-assured.

I nodded. 'Who were you expecting, given that you knocked on the door assigned to the new tutor?'

'That's fair, I guess. On the other hand, you're not quite what I was expecting to find.' He entered the room and looked me up and down. Then he walked over to the chest of drawers like he owned the place, and pulled out another towel and tossed it to me. 'You mind wiping whatever that is off your chest? Kind of looks like dried vomit. Maybe you could also put on a shirt, so we can talk like civilised people?'

I kept an eye on him as I took the jug of water off the table and washed my chest. Arex went through the rest of the drawers and pulled out a pair of trousers and a clean shirt and tossed them to me as well. The trousers were a rich black leather and the shirt was gleaming silver with purple trim. 'A little effete, I know, but your generally dishevelled look should balance it out,' he said.

I looked him over. His own robes were white silk, open in a wide v-shape over his broad chest, the rest subtly embroidered with flowers I recognised as the symbols of each of the twelve Daroman provinces. The whole affair was topped off with a bright green and gold sash. 'Who you calling effete, friend?'

I'd expected an angry retort, but he just held up his arms and grinned. 'Perils of court life. These are the official garments of my office, and I'm required to appear in them on court days, of which today is one.'

100

'And your office is what, again?' I asked, pulling on the trousers and shirt and desperately trying to think up another reason to comment on just how idiotic he looked.

'The queen's social secretary,' he repeated. 'I manage her calendar.'

I wasn't sure of what to make of this guy, who talked and looked like he could wrestle bears, but dressed only slightly more reservedly than a comfort artisan in a not very high-end traveller's saloon. 'And what can I do for the queen's social secretary?'

He glanced around the room and proceeded to sit on the sofa that was shaped like a rather large woman. 'What can you do for me? Kid, you're a disowned, disgraced, and – if you ask me – displaced troublemaker with no money, no friends and no class. I doubt there's a thing in this world you could do for me. I'm here to do something for you.'

Ah, so he wasn't here to kill me. Just to rough me up a little so as to deliver some message about who I shouldn't cross. I stretched my neck a little to get the kinks out. I never like to get beaten up with a stiff neck. I could see Reichis's beady eyes from under the bed where he was waiting to take a bite out of this guy's ankle when the time came. Somehow I didn't think it would help.

'Let me guess – you're here to give me a warning.'

Arex stared at me wide-eyed for a second, then broke out laughing. He started to speak, but then stopped again to laugh some more. 'Kid,' he said at last, 'you've got the situation all wrong. I meant what I said: I'm the queen's social secretary. I'm here to take you to court and begin the rather lengthy process of introducing you to the assembled nobles and courtiers.'

Some of the tension in my chest eased. I think my relief

was probably obvious, which only served to irritate me. 'I think I'll pass for today. I'm still tired from my trip and I've got some appointments to keep.'

The easy smile left Arex's face, just for a moment. 'They're gone, kid.'

'Who's gone?'

He sighed. 'Our relationship will progress a lot quicker if you get it into your head that I'm not one of those bumbling backwoods idiots you're used to dealing with out in the borderlands. Koresh and Arrasia aren't here. They left last night. Apparently they're on an extremely important research project.'

'For how long?' I asked.

He shrugged. 'Who knows? Could be a long time, unless things change.'

So I had no concrete evidence that Koresh and Arrasia were the ones who'd sent the langzier and no way to get any, now that they were beyond my reach. Perhaps it would be worth trying to hunt them down before I left the city, or maybe find that servant who'd led me into the trap and drag him before the queen. Unless that was precisely what someone wanted me to do. *Ancestors*. I hate politics.

Arex walked over and ran a hand along the leather seam of one of my saddlebags. 'Going somewhere?' he asked.

Something in his voice made me think carefully before I answered his question. 'Nope,' I said finally. 'Just got used to always keeping my things organised when I was out on the frontier. You know how it is.'

Arex smiled. 'Sure, makes perfect sense. Koresh and Arrasia left most of their things here in the palace when they went on their research trip, of course.'

'Why "of course"?'

'Well, because if it looked like they'd decided to, oh, I don't know, permanently abandon their duties without permission from the queen, well, then they'd be in some trouble, wouldn't they?'

'How much trouble?'

'Oh, you know, just the usual "hunted down by marshals and hanged by the neck until dead" kind of trouble. It's technically called "Desertion of the Monarch". It's an old law designed to prevent palace retainers from running if there's an attempted coup.'

I kept my expression casual. Reichis was still hidden under the bed, but I could see he was fully awake now. Arex was a big man, but we'd have the advantage that he wouldn't see the squirrel cat coming. 'Good thing I wasn't planning on leaving without telling anyone,' I said.

Arex gave me a wide-mouthed grin that hardly seemed friendly at all. 'Good thing indeed.' He removed his hand from my saddlebag. 'Oh, and watch your step around the corridors. Just a couple of hours ago we found a servant boy's body in the palace grounds.'

So much for using him as evidence against Koresh and Arrasia. 'How did he die?'

'Suicide. Apparently sometime last night he up and decided to throw himself from the seventh floor. Well, first he took the trouble to stick a knife in his own back, which seems excessive to me. Too bad really. From what I can tell, he was an enterprising young man; he'd just finished cleaning up the court baths, even though that wasn't one of his duties and they had been cleaned just hours before.'

Arex was staring at me as if he expected me to blurt out

a confession or bellow a denial. I thought about what kind of pressure the boy might have been under. Had Koresh and Arrasia promised him money? Threatened his life? Then I remembered what Reichis had said about people choosing to be servants. 'If you're waiting for me to shed a tear, it might take a while,' I said.

The queen's social secretary gave an indifferent shrug. He rose to tower over me. 'Come on, kid. It's been fun playing, but the queen's summoned you and attendance isn't optional. Let's not keep all the nice people waiting.' He paused at the door for a moment. 'Oh, and bring your pet. People will get a laugh out of him, and besides, one of the maids is liable to step on the little fella if he keeps skulking under the bed like that.'

12

The Deck of Sixty-Five

'The most important thing is to avoid embarrassing the queen,' Arex explained as we walked down a wide hallway decorated with marble busts and massive oil paintings of what I had to assume were previous Daroman monarchs, many of whom appeared to have been eating something particularly sour the day their portraits were being rendered.

'And you think I might embarrass her?'

He laughed. 'Kid, I can't imagine how you could possibly avoid it.'

I stopped and waited for him to realise I wasn't following him.

When he turned he said, 'What's the matter? Scared of something?'

Reichis gave a little growl. 'Let me show him "scared". Big damned oak tree.' It was the first thing he'd said since our encounter with the langzier. When you're worried about whether your business partner is ever going to fully recover from being poisoned by a venomous snake, having them start the day by threatening to kill the first person they meet is oddly reassuring.

Arex returned the growl with a benevolent smile. 'Better

keep a handle on that thing. Someone's liable to cook it up for dinner.'

'Keep talking like that and you might be surprised who ends up in the stew,' I said.

The queen's social secretary walked back to me. 'Yeah? You feeling frisky, kid?'

'I'm cool as a fresh stream, friend. But I'm going to have to ask you to stop calling me "kid".' Other than Ferius Parfax and Reichis, just about everyone who'd ever called me 'kid' had ended up trying to kill me.

Arex poked a thick finger on my chest. It felt like being jabbed with the back end of a spear. 'And what if I don't, kid?'

I should have seen through what he was doing, but I'd barely slept. I was angry and scared. So I got sloppy and let my temper get the best of me. Without so much as trying to distract Arex first, I took a swing at him.

He leaned back out of the way, neatly grabbed my arm and put me into a shoulder lock. Reichis growled, but Arex spun me around, using me like a shield. The squirrel cat froze in his tracks when he saw the big man's other arm around my neck. 'Best be a good doggy and sit this one out, or else your owner's headed for the grave.'

'"Doggy"? Get out of the damned way, Kellen. I'm gonna tear out this guy's tongue, wrap it around his eyeballs and make myself a sandwich.'

I tried to slip out of the shoulder lock but Arex was a skilled wrestler. I was helpless. He pushed me against the wall of the hallway and leaned in close behind me.

'Koresh and Arrasia were idiots, kid. They thought they had the queen all figured out, so they let their guard down. I'm not like them. I'm not *anything* like them.'

106

'Reichis,' I said evenly, 'go for his face.'

Arex laughed. 'Then what, Kellen of the Jan'Tep? He comes for me, I kill you. Maybe he injures me. Hell, maybe somehow he kills me. Then what? You're dead. I'm dead. The damned squirrel cat's as good as dead. So what happens to the queen?'

I didn't have an answer for that.

Arex gave me one more push, then released his hold on me and spun me back around.

'It took me all of three nasty comments to make you lose your cool, Kellen. You want to know how the queen's enemies are going to use you to embarrass her? That's how.'

I shook myself off, stared back at the big man and realised I'd just shown myself to be a blundering amateur. 'So that's what this is? A lesson in decorum?'

'Damn straight. I meant what I said, kid. I'm nothing like Koresh and Arrasia. I'll do whatever it takes to keep the queen safe.'

'You didn't seem to be doing all that great a job of it when I got here,' I countered.

A pained look crossed his face. 'Kid, I do my best, but I'm one guy and not very important in the scheme of things. Do you have any idea how many different factions of the great Daroman houses are trying to out-manoeuvre each other and the throne? I go after the royal tutors with some clumsy tactic – the kind you were probably planning before they sent their little flying snake after you – and whole nests of vipers will come out of the woodwork.'

I shook my head and started back down the hall, forcing him to follow me this time. 'The langzier's dead. Koresh and Arrasia are on the run. Seems like I did just fine without your advice.'

107

He grabbed my shoulder again, but without the wrestling hold this time. 'You're right. You did. Nobody expected that. Then again, nobody planned for you to show up in the first place. You surprised everyone and scared the hell out of them. That was day one. What have you got planned for day two?'

'I thought I might take "day two" off.'

Arex shook his head. 'Doesn't work that way. You spent last night settling your personal vendetta against Koresh and Arrasia. The rest of them, though? The court? They spent last night figuring out how to manipulate you or get rid of you. They're thinking about those markings around your eye and wondering what it all means, and how they can use it against you. You walk into the throne room with this hick frontiersman act you've got going on, and they'll box you into a corner so fast you'll find yourself chief supporter of the "bring back Koresh" movement before you know what hit you.'

'So that's what this is all about? Political power?'

Arex snorted. '"Political power",' he repeated. 'I love it when dumb people talk about politics like they're commenting on the weather.'

'Smells like rain,' Reichis said, 'in case anyone cares.'

'Fine, so explain this "political power" you're so impressed by.'

Arex looked around hopelessly, like someone had asked him to explain animal husbandry to a horse. 'First of all, political power isn't one thing. It's lots of things.'

'All right. How many kinds of "political power" are there?'

He pointed at my coat pocket. 'How many cards in one of your decks, oh, tutor of cards?'

I had a few decks on me, none of which I planned to tell him about. 'Four suits in a standard Daroman deck, each

108

with an ace, nine numbered cards, a jack, a knight, a scholar, the queen and the king. Then there's the five outlaw cards. That's sixty-five,' I replied.

'Right. Well, let's start there. If you can wrap your head around the fact that there are at least sixty-five different kinds of political power, from influence to manipulation to debt to threat . . . just start with those four and we'll see where it takes us.'

We reached the entrance to the main hall, where marshals outside stood watching people as they sauntered in and out of the large marble room. Arex stopped me there. 'This is it, kid. I'm going to take you in there and start introducing you to the infestation of snakes and rats we like to think of as the loyal Daroman nobility. What's your objective?'

'My "objective"? I don't know. You didn't tell me I needed an objective.'

'Now you know. You don't walk into court without a plan. So what's your objective, kid?'

I shrugged. 'I wouldn't mind finding a way to make you stop calling me "kid".'

Surprisingly, Arex nodded approvingly. 'Good. How're you going to do that?'

'Umm . . . wait until your back is turned, then stick a knife in your kidney?'

He shook his head. 'Flawed, since that'd be the end of you too. Come on, what's your plan?'

'Hells, I don't know. How am I supposed to figure this out on the spot?'

'Not my problem. Let's go. I'll give you a hint: threaten me.'

'All right. Quit calling me "kid" or I'll put a knife in your kidney.'

'Not believable. Try again.'

'I'll tell the queen you're an arsehole?'

He smiled. 'Closer, but that's just going to make you look like you're whining.'

I thought about it for a moment. What does a queen's social secretary worry about? What's small enough to be within the realm of possibility, but big enough to make an impression? 'How about this: call me "kid" one more time and I'll innocently turn my first conversation with the queen around to the fact that you seemed upset that Koresh and Arrasia were gone.'

Arex thought about that for a while. 'Good!' he said at last, nodding. 'That's a viable strategy. Innocent enough that you won't look like you've got an axe to grind, but aggressive enough that the comment could make trouble for me in future. Nice work. You might be a hair more clever than I gave you credit for.'

I actually felt pleased with his praise.

'Oh, please,' Reichis said. 'He's manipulating you.'

Damn it. You'd think I'd forgotten every lesson Ferius had taught me. 'This whole "lesson" of yours is just a way to manoeuvre me into thinking we're on the same side, isn't it?'

The queen's social secretary let out a big laugh and clapped me on the back. 'Now you're learning, kid! Come on – let's go meet some other folks who might want you dead.'

13

Dashing Snouts

As we entered the room, an old man in soft blue-and-silver robes announced us. 'Arex Nerren, social secretary to the queen,' he said. 'A cousin to Her Majesty, and Lord of the Eastern County of Verens. A warrior of noted skill in the arenas, he once felled two opponents while suffering a broken arm and collarbone. My lords and ladies, I present Secretary Arex.'

Arex entered the room ahead of me and received smiles and nods from various nobles and courtiers. I tried to guess which ones were his friends and which were plotting against him. He turned back to me and waited for the herald to announce me.

'Kellen Argos,' the old man said. 'Her Majesty the Queen's royal tutor of . . . ehm . . . her royal tutor of cards.' This last part sounded as if someone had forced him at knife-point to say it. 'A man of . . . unusual fashion and distinctive facial markings. He . . . ehm . . . played a most enjoyable game of cards with Her Majesty and . . . hem . . . lost with good grace. My ladies and gentlemen of the court, I present Tutor Kellen.'

'And his squirrel cat,' Arex said, looking entirely serious. 'Don't forget the squirrel cat.'

'Ehm . . . does the . . . squirrel cat have a name?' the herald asked me discreetly.

'Reichis,' I answered.

'I further present, Reichis, master . . . ehm . . . rather, a squirrel cat of, well –' he glanced down at my business partner with a look of some desperation – 'noble brown fur and . . . ehm . . . a most dashing snout.' The old man rushed through the last part. 'Lords and ladies, I present Reichis.'

People stared at the old man as if he'd gone insane. Arex smirked. Reichis laughed uncontrollably. I just tried to take it in stride and walked into the room.

'"Noble brown fur and a dashing snout"? Nicely done, Cerreck,' Arex chided the old man.

'Just you shut your mouth, Arex,' the herald replied angrily. 'What the hell has the world come to when I have to announce a squirrel cat at court?'

Arex shook his head sadly. 'Dark days indeed,' he said. 'We shall all want for "noble brown fur" and "dashing snouts" soon enough.'

Cerreck turned away, the scowl on his face disappearing as he greeted the next small group of nobles about to enter.

'You're kind of a jerk, aren't you?' I said to Arex.

'Actually, it's pretty much the only perk of my job.' He directed me towards a small group of men and women clustered around the tall, powerful figure of a military man. 'Now, speaking of jerks,' Arex said, 'let me introduce you to Leonidas. He holds the rank of major in the queen's northern army and commands a troop of the border forces.'

'All right, but why start with him?'

'Rumour has it he and Arrasia are lovers. So chances are he'll be killing you before the day is out.'

'Perfect.'

'Don't worry, partner,' Reichis chittered. 'I'll smother him with my noble fur.'

The part of me that wanted to kick the squirrel cat was still just so grateful that he was alive that all I could say was, 'That stopped being funny about three minutes ago.'

'Not to me. Maybe you need a dashing snout to get it?'

'Arex, you girlish little snot,' Leonidas boomed. 'Come to worm your way around court, eh?'

Arex's response was unlike anything I'd seen in him so far. It was, well, polite. In the extreme. 'My Lord Major Leonidas,' Arex said, no hint of accent or affect in his voice at all. 'The empire rests safely under your watch, and the court shines brighter for your presence!'

'See what I said?' Leonidas commented to his entourage. 'A worm, come in search of dirt in which to burrow.'

'We all serve as we may, lord major,' Arex replied humbly.

Leonidas strode forward and looked at Arex. They were both big men, roughly the same height. 'Look at you, Arex. You're big enough to be a soldier. What's the problem, eh? Made of fragile stuff?' Leonidas drove a fist into Arex's stomach, or at least pretended to. Arex stumbled back convincingly, but I suspected it was for show.

'My lord major, I implore you not to scare me like that!'

Leonidas laughed. 'Ah, come here, you big coward.'

Part of me was confused by Arex's sudden transformation into a sycophantic servant. Watching him get pushed around by Leonidas appealed to my sense of revenge for the way he'd manipulated me earlier, but I suspected this was some kind of act.

Leonidas gave Arex a rough embrace, designed to look as

if they were old friends. Or perhaps they were, and the show was for me? *Hells.* 'How am I supposed to survive a whole day of this?' I muttered.

'Go back to stabbing people in the kidneys,' Reichis chittered amiably in reply.

'And what have we here?' Leonidas asked. 'Someone let an animal into the queen's court?'

'That overstuffed skinbag puts a hand on me and he's a dead man,' Reichis warned.

'It is a squirrel cat, my lord major,' Arex said patiently. 'I believe it is a type of large domesticated rodent.'

Reichis gave a low growl that told me I was going to have to grab hold of him any second now, and that I was going to walk away from this morning with bite marks all over my nice new shirt.

Leonidas looked at Reichis with a bemused expression. 'That ugly little hamster? No, I was talking about this other animal here.' He pointed at me.

'This would be Kellen, the queen's new tutor,' Arex explained. 'You weren't here for his arrival yesterday.'

Leonidas nodded. 'Quite a story, if the tale is true – which it never is around here. You look Jan'Tep. Is that so?'

I nodded.

'Feeble bastards,' he said. 'And what's that filth around your eye? Someone punch you in the face already?'

'No, major, that's just an affectation from the east where I travelled as a child.'

Leonidas looked at me with a sneer on his face. 'Lying little chit, isn't he?' he commented to Arex. 'That's the shadowblack, isn't it, boy?'

Boy? He wasn't more than five years older than me.

'Saw a fellow with the demon's plague once,' he went on. 'Not a Jan'Tep like you, but a proper Daroman. Had the markings all over his face. Lived as an exile in the hills. The villagers drove him away when he was a boy and used his name to scare their children into doing their chores.'

I looked around absently.

'Need something?' Arex asked me quietly.

'Just looking for a knife,' I said.

Leonidas overheard and laughed. 'Ah, I'm just teasing you, o noble master of cards.' He threw an arm around my shoulders. 'I've no doubt we'll be best of friends one day. Isn't that right, Arex?'

Arex opened his hands as if in supplication. 'Any man would be honoured to call you friend, lord major.'

'Watch that one, boy,' Leonidas whispered in my ear. 'He's always up to something, and usually on the wrong side.' He withdrew his arm. 'Ah, I see one of my men over there flirting with a woman above his station. Can't have that.'

He turned to me briefly. 'Goodbye for now, royal tutor.' Then he nodded to Arex. 'Worm. I'll see you when I next need someone's tongue to clean my boots.'

'Don't look now, Kellen,' Reichis chittered up to me as the major strode away, 'but I think that guy's sweet on you.'

That seemed unlikely, but at least he hadn't challenged me to a duel. Or arm-wrestling or belly-butting or whatever it was they did here to demonstrate their suitability as warriors. 'How did that go?' I asked Arex.

'Not that well. I was hoping he'd ignore you. This is worse.'

'Great. How many more of these do we have to do?'

'Best take a deep breath, kid. It's going to be a long day.'

115

14

A Tutor's First Lesson

Those next few hours were a non-stop series of breaches of etiquette, false starts, near misses and overall embarrassments. Court days were, it turned out, interminably long, comprised of a sequence of meals and interviews and – once those were done – hideous rituals of group gesticulations which the Daroman nobility referred to as 'courtly dancing'. It was late evening by the time I got to bed, and I vowed to sleep for the next three days.

I made it barely an hour before midnight when someone knocked at my door. 'Master Kellen! Master Kellen!' The woman outside my room was whispering so loudly I felt as if I needed to explain how sound works.

I sighed and opened my eyes. Reichis was lying stretched out against my side, the way he does sometimes when we've been apart for a while. If you saw him that way you'd almost think he liked me. 'Get up,' I said, poking his furry belly.

The squirrel cat growled. 'Don't you need all your fingers for spellslinging?'

'Somebody's at the door. Are they here to kill me?'

He sniffed. 'Female. Adult. Horny.'

Ech. Those words have a lot more appeal when they're not being chittered at you by a grumpy squirrel cat.

I got up and opened the door. Karanetta was on the other side. 'Master Kellen—'

'*Mister*,' I said, rubbing the sleep from my eyes. 'Just "Mister".' Only Jan'Tep who pass their trials and are granted a mage's name are addressed as "Master". I didn't qualify.

'Koresh and Arrasia, they've come back. They're in the palace, in their rooms!'

I nodded. Of course they'd come back. It would've been too easy if they'd stayed away, but they'd only been gone a day and so were still protected by their status as royal tutors. I tried to imagine a reason for their return that didn't involve killing me, but there was no sense in delaying the inevitable. 'It's fine. I've got it covered.'

'They've got a man with them.' Her eyes went to the corridor outside the room even though it was empty. 'I think he's some kind of assassin.'

I found myself scrutinising Karanetta, searching for signs of deception. She was still in her nightclothes, long, blonde hair strewn across her shoulders. Anyone could tell she was terrified. 'You only got two out of three,' I said to Reichis absently.

Karanetta's eyes flickered from Reichis to me. 'Are you . . . ?'

'Just talking to myself,' I said.

The squirrel cat wandered over and sniffed at Karanetta's leg. 'Nope,' he said. 'I got it right.'

'Mister Kellen, you've got to get out of here!' Karanetta said urgently.

'It's okay, Reichis, you're getting old. Things start to slip.'

'Perhaps you could hide. Perhaps . . .' Karanetta began.

'Wait for it . . .' Reichis chittered.

'They wouldn't think to look for you in my room, would they?'

'. . . and squirrel cat one, humans zero,' Reichis chuckled, ambling back towards the bed.

Damn it.

'Karanetta, that's, well, that's very generous of you, but I couldn't risk endangering your life like that. Besides, I'll be fine. I can handle those two.'

'And the assassin?'

I nodded. 'And the assassin. Go back to bed. Don't worry about me.'

'But—'

'Trust me. It's all just a misunderstanding. We'll talk tomorrow. Over breakfast?'

She smiled shyly as I shunted her out of the room.

Once I had the door closed and locked again, Reichis hopped back up on the bed. 'So, Koresh, Arrasia and a hired assassin,' the squirrel cat said excitedly.

'I think I can take Koresh.'

Reichis snorted. 'He's bigger than you, stronger than you and he smells like an ex-soldier to me.'

'What does an ex-soldier smell like?'

'Like someone who can beat *you* up in a fight.'

I scratched my head. I really should have had a more thorough plan before I'd threatened to kill them. 'All right, put a pin in that one. Arrasia looks like she'd try to slip a knife in me when my back was turned.'

'Wrong again,' Reichis said. 'She's a poisoner. That I could smell for sure.'

Great. 'All right, let's focus on the assassin.'

'Oh, you don't have to worry about the assassin.'

'Why not?'

Reichis did his best squirrel cat approximation of a smile. 'Because I get the assassin.'

This is my life: run from all the people trying to kill me, while the two-foot-tall ball of furry insanity I call a business partner tries to murder everything in sight.

15

A Good Night's Murder

I'd figured it was a safe bet that Koresh and Arrasia would be waiting for me in one of their rooms. After all, I'd threatened their lives; they were expecting me to make a move on them. This way they had control over the terrain.

The legendary warrior-poets of Berabesq theology will tell you that controlling the terrain is the surest way to victory. They're full of crap. Surprise beats terrain every time.

Well, surprise and a lot of patience.

'He's not coming,' I heard Arrasia say. 'The coward's probably halfway to the southern border by now.'

I could make out footsteps coming towards the door.

'Stop.' Koresh's baritone voice resonated from the room.

'Why?' she asked.

'Because. I want him here, where we can control the situation.'

'Why didn't we just take a dozen men and go kill him and be done with it?'

I heard something slam against the door. I hoped it was Arrasia.

'Fool. If we did anything so overt we'd play right into that little bitch's hands. He's a tutor, do you understand that? We need *him* to attack *us*. Besides, we'd lose face if we needed twelve men to deal with one itinerant card player.'

'But you need this . . . person?'

'Ugh,' Reichis chittered quietly at me. 'Are they going to talk all night? I'm getting sleepy again.'

'Oleis is our insurance,' Koresh said. 'Besides, he keeps our hands clean. Now sit down and shut up.'

'What about magic? The card player is Jan'Tep.'

I could practically hear the grin in Koresh's voice. 'Did you not see the way all but one of his tattooed bands have reverse glyphs imprinted on them? He's an outcast. Probably the weakest mage they've ever produced. But just in case, I had my own Jan'Tep allies put abjuration spells around this whole wing. They didn't even charge me. This Kellen isn't very popular with his people.'

No kidding.

'I still don't like this,' Arrasia complained. 'The queen will demand explanations.'

'And who will give them to her? The card player will be gone and Karanetta will keep her mouth shut. No one will be able to touch us, and by the time I'm through with "Her Majesty", she'll know her place.'

A pause. 'If we push her too far, Koresh, she'll push back.'

Koresh's laughter was as vile a sound as I'd ever heard. Maybe because it sounded so much like my own father's. 'Push back? We two know the one thing about her that could destroy her. The Daroman people may be sheep these days, but there are some crimes even they won't tolerate. Why do you think she had to bring her Jan'Tep pet into the palace?'

'Are you not mad to speak of this in front of Oleis? An outsider? Use the truth to threaten the queen, of course, but

121

if the secret really got out? Koresh, the empire would fall into chaos.'

'You seem to be afraid of chaos, Arrasia. I'm not.'

The voices became quiet and for a second I was afraid they knew I was there. But soon enough I heard murmurs and realised they must have moved out onto the balcony.

'Sir?' a tentative voice whispered from far away.

I looked up and saw a servant down the hall. No doubt wondering what I was doing sitting outside the room of one of the royal tutors.

I held a finger to my lips and padded over to him in my bare feet.

'Sir,' the servant said, whispering, 'can I get anything for you?'

I shook my head. Then I thought about it. 'I could do with a whisky. Not yet though.'

'Yes, sir, but if I may ask, when would you like it?'

I looked down at Reichis. He shrugged.

'Oh, in about ten minutes, I think.'

'Very good, sir. Can I clean that up for you?' The servant pointed at the little mess I'd made in front of Koresh's quarters.

'No, it'll take care of itself. Just the whisky. Or really anything that gets people good and drunk will do.'

The servant nodded. Then he looked at me carefully. 'We all love the queen, sir,' he said. 'If there's anything else I can do to be of service . . .'

I held his gaze but said nothing.

He nodded again. 'Very good, sir. Whisky in ten minutes.'

I clapped him silently on the shoulder and padded back to my spot at the door.

'Someone comes,' a man's voice said through the door. It wasn't Koresh, so I assumed it must be Oleis.

Ah, what the hells, I thought. I knocked, then backed up from the door until I hit the wall on the other side of the corridor. Then I thought better of it and stepped a foot to the side.

The door opened and a crossbow bolt embedded itself into the wall where I'd stood a moment before. Then Koresh stepped out, dropped the crossbow and drew a soldier's short sword from his belt.

Damn it. I hate it when Reichis is right.

Koresh smiled like a starving man about to sit down to dinner. 'Card player . . .'

'Stop!' I said, holding a handful of powder in my right hand. 'One more step and you'll face the insidious death magic of Kellen Argos, arch-lord of the seventh order of shadow, master mage of the Jan'Tep!'

Reichis looked up at me, disgusted. 'You really can't stop yourself, can you?'

A man in red cloth tried to step past Koresh to get at me, but the big man held him back. 'No, he's mine,' the tutor said.

Koresh brought his sword up into line and made it clear where he was going to put it as he began to slowly bridge the three-foot gap between us. 'You stupid little boy,' he said. 'You think we don't know about magic here? Go ahead, try it. We had a true mage place abjuration wards all through this wing of the palace.'

'That's too bad,' I said, holding up the black powder in my right hand for him to see. 'Because the magic only lets me control the blast. The powder's what does all the exploding.'

123

Koresh looked at me and then at my hand. 'But . . . don't you need two kinds to—'

I pointed to the floor where he was standing in a pile of red powder. 'Should've left when I gave you the chance,' I said, and threw the black powder into the red as I threw myself to the side.

There was a modest but still respectable explosion and Koresh went up like a torch. The assassin behind him fell back from the force of the blast. Arrasia was nowhere to be seen.

'Mine!' Reichis said, and raced into the room, jumping up onto the assassin's face. I heard the man scream. It really doesn't matter how many secret fighting arts you learn; they just don't teach you how to fight squirrel cats in assassin school.

I entered the room behind him, careful not to get too close to Koresh's still-smouldering corpse. Arrasia held a long, wicked-looking knife in her hand, waving it out in front of her. 'Knife,' I said, happy to have been right for once. But Reichis was too busy skittering around, evading the assassin, who had his own blade and was doing a decent job of defending himself, despite the bloody socket where his right eyeball used to be. Reichis was savouring the aforementioned squishy sphere in his mouth as he dodged his opponent's desperate lunges. The squirrel cat had been a monstrously cantankerous little bastard even before he got the shadowblack. I was starting to worry about just how evil he was going to become. That said, I had more pressing matters to concern myself with at that moment.

'You get one chance, Arrasia,' I warned the tutor. 'I'm sure you've stuck that knife in a lot of people's backs, but you miss me just once and it's over for you.'

124

She waved the knife back and forth in a little arc. 'You're right,' she said, a smile creeping onto her lips. Then she spat in my face. A greenish-grey mist burned my skin. Even before I could scream, I felt all the muscles in my face go numb. *Damn it*, I thought as the poison set in. *The little bugger was right again.*

I kept my lips closed and held my breath to minimise how much of the toxin got inside me. It must've been some kind of paralytic, because my vision went blurry and I found myself falling to one side. Arrasia leaped forward to straddle me as I hit the ground. She brought the knife's point to my throat. I tried to shout for Reichis, but my voice wasn't working very well, and besides, when he's got the blood lust like that, he's good for pretty much nothing but eating human entrails. The worst part was that my vision was defogging, meaning the poison was already clearing from my system. If I'd had another few seconds I might have recovered.

Just as I felt the tip push into the skin of my neck I caught a blinding flash of fire followed by a deafening thunder that left my ears ringing. It also left Arrasia's blood and brain matter splattered across my face. I was horrified to discover some flecks of skull and hair had fallen inside my mouth. Her body slid sideways off me, and I got my hands underneath myself just in time to vomit on the floor instead of down my nice purple-trimmed shirt.

'Been waitin' a long time to do that,' a voice said – a deep, older man's voice with a thick frontier accent. Not quite a borderlands twang; a little more refined, but still carrying that tell-tale rustic drawl. I wiped my face and looked up to see a man in a marshal's grey riding uniform reach down to haul me up by the shoulder. My saviour was a little taller

125

than me and a whole lot older. Grey hair long enough to brush his shoulders framed a face etched with lines from sun and wind. In his right hand he held a pair of rough metal tubes, each about a foot and a half long, welded together. Smoke billowed from the end of one of the tubes.

A *Gitabrian fire lance*, I realised, though I'd never seen two banded together like that, and this was more compact than the four-footers I'd encountered last time I was in Cazaran.

'I'm Jed Colfax,' the man said, hauling me up to my feet.

'Colfax? Head of the marshals service?'

'So they remind me, on occasion.'

Everything he said managed to sound cool, like he was out for a midnight stroll instead of having just blown a woman's head off with a pair of customised fire lances. I wiped more of Arrasia's last will and testament from my face and neck before extending a hand. 'Kellen.'

He nodded. 'I know. Sorry I didn't get here faster, but then again, you never invited me.'

'It was supposed to be a private party,' I said.

'Yeah, well, we don't really take to private parties around here, Mister Kellen.' He glanced down at Reichis. 'That thing going to bite me?' he asked.

The squirrel cat swallowed something that I didn't really want to identify.

'Nah,' I said. 'He's probably pretty full by now.'

'That's one weird-looking dog, if you don't mind me saying.'

Reichis growled. I waved him down. 'I'm not the one you have to worry about offending. But he's not a dog. He's a squirrel cat.'

'Really?' Colfax knelt down – a very stupid thing to do – but I noticed he'd slid his twin fire lance into a long leather holster across his back and now held a marshal's mace in his left hand, just in case. 'Never saw a squirrel cat this big.'

'That's probably as close as you want to see this particular one.'

Colfax rose. 'You're probably right. He could use a bath.'

Reichis chittered something I couldn't make out. He's hard to understand when he gets all wound up from fighting.

'Yeah, well, I could use one too, at this point.'

The servant from earlier arrived with a tray and a glass tumbler filled with whisky. I accepted it and took a small sip before putting the glass on the floor.

'You don't like it, sir? I could get you something—'

'It's fine,' I said. 'It wasn't for me.'

The servant looked down to see Reichis lapping it up.

'Seems like a lot for something his size, don't it?' Colfax asked.

'Yeah, but if he's passed out drunk, I won't have to hear him brag all night.'

The servant gave a shy smile and left.

'Listen,' I said to Colfax, 'thanks for the save. Really.'

'Least I could do. Never had much use for Arrasia. Never had a chance to do nothing about it until now. Just got back into the capital and heard about your little card game with the queen. Figured something would be happening tonight. Would've liked to put Koresh down too, but it looks like you got to him before me.'

'Someone should probably come and—'

He waved a hand. 'Got a couple of boys on the way. They'll have the remains cleared out by morning. Same with this assassin fellow here. Looks Zhuban. Hard to be sure though, what with your little friend's, ah, proclivities.'

127

'They said his name was Oleis,' I said.

The marshal pulled out a small notebook from his grey leather coat and held it against the wall as he wrote down the name. 'That's somethin' anyway. Thanks.'

'Like I said, I'm grateful for the assistance.'

Colfax shrugged. 'Reckon you probably saved the queen a lot of grief here tonight. We've been looking for a way to deal with these two for months, but, you know, the law's the law.'

I nodded. 'Well, you can buy me dinner sometime and we'll call it even.'

Colfax shook his head. ''Fraid I can't do that, Kellen.'

'No?'

'When I said taking out Arrasia was the least I could do for you, I really meant the most. Now I'm going to have to ask you to go back to your room, pack your things and leave the capital. Matter of fact, I'd be much obliged if you kept on ridin' till you were out of my country entirely.'

My fingers slipped into the holsters at my side before I remembered it wouldn't do any good. The magical wards Koresh had commissioned would still be in place, even if he himself was dead. If I tried to use the powders right now all I'd accomplish would be to blow my own hands off.

'It's nothing personal,' Colfax went on, 'but unlike a lot of these fools, I know what that stuff around your eye means.'

Ancestors. I really couldn't catch a break in this town. 'If I was being controlled by a demon, don't you think I'd have an easier time wreaking destruction on the world?'

'Don't know, kid. How long have you had the shadowblack?'

'About two years now.'

The marshal pulled a rolled-up cigarette from his coat pocket and stuck it in his mouth. 'How long do you figure you have before those markings wind their way inside your head and your heart? How long before you wake up and both your eyes are coal-black and the nice, well-meaning kid before me is replaced by something I won't be able to kill?'

It was a question I'd been asking myself for some time, but I didn't need him to know that. Instead I gave a dismissive laugh. 'Wouldn't've expected the head of the queen's marshals service to be so superstitious.'

A little fire was still burning on the floor near Koresh's body. The marshal knelt down and used it to light his cigarette. 'You're right, Kellen, and if I was a betting man, I might even wager on it never happening. Hell, maybe it's all just stories. But this is the queen we're talking about, and I don't take chances with her. Not ever.'

'You do realise she's the one who hired me?'

'Yep. It'll break her heart when you up and run away.' He gestured with his cigarette to the still-smouldering carcasses of Koresh and Arrasia. 'Bad as those two were, Kellen, I reckon you're a lot more dangerous. Better for everyone if you leave now, before things get ugly.'

I'd come to the same conclusion after nearly getting killed by a flying snake. But I'd been pushed out of one place or another just about every day for the past six months, and I was getting tired of how easy everybody thought it would be to do it again. 'And if I decide to stay?'

'Well, then I'll respect your gumption.' He took a drag from his cigarette. 'And then I'll have to decide what to do about it.'

'You've seen what I can do. Hells, you've seen what the squirrel cat can do. You sure you want to make an enemy of me right from the start?'

129

Colfax smiled. 'Son, I've served the queen since she was born; served her father before her and his father before him. I've dealt with all kinds of threats to the Daroman throne, and I'll figure out how to put an end to you. And as for your squirrel cat? Well, I already know how to deal with him.'

'Oh yeah? How?'

He pointed to Reichis, who was passed out snoring on the floor, curled up next to the dead body of Oleis. 'Buy him a drink.'

Colfax tossed the remains of his cigarette onto Koresh's corpse and turned to walk down the hall away from me. I stood there like an idiot for a few minutes until I was sure whatever Arrasia had thrown at me had worn off. Then I reached down and picked up Reichis and stumbled back to our room. Somehow, after risking our necks and actually winning this fight, I'd managed to upgrade my nemeses, from a couple of amateur child beaters to the legendary head of the queen's own marshals service.

16

Unexpected Conversations

By mid-morning on my second day at court I was fairly sure that I'd made a tactical error in not letting Koresh and Arrasia kill me when I'd had the chance. The novelty of my presence had worn off, and no one bothered to mask their contempt for me. It turns out that 'Who brought that animal in here? Oh, no – I meant him' was the favourite joke of the court these days. Reichis loved it.

'Hey, I'm not the one who wiped blood on the Daroman flag, pal. You should be more careful next time.'

'Go hump a weasel,' I said.

Arex strode over to us. 'Didn't you see me motion for you, you halfwit? Come on. The queen has requested your presence.' He held up a finger. 'And before you ask? Yes, "requested" *is* a euphemism in the Daroman court.'

I followed behind him as we navigated our way through a smothering sea of brocade silk and velvet garments. The assembled nobles struck me as vain and overfed, but I swear I felt the hilt of a concealed dagger whenever I brushed too close to any of them. As we approached the throne, the crowd took notice of our trajectory and one by one abandoned their conversations to focus on us.

Arex bowed to the queen. 'Your Majesty,' he said.

She smiled at him. 'Cousin Arex. Are you still pestering my poor old royal herald?'

'Cerreck and I have a troubled relationship, Your Majesty. I shall endeavour to make better friends with him at once.'

'Do so,' she said. 'He's been here longer than any of us and doesn't deserve such abuse.'

Arex grinned. 'Forgive me for saying so, Your Majesty, but I believe he deserves such abuse precisely because of how long he's been here.'

The queen shook her head, though her smile widened. 'You're a terrible man, Arex. A sterner monarch would have you beheaded.'

Murmurs and angry whispers erupted from the audience. Apparently the Daroman court doesn't appreciate its eleven-year-old monarch making jokes about beheading. The queen showed no signs of taking notice of the disapproval, but Arex did. 'What, have me executed? Just like that? Can't we play a game of cards first?'

The jibe produced chortles from the crowd, and an almost palpable sense of relief. *He's protecting her,* I realised. *They don't trust their young queen, so they rely on Arex to handle her.*

She waved a dismissive hand at her social secretary. The gesture looked silly coming from a child. 'Away with you, Arex. Leave me to my new tutor of cards.'

Arex rose and walked past me, whispering, 'Careful, kid. Always remember that it's never just the two of you in here.'

'Master Kellen,' the queen began.

'Mister,' I reminded her.

'Ah, of course. *Mister* Kellen. Have you enjoyed your first days at court?'

132

I thought back to my encounter with Leonidas, which had likely put a target on my back, and the multiple breaches of etiquette that had earned me no shortage of enemies and no small amount of scorn. 'They've been . . . instructive, Your Majesty.'

'Good,' she said. 'You've so much to teach us, it's only fair that we teach you something in return.'

'Ugh,' Reichis groaned. 'She's teaching me why I find humans so pompous.'

The queen looked down at Reichis as if it was the first time she'd seen him, which was impossible since he'd been creating such a stir since our arrival. 'By my ancestors, who is this roguish fellow? I don't think I've ever seen a *felidus arborica* up close before!'

'This is Reichis, Your Majesty.'

'Your pet?'

Reichis growled, so I quickly said, 'My business partner.'

The entire court laughed at that one. Reichis didn't think it was very funny. The queen smiled warmly though. 'He's so handsome. I wonder . . . would he sit on my lap?'

'No damn way,' Reichis chittered at me.

I looked down at him with as meaningful a stare as I could muster. When that didn't work, I kicked him.

'Ow. Damn it. All right already.'

The squirrel cat ambled over to the throne, crawling reluctantly up the stairs before climbing into the queen's lap. Murmurs of 'ooh' and 'oh my' filled the room like a soft ocean wave. The queen was delighted. 'My goodness, his fur is so soft!' she remarked, stroking him gently.

Reichis endured it with as much grace as I'd come to expect from him, which is to say a fairly steady stream of curse words followed by promises of ways in which he'd get his revenge on me later.

'He does make such comical sounds,' the queen said, stroking his ear between her fingers.

'You won't be finding them comical when I'm done eating your fingers,' he warned. 'Stupid cow.'

Suddenly the queen did something very dangerous: she twisted Reichis's ear. Hard. She'd done it subtly enough that most probably hadn't noticed, but I sure did. So did Reichis. 'Kellen, these Daroman bastards are going to have to find a new head of state if this stunted skinbag doesn't take her damned paws off me right now!'

I felt my hands reach towards my holsters. Reichis wasn't stupid; he knew that attacking the queen would be the end of us. But she probably wasn't smart enough to know that if she kept twisting his ear, he'd kill her anyway. 'Your Majesty . . .'

The queen let go of his ear and then bent her head down and whispered something to him.

Reichis's ears went flat against his head even as his fur suddenly changed to a pale yellow. He looked like he'd been hit by a thunderbolt. 'Kellen!' he chittered frantically.

'What's wrong?'

His eyes found mine. I'd never seen him look so shocked. 'This bitch speaks squirrel cat!'

17

The Countess of Sorrow

I stared agape at the queen, then at Reichis, convinced that he must be playing a joke on me. But the squirrel cat's expression was deadly serious. How could this be possible? No one but me understood Reichis.

The queen caught my gaze. 'It's remarkable how expressive his little noises are,' she said. 'One almost feels as if one could understand his every word.' People laughed at the silliness of her casual remark. She smiled innocently. Reichis looked terrified. 'I shall leave it up to you, master of cards, to ensure that your noble companion learns the appropriate ways to address a Daroman queen.' More laughter ensued.

She gave Reichis a pat on the bottom and he skittered off her lap and back to me, placing a paw on my leg for reassurance. I'd never heard of anyone else being able to understand Reichis. To everyone but me he was just a brown lump of fur that made chittering and growling noises. *How did this end up being the most terrifying thing that's happened since I got here?*

'I must regretfully give him back to you, Mister Kellen,' the queen said. 'Otherwise my loyal subjects will fear I begin to play favourites.'

That turned out not to be as popular a joke. People here

seemed to take careful notice every time the queen chose to grant an audience. During the interludes between her encounters, the nobles kept score among themselves as to whose star was rising and whose was waning. I held no illusions as to my own when the queen apparently forgot even to dismiss me. I skulked away as gracefully as I could manage, which, judging by the snorts and sly looks that followed me, hadn't been particularly successful.

'You can breathe now, master card player. The axe has passed you by for today.'

I turned to find a short fellow in modest court clothing consisting of fitted, if not stylish, beige shirt and trousers beneath a white brocade coat that did a passingly fair job of masking his portly physique. He was blessed with just about the plainest, most innocuous features a man could have without actually disappearing into the background entirely. Everything about him was somewhat or rather: his posture was somewhat stooped, his hair rather thin. He was somewhat older than the other courtiers, and as he noticed my scrutiny of him, he offered up a rather friendly smile. The only definitive thing about him was that he looked almost as out of place as I did.

'Adrius Martius,' he said, extending a hand.

'Kellen. Kellen Argos.'

'Argos,' he repeated. 'That doesn't sound like any Jan'Tep family name I've heard. Are you perhaps one of those wandering Argosi who appear every once in a while to stir up trouble?' He took note of the glint of steel from the deck of cards strapped to my right thigh. 'I've heard tell of one who came through the capital some months ago. Got herself an audience with the queen in fact. Odd woman.

136

'Was it Ferius Parfax?' I asked.

'I don't recall her name,' he said.

Had Ferius been here, in Darome? A thousand questions came to mind, none of which I could risk asking without giving too much away. I'd have to find some other means to learn if it had been her, and if so, what she had been doing here. 'What do you do, Adrius Martius?' I asked.

He smiled, taking the shift in conversation in his stride. 'Oh, very little really. Like most people here, I suppose.'

I took the opening, but carefully. 'The wealthy do seem to have . . . rather a lot of time to devote to court life.'

Martius laughed. 'Well said, master card player. I see you're already learning diplomacy.'

'It seems to be the Daroman way,' I replied.

'Ah, but not always, my boy. We were a fierce people once. Not just the soldiers like Leonidas over there, but us nobles as well.'

He seemed intent on leading me somewhere. For the moment I was willing to go along. 'And now?' I asked.

'Have you noticed the necks of our beautiful Daroman ladies?'

'Not especially. No offence.'

'None taken. But if you glance around the room you'll see more silver adorning their necks than gold. Fewer gemstones in their broaches and bracelets than in the past too.'

I looked around and saw that what he said was true. I was used to travelling near border towns where money was scarce; to me these people all looked like royalty from the old stories. But the women weren't like the bejewelled figures in the old tapestries. 'I guess peace isn't always prosperity,' I said.

'Not for an empire, Mister Kellen.'

137

'So why not just go out there and beat the hells out of some other country? I hear the Berabesq have shrines lined with gold and the Zhuban hoard precious stones in their mountain keeps.'

Martius let out a long sigh. 'Once, my friend, we'd have done just that, but the queen's father signed a peace treaty and now, well, we are where we are. These days, Darome is like me: a little too old, a little too fat.' He wagged his finger. 'But always very diplomatic, yes?' He let out a breath and seemed to deflate somewhat. 'All in all, it's still a good place to retire. But what about you though? How do you find our court?'

I thought about how to answer that. *What the hells? I thought. He's probably just some low-level clerk; what will he care?* 'I'm starting to think it's quite possibly the most dangerous place I've ever been,' I replied.

Martius smiled again. 'Quite so, quite so. I see what you told the queen the other day about cards is true – a good player can see the map of all humanity.'

'That's not quite how I put it, but I'm flattered to have left an impression.'

'Oh my, of course. Most exciting thing I've seen in years. In fact . . . well, I hope you won't find this too presumptuous . . .'

'Go on,' I said.

'Well, I was wondering if you might join me for a game of cards tonight? I'm no master player like yourself, but I could try to give you a bit of a battle.'

'Sure, why not?' There are worse ways to spend an evening than swindling a bureaucrat at cards. I wondered if clerks around here made decent money.

'Count Martius,' Arex interrupted. 'Forgive my intrusion. The Countess Mariadne arrives for an audience with the queen, but you are her senior and a closer cousin. Would you like to speak to Her Majesty first?'

Count Martius?

'Oh, don't worry about me, Arex. Nice of you to ask every day, but no, the queen's got better things to do than keep me entertained.'

'As you wish,' Arex said stiffly, and left us.

'I see you already know how to keep your cards close to your chest, *Count* Martius,' I said.

'What? The title? Don't pay any attention to that.'

'And the queen's cousin.'

He shrugged. 'Well, it's a small empire really. We're all related somehow. No,' he said, patting me on the arm, 'I'm just a middle-aged man with a nice wife and a plain home. I come here because I'm expected to and because the food is good, not because anyone particularly wants me.'

'Well, either way, I'm going to keep a close eye on my money when we play cards.'

Martius laughed. 'Ah, thank you, my boy. You do honour me.'

A stirring in the hall broke into our conversation.

'The Countess Mariadne, cousin to Her Majesty the Queen,' the old herald announced loudly. 'Holder of the northern district of Sarrix, widow of the most noble Arafas.' The crowds parted to let a woman through to the throne. Dark red hair, almost the colour of wine, framed a face that would have been stunningly beautiful were it not so full of sorrow. The dark red dress clung to her body in a way that made most of the men in the room ignore that sorrow altogether. Most of all though, it was the way she walked that made my breath catch in my throat. Graceful, determined, and yet somehow even her bearing seemed somehow utterly inconsolable.

'Your Majesty,' Countess Mariadne said.

The queen rose from her throne and embraced the woman in her small arms, causing a minor stir in the assembled audience. 'Beloved cousin.'

'Forgive me for my arrival unannounced,' Mariadne said, stepping back to kneel before the queen.

'You need never apologise for coming to my home, cousin.' Then the queen gave her a stern look. 'Only for being absent too long.'

The countess nodded, fingers clasped in front of her.

'She's in mourning for her husband,' Count Martius whispered to me, pointing out the red dress.

'How long?'

'Almost five years.'

I turned to him in surprise. 'Isn't that a long time for someone so young?'

He nodded. 'It's a long time for someone of any age, and far too long for the queen's tastes.'

'You come before us in formal mourning once again, beloved cousin,' the queen said, her voice ringing through the audience. 'It brings us no pleasure to see you so determined in your grief.'

Countess Mariadne returned the queen's gaze, fire in her eyes. 'My grief will end, Your Majesty, when my husband is no longer dead.'

'You have spent too many years adrift in sadness, countess. I find myself confounded by your insistence on endless mourning.'

'Perhaps Her Majesty will understand better once she has had more years with which to understand.'

Rumbles of shock and disapproval ran through the crowd.

The queen waited until silence returned before she sat back down on the throne. 'You are in error, beloved cousin. Do you doubt my love, or do you forget that I embody two-thousand years of Daroman rule?'

'Oh my, this isn't good,' Martius warned.

'Why?' I asked.

'Because the queen's just boxed her into a trap. Questioning the queen's veracity is a treasonable offence.'

'So however she answers . . .'

Martius nodded.

The countess bowed her head. 'I doubt neither your love nor your wisdom, Majesty, merely my own capacity to benefit from it.'

The crowd breathed a collective sigh of relief. 'Clever,' Martius said.

'Very well, cousin,' the queen continued. 'I can see there is no dissuading you from your melancholy. What cause brings you to me then?'

Mariadne stood. 'Your Majesty no doubt recalls my maid Tasia,' she said.

The queen shrugged. 'I suppose I must have met her at some point. No doubt you have many maids.'

Anger and betrayal flashed in Mariadne's eyes.

'The queen just lied,' Reichis chittered.

No kidding, I thought.

'Tasia is special to me, Your Majesty. She has been with me many years. She is my dearest friend.' A pause. 'Other than Your Majesty, of course.'

'And why do you carp at me about this maid of yours, cousin? Does she require a promotion?'

The audience laughed like trained dogs.

'No, Majesty, she is due to be executed by your own marshals in six days' time.'

The room went deadly silent.

'And what crime did she commit?'

'None, Your Majesty. She was raped.'

The countess around spun and pointed straight at me. 'By that man.'

The queen and everyone else looked in my direction and my first thought was to grab Reichis by the scruff and run for it. I didn't know who this Tasia was, but I wasn't about to go back to jail for something I hadn't done.

'I believe the countess refers to me, Your Majesty,' boomed a voice behind me. Leonidas strode past me to the throne. 'The lovely Mariadne is, however, mistaken as to the facts.'

'Mistaken how?' the queen asked.

'The maid, Tasia, entered my chamber at night when I was a guest of the countess some weeks ago. My men guard the border near Countess Mariadne's lands, and we are sometimes forced by the needs of war to take our respite there.'

'And make yet another failed effort to work his way into Mariadne's bed,' Martius whispered.

'The maid tried to seduce me. When that failed, she became hysterical and attempted to stab me. It was only a small matter to me, but as Your Majesty knows, threatening the life of a military commander during times of war is tantamount to treason.'

I nudged Martius. 'Why does Leonidas keep talking about war? I thought you said there was a peace treaty with Zhuban.'

'Depends who you ask,' he whispered back. 'The queen may be sovereign, but the military have great discretion in how they defend the empire's borders.'

Coutess Mariadne, however, was having none of it, and her rage was a thing to behold. 'You lie, Major Leonidas, and Tasia pays the penalty for your false witness.'

Leonidas spread his arms wide. 'I myself urged the magistrate towards mercy, if only so as not to deprive the countess of her beloved companion, but alas, my pleas were ignored.'

'Again you lie!' Mariadne accused.

'Cousin,' the queen said, 'you vex me now.'

'Forgive me, Your Majesty, but Tasia's life is in danger, and it is two days' ride to my home. I had hoped to bring a writ from you commuting the sentence.'

The queen looked at her with little sympathy and no mercy whatsoever. 'Ah, I see. A year passes without a visit, my counsel to relieve yourself of mourning and marry again is ignored, but now you wish me to overrule my own magistrates?'

'Your Majesty—'

'No, countess. I will not do what you ask. It is not for a queen to break her own laws. I regret that your maid is to come to such an end, but if Major Leonidas has already begged for clemency and the magistrate has refused, he must have good reason.'

'But, Your Majesty . . . cousin . . .'

'You have my answer, countess.'

Mariadne threw herself on the ground, crying. 'Will you do nothing then? Will you grant me no assistance? Is Tasia to die frightened and alone a hundred miles to the north in one of your own marshals' jails and I to lose my truest friend?'

The queen sighed. 'Cousin, again your grief wounds me.'

She stepped down from the throne and held out her hand to Mariadne, who stood back up. 'I cannot alter the law to suit my whim, but since you fear for your maid's loneliness,

143

I will grant you this: I shall send someone to provide her with comfort during her final hours.'

'I . . . I don't understand. Who would you—'

'Tutor of cards,' the queen began, looking straight at me. 'You provided me with some small amusement the other day, and this felidus arborica of yours is entirely delightful. You will accompany Countess Mariadne to the jail where her maid resides and provide what companionship you can during her final days.'

'Me?' I looked around. People were stifling laughter. Leonidas looked particularly smug. But not the smug that says, 'I'm enjoying your misfortune.' More the kind that says, 'I've just figured out how to kill you and solve all my other problems in the process.' I turned back to the queen and did my best to give her a meaningful look. 'What am I supposed to do with her?'

If she caught my concern, she elected to ignore it completely. 'Why, play cards with her, of course. Isn't that what I hired you to do?'

The audience burst into open laughter. Countess Mariadne fled the room in tears.

The queen sat back down on her throne and, just like that, the audience was over.

I turned to Martius, hoping for some explanation as to what had just occurred. He shook his head. 'Well, my boy, I'm sad to say we won't be having our card game tonight. Still, the queen and many of the court are about to head north, to survey the borders to see if the Zhuban problem is as bad as Major Leonidas says it is, so I'll be spending the next several days at my villa in Juven. It's only about an hour's ride from Countess Mariadne's estate. Come see me

144

when you get the chance. If I can assist you without getting myself into trouble, I will.'

He left before I could thank him.

'Sorry, kid, that's how it plays out sometimes,' Arex said from behind me.

'What's the hell is going on, Arex? How did I just get wrapped up in this?'

'You remember how a Daroman deck has four outlaw cards – gold, silver, red and black? You know what they're for, right?'

I nodded. 'In some games, the golden outlaw in your hand makes your cards stronger. In others—'

'In others you throw the red outlaw on your opponent's pile to weaken theirs,' Arex finished for me. He clapped a hand on my shoulder. 'Guess which card you are, kid.'

Off to the side of the room I saw a tall and slender grey-clad figure leaning against the wall. Marshal Colfax touched a finger to his dusty frontiersman hat and nodded to me.

Seems everybody knew the game but me.

18

A Yellow-Haired Girl

The walk back to my rooms felt interminably long. I was tired and frustrated. Sometime between learning that a senior officer in the Daroman army was predisposed to kill me and discovering the queen I'd thought I was saving might have similar plans, my sense of equilibrium had left me. What the hell had happened to me? This past year since leaving Ferius behind, I'd survived in the frontier towns by using the skills she'd taught me to read people at a glance – to spot their intentions and weaknesses before they could figure out mine. When I gambled with my life I always played my opponents' cards, not my own. But here? In this place? I was an amateur brought to the table to feed the big fish. If that wasn't bad enough, the poncey silver-and-purple shirts Arex had told me I was required to wear at court were starting to itch.

'Slow down,' Reichis chittered, shuffling along the floor to catch up with me. 'I just got over being bitten by a poisonous snake and I don't feel like running just because you're in a mood.'

'Sorry,' I said. 'I don't know what's wrong with me.'

'It's your fleeing instinct,' Reichis said.

'What?'

'Your fleeing instinct. You said you didn't know what's

146

wrong with you. I'm saying it's your fleeing instinct. Pretty much everyone here is out to get us, and your body wants you to run, but there's nowhere to go, so you can't do anything except walk too fast.'

He had a point. Arex was clearly on the queen's side, but that did me no good since it looked as if she might not be on mine. Leonidas apparently had it in for me. Countess Mariadne hadn't even formally met me and she already hated me. Martius seemed like the only person who wasn't out for my blood, but he claimed to have no personal interest in what was going on, and people like that don't exist. Thank the ancestors that Koresh and Arrasia were dead at least. They'd made their move and it had failed.

Now I just need to deal with . . . Well, pretty much everybody else.

The memory of the langzier sent a shiver through me. As we reached my rooms I paused before opening the door, and looked down at Reichis. 'How do you manage it then?' I asked.

'Manage what?'

'Well, you said we all have fleeing instincts when we're under threat. You knew the langzier would get its fangs into you. How come you didn't panic?'

'Oh, that,' he said. 'We're completely different that way, Kellen.'

'How so?'

The squirrel cat looked up at me. 'Well, for one thing, I'm not a coward.'

Great.

'And for another, I'm not the one with my tail in a knot over whether a black mark on my face means I'm going to be possessed by demons one day. So get your head in the game or we're gonna end up dead long before we find out.'

147

He sniffed at the door. 'Probably by whoever's waiting for us inside right now.'

I pushed open the door and slipped my hands into my holsters to pull out a small pinch of each of the red and black powders. There's a reason why I don't just blow a hole in everyone who crosses my path, and it's not because they don't give me plenty of cause. The red powder is a mix of chemicals that can get pretty expensive. Still, the ingredients aren't that hard to find. The black powder, on the other hand, requires some additional unpleasantness to procure.

I scanned the room. There was no one in sight, though it was clear that the servants had been there. The sheets and bedding had been changed and I could see my clothes, freshly laundered, sitting on top of the chest of drawers. Heavily scented flowers had been placed discretely about the room, masking the smells from the night before. I stepped inside. The late-afternoon sun brought an orange glare through the window, a contrast to the heavy shadows filling the corners of the room. It would have been easy to miss the intruder, but, unlike most people, I've learned to always keep my eyes on the shadows. 'Go ahead,' I said. 'Make your move. They can always clean the room again after I've put a hole in you.'

The figure stayed where it was. I expected Reichis to pounce or growl or say something, but when I glanced down at him, he was just wandering around in circles, as if he were nothing more than a dumb animal searching for a place to sleep.

'Reichis? What the hell are you doing?'

My eye caught a tiny movement in the shadows and I raised my hands, ready to toss the powders and form the somatic shape that would do serious damage to both the decor and my visitor.

'Oh my, still with that old trick, Kellen? You're going to burn your hands off one day, and what will you use to keep yourself occupied then?'

The glare from the window was playing havoc with my vision, making it hard to discern the shape of the intruder, but I recognised her voice even before she stepped out of the shadows. Soft, a little high-pitched, dripping with a mixture of honey and pepper. The recognition only served to make me resolve to take better aim. 'Shalla?'

She stepped forward into the orange light coming through the window. The effect made her look as if she were glowing, accentuating a beauty that in recent years was fast becoming her favourite weapon. 'My darling brother,' she said, taking another step that brought her closer. The glare around her softened to reveal a green dress that nearly matched her eyes and set off her long, blonde hair to remarkable effect. Around her neck she wore the elaborate golden necklace that marked her as a Jan'Tep diplomat to the Darome empire. Somewhere in the six months since I'd last seen her, my little sister had gone and become an ambassador. She opened her arms wide. 'Sweet brother, will you not embrace me?'

I considered it for a moment, then remembered that she was family and that my vision was still dazzled enough from the glare of the sun that I couldn't make out whether her hands were forming the somatic shape for a spell. 'You should probably just tell me why you're here, Shalla. This much powder starts to itch if I leave it on too long. After about five minutes it starts to really hurt. At that point it'll have mixed with the oils from my fingers and it's probably best to fire the spell rather than put the powders back in my holsters.'

She lowered her arms, a flicker of annoyance tightening her lips. 'Don't be such a child. I could stand here for a hundred years and you wouldn't fire that spell at me. So don't bother with your lazy anger and your fool's tongue. It might make you sound clever and menacing to these Daroman halfwits but I know who you are, brother. I know *you*. So drop the act.' She walked over to the sofa. 'Or else surprise me.' She sat down, crossing one leg over the other as she stretched an arm over the back. 'Just don't bore me.'

Shalla was every inch my father's daughter and the thought of him made my fingers itch. My sister's complacent smile made me want to prove her wrong. I wanted to fire the spell, to imagine my father's face, shocked and filled with agony at the news that I had killed his daughter, despite all their conviction that I was too weak to defy them. But the image was hazy because I wasn't sure that my father loved anyone or anything enough to be hurt by its passing. Part of me didn't care. But there was another part that remembered all the times Shalla had tried to protect me, even if those occasions did always involve using me as a pawn in one of her schemes. 'Why are you here, Shalla?'

'Sha'maat.'

'What?'

'My name, brother. I completed my trials and earned my mage's name. I am no longer Shalla. Now I am—'

'Sha'maat,' I said, trying the word out on my tongue. Somehow those two syllables felt as if they'd stolen something precious from me. I let the powders fall back into the holsters. 'What have you done to Reichis?' The squirrel cat was sniffing around the room now, looking for food.

'Silk magic. A simple spell actually.' A slight theatrical pause

150

as she brushed an imaginary speck of dust from her dress. 'For me, anyway.'

'Well, when Reichis comes out of whatever trance you've put him in, he's going to want to kill you, so maybe you should tell me why you're here.'

She patted the seat next to her on the couch. 'Because it's your birthday, of course. I've brought you a present.'

I couldn't see any signs that she was readying a spell, but while the penalty for one Jan'Tep murdering another is usually death, the penalty for killing a shadowblack typically involves gifts and a three-day feast. I walked over to the bed and sat on the corner a few feet away from her. Her bemused expression made me feel like a stubborn child.

'I was there in the court, you know,' she said.

My spine stiffened and my mind went hurtling back through the past few days, trying to see her face among the crowds of nobles and courtiers. How could I have missed her? The thought that someone from my family could get so close to me without my noticing them chilled me. 'When? Today?'

'Today. Yesterday and the day before as well, actually. That was quite the performance you and Ginevra put on.'

'Ginevra?'

'The queen, silly. You should probably take the time to learn her name if you're going to be of any use to us at all.'

'I can't think of anything I want less than to be of use to our family, Sha'maat.'

She sighed. 'It's never been about what we want, sweet brother. You are Kellen of the House of Ke and will do wh—'

'My name is Kellen Argos now, sister. It has been for a while. You might as well get used to it.'

'No, brother, I will not,' she said. Her voice had an edge

151

to it. 'Besides, Kellen is a child's name, just as Shalla was for me. It's long past time you grew up.'

It was my turn to be angry. 'I would have happily taken a man's name, Sha'maat, but our father forgot to persuade the council to offer me one. Perhaps because he was too busy trying to have me killed.'

She rose, gracefully, as if she'd rehearsed it just that way, the way she did everything. She walked over to the bed and placed a hand gently on my cheek. I felt an overpowering desire to put my hand against hers, to feel connected once again to the yellow-haired girl I used to argue with when we were children. She leaned in and whispered, 'Let's not quarrel, brother. Don't you want to see your present?'

The slight sound of silk fabric shifting made me look up. She pulled a card from inside the top of her gown with a length of string attached to it. The card was a little bigger than those of my Argosi decks. In fact, I'd only ever seen one card that particular size before. 'Let me guess. You brought me another of Father's scrying cards, so he can spout more of his edicts at me?'

'Better than that,' she said, stepping away from me and glancing about the room. 'I'll need a candle. A lantern would be better actually.'

There was an oil lamp on the table next to the bed. I lit it using a few grains of powder and handed it to her. She balanced it on the arm of the sofa, then held the card by the string, dangling it in front of the flame. With her free hand she flicked the card, making it spin. Light from the lamp began to pass through the card itself, casting shadows against the wall.

My sister looked at me. 'Would you like to perform the spell?'

152

'You know I can't work silk magic.'

She shrugged and made a series of somatic gestures with her right hand before speaking the incantation. I could match every movement and shape and utter the same syllables perfectly, but for me it would produce no result. '*Rhea naphan*,' she said.

The lamplight flickered as if the flames themselves were dancing. Without Sha'maat having to touch it at all, the card began to float by itself, spinning faster and faster. The shadows on the wall shifted and twitched as if a rough charcoal sketch were being drawn and redrawn faster than the eye could follow. I had expected to see a face, but what appeared instead was a mansion of the Jan'Tep style, bigger than most, as befits a noble family. Though the projection was all in blacks, my mind filled in the copper-coloured roof, red-brown steps and white marble walls. Kath trees swayed, their long strands of thin rope-like branches shifting in the wind, arrow-head leaves like gentle hands beckoning to me. It was a sight I had not seen in over two years.

'Home,' I said, the word barely loud enough to reach my own ears. 'You've made a scrying card for our home . . .'

I felt her arms reach around me and hug my chest. 'Happy birthday, brother,' she said.

'This . . . This must have taken months to create. Why?' I wanted to see what was in her expression, but try as I might I couldn't pull my eyes away from the projection.

'Because I know how much you miss it. Because it's your birthday and even after all the foolish things you've done, I love you.' Her hands released me and I heard her step back to the table. A moment later the flickering shadows stopped and the image disappeared from the wall.

I turned to see her standing before me, holding the card for me to take. It felt warm to the touch. 'Now you can see it whenever you want,' she said.

'You know I can't do the spell, Sha'maat. It's just a card to me.'

'Then send for me, dear brother, whenever you want to see it again, and I'll come do the spell for you.'

Of course. Another trick, another game, another tool with which to control me. I went to turn away from her, but the gentleness of my sister's voice held me back. 'Or simply return with me, and have no need for such devices ever again.'

I spun around, searching her face to see if she was mocking me, but her expression was full of earnest longing. 'What are you saying to me, Shalla?'

'You have to call me Sha'maat now, brother.' She took a careful step towards me, the way you might handle a shy animal about to bolt. 'And my name isn't the only thing that's changed. You don't have to be alone any more, brother. You can come home.'

Home.

The word came on me like the blade of an assassin who has struck before you even knew you'd pissed anyone off. It passed through my skin and slipped between my ribs to reach my heart before I could harden myself to it. How could I want something so badly that had never brought me anything but misery and pain?

I looked at my sister again, her green eyes staring back at mine. She could read me so easily, even when we were children. Whatever I was feeling or thinking or planning, she picked up on it. Usually it put me off my game and made me nervous and awkward. But now, because I saw in her face the recognition of how close I was to bending to her will, I realised I could see through her too.

'He sent you here, didn't he?' I asked.

When she didn't answer I pressed her again. 'Answer me. Did Ke'heops send you here?'

She nodded, her eyes still hopeful. 'I would have come regardless, so long as he didn't forbid it. But yes, Father sent me to you.' She rushed through the words just a little.

'I don't believe—'

She came to me and put a hand on my chest. 'Brother, it is true, I swear. Father is the mage sovereign of our people now, and he says you can come home. You'll be Jan'Tep again, among your people, welcomed and loved.' Sha'maat hugged me and rested her head against my shoulder, her mouth close to my ear as she whispered, 'He'll give you your name.'

I felt her hands linking around my back, pulling me closer. She was offering me something I had never believed possible so had never dared think I wanted. My name. My mage's name. Would my father really take me back?

Ancestors, what's wrong with me? Ke'heops had counter-banded me, denying me any chance at a mage's future. He'd allowed the council to put a spell warrant on my head. He'd sent my own best friend, Panahsi, to kill me. Now the faint promise of my family's acceptance was enough to make me this weak?

The love and warmth in Sha'maat's embrace told me she knew I was more than half hers at that moment. She'd always known me better than I knew myself. But I had always understood our father better than she ever could. 'What does he want?' I asked, pushing her gently away.

If there was a trace of sorrow or regret in her eyes, I couldn't

155

find it. She simply held my gaze evenly, confident as always that, despite the fact that I was two years older, she knew better than I did. 'Ke'heops has a mission for you, brother. A few simple duties for you to complete before you return home.'

'Duties?' I almost choked on the words. 'Father has *duties* for me?' I felt betrayed by my own heart that I couldn't blast a hole in my beloved sister then and there. I even felt angry at Reichis for failing to voice my rage. 'Sha'maat, I swear, if you say his name to me again I may just pull powder and surprise you at last.'

She ignored me, as she always did when I threatened her. 'Like it or not, brother, he is the mage sovereign of our people and the head of our household. I know how hurt you were by . . . some of the actions Ke'heops took, but he had no choice.' She reached out a hand and traced a fingertip along the elaborate lines of the shadowblack around my left eye. 'None of us had a choice.'

I pulled back. 'But now? Now you've all decided I'm okay? That I'm not demon-spawned or devil-possessed or whatever other nonsense. Now I'm suddenly Jan'Tep again?'

Sha'maat looked into my eyes. For an instant I thought I saw the yellow-haired girl of our youth again, but she disappeared from view, replaced by the Jan'Tep diplomat, the mage and oh-so faithful daughter. 'Those things haven't changed, brother, how could they? But now . . . now you have altered your circumstances and we have more pressing matters.'

I shook my head, trying to clear my thoughts. The fact that she could stand here and say these things to me infuriated me almost as much as the fact that I lacked the spine to walk out of the room without asking the obvious question. 'What exactly does he think I'm going to do for him?'

Sha'maat nodded, as if we could get down to business. 'The situation in Darome is changing, brother. We can no longer afford to sit back and watch our own numbers dwindle away as the child queen consolidates power. We believe there is a weakness in her, something we could use to control her, but we can't discern it.' She waved her arm at the stone walls of the palace. 'These damned Daroman with their iron and stone. Do you know they import it from across the sea? It makes certain forms of magic harder to work here. We had hoped our other agents might have gradually given us the means to control Ginevra, but your arrival has made that more complicated. Brother, you will use your position to gain control over the queen. You'll put her in a position of weakness and uncover what secrets we can exploit.'

She walked over to the window and gazed out at the fading sun. 'Oh, and when the time is right, you'll execute the Countess Mariadne.'

'What? Why would the Jan'Tep go after her? What has she done?'

'She rejected certain overtures Father made. We cannot afford for her to gain more influence.'

'Then why doesn't he just assassinate her himself? It's not as if he doesn't have the power. When she leaves the palace he could reach out with one spell and extinguish the life from her as easily as you put out the flame of that lamp.'

She shook her head. 'You've never understood the higher forms of magic properly, brother. There are . . . costs to such actions. Father's soul must remain untarnished.'

The hypocrisy of my family's beliefs never ceases to amaze me. 'And what about my soul?'

157

'Brother, I love you, but your soul already has a claim against it; you know that.'

I flinched at the words. The harsh, simple, almost casual truth of it. I was shadowblack and thus condemned to the eternal blood-red ending that awaits a blackened soul. I couldn't be saved, so I might as well be useful. I was no different than the horses that pulled the tillers across my family's fields or the boot-jack they used to remove their shoes.

A part of me expected to hear Reichis snicker at the way I let myself be manipulated, or maybe growl at Sha'maat. But he was rolled in a ball, sleeping in the corner like somebody's pet. Even though I knew that this thing that happened – whatever it was – wasn't his fault, I hated him for just a second. Then I hated myself for much longer. Finally I said, 'I'm not going to kill off some widow just because she had the good sense to refuse our father.'

'She's a fool,' Sha'maat said. 'His offer was better than she deserved.'

I wanted to hurt her, so I said, 'Not everyone has the same degree of desire for our father's offerings as you do, Sha'maat. Some of us even find them . . . unseemly.'

She looked at me and in her face I couldn't find the slightest injury, just a tiny smirk at the corners of her mouth. 'And here I thought you said you were incapable of projection spells, brother.'

'Nevertheless, the answer is no.'

She took a deep breath and sighed. 'I see you need some time to consider the way of things. I will leave you here with all your illusions intact.'

As she turned towards the door a thought occurred to me. *Other agents.* She had said they had other agents they'd been using against the queen. 'Koresh and Arrasia – were they your creatures, Sha'maat?'

She turned and nodded slightly, but then tilted her head. 'Not precisely. Though they were serving our purposes. It's more accurate to say that they were cooperating with our interests, though they were not, perhaps, entirely aware of them. But you interfered in that.'

There was a question forming in my mind. I looked back at Reichis again and thought about how close he'd come to dying. If she answered the next question with a yes, then every chain of resistance would be gone from me. I would kill my sister here and now. 'Did you help them set the langzier on us?'

'Not exactly.'

My fingers itched to feel the burn of the red and black powders. 'It's a yes or no question.'

'The langzier was never meant for you, brother. Had it been, you would never have survived. Arrasia must have had someone refocus its intent towards you instead of its original target. There are always mages around ready to perform minor magics for the right price. Be assured, brother, it was not I who cast the spell.'

'But you gave them the snake.'

'Months ago and to use at the right moment, for the right purpose. Not for some petty vendetta against you. I informed them that I was withdrawing my support. Immediately.'

So that's why they'd gotten so desperate, probably hiring the first assassin they could find. Had they been counting on magical help to protect them from me and she'd abandoned them? I wondered if she'd told them that she was my sister. 'All these schemes. All these plans you and Father have.' I

159

held the card out to her. 'I'll have nothing to do with them, Shalla.'

'My name is Sha'maat!' The anger in her voice was jarring. Brittle. She stood there a few moments, just breathing, before she said, 'You have to get used to saying it, brother. You have to . . .' Her voice trailed off. She walked back to me and then wrapped her hands around mine, closing my fingers on the card. She kissed it lightly, and then me. 'You will do as your mage sovereign commands, though it may take you a little while to accept it. You'll do so because you're Jan'Tep, no matter how foolishly you prance about with your Argosi pretensions, dressed like a frontier herder in that preposterous hat with its silly superstitious symbols. You'll learn the queen's secrets for us and, when the time is right, you'll kill the countess. Then you'll come home to our family. To me.'

The calm certainty in her voice was like an edict uttered by a magistrate, as if a thousand men in steel plate were standing by, ready to enforce it. As if I was one of them. It was almost overpowering.

'Why?' I tried to make the question a taunt, a dismissal – at least the start to another argument. Instead it came out sounding hurt, and utterly genuine.

Sha'maat's eyes glimmered with the barest touch of tears. 'Because despite everything you think about yourself, for all your cleverness, you have one great weakness, brother. You yearn for a family. You crave love. They will discover that about you, these Daroman barbarians. Be careful that they don't destroy you with it.'

As she closed the door behind her, my sister said, 'Happy birthday, Kellen. I wish I had better presents to bring you.'

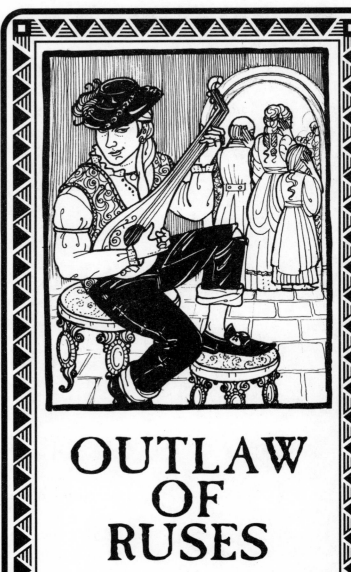

OUTLAW
OF
RUSES

The trouble with house-training an outlaw isn't getting them to stop lying; it's getting them to understand that just because they used to lie for a living, doesn't mean other people aren't a whole lot better at it than they are.

19

Imaginary Conversations

The carriage barrelled its way along the Northern Daroman Imperial Way, the trees and foliage lining the route becoming ever sparser as we reached colder climes. The countess's carriage was pretty to look at, its black lacquered exterior accented with silver gilding and the elaborate crimson rose-and-sword sigil of her house embossed into the doors on either side, but entirely unsuited to the rigours of long-haul travel. The rougher the road became, the more the wheels of the carriage diligently relayed every bump and dip directly to my buttocks. Nevertheless, the unforgiving wooden seats were nothing compared to my travelling companion as far as giving me a pain in the arse was concerned. Countess Mariadne's silences were decidedly loud in their effect, and by the second day I'd had just about enough.

'Any reason why your driver is trying to outrun the wind?' I asked.

The countess kept her face in her book despite how little light was coming in from the late afternoon sun. 'The faster we get there, the sooner I'll be done with this farce,' she said. 'And with you in particular.'

'Me? How exactly am I to blame for your predicament, countess?'

'Oh, on that account you may take comfort, Master Kel—'

'Mister,' I corrected.

Reichis grumbled. 'Of all of Ferius's stupid habits, this is the one you want to adopt?'

Countess Mariadne wrinkled her nose as though the squirrel cat had just farted. Maybe he had; the interior of the carriage was smelling a bit ripe. 'As you please. Regardless, you have my assurance, *Mister* Kellen, that you are not even the slightest bit to blame for my "predicament", as you call it. The loss of my husband these five years, the constant attacks on my border, the fact that my own cousin, the queen, refuses to overturn the unfair and unconscionable sentence given to my closest companion – these are the sources of my torment. You, by contrast, are nothing more than the queen's fool, sent to entertain himself at my expense.'

'Entertain myself?' I leaned forward in my seat just enough to make her uncomfortable. 'Lady, you seem to be under the impression that I want to be here instead of back at the palace where I have a comfortable room and at least the vague possibility of pleasant conversation. Allow me clear things up for you: in the past eight days I've had lightning thrown at me by a war mage, been knocked unconscious by a marshal's mace, almost had my face taken off by a Zhuban fanatic, been condemned to the gallows for accidentally wiping blood on your people's stupid flag, and – because up till then it had been a light week – been attacked by a damned flying snake. None of which, your ladyship, holds a candle to the raw unpleasantness of your company.'

The countess looked dumbstruck by my tirade. I took advantage of the situation to lean back in my seat, lowering my hat just enough to cover my eyes and end the conversation.

Reichis snorted. 'Good to know your winning streak with women is holding solid.'

'Go sniff your own backside' I muttered.

'What?' Mariadne shouted, slamming her book down on her lap.

'I was talking to him,' I said.

She looked around briefly, then her eyes settled on Reichis. 'Ah. Of course. You talk to your . . . rodent.'

'Squirrel cat,' Reichis said with a warning snarl.

'Is it wild? I think it's growling at me.' She sounded not so much afraid as affronted.

'"It" is a squirrel cat, not a rodent,' I corrected, with as much imperiousness as I could muster. 'And "it" has a name, which happens to be Reichis.'

The countess looked from Reichis to me as if I was making fun of her. 'And you talk to this . . . squirrel cat, do you?'

I nodded.

'And does he talk back?'

I snorted. '*All* he does is talk back.'

'Leave me out of this,' Reichis chittered, sticking his muzzle out of the carriage's side window.

Mariadne let out her breath and made a show of pausing before speaking. 'Master Kellen—'

'Mister. Among my peop—'

'Whatever. *Mister* Kellen, has anyone ever suggested that you entertain the possibility that your pet rodent – or squirrel cat, or whatever you want to call it – is an animal, that animals don't talk, and that you're just imagining that this one talks to you?'

I started to reply, when an uncomfortable thought occurred to me. Despite what happened when Sha'maat was around,

I'd never really questioned the fact that Reichis and I could talk to each other. On the surface, it seemed completely natural. After all, mages communicate with their familiars through their thoughts. Why shouldn't I be able to talk to Reichis? But then, I'm not a proper mage and would never be one. When I thought about it, I couldn't think of any other magical adepts who actually spoke – not thought or projected or whatever it was they did, but used actual words – back and forth with an animal. But the queen had spoken to Reichis too, hadn't she? Unless I really was out of my mind and she'd just been making fun of me. I thought back to the last two years as I looked over at the squirrel cat.

'Don't look at me,' Reichis said. 'I always thought you were crazy.'

Countess Mariadne gave me a look that was half genuine concern and half triumphant smugness. That's when I noticed the redness around her eyes and the dampness of her cheeks. She'd been crying; *that* was why she'd been keeping her face behind that book the whole trip. She noticed me staring at her, and embarrassment quickly turned to outrage. 'How dare you look at me like—'

I was rescued by Reichis chittering loudly. 'Horses coming, Kellen!'

'What? Who? How many?'

He sniffed out the window. 'A lot.'

'What is it?' Mariadne asked.

'Someone's on our tail,' I said, pushing Reichis out of the way so I could stick my head out the window. About two hundred yards to the right of us I could just make out a dirty brown cloud getting closer. Whoever they were, they were riding hard, just off-road and on a path to intercept us.

I pulled my powder holsters out of my travel bag and attached them to my belt. Next I strapped my deck of steel throwing cards around my right thigh. Finally, I unpacked the pair of long knives I'd taken off good old Merrel of Betrian and stuck them in my belt.

'How can you tell we're being pursued?' Mariadne asked. 'I don't hear anything.'

I jabbed my thumb at Reichis. 'My imaginary talking rodent told me.'

The countess snorted and started to speak but another voice interrupted her.

'Men coming, my lady,' the driver shouted down to us. 'Bandits, I fear. At least six of them.'

Six bandits on horseback. We were screwed.

I flipped open the covers of my powder holsters and then spat on my fingers, then lightly rubbed them on my trousers. Wet fingertips are a bad idea, but damp ones make it easier to hold the powder.

'What are you doing?' Mariadne asked.

I opened the door and found a grip for my right hand on the inside edge of the carriage. The wind slapped at my cheeks as if it were trying to get my attention. Maybe it was trying to warn me that this was all a little too inconvenient even for my luck.

'Getting ready to kill our new friends,' I replied.

Barely two days out of the palace and we were being attacked by just enough men to prevent our escape. It didn't strike me as coincidence. Sha'maat could have arranged this to ensure the countess was killed. If that was the case, there was a good argument for jumping off the carriage and making a run for it before I got caught up in the attack. On the other hand, Colfax might have hired men to see *me* dead, and leaving the carriage would just make it easier for them to run me down.

'You're being ridiculous,' the countess said. 'This is Darome. We have laws. Whoever they are, they don't dare harry us on the queen's highway.'

'We're almost two days' ride from the capital, your ladyship.' I set my foot against the window of the open door and began pulling myself up to the roof. 'I've been wandering the long roads a while now, and one thing I've learned in that time: laws count only where there are men and women who care to enforce them.'

20

Horseplay

It took a moment for my eyes to adjust to the glare of the late-afternoon sun. The rush of air atop the carriage threatened to separate my hat from my head. The thunder of hoofs getting ever closer threatened to separate my head from my neck. 'Keep your speed up,' I told the driver.

The old man nodded once, his eyes on the road and his hands on the reins. 'Name's Erras,' he said.

'Kellen.'

'Have you a plan, Kellen?'

I pulled the two knives from my belt and jammed the points into the seat next to me so the handles were sticking up.

Erras glanced down at the knives. 'There's at least six riders following us. You got any more knives?'

I tapped the leather deck case strapped to my thigh.

The retainer raised an eyebrow. 'You're going to gamble them to death?'

The wind shifted direction and the specks of dirt from our wheels billowed up to cover us in a fog of dust and grit. The terrain was the same as it had been before, sparse silvery-barked trees and bare bushes whistling past, but the shrinking

171

distance between us and our pursuers made it feel as if the world were collapsing around us.

'They'll be on us any minute now,' the driver warned.

I gave the old man credit for the even tone in his voice. When bandits run down a carriage, they often take the passengers for ransom. Drivers? Not so much. The best Erras could hope for, if we were overpowered, would be a swift blade to the belly. As for me, I was starting to miss that itchy, silver shirt Arex had given me; at least if I were clothed in poncy finery I might look wealthy enough to capture instead of kill.

Reichis crawled up between us on the driver's seat. They say human beings are the only creatures that smile. Whoever 'they' are, they haven't met my business partner. The little monster loves a nasty fight.

Mariadne shouted up to us. 'Erras, stop the carriage. I'll talk to these men, whoever they are.'

'My lady—'

'I said, stop this carriage!'

Erras looked at me helplessly and started pulling back on the reins. I pushed his hands forward to let the reins slack again.

'You stop this carriage and she's dead,' I said.

'She's my—'

'Would you rather work for an irate employer or a quiet corpse?' I asked.

Erras shook his head hopelessly and whipped the reins to keep the horses at speed.

The first man broke through the cloud of dust to our right, riding hard to intercept us. He had a hard steel cap over his head, and billowing fabric around his shoulders and face kept in place by leather straps. His sword had a nasty double-curve to it. This guy wasn't some highway bandit. 'Zhuban warriors,' I said, reaching into my holsters.

Whatever hesitation Erras might have felt moments ago disappeared when he heard that. 'Hyah!' he shouted to the horses. 'Hyah, hyah!'

The Zhuban swordsman was about thirty feet away, weapon held straight out at us. *He'll try to spook me with a feint, then slash at the horses. If he injures one of them it'll fall into the other and the carriage will go down. Then he and his friends will have all the time in the world to slaughter us at their leisure.*

'*Carath Toth!*' I shouted, tossing red and black powder into the air as I made the somatic gesture. The problem with spellslinging on a moving carriage is that if you misjudge the wind, you end up sending your own hair up in flames. A bolt of fire and hate shot out and blessedly struck the man straight in the face. His body slumped back but his horse kept coming, and I heard Mariadne scream as she saw the bloody wreckage of his still-burning skull slam against the window of the carriage.

Our own horses, ignoring the fact that I'd just saved their lives, nearly took us over the steep ridge on our right side. Erras pulled hard on the reins, bringing the beasts back into the middle of the road.

'Two more coming in,' Reichis said, his body coiled to jump off the right side of the carriage at one of the approaching attackers.

'Not yet!' I shouted. 'You'll end up too far behind us when the others get here.'

A pair of warriors came up on our right side, one slightly ahead of the other. I dipped my hands back in my holsters.

173

The trouble with my blast spell is that it requires two separate powders to work. I need both hands to cast it, which means I can only target one enemy at a time. Right now I had two Zhuban swordsmen coming for me, both equally keen to soak their long, double-curved blades with my blood. One of them had a particularly excited gleam in his eye, though, and since enthusiasm for one's work should always be rewarded, I decided he'd be heading for the great Zhuban Wheel of Destiny first.

I aimed carefully, using the lesser variant of the spell to preserve my own fingers. 'Carath,' I intoned. My first shot missed, leaving me with barely enough time to pull powder and try again before the two warriors would be on us. 'Carath,' I said a second time, a distinctly pleading tone to my voice. My ancestors rarely show much affection for me, but they must have found my pathetic plea entertaining because the blast took my opponent right in the throat. He died without so much as a scream. Better still, his horse careened into that of his fellow warrior, knocking the other man from his saddle. I hoped the faltering beast would land on top of him and save me the trouble of killing him later.

'What's happening? Who are these men?' Mariadne shouted to us, leaning her head out of the right-side window, practically daring some enterprising swordsman to take her head.

'Just stay in the damned carriage,' I shouted back.

'The other three are coming around behind us, Kellen,' Reichis chittered. 'I'm taking the one in the lead.'

'Be careful,' I warned. 'These aren't sandal-wearing grunts. They look like Zhuban Front Cavalry.'

The squirrel cat snorted. 'A skinbag is a skinbag.'

As the leader came up close behind us and started reaching

174

for the back of the carriage, Reichis leaped up from the bench, his limbs spread wide to catch enough breeze to glide right onto the warrior's back. 'Death strikes from above!' the little monster roared joyously as he started ripping chunks out of the back of his enemy's head and neck. 'No stinkin' human defeats a squirrel cat!'

I ignored the screams as I pulled powder from my holsters and aimed at the last two of our attackers. They were trying to swing around the left side where they could kill Erras and drive the carriage over the ridge. Reichis's opponent was still in front though, swinging his blade wildly while screaming a series of what I suspected were rather insistent Zhuban curses. His confused and terrified horse weaved all over the road, getting in the way of the two warriors behind. The little squirrel cat was spitting bits of human flesh at them even as he dodged the desperate swings of his victim. *Show-off.*

The other two quickly abandoned their comrade. I took a gamble and pulled two heavy pinches of powder. The Zhuban warriors were just close enough to each other that I could try for a blast big enough to cover them both. The more powder, the more dangerous the spell, and the more likely that I'd just blow my own hands off. I made the gesture carefully – index and middle fingers pointed straight towards my enemies, ring and small fingers pressed hard against my palm, thumbs up to the sky.

'*Carath Toth!*'

The blast was bigger than I intended – enough to feel the sparse whiskers on my cheeks stinging. But at the last instant the two men had split apart, each heading for opposite sides of the carriage, the red and black fires of my spell splitting the air cleanly between them. I'd missed. Worse, I couldn't

175

try another shot – my fingers were too singed and there was no way I could attempt the spell again so soon. I flipped open the leather pouch holding my steel throwing cards and drew a pair. 'Go to the left side!' I shouted to Mariadne.

'What? Why? What are you—'

I rolled over the top of the carriage roof and got to my feet just in time to find a Zhuban warrior standing on his horse's saddle, sword held high. He delivered a slash that would've sliced off my ankles had I not leaped up in time. I landed awkwardly though, stumbling on the roof of the carriage, desperately trying to regain my balance as my opponent brought his sword around for a second attack. *Screw it*, I thought, and let myself fall even as I flicked my wrist to send a pair of steel cards spinning through the air. I'm a pretty good shot with the cards – not as good as Ferius, of course, but I can reliably hit the bullseye on a saloon dartboard from ten paces away. Of course, the dartboard isn't usually riding a fast horse and the floor of the saloon isn't tossing me up and down relentlessly.

The warrior's sword whipped out and nearly took my eye right out of its socket, but I rolled to the other side of the carriage roof and got away with just a scratch on my shoulder. He came around again. I took a second to aim and then threw another card. Some local whisper spirit must've smiled on me, because as I landed hard on the roof of the carriage, one of my cards bit into the meat of my opponent's sword hand and the other caught him in the thigh.

Even as his weapon dropped to the ground, the Zhuban warrior was reaching for a second scabbard strapped to the back of his saddle. His horse picked up speed, coming up on our left side again. 'Your ladyship, open the door now!'

Surprisingly, given how uninterested she'd seemed in my suggestions thus far, she kicked the carriage door open, swinging it wide just as the horse came up alongside. In a better world, the beast would've panicked and thrown its rider, but Zhuban warhorses are the best trained on the continent. The animal kept its cool, and its rider drew his second blade.

I tried tossing three more cards, but my luck had run out and not one of them found their target.

'Erras!' I called out. 'Toss me one of those knives.'

'*Toss* you a knife?' he shouted back as he struggled to keep our own horses steady. 'What if I miss?'

'Then toss the other one.'

The old man's first throw did, in fact, go wide, sending the long-bladed knife over the side. He didn't hesitate though, and a moment later the second one was spinning in an arc over my head. One good thing that comes from spending your entire childhood obsessively practising somatic shapes for spells that, as it turns out, you'll never get to cast is that you develop real fast hands. I snatched the knife out of the air just in time to parry a slash from the Zhuban warrior's second sword. To say the guy was stronger than me would be an understatement, and the force of the blow nearly knocked me off the carriage roof. He brought his weapon back for a second try, only to have a lithe leg appear from the open carriage door as her ladyship, Countess Mariadne, tried to boot his two-thousand-pound warhorse out of the way. The warrior grinned, and said something which I hoped was Zhubanese for, 'You show great courage, and thus we are no longer enemies.' Unfortunately, the way he was bringing up his sword in line to chop off her foot made me question my translation.

'Mariadne, watch out!'

She pulled her leg back just in time to avoid losing it. The horseman nudged his horse forward, and I knew then he'd tired of playing with us and was now going to kill Erras before driving our own horses over the ridge.

Guess I never should've cheated old Merrel of Betrian at cards. With his knife in hand, I leaped from the carriage, slamming into the Zhuban warrior's side and very nearly taking the two of us – along with the horse – to ground. The beast careened back to the right, slamming into the side of the carriage. The impact made my leg go numb. I hoped it might have the same effect on the Zhuban, but he didn't look troubled at all.

This man was big, and masterful in keeping control of his mount. I slid behind him and jabbed my knife into his back over and over, as fast as I could. The Zhuban wear a type of armour made of tough leather straps that can withstand just about anything. The trick is to stab enough times that your point goes between two of the straps. I felt the tip sink into soft flesh and jammed it in as hard as I could. All I got for my troubles was a grunt from the warrior and his left elbow coming around to jab me in the ribs.

I ignored the pain and just kept mindlessly stabbing at his side, taking whatever blows he dished back at me even as we lost pace with the remaining warrior and the carriage. It was an awkward, cowardly way to fight, but it was perfectly suited to my temperament. Pretty soon we were both spattered with his blood.

At last my opponent slumped over his horse and I pushed him out of the saddle. A hundred feet ahead of me I could see the carriage pulling to a stop. I heard a scream. The last soldier had managed to force himself partway in through the carriage window.

'Hyah!' I shouted, kicking the horse's sides, but he ignored me and came to a stop. Zhuban mounts are trained to respond only to their master's instructions. I leaped off the horse and ran to the carriage, but I knew I was already too late. The carriage had halted and Erras was struggling to make his way down to try to fight off the last warrior.

'Stop!' I screamed – one of the few words I knew in Zhubanese – but the warrior ignored me. I knew then that I'd been irrelevant to their mission. They had come here with one purpose: to murder Countess Mariadne.

As I reached the carriage the door opened, carrying the warrior's body with it. His legs dangled in the air and I caught sight of his face just as the last of life's colour drained from it. The weight of his body strained the door's hinges, and his head lolled to the side. From his throat protruded a short knife. The countess slipped out of the carriage, her whole body shaking with a mixture of shock, fury and grim satisfaction.

'My lady!' Erras said, his voice full of terror at the sight of her.

'I'm . . . I'm all right, Erras.' She looked down at the blood on her dress. 'I mean, I think I'm all right. I don't think he cut me. The carriage jolted and one of his blades fell from his cuirass. I grabbed it and . . . I'm not sure if I stabbed him or he fell into me or—'

'It's over now, my lady,' Erras said gently, his arm around her shoulder.

'Best get a blanket on her,' I said to the old man. I offered my arm to Mariadne for support. 'That the first Zhuban cavalry you've killed, your ladyship?'

179

Her eyes were wet, but defiant. 'I live near the borderlands, Mister Kellen. We know how to defend ourselves.'

But why had this raiding party been targeting Mariadne's carriage in the first place? I couldn't believe some Zhuban philosopher warlord cared enough about a Daroman countess to send assassins after her. A thought occurred to me and I went back to the man hanging off the carriage door. Though the Zhuban live in the north, they tend towards a dark skin tone. This man was deeply tanned, but he could just as easily hail from the southern reaches of Darome. His weapons and armour could have come from captured raiders. What if these men weren't Zhuban at all?

'We've got more troubles, Kellen!' Reichis shouted.

I looked back to find him racing towards us, a cloud of dust following behind. I reached into my holsters and carefully pulled more powder out, hoping enough life had returned to my fingertips to do the spell again.

'You're gonna need a lot more powder,' Reichis said as he reached us.

Out of the dust cloud rode almost forty men. But these weren't Zhuban; they were Daroman soldiers, steel helmets shining in the sunlight as the brace of short plumes on top flicked in the wind.

Within moments they had surrounded us, like hungry foxes cornering a trio of fat rabbits. A moment later the soldiers parted and their leader came forward. Major Leonidas dismounted and walked towards us, a freshly polished sword in hand.

21

The Unwanted Rescue

Reichis's hackles went up and his fur turned black with red stripes. He gets like that when he's angry, but also when he's nervous. Much as he loves a good fight, he can't stand being surrounded. I didn't blame him. My fingertips already stung from holding on to the powders too long, but I needed to be ready to fire the spell.

'My lady,' Leonidas said as he jammed the tip of his blade into the ground in front of her.

'Major Leonidas,' she said, voice flat, back straight as the major's sword. 'What brings you here?'

Leonidas's eyes went to the blood on her dress. I really think that someone staring at blood clinging to a woman's dress shouldn't look so. . . aroused. 'We had word of Zhubanese outriders crossing the border nearby. I knew your carriage was coming this way and feared for your safety. Despite your harsh words for me at court, I hope you know I crave nothing so much as your well-being –' he spread his arms wide, looking passably beatific – 'and your happiness.'

Mariadne stepped back to avoid his embrace. 'I am fine, major. You are too generous with your concern.'

'Generous?' Leonidas smiled, a big arrogant grin filled with shiny white teeth that made me want to reach for a big rock. 'Genrerous indeed, my lady, for I've brought you a gift.' Leonidas motioned to one of his soldiers, who handed him a brown sack. He stuck his hand in and withdrew the bloody wreck of a man's head. 'I have slain your enemies for you.'

I couldn't stop myself. '*You've* slain her enemies? You mean the only guy left – the one who fell off his horse?'

Leonidas's head spun towards me. 'The others weren't all dead. Merely wounded. I dispatched them myself.'

'And then had time to polish your sword?' I muttered.

You'd have to work long and hard to come across more guilty than the major did right then. And yet, would someone so blatant and clumsy really have risen so high in the ranks of the Daroman army? Had Leonidas set this whole thing up, wouldn't he have simply picked up one of the Zhubanese swords and stabbed Mariadne then and there? There were more than enough corpses to make it look as if the raiders had killed us before the major's troops had prevailed.

Two of the Daroman soldiers walked to the carriage and hauled off the corpse hanging from the door before dragging it away. Leonidas made a show of supervising their bloody work.

'Kellen, tell those guys to leave our kills alone,' Reichis growled. 'Or at least save me the eyeballs.'

Leonidas looked down at the squirrel cat. Other than the queen, I've never met anyone else who could understand Reichis's actual words, but his tone has a way of conveying his meaning that occasionally bypasses the need for language.

'Would someone get rid of that weasel? Its braying offends me.'

I was about to point out that weasels don't bray when one

of his soldiers stepped forward and pulled a short sword from its sheath. I pressed my ring and little fingers into my palms and aimed my fore and middle fingers at the soldier as I addressed Leonidas. 'Tell your lackey to back off or you'll be writing a very sad letter to his wife.'

The soldier froze. Spellslinging isn't very common, but enough people had probably run across Jan'Tep exiles to know we had a few tricks up our sleeves. The major pulled his sword out of the ground.

'Major! Leonidas, please,' Mariadne protested, rushing to him and pressing her palms against his broad chest. 'This man saved my life!'

Leonidas looked at me with a hunger in his eyes I usually only find in my own people. Nobody likes spellslingers all that much, but military men have a particular hatred for us. I guess firing bolts of red death from your fingertips must look like cheating to someone who's spent a lifetime practising hand-to-hand combat. 'He threatened a Daroman soldier in the conduct of his duty.'

'Please,' the countess repeated. 'Leave him be. Look at him, barely more than a boy. He is of no consequence to the two of us, my lord.'

That 'two of us' seemed to please Leonidas mightily. The way Mariadne's eyes gazed up at the major, lips slightly parted, fingers tracing the ridges of the eagle adorning his steel breast-plate, could easily have been interpreted as ardent desire. But I'd spent almost two years with Ferius Parfax, learning the ways of the Argosi arta precis – the talent of perception. The stiffness in Mariadne's limbs and the tightness in her voice spoke of intense disgust. That, and fear. She'd done everything she could not to have to touch him up until now, but my

183

little confrontation with the major had forced her to debase herself before him and his soldiers. Unfortunately for both of us, it didn't work.

'The wretch is a Jan'Tep shadowblack and, if the rumours are to be believed, an Argosi spy.' He pushed Mariadne aside and spun his sword in the air, catching the grip neatly in his right hand. 'Do you know what we do when we find an Argosi sniffing around our borders, boy?'

'Come on, soldier boy,' Reichis chittered, his fur turning blood red. 'Try something.'

'Shut the hell up, Reichis,' I said.

Leonidas laughed. 'Look! The boy talks at his weasel! Perhaps he was raised by one and thinks it to be his brother!'

Forty men laughed. I suppose it's nice having people trained to laugh at your jokes.

'Major, we thank you for your generous assistance,' Mariadne said, taking advantage of the temporary levity. 'Truly we would have been lost without you and your brave men. Now I must take my leave, for the afternoon grows late and we still have many miles to travel.'

Leonidas smiled down at her. 'Nonsense. You will be my guest tonight, Lady Mariadne. I shall have my men set up my tent for you and I myself will stand guard outside your door. I swear no man or woman shall get past me.'

Not sure where the 'woman' in question would come from. While both men and women are required to serve in Darome's military, so far as I could tell there were only the former among the major's troops.

Mariadne smiled. 'A most generous offer, major.'

'Good, then—'

'Alas,' she interrupted, 'it is one I cannot accept. I have

184

pressing business at my home in Sarrix and can afford no delay.'

The look that crossed Leonidas's face wasn't pretty. 'Very well,' he said at last. He sheathed his sword and started walking towards his horse. 'Goodbye, rodent boy. I trust you'll keep your weasel from peeing on the lady's carriage.'

'Squirrel cat,' Reichis corrected.

'Goodbye, major,' I said. 'I don't imagine we'll run into each other again anytime soon.'

Leonidas mounted his horse and grinned down at me. 'Oh, I wouldn't say that. I have every intention of ensuring that you and I meet again exactly one more time.'

He kicked his horse and headed down the road away from us, and I briefly wondered if it might not be worth trying to shoot him in the back.

22

Bathwater

We stopped at one of those small travellers' inns that litter the northern countryside, with their badly thatched roofs, freezing cold breeze-inviting stone walls and watered-down beer. Erras rented one room for the lady and a second that he, Reichis and I shared. Part of me worried that Leonidas might come find us here. The other part felt fairly sure he wouldn't notice a place like this even if his horse ran right into it. 'I thought she wanted to make Sarrix by nightfall,' I said as I sat on the bed in a towel and began scrubbing the remaining blood off my shirt.

Erras had allowed me first use of the bath since he'd avoided most of the blood spatter in the attack. I was grateful, and a bit surprised, since it meant he would have to bathe in dirty water. Reichis had dipped a paw in after I'd finished and decided it was still too hot, which saved me a prolonged, bite-filled argument over why the 'useless old skinbag' was getting to bathe before the 'noble squirrel cat who saved everybody's lives by single-pawedly taking down fifty Zhuban Elites'.

'Wouldn't do much good to arrive in town this late,' the old man said, craning his head back in the bath as the steam gathered around his face. 'The marshals won't let us into the jail to see Tasia until tomorrow.' He sighed, but not from contentment. 'If they let the countess in at all.'

'What happens if they refuse?'

Erras raised an eyebrow. 'My lady will quite possibly do something you and I will both regret.' He nodded towards the powder holsters sitting on my bed. 'Don't suppose you could just blow a hole in the jail the way you did with those Zhuban, could you?'

I dried my hands on a towel before checking the holsters. 'I used up most of what I had on the Zhuban. Besides, the powders don't like it much when you use them on things other than people.' That wasn't exactly strictly true, but I preferred not to share more than necessary about the weapon I most rely on to keep Reichis and myself alive.

'Mind if I enquire as to what those powders are made from, Mister Kellen?' Erras asked.

I tapped the left holster. 'The red powder is crow's root and ground-up sparkrock, mixed in with a few ingredients I like to keep to myself.'

'And the other?'

'Dead man's tongue, mostly.'

Erras stared back at me, likely trying to see if I was having fun with him, then said, 'So you rob a lot of graves then, I take it?'

I shook my head. 'In a pinch any corpse will do, but it works best if it comes from someone whose death is connected to me somehow.'

'Then why didn't you collect some from the Zhuban you killed?'

'Believe me, I wish I had, now. But desecrating the dead is

187

a crime in Darome. Leonidas would've used the excuse to set his men on me, which would have been . . . inconvenient.'

Erras nodded. 'The major is nothing if not inconvenient.'

He stood up out of the bath, old and skinny and shrivelled in all the ways you would expect, but without a lick of embarrassment.

I tossed him a towel and resumed cleaning my shirt when a thought occurred to me. 'Countess Mariadne told Leonidas we needed to be in Sarrix tonight. She lied to him.'

Erras grew a grim little smile. 'My lady makes something of a career of it.'

Reichis grabbed at my shirt. I put it down and he hopped up on my lap so I could brush his fur. He's not fastidious by nature, but he does like to have his coat brushed now and then. 'If Mariadne can't stand him, why doesn't she just tell him to bugger off?' I asked.

Erras sighed. 'There are times that I wish she would, you can be sure of that, Mister Kellen, but Leonidas commands the north-east border. Zhuban raiders come across every other week lately, and when they do, the countess's domain is the first place they strike. If the queen's soldiers don't come in time, well, we lose people.'

'So Leonidas . . .'

'Major Leonidas is someone that my lady must, shall we say, humour when possible.'

'And Tasia? Could Mariadne have ordered her to . . . ?'

The retainer shook his head. 'My lady would never do such a thing. In fact, she commanded Tasia be kept away from Leonidas and his men. Tasia's been with her since they were children. When Arafas died . . .' The old man sighed. 'A bad business, that. Poor boy. He and Mariadne were just seventeen when they wed. She loved him like . . . well, I'm no poet. She just loved him, that's all. Plain and true.'

I had trouble imagining the haughty, condescending Countess Mariadne as a doe-eyed maid. 'What happened?'

Erras chewed on his lip a while before answering. 'A year after they got married, Arafas was attacked by Zhuban raiders on his way home. They strung him up from hooked wires set across two trees. Ritual murder it was. No reason for it. The Zhuban, well, I guess they just decided it was his destiny. My lady . . . when they brought her husband's body, it was like all those sharp hooks we took from his flesh became embedded deep into her soul, still pulling at her long after we lay Arafas to rest.'

'Shoulda killed 'em all or else quit whinin' about it,' Reichis muttered as he curled up on my lap. It's not that squirrel cats aren't sympathetic – I mean, they aren't really – but mostly it's that they don't grieve for the dead the way humans do. That's what Reichis says anyway.

Erras went on. 'I didn't think my lady would ever recover, but Tasia, she was like a lioness looking after a wounded cub. Never left her alone, never let her give up. Refused to heed anyone who tried to stop her, even the countess herself.'

Reichis gave a little grumbling growl. 'Exactly. That's how you do it. Fight for the livin' not the dead.' The last part came out more a snore than anything else.

The old retainer's mythologising of the maid raised an obvious question. 'You think Tasia might have slept with Leonidas of her own accord – maybe to get him to leave Mariadne alone for a while?'

Erras scowled at the mere suggestion, but then the breath went out of him. 'I've been asking myself that question since

189

this whole mess started. But it doesn't make sense. Does Leonidas strike you as the kind of man who would settle for a lady's maid?'

No, I thought, *not one bit.* He seemed like he was after more than just Mariadne's virtue. Leonidas struck me as an ambitious man, hungry for power. He was a soldier with a rising star, to be sure, but still a soldier. No great name, no wealthy household. A marriage to a widow like Mariadne, cousin to the queen, would open up a lot of doors for him. Sleeping with the maid was an embarrassment, and gave Mariadne an excuse to keep him at bay for a while. I couldn't believe a military commander would make that big a tactical error. As much as I would've liked to pin everything on Leonidas, someone else had a hand in all of this. So had Mariadne pushed Tasia into pursuing Leonidas? Or had the maid done it herself to protect her employer, knowing it could end her own life?

23

The Jail

One glance at the lavish, indigo-peaked stone towers of the settlement of Urbana Sarrix was all it took to understand why it was the target of Zhuban raids. The town stood high atop a mountain ridge, a flower in the snow, begging to be plucked. As Daroman outposts went, it wasn't especially big: three large keeps, like little castles, surrounded by a hundred smaller buildings. A population of two thousand souls split between the town proper and the smaller homes on the outskirts. The streets were flagstone, likely imported from the south to remind people that the queen's roads extended from the capital to all parts of the empire. Flowering trees grew in pots along the main street, requiring constant care to survive the harsher northern climate – another insult to the Zhuban for whom enduring the rugged terrain of their lands was a matter of individual struggle.

'This was once a place of peace, if you can imagine it,' Mariadne said as she guided me down the avenue towards the marshals' garrison.

Erras kept a polite distance behind us. Reichis didn't care about etiquette and skittered around as he pleased, taking special care to piss on every statue and monument we encountered.

The mid-morning sun was bright, though the air was chill, a nasty combination for my left eye so I kept my hat low on my brow. 'I'm not sure the Zhuban got the joke,' I said.

'You don't understand. Sarrix was built as a place for the Zhuban to visit, to wander our streets and receive food, supplies, even books without paying for them.'

'Get to know the Daroman way of life? Maybe start to see how they might benefit from assimilation?'

She smiled, just a bit, but enough for me to think that maybe she didn't actually despise me any more. 'Perhaps. But I prefer to think of it as a gentle place where two cultures could meet without hunger or thirst or fear of violence.'

Reichis snorted. 'Well, I'm hungry and thirsty and I may get violent if I keep having to listen to this.'

'Shut up, Reichis.'

Mariadne looked at me and shook her head. 'I still . . . No, leave it aside. You did us a great service yesterday, master card player.' Then she eyed Reichis. 'And your . . . squirrel cat too. He is a fierce creature.'

'Got that right, lady,' Reichis said.

She leaned into me. It was an odd sensation that I found I liked. 'Have I angered it?' she asked.

'"Him", not "it". And no – he just growls when he's boasting.'

She smiled and started to laugh before composing herself.

'What?' I asked.

'Oh, it's nothing, really. Tasia sometimes claims I sound as if I'm barking when I become angry.'

The thought made me smile. My sense of self-preservation made me keep my mouth shut. That, and the fact that she was still walking very close to me. Her unassuming grace and elegance were intoxicating.

'Hey,' Reichis said, pulling at my trouser leg. 'No making hump-hump with the stuck-up bitch, all right?'

'I wasn't—'

'What?' Mariadne asked.

Reichis tapped his snout. 'I can smell it, Kellen. I can also smell her, and she's just playing you.'

'It's nothing,' I said to the countess. 'Just remembered I haven't bathed the squirrel cat in a while.'

'Well, that will have to wait,' Mariadne said. 'We're here.' She pointed to a set of four nearly identical single-storey buildings, each made from the same dull grey stone. One for the barracks, one for the jail cells, one for the magistrate's chambers, and one for the gallows. I'd travelled the length and breadth of the borderlands in the past couple of years and I swear every Daroman marshals' garrison looks exactly the same, including the spiked iron fence surrounding the compound with the gate bearing their six-pointed star and the phrase 'Trajedam necri sodastium frigida'. *The trail never runs cold.* The only difference I'd ever noticed was the number of marshals stationed there. This one had two: a big, senior marshal named Bracius, and her junior, named Fen. Unfortunately, both seemed to know the countess quite well.

Bracius came right up to the gate and held a meaty hand out in front of her. 'I'm telling you right now, your ladyship,' she intoned, a surprisingly smooth contralto voice making her jowels flutter as if they were about to take flight, 'under no circumstances are you going to meet with the prisoner again.'

Mariadne's fury ignited instantly. 'How dare you! How dare you hold that poor girl with intent to take her life, and refuse me the chance to give her what little comfort I may!'

193

'My lady, I'm going to ask you to take your hands off the bars and step back. You violated the law when you tried to break your maid out, and we're not letting you in again for a second try.'

'The queen—'

'You're the queen's cousin. We know.'

Her partner, Fen, nodded. 'You've certainly reminded us enough times,' he muttered, and wiped a dirty handkerchief across the oily surface of his pockmarked forehead.

Bracius gave the younger marshal a dirty look. 'My lady, we know your rank and your relationship to Her Majesty. You should be glad we do, otherwise you'd have been arrested by now. The prisoner has rights, and one of those is to refuse visitation by anyone, no matter their rank.'

'Wait,' I said. 'You're telling me Tasia doesn't *want* to see the countess?'

Marshal Bracius gave me a warning look as if I'd just brought a match to a mountain of dry tinder.

'It's a lie!' Mariadne cried, slamming her palms against the bars. 'Why would Tasia refuse me?'

'You'll have to take that up with the magistrate, your lady-ship,' Bracius said, not unkindly.

'Garran?' Mariadne spat the name. 'That fool won't even let me see the writ of judgement against her. He just spouts on and on about the ineffable majesty of the law and how even the highest among us must accept . . .' The rest of that sentence died on her lips. She turned away and leaned into Erras, who embraced her sympathetically while giving me a look that made me feel as if this were all my fault. What is it about old people that makes them think that just because they're willing to die for a cause, you should too?

194

I sighed. 'Any reason why I can't see the prisoner?' I asked Marshal Bracius.

She looked through the bars at me appraisingly. 'Depends. Who the hell are you?'

I pulled the credentials the queen's social secretary had given me out of my coat, and handed them to the marshal. She took the papers and rubbed the vellum between thumb and forefinger before reading them. When she was done, she gave a snort before passing them to Fen.

'The queen's tutor at cards?' Fen asked. 'Seriously? You teach Her Majesty to play card games?'

'It beat the only other means of employment they offered me.'

Bracius took the credentials from him and handed them to me through the gate before pulling out a set of iron keys and opening the lock. 'Fine. Fen, check him for weapons and let him in.'

Fen stood back as the gate opened, eyeing Countess Mariadne warily and then looking down at Reichis, who was following me in. 'That thing bite?' he asked.

'Yeah, but he ate a guy's face yesterday, so he's probably not hungry.'

Fen's reaction made his partner snicker. Finally the junior marshal made a sour face and stepped aside. 'Fine. You and your weasel've got an hour.'

'Does no one in this brain-dead country know what an actual weasel looks like?' Reichis chittered as he walked by him.

195

24

The Maiden of Cards

Tasia's cell was as plain as a grey cloud on a dreary day –
stone walls, iron bars set into the frame of a small window
that was too high to provide any view of the town beyond
an equally grey sky. A small sleeping pallet occupied one wall
and a little wooden table with two chairs took up the rest
of the floor space.

'Who are you?' the maid asked, once Fen had left us.

'Wait,' I said to her, holding up a hand.

Reichis sauntered over to the door and squeezed himself
with some difficulty through the bars. I resisted the urge to
comment on his weight. 'It's clear,' he said.

'Go check out the rest of the jail. Find out how many other
prisoners are here and how well secured the place is.'

Reichis left and the maid looked at me quizzically. 'Are
you a mage? You don't look Jan'Tep to me. Who are you?'

'No, I am, and Kellen, in that order.'

'May I ask why you're here?'

I looked at this woman who was a few days from execution.
Tasia was maybe a few of years older than me, taller too, with
skin as pale as mine would be were I not tanned from two
rough years on the road, most of them spent in deserts. She

was pretty, though not as conventionally beautiful as her mistress. But she had an unassuming charm that was just as alluring.

Stop looking with your eyes, I imagined Ferius cajoling me. *If you want to see what's going on, look with everyone's eyes but your own.* It was the typical Argosi nonsense she traded in, but at this particular moment it made a lot of sense. *How would Leonidas see her?*

I didn't know the major particularly well. I'd never been a soldier, I'd never been particularly big or strong. My ambitions had never been towards any kind of political advancement. *See, Ferius?* I thought bitterly. *Another Argosi trick that doesn't work.*

Had she been there, no doubt she would've pulled out a smoking reed from her waistcoat, made a match appear from her shirtsleeve to light it with, let out a long puff of smoke and said, *Kid, if you're just gonna stand there tellin' yourself tall tales, surely you can come up with fancier ones than that?*

She'd've been right too.

I may never have been in the military or aspired to any kind of courtly position, but I knew what it was to want things. To want power. To want people. Had I never lost my magic – more importantly, had I never met Ferius and Reichis – I'd've turned out just like the rest of my fellow initiates back in the Jan'Tep territories. I'd've become my father's son.

Appealing enough, I could hear Ke'heops saying, as if he were standing right there beside me. *The shape is reasonably trim and womanly. The face doesn't turn the eye away. Worthy of an evening's entertainment, though not much beyond that, and only for a young man seeking distraction, nothing more.*

The way Ke'heops would have viewed Tasia was foul. Clinical. Unfeeling. Yet I was almost positive he'd be right in at least one sense: a man like Leonidas, so carefully cultivating

197

his future, wouldn't risk his ambitions on her. Not if it meant jeopardising his chances with Mariadne.

'Seen enough?' Tasia asked, crossing her arms.

'Sorry,' I said. 'Occupational hazard.'

'And what is your occupation?'

'Mostly people try to kill me,' I said, pointing at the shadow-black mark on my left eye. 'When they fail, I take their money.'

'How noble,' she said, her tone reminding me of Mariadne. For a second I could see the spark Erras had alluded to back at the inn.

'Beats prison,' I replied.

She stuck her tongue out at me, which caught me off guard and made me laugh. 'Is that how you greet all your visitors?' I asked.

'I've discovered that a death sentence can be somewhat liberating for someone who's spent their life curtsying.' There was an edge to her voice – like the first stirrings of one of Reichis's warning snarls – before she shook her head. 'Forgive me. My manners quite escape me. Why exactly are you here, Master Kellen?'

'Mister Kellen,' I said, since Reichis wasn't there to complain. 'Or just Kellen. I'm the queen's new tutor.'

'How is Her Majesty?' Tasia asked. Her voice carried more concern than I would've thought a condemned maid would have about her monarch.

'You know the queen?'

'She came often to my lady's home when she was younger. I cared for her during her visits. The last I saw her was a few months ago.'

'Her Majesty's fine,' I said. 'Though a bit low on tutoring these days.'

198

The maid's eyes flared. 'Koresh and Arrasia . . . ?'

'Took a leave of absence. From life.'

She nodded and the smile that passed over her face definitely reminded me of Reichis. 'Long overdue.'

'Karanetta's still there.'

Tasia snorted. 'Karanetta.'

'Seemed nice enough to me.'

'She's an ignorant cow. That snivelling craven. She let them – she let Koresh and Arrasia – do those awful things! To the queen! To a little girl trapped in a stupid, stupid world!'

'What was she supposed to do?'

Tasia came to her feet and got in my face. 'Take a knife and slit their damned throats. Take them in their sleep. Take them when they were having a bath, or when one of them was sick and couldn't defend themselves. Find the opportunity and end them! She's the damned queen of Darome. Someone should have killed them for her.'

I was surprised by the vehemence of her reaction. She took in a deep breath and let it out again before sitting back down. 'And yet,' I said, thinking back to Shalla's reference to the queen's having a weakness that could be exploited, 'no one did.'

Tasia shook her head. 'Oh, we are a proud and honourable people, we of Darome. Far too noble to ever do the hard thing when it needs to be done.'

'Is that what you tried to do with Leonidas?' I asked. 'Do the hard thing and end him?'

Her eyes were suddenly as unyielding as the iron bars of the cell.

'Were you protecting Mariadne?' I asked.

Her expression was flat. Not even a trace of anger or fear.

199

'Were you protecting yourself? Did he attack you?'

'Why are you here?' Tasia demanded.

'The queen sent me.'

'I don't believe you. The queen would never do anything so foolish.'

'Why wouldn't she?' I asked. 'And why won't you allow Countess Mariadne to visit you?'

'Both questions have the same answer.'

Her eyes glared back at me with the same unyielding grey resistance as the walls of her cell. She wasn't going to reveal anything to me, not yet. Pushing her further would get me nowhere, and I wasn't going to give her the satisfaction of asking a second time.

Tasia's expression changed, just a little as she watched me. 'Not without wits then,' she said finally.

Our staring contest came to an end when Reichis squeezed back in through the bars. 'No other prisoners. Security's tight though. We aren't breaking in or out of here without a lot of help.'

I nodded.

'Does your felidus arborica really talk to you, Master Kellen?' Tasia asked.

'Mister,' I said. 'Just Mist—'

She cut me off. 'Do you correct people every time they make that mistake, *Mister* Kellen? And if so, has anyone taken the time to inform you of just how annoying it is?'

Reichis started chortling so hard he fell back on his rump.

'Is he all right? He seems to be having some kind of seizure,' Tasia asked.

'He's fine. Probably just has worms again.'

'Oh, I doubt that. He seems a handsome and well-groomed

little warrior to me.' Tasia sat down on one of the two chairs before reaching out a hand towards Reichis, who got up and sauntered over to sniff her.

'I like her, Kellen. She's got fire in her.'

He climbed up into her lap and closed his eyes. My jaw was hanging open.

Tasia looked at me with a small smile on her face. 'Friendly little fellow, isn't he?'

'You have no idea,' I said.

Something eased in her at last, as if she had been holding too tightly to a heavy bundle of sticks and was finally ready to let them fall to the ground. 'You said the queen sent you to me. If that's true, then for what purpose?'

No damned idea, I thought, but decided to tread carefully. 'She told me to keep you company. She said I should play cards with you.'

Tasia's face softened. She started to speak and then stopped. I saw the beginnings of tears in the corners of her eyes. Was there some connection between the queen and Tasia and playing cards? Was it possible that there'd been no secret plans, no hidden motivations for my being sent here? Was I really here just to comfort a woman facing execution? 'Do you want to play cards for a little while, Tasia?' I asked as gently as I could.

She nodded, and wiped her eyes on the sleeve of her dress. 'For a little while. That would be nice.'

So we did just that. I pulled out a deck of cards and we spent the remainder of the hour playing hands of Country Harvest while Reichis lay snoring on Tasia's lap and the afternoon sun brought a little warmth through the bars of the window.

25

Hospitality

That night I accepted the hospitality of Countess Mariadne's keep. As northern fortresses went it was warm, elegant, and altogether inviting. A wiser man would've slept outside in the cold.

'You played *cards*?' the countess asked for what must have been the third time, finishing her meal by setting her cutlery back down on the table with the considered precision of someone who may want to stab you with it later.

The meal had been simple but plentiful, culminating with roast pheasant in a sort of winter berry sauce that I'm certain would have tasted delicious to anyone not being castigated every time they brought a spoonful to their lips. 'Playing cards is what the queen ordered me to do,' I said.

'"Playing cards is what the queen ordered me to do",' Reichis repeated, mocking me as as he tore into the massacred remains of a second pheasant. The servants had categorically refused to feed him at the table, which had turned out to be for the best since the squirrel cat had created a battlefield's worth of slaughter on the dining-room floor re-enacting his imagined stalking, pursuing and slaying of the 'much more dangerous that you might expect' pheasant.

Mariadne went back to toying with her cutlery. A servant entered the dining room, no doubt with the intent of retrieving our dishes, only to surreptitiously back away into the outer hall when she caught her mistress's expression. The countess, evidently aware of the effect she had on her staff yet determined not to spare me one ounce of her ire, said more quietly, 'That girl is four days from the hangman's noose. I travelled over a hundred miles to beg the queen for help, subjected myself to the depridations of that horrible court of hers, and you're telling me the sum total of your efforts on Tasia's behalf will consist of nothing more than a few hands of cards?'

I don't really know what to do with righteously furious people when they aren't actually trying to kill me. My instincts are all based on the premise that the best way to assuage their anger is to blast them out of existence. 'Countess, you knew the limits of my involvement here from the moment we left the palace. It's one of the reasons you hate me so much, isn't it?'

She hesitated. 'I thought . . .'

'You thought what, precisely?'

'Out on the road, when those men attacked, you fought – not entirely without skill – to protect me. Is a maid's life worth so much less to you?'

'You want an honest answer?'

Her jaw tightened even as she kept staring at her plate. 'If you think yourself capable of one.'

'I wasn't trying to save you, countess. Had I been standing by the side of the road minding my own business when those men attacked your carriage, I'd've run in the opposite direction. I was saving myself.'

Her next words came out softly, almost resignedly, as if all the air were emptying from her lungs. 'So you're a coward.'

Somehow the lack of outrage in her voice only served to make me more defiant. 'Had I not made that clear yet?' I got up and went to stand over her. 'Who do you think I am, countess? I'm an exiled spellslinger with one good spell and a couple of dirty tricks. I have no money, no political power, and a bounty on my head in half the countries on this continent. I play cards and occasionally kill people with my one good spell, two holsters of powder and as much luck as my ancestors choose to grant me on any given day. I've got no friends, except a squirrel cat for a business partner who mostly steals from m—'

'Don't drag me into this,' Reichis growled. He was standing on his hind legs, propping himself up against my right leg and was in fact, at that precise moment, pilfering a coin from my pocket.

'Shut up,' I said.

Mariadne must've thought I was talking to her. She rose up to face me, sending her chair screeching across the floor, glaring at me with eyes wide and cheeks flush with fury just waiting to be released.

I didn't bother to explain. Instead I ended my tirade with, 'Given everything you know about me, what precisely have I done to make you think I'm a hero, countess?'

Despite her anger with me, her response came haltingly, almost timidly. 'At the royal palace, before my audience with the queen all anyone wanted to talk about was the brazen outlaw the queen had hired to be her tutor; the deadly spellslinger who turned up at court and put an end to Koresh and Arrasia – something no one else would've dared attempt.

After the queen reacted to my plea with such callous indifference in front of her nobles, I thought . . . I hoped perhaps she'd sent you here to pursue some clever, clandestine course of action that would free Tasia.'

'How, exactly?'

She didn't reply, but her eyes betrayed her. They went to the powder holsters at my sides.

And there it was. The length and breadth of Countess Mariadne's newfound respect for me, defined entirely by the degree to which I was willing to kill for her. 'I thought you might be able to blow the wall somehow,' she said awkwardly. 'If you could just get Tasia out of that awful place . . .'

'Sure. No problem. Blow a hole in a two-foot-thick stone wall. I could probably do that.' I was lying. In a thousand years I couldn't break through a wall like that. Still I asked, 'And after I get her out? Then what?'

A flicker of hope appeared in Mariadne's expression. 'Tasia could run. I could help her get away from Sarrix, and then—'

I couldn't help but laugh, even though it was cruel to do so. 'Guess you've never been pursued by the queen's marshals service, have you, your ladyship?' I shook my head. 'How can you live your whole life in this country and never have learned what everyone in the borderlands knows? The marshals are some of the best trained, most dangerous men and women on the continent. You know why people fear the Daroman empire? It's not your armies. It's because everyone knows that if the queen sends her marshals after you, they'll track you to the ends of the earth. "Trajedam necri sodastium frigida". *The trail never runs cold.*' I should've stopped there, but I'd narrowly avoided death one too many times lately, and fear and frustration got the best of me. 'And if none of

205

that dissuades you from this insane course of action you want me to take, consider the fact that not only has Tasia shown no inclination whatsoever to leave her cell or cooperate with your efforts to secure her release, she won't even let you visit her.'

I braced myself for a slap in the face. Actually, a dinner knife to the throat was more likely. Neither came though. Mariadne just turned away from me and wrapped her arms around herself. 'Then it's over. I've failed Tasia. The one true friend I ever had is going to die, and the marshals won't even let me say goodbye.'

An uneasy feeling spread out from the centre of my chest. My gaze went to Reichis, who appeared to be searching for a place to hide the coin he'd stolen from my pocket. Would I ever leave him to rot in a cell waiting to die, even if I knew nothing good could come from trying to free him?

The squirrel cat looked up at me and clacked his teeth a few times in quick succession as he tilted his head from side to side. I'd learned that this was how one squirrel cat calls another a coward. I hate it when he does that.

26

Charades

They put us in a guest room on the top floor, in what Erras informed me had once been the countess's late husband's study, which gave Reichis the creeps. The squirrel cat claims his kind don't believe in ghosts ('If they were real, we'd just kill 'em again'), but he's got a superstitious streak. Given how poorly the meal had gone I would've left the keep and sought out a travellers' saloon outside town, but Mariadne's resentment and disappointment in me had settled into such inconsolable grief that leaving felt like an act too craven even for me.

'No making hump-hump with the bitch countess, remember?' Reichis warned. He was sitting on his haunches rather precariously on the balcony railing outside our room, holding a handful of small rocks in one of his paws.

'You have a problem with Mariadne?' I asked.

Reichis tossed one of the pebbles at a crow's nest lodged in a small gap in the roof. It missed by a good three feet. 'I don't care about her one way or the other. What I have a problem with is you gettin' distracted.' He tossed another rock at the nest. 'And crows. I hate crows.'

Crows also hate Reichis, and I suspected by morning they

would have found a whole range of unpleasant ways to communicate their views on the subject. Reichis claims to speak crow, though when he talks to them it sounds as if he's chittering the same insult over and over again. This also seems to be the case in the other direction.

'You need a different hobby,' I said.

Reichis paused in his assault to look at me. 'Why? I like this one.' He turned and threw another rock, this one landing even further away from the nest.

'Distracted from what?' I asked.

Reichis made a little 'hrumph' sound that went up just a bit in pitch at the end. This is squirrel cat for, 'Are you still talking? I thought you were done talking. Maybe you should stop talking.' Theirs is an economical language.

'You said I was getting distracted. What am I supposedly getting distracted from?'

Reichis let all but one of his remaining pebbles fall over the side of the balcony. 'From doing the queen's dirty work, Kellen. That's what you signed us up for.'

I didn't like the phrase 'dirty work', but I let it slide. 'I'm here, aren't I? Played cards with Tasia just like I was ordered to.'

'Don't act dumber than you already look,' he said, throwing the remaining stone at me. He has remarkable aim when I'm the target. 'You're tryin' to figure out how to help the maid. Or the countess. Or maybe how to get in bed with the countess. Or the maid. Or both. None of those are good ideas, Kellen. Whatever it is the queen really sent us down here to do, it's a safe bet it doesn't involve anything that makes you or anyone else happy.' He made a little growling noise. 'You're the one who decided to risk our necks for a chance that the queen can find you a cure for the shadowblack, Kellen. It's a little late to grow a conscience. Or an erection.'

Reichis was right. I'd bet on the queen, hoping she could help me. If the ruler of the Daroman empire can't find you a cure, then chances are no one can. Now I needed to focus on delivering on my end of the bargain. But what was I supposed to be doing here? I thought back to the day at court when Mariadne had pleaded for clemency for Tasia. *Teach her to play cards*, the queen had said. And then two days later we'd been attacked by Zhuban raiders intent on murdering the countess. Had Leonidas engineered that by himself? Or Marshal Colfax? He'd wanted me gone from the palace, and the queen's orders had certainly accomplished that. *Ancestors*, I thought. *What if it's the queen herself who wants Mariadne dead?*

Reichis glanced up at me, fuzzy muzzle contorted into an expression that I assume was meant to convey disgust at my troubled ruminations. 'Why don't you use your –' he tapped a paw against the twisting markings around his left eye – 'enig . . . um . . . eniggy . . . enigmarismitipitopystupidism?'

'I think you mean "enigmatism".'

One corner of his lip curled up into a snarl. 'That's what I said.'

'Right, sorry.'

It wasn't as if I hadn't thought of that, but no matter how many times I tried to make the shadowblack markings around my left eye twist and turn to unlock the visions that would reveal the secrets I was trying to uncover, I just couldn't seem to find the right question.

'All right,' I said at last, sitting down on the smooth stone of the balcony floor. 'Let's play a round of Lousy Rotten Bastards.'

"Lousy Rotten Bastards" was the name Reichis had chosen for the method we'd once devised for figuring out why other people were screwing with us.

He hopped down from the railing and ambled over to sit across from me. 'Fine. Who am I?'

'The queen.'

'Okay, who are you?'

'Unfortunately I'm me.'

He shook his furry head. 'No, no point. We don't have anything to go on.'

'All right. Who am I then?'

'The countess,' he said. 'Try not to enjoy it.'

I let the comment slide. 'Fine. I come to you to—'

Reichis put up a paw. 'After an entire year.'

'So you're offended?'

'Of course I'm offended. I'm the Daroman queen, you ungrateful sow. You come see me on a regular basis or else—'

'Or else what?' I asked.

'Or else . . . I don't know. Maybe it makes me think you don't care about me as much as you should.'

I thought about that for a moment. Peevishness might be the reaction of an eleven-year-old girl, but a two-thousand-year-old monarch? I remembered the fiddling with her collar and the cuffs of her dress when we first played cards, showing me the burns and bruises. Why had she put her trust in a shadow-black outcast over everyone in the palace? Was she really that alone?

'The tutors,' I said, momentarily falling out of character. 'Maybe the queen thought Mariadne could have helped her with the tutors.'

Reichis sniffed. I've noticed that he does that sometimes

when he's trying to remember something he's been told, as opposed to seen himself. It's weird, I know.

'You should have fought for me,' he said. 'You're supposed to be my "beloved cousin", so why didn't you protect me?'

'I didn't know,' I said. 'How could I know?'

'Right . . . No, wait. Tasia knew. She said so in her cell. So you had to have known.'

I shook my head. 'Tasia never told me.'

'Rabbit droppings!' Reichis chittered. 'You expect me to believe that the maid who's willing to kill a military commander and go to the gallows on your behalf keeps secrets from you?'

'All right. She told me. What the hell was I supposed to do?' I thought about it more. Mariadne's right on the northern border. Her husband's dead and she's dependent on the military. Leonidas is pressuring her into marriage – a marriage that's not likely to be fun for anyone but Leonidas. What happens if Mariadne goes to the capital and starts sticking her nose into the affairs of powerful nobles and tutors who can't be prosecuted? I shook my head. 'I can't risk helping you. If I try, chances are my life is over. You're supposed to be some all-powerful monarch with the wisdom of a hundred generations, but you put all this on somebody else? Someone who's in just as much danger as you? Solve your own damned problems!'

Reichis chortled. 'Sorry, are you the countess now? Or are you back to being you?'

'I'm the countess. I'm your favourite cousin. So why haven't you come to help me? Or why haven't we figured out how to help each other?'

Reichis sat back on his haunches. For a second I thought

211

I might have stumped him. But then he raised a paw. 'Because we can't trust each other.'

'Why not?'

He got up and started pacing around. 'Because . . . Because if I'm this weak at the palace, it means somebody's betraying me – somebody's sold their influence. How can I know it's not you?'

It was my turn to get up and stretch my legs. 'Why shouldn't I suspect the same of you? Why haven't you gotten Leonidas off my back?'

Reichis shook his head. 'Can't. He commands the northern border army.'

'And why do you care so much?'

'Because those stupid skinbag Zhuban raiders creep across the border every second day.'

Reichis climbed up onto the wide balcony railing and started pacing back and forth. Try to imagine a short, slightly tubby lump of fur ambling along earnestly on his rear legs, periodically scratching his ear with one paw, and you'll understand why I had trouble not snickering.

But he was right. With all the problems going on, the queen couldn't risk pulling Leonidas. It would weaken the northern border, and that could mean Darome being invaded by the Zhuban. The queen seemed like a sweet girl and all, but in the end a monarch's job is to protect the realm. For all its military might, Darome hadn't fought a war in decades, while all the Zhuban ever do is prepare to do battle in the name of their bizarre philosophies. The queen would have to be very careful of how she managed her army right now. So Mariadne's problems would have come second to her own . . . or maybe it was even worse than that. Crap. 'And how do I know that you aren't already trading away my freedom for some kind of deal with Leonidas?'

Reichis stopped in his tracks and turned to face me, beady eyes gleaming in the dark. 'You can't. Neither of us can.'

'So we're both playing lousy hands. And someone . . . someone is holding all the cards we both need.'

He hopped off the railing onto the balcony. 'Who?'

I thought about all the players at the table. Koresh and Arrasia were dead, but who had they been working for? Arex appeared to know the ins and outs of the court better than anyone, and he was technically in line for the throne. Then again, everyone seemed to be in line for the throne; the queen had no end of cousins. Countess Mariadne herself was one. Count Martius was one, too. He was older than Mariadne and closer to the front of the pack. Then again, maybe the marshals were tired of following the orders of an eleven-year-old queen and old Colfax was ready for a coup? What if it was my own family? Ke'heops, mage sovereign of what few clans remained of the Jan'Tep, had no love for anyone but his own people. Only . . . the Zhuban despise magic. They'd happily wipe out the Jan'Tep if they could. Whatever Sha'maat was up to at court, it probably wasn't designed to let the Zhuban pour into Darome.

'Damn, Reichis,' I said. 'There are more people with cause and means to bring down the queen than there are fleas in your fur. Maybe we should – Ow! Stop that.'

Reichis pulled his teeth out of my leg. 'Fine, so the countess is screwed and the queen even more so.'

I nodded. 'And Tasia is caught in the middle. She's the one person with neither power nor influence here.'

Reichis started picking at his fur. I shouldn't have made

213

the joke about fleas. He can be remarkably sensitive at times. After a few seconds he chittered, 'How in the thirteen squirrel cat hells are we supposed to figure this out when everybody – *everybody* – in this freakin' country is lyin' to us?'

'*Juridas averso ombrix*,' I said.

Reichis looked up at me. 'What's that supposed to mean?'

'It's the inscription on the bottom of every magistrate's gavel. It means, "Justice abhors shadows". The Daroman legal system favours openness and transparency.'

Reichis went back to cleaning himself. 'These skinbags sure do have a lot of fine-soundin' sayings. Too bad they don't live up to them.'

'What do you mean?'

'Back at the marshals' garrison, didn't Countess prissy-face say somethin' about the magistrate refusing to let her see the writ? How "open and transparent" is that?'

I hadn't considered it at the time, but Reichis had a point. To keep a writ of execution secret? From the noblewoman who rules the very district in which you're a magistrate? I doubted any lone backwoods judge would do that of his own accord. Finding out why he'd done it would be a big step in untangling this mess.

'Ah, crap,' Reichis muttered, sauntering by me to go back into the room.

'What?'

He hopped up onto the bed. 'You've got that dumb look on your face that tells anyone with a pair of eyes that you're planning somethin' stupid. Can't believe you manage to beat other skinbags at cards.'

I joined him inside, closing the doors to the balcony behind

214

me. 'Help me get Mariadne a look at that writ, partner, then we're out of this town and back to the palace, alright?'

Reichis curled himself up into a ball. 'Only the writ is secret, so how exactly do you plan on persuadin' the magistrate to let you see it?'

I pulled one of the Daroman decks I'd been carrying with me from my pocket. 'By doing what the queen sent me here to do in the first place: play cards.'

27

The Royal Deception

The magistrate's chambers consisted of a courtroom, an office and a records room that occupied the eastern side of the marshals' compound – just in front of the gallows: a testament to Daroman frontier efficiency. Unfortunately, Magistrate Garran wasn't there. Even worse, Bracius and Fen were the ones in charge while he was away.

'You again?' the big marshal asked, her hand drifting to the mace at her side.

I shrugged. 'I'm just trying to keep her off my back.'

Mariadne shot daggers at me with her gaze. I'd managed to convince Marshal Fen to let her accompany me on the guarantee of the queen's tutor of cards that the countess wouldn't try to break out her maid and the further assurance that she wouldn't so much as utter an angry word until we'd left the garrison. Turns out some people don't appreciate my negotiating skills.

'Where's your . . . whatever that weasel-thing was?' Fen asked.

'He's outside,' I said. 'I think he's afraid of you.'

'He better be.'

Bracius pushed him aside. 'All right, Fen, you've shown us

all how tough you are.' The marshal turned back to us. 'Now, what do you two want?'

'Is that the records room over there?' I asked, pointing to a door behind the counter.

She nodded. 'What do you want?'

'So that's it there,' I said, louder than I probably needed to. 'On the south-east corner?'

Bracius looked at me like I was an idiot. So did Mariadne. 'Yes,' the marshal said, just as loudly. 'Do you need me to draw you a map?'

'Nope,' I said. 'But you could let us see the writ of judgement against Tasia.'

The marshal shook her head. 'It's been sealed. Only by application to the queen or the presiding magistrate can it be *unsealed*.'

'Fine,' I said. 'We'll wait.'

The marshal sighed. 'He might not be back today, and even if he is, he's not going to let you see it.' Her gaze went to Mariadne. 'As I've told you on roughly five separate occasions, countess.'

'Well, doesn't hurt to let us wait a little while, does it?' I pulled out my deck of Daroman playing cards. 'Say . . . either of you enjoy a good card trick?'

Fen looked up. Don't know what it is about Daroman marshals, but I swear they're all addicted to gambling.

'You sure I can't persuade you?' I said, dropping a fat silver coin on the desk.

Fen reached for it but Bracius slammed her fist down. 'You know what the penalty for attempting to bribe a marshal is, friend?'

I put my hands up. 'No bribing here, marshal. Just thought

217

you and Fen here might like to play a game while we wait to see if the magistrate turns up.'

Bracius snorted. 'Yeah, like we're going to make bets with the queen's tutor of cards.'

'Tell you what – let's make it easy. I'll show you a little card trick like this . . .' I flipped the outlaw of chariots from the deck along with the knight of blades and the knight of arrows.

'This game here's called Prison Break,' I said, flipping the cards face down and switching their positions back and forth. 'All you have to do is help the outlaw escape. Don't worry – he's innocent after all.'

Bracius laughed. 'That's what they all say.'

I've done this trick on a half-dozen occasions with marshals on the borderlands, and I swear to you, they make that joke every single time. 'All right then – where's our prisoner?'

Fen put a finger down on the middle card. I flipped it over. It was the outlaw.

'Well now, see? That's all there is to it.'

Fen smiled. 'So I get the coin now, right?'

'I was going pretty slow that time. How about we do it for real now?'

'Okay,' he said, leaning in so his face was six inches from the cards. I flipped the cards back and forth twice as fast this time. When I stopped he put his finger on the middle card again.

'You sure?' I asked.

'That's the one,' he said.

I flipped it over. Sure enough, it was the outlaw of chariots.

'Well, all right!' he said, and took the coin. 'So much for Mister Fancy Card Player!'

218

I smiled. 'Come on now – let me have a chance to win it back.'

I dropped another silver coin on the desk.

'Just walk away from it, Fen,' Bracius warned.

Fen looked at me, his tongue working its way like a snake in his mouth as he considered his odds. 'I think I can do it.'

'Good man,' I said.

I pulled the same trick again. And again Fen pointed to the middle card. I flipped it over and it was the outlaw of trebuchets.

'Ha! See that, Bracius? That's two silver for me.'

Bracius looked at me suspiciously. 'Guess you're buying drinks tonight.'

'Maybe. Maybe not,' Fen said, a big, dumb smile lighting up his face.

I put another silver on the desk.

'Oh no – I think two'll do just fine, Mister Card Player.'

'Ah, come on,' I said. 'You're a natural at this. Besides, what's the worst that can happen? Even if I win this round, you still walk away with a silver.'

'I don't know . . . Ah hell, let's do it. I'm feeling lucky!'

'Here we go,' I said. This time I spun the cards around faster than all the other times. I did it longer too, whirling them back and forth faster than the eye can follow. When I finally stopped, Fen looked angry.

'You tryin' to cheat me?'

I shrugged. 'You agreed. Never said I couldn't go faster.'

Bracius didn't look too pleased either.

'Well, come on now, pick your card.'

'Don't rush me,' Fen said.

He stared at the backs of the cards like he thought he

could see through them if he just tried hard enough. Eventually he stuck his finger on the one on the left.

'Okay, here we—'

'No,' he said. 'You went for that too quick. I want this one.' He put his finger back on the middle card again.

'You sure?' I asked.

'Damn straight,' he said.

Reluctantly I flipped the card over, revealing the outlaw once again.

'Whee-hoo!' Fen shouted. 'That's a week's wages, Bracius!'

Bracius shook her head. 'Hell, Fen, I got to admit, that was pretty impressive. How did you do it?'

'I got the family eyes,' he said proudly. 'My pa used to be able to shoot an eagle with a crossbow from two hundred yards. Fast eyes – that's what Mister Card Player here didn't count on.'

Nobody, not with any crossbow ever made, has ever hit a moving target from two hundred yards away. 'One more try?' I suggested.

Fen looked like he was considering it, but Bracius stepped in. 'No way. That's enough fun for one day, and I know how folks like you work. No, sir – just walk away from your losses, friend.'

I sighed. 'All right, but don't you think the least you can do is let me see the writ, just for a second?'

Bracius shook her head. 'Out,' she said. 'Come back tomorrow and try the magistrate again.

'And bring more money with you,' Fen said, cackling. 'I could use some new leathers.'

* * *

220

Mariadne had the decency to wait until we were outside before she started yelling at me. 'That was your big plan? Lose money to a half-brained thug who only ended up in the marshals service by being arrested for drunkenness and then getting lost on the way to his jail cell?'

'They were never going to give us that writ,' I said. 'Best to keep things friendly.'

'I don't even understand the point of the trick! You just shuffle the same three cards around over and over, trying to hide an outlaw he had no trouble finding!'

I snorted. 'You kidding me? That guy missed the outlaw every time! The trick was convincing him he'd actually landed on the right one.' I stuffed the deck back in my pocket. 'Actually, I screwed up on the second turn and showed him the outlaw of trebuchets instead of chariots, but nobody pays attention when they're winning.'

The expression of befuddlement on Mariadne's face was actually rather endearing. 'So you devote what I assume must be considerable skills at sleight of hand for the purpose of *losing* money?'

'Keeps everyone friendly while the time passes.'

Across the street, Reichis was marking his territory against the trunk of what looked to be a very expensive to maintain finberry tree. 'I see your animal is hard at work too,' Mariadne said.

'Any luck?' I asked the squirrel cat as I walked over to him.

Reichis gave me one of those looks of his that says that 'luck' was something only skinbags required. He scratched away at a little mound of dirt to reveal a crumpled sheet of vellum. I retrieved it and handed it to Mariadne.

221

She looked at the writ, then at Reichis, in shock. 'It's true then? He really does understand you?'

I shrugged. 'Who knows. Maybe he just gets lucky a lot.'

'I . . .' Mariadne looked at me with a confused expression that eventually settled into something faintly apologetic. I've learned over the past year not to be tricked, bewildered or otherwise boondoggled by beautiful women. The ones who aren't disgusted by my shadowblack soon learn to be when they see other people react to it. But something about Mariadne and the way every thought in her head seemed to write itself across her features one by one made her hard to resist. For all the privileges of her birth, those same circumstances had threatened to steal all the joy from her life. 'Apologise later,' I said. 'What's in the writ?'

She read over the document and then handed it to me. 'Damn him. Damn him to hell!'

'Who?'

'Leonidas! He lied, just as I suspected. He told the queen that he'd urged the magistrate to clemency, but it says here that he swore an oath that Tasia's attack had been intended to *undermine the security of the Northern Border Forces. That's* why the magistrate treated the attack as a treasonous offence.'

Having had some experience with the Daroman propensity for charging treason in cases involving honest mistakes like wiping blood on the flag or trying to stab military commanders, I read through the document carefully. Daroman writs are pretty comprehensive, detailing what evidence was considered by the magistrate, what was deemed credible, what factors determined the sentence and who signed off on the execution . . .

'Okay, so this is bad,' I said.

222

'What? What is it?'

'We have a bigger problem than Leonidas.'

'Well, tell me!'

I'd been wondering why a petty local magistrate would risk executing the companion of a noblewoman with close ties to the queen. All he'd had to do was lower the charge from treason to armed assault or even attempted murder and sentence Tasia to life in prison. Yet he'd gone ahead and sanctioned her execution – something that under normal circumstances would require the guilty to be taken to the capital and put before the monarch for final sentencing. I handed Mariadne the writ and pointed at the execution order. On the bottom line was a seal and a signature that read, *By order of Ginevra, Imperial Majesty of Darome.*

28

The Fortune Teller

Countess Mariadne was capable of vastly more indignant fury than I'd previously assumed. It was in hopes of keeping her from picking up the nearest pitchfork and walking all the way back to the capital to personally declare war on the queen of Darome that I went to the considerable trouble of convincing Marshal Bracia to let me visit Tasia a second time.

'You care about these women?' the marshal asked me as she led me down the jail's narrow hall, her gruff but almost gentle tone making it seem as if we'd suddenly become old friends.

'Not in the slightest,' I replied. 'Just trying to do my job.'

'Which is what, exactly?'

'Yeah,' Reichis chittered. 'I for one would love to hear it.'

I shrugged. 'I'll let you know when I figure it out.'

Bracia chuckled, and slapped me on the back in that way that says, 'You seem like a nice fella, sure would be a shame if I had to smash your face in with my mace.'

When we finally reached Tasia's cell, the marshal paused after unlocking the door and quietly said to me, 'She's a good girl, this one. Don't know why she done what she did, but it weren't from cruelty nor cowardice. If you reckon you can help her, best be doing it soon.'

'Yeah? And if I could bust her out of here, what then?'

Marshal Bracia glanced back at me, and gentle compassion shone in her eyes, but it couldn't hold a candle to the unyielding determination behind them. 'Then we hunt you down, boy, to the ends of the earth.' She turned and headed back down the hall. 'It's a big world, though. Might take us a whole month to find you.'

The smile that lit up Tasia's face when Reichis and I entered the cell, her gaze going from me to Reichis and back again, made me reassess her looks. She was, in her way, as pretty as any woman I'd ever met.

Beauty is what you see when your eyes stop focusing on the details and you begin to see the whole person. Ferius's typically bizarre axiom was starting to make sense. A little.

Regardless, I had trouble imagining that Leonidas had seen her the way I did now, and I doubted he'd risk his future just to get her into bed. But the plain truth was, Tasia was stuck in here, and that smug, self-important bastard Leonidas was walking free, and those facts made me want to stick a knife in him.

'Thank you,' Tasia said to me as I sat down on one of the wooden chairs.

'For what?'

'For these.' She pointed at one of the decks of cards I'd left her. 'I'd forgotten how much I loved cards.'

As Reichis crawled up on Tasia's lap I picked up a standard Daroman deck and started shuffling. 'You've played a lot of cards?'

225

'Enough to win a bet here or there,' she said, the left side of her smile tilting up. She made a silver coin appear from the sleeve of her dress.

A surprised laugh came out of me. 'You gambled with Fen, the marshal, didn't you?'

Her smile widened. 'He's really not very good.'

'You ever play with Mariadne?'

'Oh no, the countess isn't one for cards. Her husband Arafas used to play once in a while before . . .'

'Before Leonidas had him killed and blamed it on Zhuban raiders?' I asked.

The smile disappeared and her silence let me know that no response would be forthcoming.

I laid out a hand on the table and decided on a different approach. 'You've played with the queen too, right?'

Tasia picked up her cards and examined them, shielding them from me. 'Often – when she was younger and visiting the countess.'

'Would you say the queen's a good card player?'

'You've played her, haven't you?' she asked.

'Yes, but the question of who beat who is a bit uncertain.'

Tasia's smile returned. 'Isn't that what they say though? When you can't tell who the fool is at the table, it's probably you.' She tilted her head as she gazed at me. 'Why did you choose to become a card player by profession, Kellen?'

'I didn't really. I just found myself . . .'

'Found yourself what?'

There's something about knowing a person's going to die that makes lying to them feel wrong somehow. 'For a while now I've been telling myself that gambling was as good a way to make a living as any. Better than most actually, since it

226

meant taking money off people who I don't like and who don't like me. The truth is –' I flipped my cards between my fingers, making them dance, listening to them rustle against each other – 'when I shuffle the deck, I hear her voice.' I fanned the cards open and closed. 'When I look at my hand, I see her grinning back at me.'

Tasia's voice was very quiet. 'You must have loved her very much.'

'It's not like that,' I said. 'It's . . . She made me believe I could be someone worth knowing.'

'And now?'

'Now I don't know who I am any more. I just know I don't like the person staring back at me from the mirror.'

I put down my first card face down and she did the same. Thieves' Sleeves is played by setting up two columns of cards. Only one suit, in this case chariots, add to your score, but with a trebuchet you can steal the other player's chariot. If they put down an arrow when you put down a trebuchet card, your trebuchet gets taken. Lose ten points worth of trebuchets and the game's over. If you're wondering what the blades are for, each one you're forced to play removes a chariot from your own stack. In Thieves' Sleeves, as in life, throwing a blade just gets you into more trouble.

'So you've made yourself as much a prisoner as I am,' Tasia said.

'The difference is,' I said, 'when the game's done, I get to leave.'

We flipped the cards over. Both of us had played trebuchets.

'Maybe,' Tasia said. 'But if you think either of us is truly a player in this game, Kellen, then you really are the fool at the table.'

227

She put down her second card face down and I did the same.

'Fine,' I said. 'Then what are we? The audience?'

She shook her head. 'No, we're just cards in someone else's hand.'

'And which card are you?'

Tasia flipped over her card. It was a two of chariots. 'Nothing important, Mister Kellen. Just a girl trying to do her best not to be someone's blade.'

I reached to flip over my card, but she put her hand on mine. There were calluses on her fingers but all I could feel was the electricity from her skin. Was this what Leonidas had felt? I looked into her eyes. 'Who are you trying to protect, Tasia?'

'Right now? Maybe I'm trying to protect a fool who doesn't know who he is.'

I pulled my hand away. 'And who am I?'

'Are we playing cards or playing games? Flip over your card. The marshals said I only get an hour with you, and I'm bored of solitaire.'

I may not be the best card player in the world, but I know people and I'd known that she would play another chariot, so I'd put down the seven of trebuchets. But when I turned it over, my card was the seven of blades. She'd pulled a trick on me while I was focusing on her face. 'Be careful what you do with your blades, Kellen of the Jan'Tep. They cut both ways.'

It was a good trick, but I was tired of tricks. I was trying to help this woman and all she'd done was spin me around in circles. I tossed my cards down on the table. 'Fold,' I said.

'Already?'

'Seems to be working for you.'

Tasia picked them up and flipped them over back on the deck. She shuffled and laid out seven cards face down.

'I think I'm done with card games for now, Tasia.'

'It's not a card game,' she said, placing the rest of the deck back down on the table.

Reichis opened one of his eyes from where he sat curled up on her lap. 'Never seen a seven-down game before,' he muttered.

'What is it?' I asked Tasia.

'Did you know that hundreds of years ago Daroman wise women used cards to pierce the veil of the stars?'

'What, you're going to tell my future?' My people have all sorts of magic, but even we know divination is a con game.

'Maybe,' she said, turning over the first card. It was the ace of trebuchets. 'Sometimes it tells the past too, or the present.'

'How is that helpful?' I asked.

'You want to know why people are doing what they're doing, but you don't even know who the players are.'

I picked up the card and held it out towards her. 'So what does this mean?'

'Aces represent emotions. The forces behind our actions. The suit of chariots represent the drive for change, sometimes anger too. Arrows are love, blades violence. Trebuchets determination, but also self-interest.'

'So I'm feeling self-interested, is that it?'

She smiled. 'I tell you two meanings and you choose to believe the worst.'

'Occupational hazard,' I said.

'Well then, you see – the cards are already revealing the truth of your life.'

229

She flipped the second card. It was the two of arrows. 'The numbered cards can represent people or actions.'

'So if it's a person?' I asked.

'Then it's a loving person of low means. The higher the number, the more powerful the person.'

I wondered where I would sit on that scale.

Tasia went on. 'But the numbers can also represent actions. Two for conflict, three for peace, four for advance, five for withdrawal, six for conspiracy, seven for revelation, eight for imprisonment, nine for release.'

'And ten?'

'Ten for the end of things,' she said.

'So does the two represent a person or an action in this case?'

Tasia frowned as she looked at the card. 'I'm not sure. But my intuition tells me it means a conflict of two loves.'

'Now I know you're making this up.'

She shrugged. 'The cards always tell the truth. It's up to us how we understand it.'

She flipped over the third card.

'Ah. The queen of arrows. This, I believe, would be the queen herself.'

'I thought it was the numbered cards that represented people.'

'They can, but as I said, they just as often symbolise actions. But the face cards always represent the people in our lives.'

She turned over the remaining cards one by one. The six of trebuchets, the knight of blades, the king of chariots, the eight of blades.

'Oh my,' she said.

'What does that mean?' I asked.

Reichis opened his eyes and looked down at the cards. 'From her tone, I'm guessing it means you're screwed.'

'A man of violence intends you harm, Kellen, and it's because of the queen. He has another man, a man of secrets, with him. They seek to imprison you.'

I leaned back in the chair and shook my head. 'Sister, you didn't need cards to figure that out. I've had people chasing me every day of the past two years, and half the nobles at court probably want me dead, just on principle.'

Tasia reached out to take my hand. 'You should take this seriously, Kellen. A knight and a king of different suits close together are never a good thing. These men are dangerous. Promise me you'll be careful.'

I heard the sound of footsteps and realised our hour was up. Reichis hopped off her lap and sniffed the air. 'It's the skinny one who nearly pisses himself every time he sees me.'

That would be Fen.

'You know what I think, Tasia?' I said. She folded her hands and kept her eyes down. 'I think you know exactly who the knight and the king are – the man of violence and the man of secrets. I think that if those men knew what you know, then they'd get exactly what they wanted. So you're going to sit inside this cell and wait to die, just to protect the queen who sanctioned your execution or the countess who got you into this mess in the first place or whoever the hell else you're covering for, because you think that somehow that's going to lead to your salvation.'

'We all die, Kellen. Is it so wrong that I want my death to make the world a better place, rather than a worse one?'

'If you believe your death is going to make any difference

231

to this world, Tasia, then you might be good at card tricks, but you're a lousy fortune teller.'

I stood up but she grabbed my arm. 'Believe what you want. But promise me you'll be careful. Promise me you'll watch out for these men.'

'I—'

'Promise me, Kellen.'

She looked so upset that I promised her. It seemed to give her some small comfort, and it didn't really matter. In a few days she'd be dead, and besides, I hardly ever keep my promises anyway.

29

Patronage

'What now?' Reichis asked as we left the jail.

It was only a couple of hours into daylight and already the sun was irritating the black marks around my left eye. 'I don't know,' I said, pulling my hat down. 'This is all way beyond us.'

Mariadne was sitting at a bench some thirty yards down the street, waiting for us. What in all the hells was I supposed to tell her?

'So we run?' Reichis asked.

I hesitated. I knew it was the right thing to do. This was law and politics and intrigue. Everybody seemed to have a stake in everything. Me? I was just a card player with a talking squirrel cat and a guilty conscience.

Reichis sensed my discomfort. 'You want to try to bust her out?'

I shook my head. 'Those locks are too heavy for my castradazi coin to pick. Even if we could, she's got no money and nowhere to go. She'd need help, maybe even royal help, to get out of this.'

'So we go see the queen?'

'And do what? Ask her for a favour? No, she's deep into

this. We go making trouble with her without a plan, and I'm liable to wind up back in my own Daroman cell.'

We walked past a potted tree on the street and Reichis paused to pee on it. I guess he'd missed that one earlier. 'Well, there's one obvious thing we could do,' he said.

'What's that?'

'Let her die.'

I looked down at him. I was going to ask if he was serious, but I really didn't need to. Reichis is a survivor. He'll take on just about anything for me – that's just a part of our business arrangement. But with Reichis you're either part of the deal or you aren't, and if you aren't, well, then you're on your own.

'I can't do it,' I said. 'Whatever's going on, Tasia's not to blame for it. Somebody's using her, and now she's going to die for no damned good reason.'

'All right,' he said, shaking the dust from his fur. 'Then saddle up a horse, pull some powder and let's kill us a few marshals.'

'And then what? We spend the rest of our short lives running from the long arm of Daroman law?'

Reichis snorted. 'See, this is what you always do, Kellen. You talk yourself in circles until you run out of options and somebody's pointing a sword at your belly.'

'So what do you think we should do?' I asked.

'Well, the way I see it, if we can't break her out, then we need help – political help. So who do we know who's got political clout and doesn't hate us yet?'

Damn. I hated to admit it, but the little bugger was right. 'Martius,' I said. 'Count Adrius Martius.' Back at court he'd told me he'd be staying in Juven, not ten miles from here. 'Let's borrow one of Mariadne's horses and go get us a patron.'

234

30

The Bravery of Fools

Ten miles isn't a long way unless it leads you nowhere.

Count Adrius Martius shook his head regretfully, his somewhat jowly face wiggling along in an expression that was rather like sympathy. 'I said I'd help you, Kellen, but only if I could do so without getting into trouble myself.'

I leaned back heavily in the plush chair. Martius's villa was a lot like the man himself: somewhat stately and rather old-fashioned. 'But you're a count, and one of the queen's cousins.'

'Yes, and I aim to keep it that way. Getting involved in these kinds of machinations isn't practical for a man like me. The queen has many cousins and many supporters.'

It occurred to me that if the queen was removed, noblemen like Martius would have to choose sides. Maybe keeping on good terms with everyone was a way of keeping the path open.

'Hah!' he said. 'I do believe we must play cards soon, Mister Kellen. To answer the question written on your face, just take a look at me. Can you imagine anyone cares what I think or whom I side with?'

'So you just don't believe in taking a stand?' I said.

'Kellen, my boy, I take a stand every day. I stand up to go

to the kitchen, I stand up to go to the bathroom. Some days I even stand up to look at the night sky. What I don't do is stand up on the gallows so the hangman can put a noose around my neck. You shouldn't either.'

'Where's all that nostalgia for the good old days when Daroman nobles were all warriors striding across the continent?'

He laughed and patted his belly. 'Do I look like I'm up for a lot of striding? No, son, that's for men like Leonidas now.'

'Any striding he does seems to involve forty men gathered closely around him. You'd think the queen would have a problem with a commander using soldiers as his personal valets.'

'Ah, those. Those aren't regular soldiers.'

'They dress like solders. They carry swords.'

'They want to kill us the way soldiers usually do,' Reichis added. 'We run away from them the same way we always run away from soldiers.'

Martius looked a bit surprised. 'Is your friend all right? He's making very odd noises.'

'Probably just has gas,' I said.

'Ah. In any event, these particular soldiers are technically mercenaries.'

That threw me. 'Why would a Daroman military commander need mercenaries? Don't you have the largest conscripted army in the world?'

'We do,' the count said. 'Though it's not nearly as large as it used to be. But the mercenaries are more of what you might call the major's personal guard.'

'Isn't that expensive on a military man's salary?'

Martius pulled some coins out of his pocket. 'You see this bronze piece? That's what a regular soldier makes in a week. You see the silver one? That's what one of Leonidas's personal

236

guards earns in the same week. They're better trained, completely loyal to their commander, and willing to do things regular soldiers might find disagreeable. You should probably stay away from them. And from Leonidas.'

'So how does he afford it?'

Martius closed his hand on the coins and made a show of making them appear in the other palm. Maybe it's because I play cards for a living, but people always seem to want to do tricks for me. 'Friends, dear boy. Wealthy friends.' He put the coins back in his pocket. 'The kinds of friends you should be cultivating. Leonidas is good at making friends.'

'He's good at making enemies too.'

'Now, Kellen, don't go underestimating the man. He's an extremely capable soldier, and a lot smarter than he looks.'

'That isn't hard,' Reichis commented.

'I think your squirrel cat is hungry,' Martius said. He motioned to a servant and a few moments later food arrived, plenty for us all.

After a while Martius gave a contented sigh that turned into something else. 'Look, Kellen, I can't take a direct hand in your business with the queen. But maybe I can give you some advice that will help.'

'What would you suggest?'

'Well, my first piece of advice is to get out of Darome as fast as you can.' He held up a hand before I could speak. 'I know, I know, you're not going to listen to that kind of advice. Fine. My second suggestion then is that you make your case to the queen. She's encamped about fifteen miles from here, near the border. Leonidas is giving her, and much of the court, a tour, walking them through the business that's been going on with the Zhuban.'

'But she's the one who signed the execution order.'

'And why did she do that?'

'I don't know. That's what I came to you to find out.'

'Take a guess.'

'Political expedience?'

'Well, that's a bit cynical, my boy, but you're on the right track. She did it because a monarch's job is to keep any troubles from bubbling up to the surface. What she wants is to avoid any political complications. So what do you need to do?'

'I . . . need to make it so that carrying out the execution makes more trouble than it's worth.'

Martius tapped a finger against his nose. 'Now you've got it.'

'Making trouble for a queen doesn't sound like a healthy habit to get into.'

'Then you should walk away. But if you won't, look at it this way: you don't have to actually make trouble for her. You just have to make her see that you *could* make trouble.'

'So what makes more trouble for the queen than a maid who might reveal a conspiracy?'

'Wrong question. A better one would be, what troubles does an eleven-year-old monarch have?'

I thought about that for a minute. From my brief spell at court it appeared she had people well in hand. I thought about Leonidas and all the nobles who regarded him like a god walking the earth. Then I remembered something Martius had said. 'Didn't you tell me that her father signed an unpopular peace treaty with the Zhuban?'

He nodded. 'And your Jan'Tep people too.'

'And now the Daroman borders are getting walked all over by the Zhuban. They're getting bolder by the day.'

Martius nodded again. 'Go on.'

'So what she fears is looking weak. If the nobility fears the Zhuban enough, and can't trust the queen to protect their lives and property, eventually they're going to start looking for an alternative.'

'Now watch what you say there, Kellen. Remember, the queen is a fine young lady. She didn't make all of this trouble happen – that was her father. I can't imagine, and neither can you, what it must be like for her. No child should ever have to face such dilemmas.'

A thought occurred to me. 'I still have the writ,' I said.

'What writ?'

'The writ of execution. The one she signed. If it were to come out that she had signed it herself, it might look like she was currying favour with Leonidas – that she needed to appease him. If it were to come out that she was behind Tasia's attempt to seduce, and later kill, Leonidas, the queen would be ruined. But if people knew she had signed the writ, after having seemed to be unaware of the case when Mariadne brought it up at court, she would seem to be plotting with Leonidas.'

Martius shook his head. 'A dangerous game, Kellen.'

'So you don't think I should use this against her?'

Martius shrugged. 'I think you should follow your conscience, son. That's what we all need to do in these troubled times.'

I considered my options. They all still came back to either taking a chance on the queen or letting Tasia die. But I wasn't willing to let an innocent woman hang for the political gambits of the court.

Martius looked at me, shook his head and gave a laugh. 'For a card player, you have a terribly easy face to read. I'll send for my carriage.'

31

The Queen's Hand

'I find myself displeased by my tutor of cards,' the queen said.

Well, you're the one who hired me, lady, I thought, but bringing that up seemed like a bad idea at that particular moment. Her Imperial Majesty, the Queen of Darome, sat straight-backed in a kind of portable throne in the centre of a richly furnished tent that stood roughly five times the height of a man and was large enough to hold the queen, half the nobles from the court and a contingent of Leonidas's soldiers.

'You have but to say the word, Majesty, and I will deal with the boy,' Leonidas said.

She looked at him sternly. 'Have you forgotten, major, that Kellen is one of my royal tutors? As such he cannot be harmed nor charged unless four-fifths of the court dismiss him from my service.' She leaned forward slightly. 'I wonder that you showed such deference to my previous tutors.'

Leonidas looked around at the reaction of the nobles in the tent, his face reddening.

'She's none too happy with him,' Martius whispered to Mariadne and myself. He'd insisted on picking her up before we came, seemingly for the purpose of instructing both of us on the intricacies of royal politics. 'He's been pushing the queen hard during this trip on the need for even more soldiers under his command.'

'Your Majesty knows I am her humblest servant and defer to her wisdom in all things,' Leonidas said, though I noticed he didn't bow.

The queen appeared unconcerned by his lack of deference, but there was a very slight hesitation in her voice. 'Good. Then please do so now as I try to sort out this mess that you and Countess Mariadne have put before me. You have seen this writ, Master Kellen?'

Mister, I thought, but again figured this was a poor time to be correcting the queen's grammar. 'I have, Your Majesty.'

'And you claim that Major Leonidas did not, as he earlier claimed, call for clemency, but instead demanded the maid be executed for her crime. Was there anything else of note you observed in this writ?'

This, right here, was the moment I would either confirm I had leverage over her, or swiftly find my head separated from my neck. 'Well, you see, Your Majesty, that's the funny thing. I'm almost positive I noted at least one other remarkable thing about the writ, but in all the rush to get here, I'm afraid it's slipped my mind.'

'You've forgotten?' she asked, the beginnings of a laugh coming fast on the heels of her question. She stifled it, though, which was smart. Fake laughter is actually quite easy to detect.

'Yes, Your Majesty. My memory's never been all that good.' Actually my memory is excellent, and I kept my eyes on hers to make sure she knew it.

The queen seemed to ponder my words. 'I understand this writ is now lost?'

'Yes. I found it quite by accident outside the magistrate's

241

office. No doubt the wind had blown it from his desk and out the window.' In fact it would've had to blow under a locked door, down a hallway, around a corner, through two sets of bars and *then* out of a window – which had been closed at the time. Or stolen by a squirrel cat who's particularly good at picking locks.

'And you subsequently lost it yourself?' she asked.

I spread my arms helplessly. 'Flew right out of my hands, Your Majesty.'

'Quite a magical wind you've been encountering, tutor of cards. Let us hope it hasn't accompanied you on this journey or it might well blow this very tent away and leave us all standing outside in the cold.'

The courtiers and retainers laughed. Leonidas gave a particularly loud – and patently fake – chortle. 'What a shame your grip was too weak to hang on to the document, boy,' he said. 'That way we could've all known if you were lying.'

I didn't bother turning to him. I kept my gaze on the queen. 'You never know. The thing about magical winds is that there's no way of predicting when they're next going to blow. The writ could remain lost forever . . . or drop right into our hands any moment now.'

Nothing in the queen's expression betrayed anxiousness or acquiescence, but she nonetheless did as she knew I wanted, and addressed Leonidas. 'Well, major, it seems you and I are united in our inconvenience. Do you still maintain that you asked for clemency for the girl?'

For a big, dumb guy, he wasn't *that* dumb. 'I . . . I do not quite recall, Your Majesty. It seems to me that I did, but it is possible the magistrate failed to understand my meaning.'

'What poor memories everyone suffers from today. Perhaps

the magistrate, being busy with so many cases and in great haste to administer judgement on behalf of the worthy citizens of Urbana Sarrix, momentarily misunderstood your carefully worded request. That would explain things to everyone's satisfaction, wouldn't it?'

Leonidas frowned. 'And yet, Your Majesty, should we not consider that if the magistrate, with all his long years of judicial experience and wisdom, instinctively deemed that the girl should suffer the penalty prescribed by law for attempting to murder a military commander during times of war, is it proper for you or I to second-guess him?'

The queen looked thoughtful.

'Watch,' Martius murmured. 'He's pushed her too far now. He's tried to embarrass her and now she's going to prick him – but not too much. She's a clever girl. She'll thread the needle just right.'

'Are we at war, Major Leonidas?' the queen asked finally.

'Are we at . . . ?'

'You said it yourself, quite plainly, here in front of my court: "The girl should suffer the penalty prescribed by law for attempting to murder a military commander *during times of war*."'

'What I meant was—'

'If this is so,' she went on, cutting him off before he could dig himself out of the hole, 'I have not been informed of it. In fact I'd believed that the peace treaty with our neighbours to the north, signed by my father prior to his death and affirmed by myself, still held the force of law. Is it possible, major, that you have declared war against the Zhuban without consulting me?'

Leonidas straightened. 'A poor choice of words, Your Majesty.

243

We are, of course, not at war. Your honoured father did indeed make a treaty with the Zhuban, though some of us continue to find such concessions . . . troubling. However, they harry our borders repeatedly, forcing those of us whose sworn duty is to protect this empire to fight, and all to often, to shed our blood to preserve Your Majesty's peace.'

Nice double-entendre, I thought, *Your Majesty's peace* could refer just as easily to the treaty or to the easy comforts enjoyed by an idle monarch.

Cautious grumbling rose from the audience. 'Cleverly done,' Martius noted. 'The nobility have always resented the queen's father betraying his promise to renew the wars of expansion.'

It looked as if the queen had overplayed her hand. Perhaps she really was just an eleven-year-old girl pretending at being a two-thousand-year-old soul. I could make out snatches of side conversations in hushed tones among several small groups of the assembled nobles. *Is this how fast it happens?* I wondered. *Am I about to see an empress lose her throne just because I came to box her in and force her to release a lowborn maid?*

The queen raised a hand for silence. Quiet came grudgingly over the court. 'Very well, Major Leonidas, I have but one more question for you.'

He was practically gloating already. 'Yes, Your Majesty? Shall I explain once again –' I noted how he hung there a while, implying she hadn't understood his apparently many prior attempts to instruct her on Darome's precarious military situation – 'the complexities surrounding our situation with Zhuban?'

'No, no,' she said with a smile. 'I've found your expositions on the subject of your many valorous missions along the border and the many, many dangers you personally have faced to be more than sufficient.'

An unexpected burst of laughter from the audience. *Nice one, kid*, I thought.

'No, Major Leonidas,' the queen went on. 'My question is simply this: at any point during your . . . encounter with the maid Tasia, were you in peril of being overcome by her?'

'"*Overcome*"?' the major demanded. 'By a *maid*?'

'Yes. Was she a particularly formidable fighter? Did she present a credible threat to your life?'

Leonidas looked like someone had just made him eat a frog. 'I . . . That is, Your Majesty, it's not for me to question the magistrate's interpretation of wheth—'

'Come now, major, the question is simple enough: were you, with all your military tactics and experience, with your very impressive sword and legendary martial prowess, in danger of being overpowered by a hysterical scullery maid's kitchen knife?'

The major found himself surrounded by the eyes of his superiors, his peers and, worst of all, his subordinates, all wondering the same question: was Leonidas perhaps not quite the man he'd always presented himself to be.

'Never!' he declared, loudly enough that had there been a table near him I'd no doubt he would've slammed it with his fist. 'I have led a hundred skirmishes. I have killed Zhuban Elites with my bare hands. Had that simpering creature been armed with every trebuchet and cannon in Darome, still she would not ha—'

'That's fine, major,' the queen said. She pretended to a thoughtful expression before sighing and leaning back in her chair. 'Well then, I find myself confounded. If the maid was never a threat to you, and we are not in any event at war, then how came she to be charged with treason?'

'Your Majesty would have to address such questions to your magistrate,' Leonidas said defensively, already beginning to turn away in preparation for what would no doubt be some impressive stomping out of the tent.

'And do you feel that would be a suitable use of my time, major?' the queen asked, freezing him in his tracks.

At long last Leonidas realised he had lost this round. 'No, Your Majesty,' he replied, turning once again to face her. This time he *did* bow. 'In fact I would counsel that you dismiss this matter immediately so that we might return to the discussion of the need for more troops along the northern border.'

The queen nodded sagely. 'You are quite correct, major. As I suspected, this is too small a matter for my attention. The question is dismissed.'

Mariadne started to protest, but Count Martius grabbed her wrist. 'Wait for it,' he said.

The queen motioned to one of her marshals, a lean woman whose eyes surveyed the room as if she were making a list of everyone who'd slighted her monarch that day. 'Lirius, you will obtain a writ of cessation for my signature. The maid Tasia's sentence will be commuted to one year in prison for – how should we put it? – bringing distress to the Lord Major Leonidas during . . . stressful times.'

The marshal nodded and left. Leonidas looked furious. I thought she'd pushed him further than necessary, but then I discovered he wasn't quite done with her. 'Shall I assume, Your Majesty,' he began, 'that from your description of our situation you do not see fit to grant me the additional forces I requested to secure the border?'

'And the additional monies,' she said absently.

'Your Majesty?'

'You forgot about the additional monies you requested as well. They are substantial. Why, with so many soldiers under your command and so much wealth at your disposal, there are no end of things you might achieve.'

'I only seek to protect the people of Darome from the dangers that others have created.'

The queen's gaze was as cold as ice. 'Are you informing me, Major Leonidas, that the border is now not secure under your leadership?'

'I . . . No, Your Majesty. Forgive me – it was a poor choice of words.'

She shrugged – an odd gesture for a queen. 'Since you ask, I will forgive your poor choice of words. It seems I'm doing a great deal of that lately.' Had her eyes flickered to mine for just a second there? 'In any event, Major Leonidas, I confess that I grow concerned with the poor choices you make – with your words as with other things.' She rose from her chair. I swear Leonidas looked like he was actually in danger of cowering before a girl a third his size. However, she soon relented. 'Nonetheless, you do a passable job of pushing back the occasional Zhubanese incursion. In fact, I'm quite sure that most pressing tasks must be calling to you even now. I would consider it unconscionable to delay you further from your duties. Unless there are any more court matters for me to consider?'

Leonidas stood stiff as a stone column. *Walk away, you idiot*, I thought. *You're not holding any more cards, so stop putting coins on the table.* He didn't, though. The major was what I like to call an 'honourable fool', with the honourable part

247

almost always being redundant. 'There *is* one more matter, Your Majesty.' He jabbed a finger in the direction of Mariadne and myself and his next words were gloriously outraged, as though he meant them to be preserved for all time. 'I have been insulted by this woman. I have done nothing but risk my life and that of my troops to protect her and her home, and in return she has sullied my name and reputation – in *your* presence, no less. Does a military man's honour count for nothing in Darome these days?'

'You ask that I take some action against the countess, major?'

He did a decent, but incomplete, job of hiding his smirk. 'Your Majesty, I would never ask you to find cause against a cousin whom you clearly love beyond measure.'

The queen went back to her throne and sat back down. For a long while she didn't speak, instead allowing the major's insinuation to spread about the nobles and soldiers like a bad smell. It was an interesting calculation, I thought: she was betting that, given a few seconds to think about it, they'd decide that his public whining about his honour counted against him more than the implication of the queen's favouritism towards Mariadne weighed on her. It was like watching someone go all in on a pair of threes.

It wasn't at all clear who would win the hand. Everyone in the tent looked uncomfortable, then suddenly the silence was broken by a single snort. I'm not sure where came from, but it spread quickly, accompanied by giggling, sidelong glances at the major. The jury, it seemed, had rendered their decision, and found him guilty of being a giant prat.

Damn, I thought, watching the queen sit placidly on her throne. *Maybe she really could beat me at cards.*

'Well, major,' she began, 'we have all heard your concerns,

and while the court feels terrible at the many insults you have suffered, I believe we would all feel much better if you returned to your duties.'

Leonidas left the room without bowing to the queen, but not before giving me the full benefit of his rage with a look that told me I'd better get out of the northern region as soon as possible. There was something else in his eyes too. It reminded me of someone anticipating the satisfaction of a particularly enjoyable meal, and it scared me a lot more than his anger. His soldiers followed him out, and I wondered if the way this had all shaken down meant everyone else had just made peace and I was screwed. Well, not me alone, as it turns out.

Mariadne ran to the throne. 'Beloved cousin, I thank you—'

'You are dismissed as well, Countess Mariadne.'

'I—'

'Is there anything else, countess?' the queen asked, her young eyes looking positively baleful. 'Perhaps a butler or cattle-thief you wish to have me set free?'

'N-no, Your Majesty, I am most grateful for everything you've done.'

'Then you are dismissed from our presence, cousin,' the queen said.

Mariadne rose and headed for the door of the grand tent, then turned and said, 'I promise, Your Majesty, I will come soon to the palace to visit you once again and renew our friendship.'

'I find, Countess Mariadne, that court is very crowded these days and you would find the weather inclement. In fact, I would feel most reassured if I knew that you were staying at your home in Urbana Sarrix from now on. Should I feel the climate is more agreeable to your disposition, I will summon you.'

She whispered to one of the marshals and he announced, 'This day's session is at an end. The court will disperse.'

The crowd shuffled out of the tent and I started to follow them.

'Not you,' the queen said.

Yeah, I was definitely screwed.

32

Trust and Loyalty

She waited until the tent had cleared out. Martius was one of the last to go, leaving me with a sympathetic look and a brief squeeze of my arm before joining the others in whatever revels await those not about to get their arses handed to them by a child.

I walked over to the throne. Reichis followed behind me. Even he kept his tail down low.

For a moment the queen said nothing, waiting instead until the last stragglers were out of earshot. 'I had thought you my friend,' she said.

'Your friend?' Despite myself I was taken aback by her words. I'd expected anger, fury, even threats, but not the distressed plea of a sad and uncertain eleven-year-old girl. 'It wasn't my intention to harm you,' I said at last. It sounded exactly as lame spoken out loud as it had in my head.

'But harm me you have. You've weakened me before the court and further divided me from a powerful segment of my armies.'

'Again, that wasn't my intent.'

'Then you're a fool who acts without thinking.'

Well, that much is true anyway. 'You didn't leave me much choice, Your Majesty.'

She slammed her little fists on the arms of the throne. 'All you had to do was leave it alone!'

'And let Tasia die?'

'Yes! And let her die! People die, Kellen. In fact, as I understand it, sometimes they die because you kill them!'

'She doesn't deserve it.' I hesitated, unsure whether to say the next part. I really *wasn't* trying to hurt the queen, or even coerce her through guilt, but in the end I couldn't stop myself. 'Tasia's been covering for you. She seems to love you greatly.'

The queen looked heartbroken, but she quickly steeled herself. 'And I love her, Kellen. The Countess Mariadne wasn't always my favourite cousin, you know. When I was young I was terrified of her. You may have noticed that she has something of a temper. It was Tasia who took care of me when my father brought me for visits.'

'Then—'

'The law is the law, Kellen. I don't get to break it on a whim. In fact, a queen must follow her laws closest of all.'

'Why did you send me there then?'

'I told you – to give her some comfort in her final hours.'

'She's lying,' Reichis said.

The queen's eyes flared angrily.

Reichis's tail twitched. 'Give me all the stink-eye you want, kid, I'm a squirrel cat.'

The queen turned back to me. 'Are you loyal to me, Kellen?'

'I . . .' How do you answer that question? With a lie, obviously. *Why, yes, Your Majesty, of course. I mean, I barely know you at all and I'm pretty sure you're using me and will discard me just as quickly as you have Tasia, but let there be no question*

252

of my absolute loyalty to your royal person. 'No, Your Majesty,' I said. 'I'm not loyal to you. You're queen of the most powerful country in the world and I'm a guy whose only friend is a squirrel cat.'

'Business partner,' Reichis corrected.

'Business partner,' I repeated. 'I'll do my best not to betray you, Your Majesty, but in the end I have to look out for myself and Reichis.'

'And that means we can't be friends?' It was like being scolded by the loneliest girl in the world. 'There's no one here I can talk to, and no one in my palace in the capital. Not in my entire country. Not really. There's not a single person I can trust.' Her eyes met mine. 'I hoped I could trust you, Kellen.'

One question in my mind had been bothering me since the day I first met the queen and every day since. Martius's mention of an Argosi consulting with the queen came back to me. 'Why? Because some wandering Argosi turned up at court and happened to mention me?'

The queen looked at me wide-eyed for a moment, then chuckled. 'I assure you, Kellen, while the Path of Thorns and Roses did, indeed, mention you, it was *not* to counsel me to take you into my service.'

The Path of Thorns and Roses? Rosie had been to the Daroman court, not Ferius?

'The Argosi meet with any monarch who will give them audience,' the queen went on. 'They bring news of the world outside our borders, drop enigmatic hints about plots and machinations that might steer the continent towards war. My father used to heed their counsel. I have tried to as best I can.'

253

'And what did the Path of Thorns and Roses advise you this time, Your Majesty?'

'She dealt her Argosi cards for me.' The queen's smile faded. 'The suit of shields represents the Daroman civilisation. No matter how she arranged the cards, every hand, every configuration, showed the same path ahead. I would never reach the age of thirteen. I would never truly lead my people.' Her eyes met mine. 'Not unless a new card came to my hand. A discordance.'

It made sense. Ferius always said the Argosi weren't fortune tellers, but, so long as their decks accurately reflected the structures of power within a people, the inevitable ways in which those forces would collide could be discerned. In a culture committed to empire, weakened by stagnation and its own corruption, there was no way for an idealistic eleven-year-old to survive long enough to find a way forward for her troubled nation. She needed something else. Something that could change the game itself. 'Why me?' I asked. 'All you know about me is that I'm a disgraced Jan'Tep cursed with the shadowblack. I don't have allies or money or power. My own father once put a spell warrant on my head. I'm as good an example of walking, talking trouble as you could imagine. Any sane monarch would've had me executed the day they met me.'

'We're not as different as you think,' she said.

I wanted to laugh at that. I almost did. But the sorrow in her eyes stopped me. 'Why did you send me to Sarrix, Your Majesty?'

'I sent you to Tasia because I thought . . . I suppose I hoped you might—'

'Break her free?'

She nodded.

Oddly I felt guilty – as if I should somehow have figured that out on my own. Maybe some part of me *had*, but it had been easier to believe some other, more nefarious plan was at work, one I wasn't morally compelled to enact. 'Breaking someone out of jail isn't nearly as easy as they make it sound in the stories, Your Majesty. You know the marshals service is relentless in pursuing escapees – especially ones due for the gallows. To say nothing of the fact that Leonidas would probably use his men to hunt her down himself. Tasia wouldn't last a week without a lot of money and a lot of friends, and I'm pretty sure she has neither.'

'Then you should have left well enough alone.'

'And you should never have sent me to her.'

The queen sighed, a sad sound that made me want to reach out and comfort her. But just as quickly the sorrowful child disappeared and the imperial monarch had returned. 'Go then, my tutor of cards, and reap the harvest we two have sown.'

33

The Sister's Hand

'Well, what now?' Reichis asked as we left the queen's tent. He was glancing around in that way of his that tells me he's on the prowl for something to steal or kill. Squirrel cats can only seem to go so long before they have to get themselves – and you – in deep trouble.

The reflection of the midday sun in the expanse of smooth, shale-like rock cast a blue-grey tinge on the thin layer of snow covering the dozens of tents set up for the various contingents of court nobles, their retainers and Leonidas's troops. None of the other tents were as grand as the queen's, of course, but from the absurdly rich fabrics and architecturally questionable structures, it didn't seem to be for lack of trying. There were pennants hanging everywhere, adorned with colours and sigils that no doubt were of great importance to the hundred or so people milling about outside. Nobles chatted to soldiers in admiring tones as if they gave a damn about them. Servants carried polished golden platters that mirrored the sunlight from above, forcing them to squint as they smiled and bowed while offering steaming mugs of some kind of hot drink that smelled of cinnamon and yellowberry to the queen's guests.

The only thing anyone offered me was a dirty look.

'We'll ride back to Sarrix,' I informed Reichis. 'Make sure nothing about the queen's orders have been lost in translation. Then we'll ride as fast and far away from this lunatic country as we can.'

Reichis sniffed the air. 'I smell Jan'Tep stink,' he said.

'I'll have a bath when we get back, all right? You're not exactly a basket of fresh-cut roses yourself, partner.'

He gave a low growl. 'It's not from you. It's from them.'

Two men approached us. Both had blond hair and pale skin offset by midnight-blue coats with gold inlay and a thick sable trim around the collar. 'Brethren,' I greeted them.

'I am Phe'tan,' the older of the two said.

'I am Phe'trist,' the younger one followed. 'And we are not your "brethren", spellslinger.' He lent that last word a remarkable amount of disgust. And phlegm.

'Gentlemen. Nice to see friendly faces out here among the barbarians.'

Phe'trist snorted. He was a little too refined – and phlegmy – to pull it off.

Reichis snarled in response. The only use he has for any Jan'Tep other than me is as something to clean his teeth with. Phe'trist's fingers twitched several times, resting on a somatic shape I recognised as an unpleasant iron spell. I popped open my powder holsters. 'Ready to find out the secret-of-all-secrets, friend?' I asked.

Phe'tan put a hand on his fellow's shoulder. 'We will all meet in the Grey Passage when the ancestors call our names,' he said to me. 'Right now, *she* wants to see you.'

I glanced around. *Hells*, I thought. *How does she do that?* 'Where exactly is my sweet sister?' I asked.

'We will take you to her,' Phe'trist said. He looked down at Reichis. 'The nekhek will stay here and lie on its belly like the lowly creature it is. If he tries to follow, or disturbs us in any way, I will use iron and ember to skin him and line my boots with his fur.'

There's a difference between the sort of idle insults that constitute the bulk of Jan'Tep diplomacy and an actual threat. Phe'trist had just crossed that line. I didn't wait for Reichis to react. Situations like this call for a more calm and civilised approach to resolving the conflict. I drove the palm of my right hand into the side of Phe'trist's nose hard enough that a satisfying crack filled the air. The spray of blood that painted the rocky ground at our feet was a curved red line that formed a smile, which was pretty impressive, I thought, even if I hadn't planned it that way.

Phe'tan had his hands forming a steeple shape, a spell on his lips.

My hands were in my holsters. 'Say the first syllable and I'll put a hole in both of you, brethren.'

Phe'trist spat. 'You think your child's tricks and powders have one-tenth the power of our magic, spellslinger?'

I tossed a minuscule pinch of the twin powders, formed the somatic shapes with my fingers and angled my hands down. '*Carath*,' I said. The narrow blast of red and black flame charred the snow-covered ground, adding a burnt-out eye to the smile.

'Heh,' Reichis chuckled. 'That's cool.'

'No, gentlemen,' I said amiably to Phe'trist and his brother. 'I've no doubt your magic is vastly greater than mine.' My hands were already back in my powder holsters. 'I'm just a little faster, is all.'

'Enough,' Phe'tan said. He nodded towards the crowds of the nobles and soldiers who had begun to take notice of our exchange. 'Not in front of the barbarians. Sha'maat will not be pleased.' He pulled a handkerchief from his pocket and handed it to Phe'trist. Then to me he said, 'The diplomat to the Daroman empire, envoy of the mage sovereign of the Jan'Tep, has summoned you. Will you come?'

'Sure,' I said. 'I always have time to see my sister.'

He turned to Phe'trist. 'You will wait here, in the cold, with the barbarians. Perhaps you will learn manners from them.'

I looked down at Reichis. 'You stay here and keep him company.'

Reichis grinned. Phe'trist didn't.

Sha'maat waited for us in one of the smaller – though no less ostentatious – canvas tents situated about a hundred yards from the queen's. When I entered, I found her standing by an ornately carved wooden table, filling two long-stemmed glasses with something that might've been wine, or perhaps poison. She wore a blue and gold brocade gown which I imagine was intended to be described as 'resplendent'.

I was prepared to be civil. This was my sister, after all, but something about her manner, the way she'd shed every last trace of her old self in favour of something more . . . I couldn't quite find the word, so I said, 'Any particular reason you're dressed as a low-rent saloon's least popular comfort artisan, dearest sister?'

Phe'tan's face went from pale to ashen. Shalla – *no, she's Sha'maat now. Don't let yourself forget* – merely smiled. 'Sweet brother, won't you share some wine with me?'

259

'I'll pass, thanks. I've got a long ride back to Sarrix and being drugged tends to upset my stomach.'

Phe'tan's mouth made contorted shapes that didn't flatter his features. His fingers were twitching. 'You would dare accuse—'

'Oh, don't be discomposed, loyal Phe'tan,' Sha'maat said. 'This is simply my darling brother's way.'

The oddly sensuous way she spoke to him, this new royal bearing she'd adopted, made it hard for me to be in her presence. *Ancestors. She's turned into some kind of perverse version of our father.*

'Yeah,' I said. 'We're all—'

She interrupted me. 'You see, this is how Kellen survives a world that is so set against him; he makes his opponents lose their composure in the desperate hope that from this he can glean some advantage.' She reached out a hand and placed it against the side of my face. One of her fingertips touched lightly behind my ear near the top of my jaw. The softness and unexpected intimacy made me shiver uncomfortably. 'He's quite predictable really.'

Phe'tan nodded. 'I shall take my leave then, *carreva*.' He turned and left us alone in the tent.

'Carreva?' I said.

Sha'maat took her hand away and smiled. 'Isn't it wonderful? Father sent me word yesterday.'

'I suppose. But what good is becoming heir to the Jan'Tep throne when there isn't a proper Jan'Tep throne to inherit?'

'Oh, pooh. Don't try to take away my fun, brother. One day our people will be strong again, and when that day comes I will have a palace and be surrounded by servants to take care of my every desire.' She picked up a glass of wine from the small table in the centre of the tent and took a sip. 'Can't you be happy for me?'

'Well, you've already got a tent at the edge of the tundra and two morons ready to take a knife for you, so you've made a start anyway.'

She leaned over and kissed me on the cheek. 'See? Now was that so hard?' She made a show of looking around. 'And where is your pet? I hope nothing untoward has happened to him?'

'Reichis is busy pondering something.'

'And what would a filthy nekhek be pondering?'

'Whether you can make do with just one moron serving your every whim.'

She laughed. I wondered what Phe'trist would've thought about her level of concern for his well-being.

'And what are you pondering, sweet brother?'

'Me? I'm wondering what the hell you've allowed Ke'heops to turn you into, Shalla.' This time I intentionally used her old name. Maybe it would break through this new shiny shell she'd cocooned herself in. 'What are you doing out here?'

She put down her glass and motioned with her hand to where the sun's rays were casting a long shadow against the flap of her tent. 'Like everyone else who spins in orbit around the little queen, I am keeping close watch on the time and guessing how long until darkness falls on her reign.'

'Is that why you summoned me, Sha'maat? To tell me what time it is?'

'No,' she said, taking my hand and kissing it. 'I summoned you to congratulate you. Father will be very pleased with your progress.'

261

I pulled my hand away. 'For what? I haven't done anything you asked, and I don't intend to either.'

'Nonsense,' she said. 'You've done a wonderful job of weakening the little queen. Through that odd and awkward charm of yours, you've wormed your way into her trust. If she counts on you a few more times I dare say you'll be able to bring down the Daroman empire all by yourself.'

'Don't play head games with me, sister. All I'm trying to do is help the maid who's been caught in the middle of a political game.'

She clapped her hands excitedly – an affectation far more childish than anything she would've done the last time I saw her. 'But of course you are, brother! You're playing the tragic hero, which you do so very well these days. You know, it used to annoy me, but now I think it's what I love most about you.' She tapped a finger against my chest. 'Underneath all this anger and belligerence, you . . . how would that vulgar Argosi you used to follow around have said it?' My sister's voice took on a preposterous drawl. 'Ya jest wanna dew the raat thang.'

She laughed uproariously at her own joke and at my expense. Two years my junior and she still managed to act as if I'm *her* little brother. But Sha'maat was carreva to the throne now. I took small solace in the fact that Father would likely marry her off to whichever fat, toad-faced man had the strongest bloodline and the most power to offer the House of Ke.

Sha'maat caught my expression. 'Oh, don't be so serious, brother. Keep on doing what you're doing. Try to save the maid. Save all the maids in Darome if you like. I approve.'

'I saved Mariadne's life,' I said.

Sha'maat picked up her wine glass again and took a sip. 'Hmm?'

'Mariadne. You told me Father wanted me to kill her, but I saved her life instead. Are you going to tell me that's all according to plan?'

'Mariadne? You're on first-name terms with her now, are you? Have you bedded her yet, brother?'

'No, of course not. She—'

Sha'maat stood even closer to me, practically whispering in my ear. 'Come now, brother. She's certainly beautiful. And you'd probably be doing her and everyone else a favour if you got her out of that dour red mourning dress at long last.' She turned away and drank the rest of her wine before spinning back to me. 'Yes, I do believe I approve of this. You will bed the countess. In fact, make her fall in love with you if you can. That will make it all the sweeter when you put an end to her.'

It was my turn to laugh. 'You know, I think I've finally figured out the grand strategy by which you and Father plan to take over the continent: just keep pretending, no matter how many times you fail, that everything is going according to plan. Then maybe everyone else will become so confused they'll accidentally make you emperors of the entire world.'

'It's you who blithely ignores the obvious, brother. Darome is in the twilight of her power. These people aren't mages like we are. They aren't explorers or inventors like the Gitabrians or even hunters and farmers like the borderlanders. Militarism and brutality are in the very blood of Darome. Without war, this empire of theirs will sink into a sleep from which it will never wake.'

'Maybe the queen has something else in mind.'

263

'Indeed she does, and that is why she will never be allowed to rule. Her father had promised his nobles a war – a chance to expand and fill their coffers. But he became soft, as old men do. And when Ginevra was born he used her as an excuse to make peace. Look around at the nobles out there, bowing and scraping as they utter curses under their breath. The Daroman nobility are jackals, brother, and the jackals are hungry.'

'So you're waiting until the jackals pounce to see what scraps they leave for the Jan'Tep? Does the mighty Ke'heops mean to make buzzards of our people, picking at the remains left by braver scavengers?'

She ignored the insult to our father. In fact she seemed to ignore everything I'd just said. 'Now, brother, timing is all important here.' She held up a finger. 'You must not kill the countess too soon. There are other players in this game who we require you to eliminate first.'

With every shred of arta precis I'd learned from Ferius, I tried to see through Sha'maat's pretension. How much of her confidence was real, and how much was posturing? My family seemed convinced that I was still the runt of our litter, ready to beg and perform tricks for them in exchange for whatever scraps they'd give me.

I turned and opened the flap to the tent. 'You know something, sister? I know our people don't believe in hell . . . but go to hell anyway.'

As I started walking out she said, 'Oh, don't go away angry, sweet brother. I have some information for you.'

'No, thanks.'

'Really, you'll want to hear this.'

'Fine,' I said, still looking out at the mountains in the distance. 'What is it?'

'These Daroman, these barbarians,' she said, 'their lives are governed not by power, but by the perception of power. The queen, Leonidas, the army, the nobles. All of them.'

'And?'

'Major Leonidas has been shamed in this matter with the maid. He cannot allow that to stand. When he makes his move, you must stand aside for your own good.'

Now I turned back to face her. 'You think he's going to find a way to kill Tasia? Even while she's inside a marshals' jail?'

For just a moment Sha'maat's expression softened. 'Brother, everyone but you knows that the maid died days ago. The breath simply hasn't had time to leave her body.'

34

Return to Sarrix

Reichis and I returned to Sarrix alone, on a horse borrowed from one of Martius's retainers. I spent most of that time considering my predicament, and, in my own defence, almost a full minute remembering that I wasn't the one stuck in jail.

'Quit yer moanin',' Reichis grumbled, his eyes still closed. How he can balance while lying on his back in the saddle of a horse I'll never comprehend.

'I didn't say anything.'

'Didn't have to. When you get like this you reek of angst and self-hatred.'

'What do I smell like the rest of the time?'

'I'll let you know if it ever happens.'

We rode on a little way further in silence, but eventually I realised the squirrel cat was right, if not in the way he seemed to think. Reichis doesn't suffer from self-doubt. He instinctively knows what he wants, who he wants to protect, and who he wants to kill. Me? Somewhere on the long roads this past year away from Ferius, I'd lost my moral compass. It was getting harder and harder to think about anything other than how to save my own skin. 'What do you think

266

we should do?' I asked Reichis. 'Even with the queen changing the writ, you think Tasia deserves an entire year stuck in that jail with no one to look out for her? You think Leonidas is going to leave her alone?'

'No, she does not deserve it, and, no, that skinbag will definitely not leave her alone.'

'So?'

'I reckon she needs to find herself one of them . . . what do you call them things? Somebody who does brave deeds and fights for good causes?'

'A hero?'

Reichis lifted a paw and briefly opened one eye. 'That's it, a hero.'

I let that hang in the air for a while, but finally I had to say something. 'You don't think I could be a hero?'

The squirrel cat snorted. 'You? Kellen, I love you like a, well, like a business partner. But you ain't been on a hero's path for years now.'

'You realise I'm only eighteen and you met me when I'd just turned sixteen?'

'I was talkin' squirrel cat years.' He wriggled around until he was sitting on his haunches, facing me on the horse's neck. 'Look, I get it. You're a human, Kellen, and that means you ain't built for bein' heroic even when most everyone we meet wants to kill you.'

'Ferius does it. She's been at it a lot longer than me.'

'Pretty sure she's got some squirrel cat blood in her. Anyhow, you ain't gonna be much good as a hero so long as you got this.' He tapped a paw at the black markings that wound around his left eye, an echo of my own.

'The shadowblack?'

He shook his furry head. It's not a normal way for squirrel cats to communicate, so he always does it in a comically exaggerated fashion. 'No, the fact that you use the shadowblack as an excuse for being a coward.'

Other than crocodiles and langziers, I hadn't seen much that scared Reichis, so I found it irritating the way he so glibly called me a coward, even if I was one. 'Maybe you'd feel differently if you'd spent the last two years of your life being hunted by your own people.'

He gave a snort – another means of non-verbal communication that he should probably avoid when making a serious point. 'Idjit. How many other squirrel cats do we ever run into? My kind have been hunted almost to extinction. I don't have to worry about my "own people" hunting me, because everybody else's "people" are already doing it.'

I thought about that for a second. Reichis never talked much about his own kind, or what the Jan'Tep had done to them. Whenever I brought it up, I got bitten, and I was tired of tooth marks in my shirts. We were almost at the city limits of Sarrix, and the glimpse of tall, expensive-looking homes beyond the walls gave me an idea. 'Well, since I'm such a coward, instead of picking a fight with half the Daroman empire, how about you and me put together some money and get Tasia help that way?'

'You ain't suggestin' bribin' the marshals service, are you? Cos even I know that's a bad idea.'

'No, I'm thinking the magistrate – what was his name? Gerran? We see what he's willing to do for a little cash. Maybe we go on a couple of heists of the more prominent Daroman noble families around Sarrix and then we—'

Reichis cut me off with his version of a sigh. 'That's the

268

problem with you, Kellen. You always try for the easy play. You never go all in.'

'I go all in every time I'm in a fight, Reichis.'

'You go all in when there's absolutely no other choice left. That's why we're always on the run. You fight when you have to, not when you should.'

'Well,' I said, 'that's what you call a distinction without a diff—'

'Shut up,' Reichis growled. 'Someone's comin' for us.'

Marshal Fen, the skinny one who'd by now probably gambled away the rest of the silver coins I'd given him, was riding up the slope of the road towards us. I imagine he'd figured out we'd stolen the writ from under his nose. 'You're comin' with me, Mister Card Player,' he said, pulling his horse up in front of us.

'Listen, if this is about the writ, the queen's already—'

'It ain't about that. Lirius just got word to us. Leonidas and his men have rolled into town. They went straight for the Countess Mariadne's home. They've got her compound surrounded.'

'What? Can they do that? Why didn't you stop them?'

Fen looked at me as if I was an idiot. I guess I was. 'There's just Bracius and me here,' he said. 'Most of the Northern Detachment are with the queen. Besides, we don't go around arresting the military.'

'Where's Bracius?' I asked.

'Already at the countess's home.'

Good, I thought. *Maybe she can talk some sense into that idiot major.*

'She's been asked to oversee a duel,' Fen said.

'What?!'

Fen nodded. 'Major Leonidas just challenged Mariadne's house on grounds of insult to his reputation. She's got to field a champion against him or forfeit her . . . well, I'm not rightly sure what she has to forfeit, but I doubt it's gonna be something she wants to give up.'

Truer words had probably never been spoken. Reichis's fur changed colour, shifting from the soft, sleepy brown to an angry red, the hackles rising. 'Well, Kellen,' he said in a low growl, 'guess it's time to decide if you plan on being a hero.'

35

The Hero's Duel

By the time I reached Countess Mariadne's home, all hells had broken loose. Leonidas and his soldiers stood inside the gate in the broad courtyard. Mariadne was screaming at him, with the old retainer, Erras, doing his best to hold her back.

'I'll never marry you, you pig. Never!'

'Then send your champion, countess, for I do take offence at the false accusations you have made of me in court, and I demand redress.'

Reichis and I snuck around the courtyard and entered by the servants' gate so we wouldn't have to go through Leonidas's soldiers. 'Thank goodness you're here,' Erras said the moment he saw me.

'What's going on?'

He gestured helplessly. 'The major claims the accusations the countess made at court cast a slur upon his honour and that he cannot rightfully lead his troops on behalf of the crown until that stain has been removed.'

'He's out of his mind then,' I said. 'The queen'll have him hanged for this.'

Erras shook his head. 'No, she won't. Oh, she'll quite likely reprimand him, ensure he never rises further in the military

271

or in Daroman society. But I suspect she's already done too much to embarrass him publicly, and Leonidas has no further reason to seek her support. I believe he'll have made the calculation that he's better off appealing to older and less refined Daroman traditions, seeking support from those who believe we have strayed too far from our more aggressive roots.'

'So what now? Can he seriously force the countess to duel him? She's not a trained warrior, is she?'

Erras shook his head. 'No, but just because she cannot fight him herself does not mean she can say anything she wants with impunity. When she speaks, she does so on behalf of her house. If Leonidas insists on a duel, the house champion must accept.'

'Who's that?' I asked.

'There isn't one. When Arafas was alive it would have been his role to defend his home and family. Since he died, the countess hasn't wanted to hire one for fear they might seek to use their position to pressure her into marriage.'

'Then she just has to back down and apologise.'

He shook his head. 'It isn't so simple as that, not in Darome. If she admits fault she will be weakened politically and owe Leonidas a debt. She may as well marry him right here and now as apologise.'

I looked over at them. Mariadne was hurling insult after insult at Leonidas. For his part, he was becoming more and more confident in his position.

'So what do we do?' I asked Erras.

He looked at me. 'You have to challenge him.'

'What?'

The old man gripped my arms. 'You can take the role of

house champion on Mariadne's behalf. If she accepts, you will fight Leonidas.'

'What good will that do?'

'If the house champion fights, then even if he dies, honour is satisfied without the countess having to make any admission of fault. Leonidas will have improved his standing, politically, but the countess will remain free of obligation to him.'

'Old man, you've lost your mind. I'm not going to get myself killed because her ladyship can't keep a polite tongue.'

'Are you afraid then?' Erras said, visibly disgusted with me.

'Terrified,' I admitted.

The old man chewed his lip a while. 'Fine. Then just wait here and keep her from doing anything rash.' He spun on his heels and stepped back into the house.

I walked towards Leonidas and Mariadne to see if I could calm things down.

'Ah, perfect. The tutor. I see you consider a Daroman military leader beneath you, countess, but a filthy card-playing shadowblack is worthy of your bed.'

'You've got it all wrong, Leonidas,' I said.

He backhanded me so hard I fell to the ground. Reichis leaped in front of me, growling. 'Shut your damned mouth, boy. And get your animal out of my way before I break its neck.'

'Reichis, back off,' I said, rising to my feet. 'Your ladyship, go inside. I'll talk to the major here and work something out.'

That did not produce the grateful reaction I'd been expecting. 'You? *You?* How dare you presume to speak for my house?'

Leonidas was delighted at my upbraiding. 'And what will you say to me, weasel boy?'

273

I rubbed at the already swelling left side of my jaw. 'I'll tell you that you just struck one of the royal tutors, and the queen is probably going to want to have words with you.'

'The queen? You'd hide behind the skirts of a child? The Zhuban have a word for men like you. It's *shozia*. It means "eyes-down". It's what they call cowards. Besides, as I hear it, you just publicly humiliated the queen to save a whore maid. I doubt she'll much mind that I gave you a light tap.'

His words were confident, but his tone was more tentative. He wasn't sure how much he could get away with. As long as I wasn't stupid enough to challenge him, I might be able to get this situation under control. That's when Leonidas suddenly let out a barrel laugh so loud I thought the walls of Mariadne's compound would start tumbling. 'What have we here? A mighty hero from the old legends?'

I turned to see Erras emerging from the main house. The old man was attired in battered, rusted armour that looked three sizes too big. His right hand trembled from the effort of holding a broadsword far too long and heavy for him. 'You come to challenge the House of Mariadne, Countess of Urbana Sarrix. Your challenge is met, major.'

Leonidas's men were laughing their heads off. Erras ignored them and continued advancing.

'Go back to your sewing needles and cooking, old man. There's nothing for you here but a sound beating.'

Erras didn't flinch. 'I stand ready,' he said.

Reichis reared up on his hind feet and gave a series of oddly deferential growls towards Erras.

'What are you doing?' I asked quietly.

'I'm acknowledging him as a warrior. He has the heart of a squirrel cat.'

Maybe, I thought. *But the body of a man too old and too fragile to be fighting Leonidas.*

'Do you accept me as your opponent, major?' Erras asked. 'Or do you need time to gather your courage?'

Leonidas's hand shot out and grabbed Erras by the neck, very nearly lifting him off the ground. Erras's sword clattered to the ground and he gasped for air.

'Stop!' Mariadne said.

Leonidas ignored her. He kept his grip tight – not enough to kill Erras, but enough to make breathing difficult. His eyes burrowed into the old man's. 'You pathetic old fool. What did you hope to accomplish here?'

'I beg you, release him,' Mariadne pleaded.

'Let him go, Leonidas. You don't need to do this,' I said.

'Quiet, weasel boy. I'll get to you soon enough.'

Erras looked as if the life was draining out of him. I flipped open my holsters, but two of the soldiers grabbed me and held my arms behind my back.

'Did you truly think you might defeat me?' Leonidas asked Erras. 'But no, that wasn't your plan, was it? You thought to simply die during the duel and absolve your mistress from her obligations.'

He pulled Erras closer. 'You made a mistake though, old man. We haven't started the duel. The marshals aren't here to oversee it yet. All you did was attack a military commander on duty. I can kill you and it won't make a bit of difference to your lady's situation.'

'I'll marry you!' Mariadne screamed. 'Don't kill him. Let Erras live and I'll accept your proposal. You've won, damn you. You've won!'

Leonidas smiled. Then he let out a growl of pain. Erras

had buried a knife in his shoulder. If he'd had a longer reach, he might've got his neck or belly. Leonidas squeezed once, and I heard the old man's neck crack. The withered mess of skin and bones that was Erras of the House of Mariadne fell to the ground in a heap.

'Your pardon, countess,' Leonidas said, pulling the knife out with a grunt. 'What were you saying?'

Reichis leaped at Leonidas and got his teeth around the bare skin of his arm. Leonidas flung the squirrel cat off and I watched his little furry body fly through the air until it hit the outer wall of the keep. Reichis rose unsteadily, but he proudly displayed a piece of skin in his mouth.

Leonidas held up his arm. 'Look, the little weasel did more damage than the old fool!'

His men cheered on cue.

Ancestors damn me for a fool and a coward a thousand times over. 'You're a dead man, Leonidas,' I said.

He laughed. 'What? You're going to challenge me now? At what? Cards?'

I didn't reply. I didn't need to.

Leonidas nodded. 'Very well then, card player. I will return in the morning and you can fight on behalf of this shameful house.'

He motioned to his men to release me, and started towards the gate. Then he turned briefly and said, 'It's too bad you didn't take the challenge earlier. You might've saved the old man from a meaningless death.'

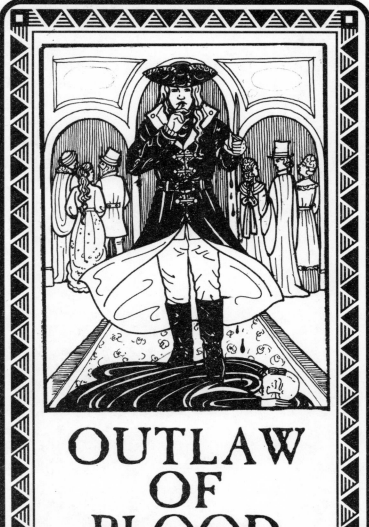

OUTLAW
OF
BLOOD

The worst deception of all is when people forget who you are – when they tell themselves that maybe you're not so bad. Maybe you're just rough around the edges. Maybe you can acclimate to polite society. That changes awful quick the first time they see the blood on your hands.

And the gleam in your eye.

36

Oraxian Root

Hours later I found Countess Mariadne standing solitary vigil over the body of Erras in a small grey room beneath the keep, with cold stone walls and flickering candles.

'Thank you for coming,' she said. On a stone pallet lay her old retainer in the Daroman position of repose – arms on his chest with one hand on top of the other, a single red flower between them as greeting to his ancestors when he is reunited with them. 'He was old when I was a child.' She reached out a hand and her fingertips brushed the dead man's lips. 'He seems no older now than he was then.' She turned to me. 'Did you like Erras, Mister Kellen?'

I nodded. 'What I knew of him. He was brave when the carriage was attacked, braver still when he went after Leonidas, and he seemed to love you above all things.'

Mariadne nodded.

We stood in silence for a moment then she handed me a small piece of paper. 'I found this in his pocket.'

I took the note and unfolded it. There were only two brief lines on it: *Sold to Kellen, Tutor of Cards of the Queen's Court – One dead man's tongue. Paid in full.*

'Did you read this?' I asked.

She shook her head. 'I do not care what it says. I know Erras well enough to know what his intent might be – to goad you into fighting Leonidas.' She turned to me. 'I do not want you to fight.'

Yeah. Me neither. 'Not much either of us can do about that now, your ladyship.'

She put her hand on my arm. 'Run. You can run. I don't want anyone else's death on my conscience. I will wait for Tasia's eventual release so that I can give her what she needs to get out of the country and start a new life. Then I will inform Major Leonidas that I will wed him at his convenience and begin mine.'

'You'd let him bully and threaten you into marriage?'

'I've been a bit of a bully too at times. I can stand up for myself when I need to. Perhaps Leonidas and I are better matched than either of us realises.'

'If you believe that, countess, then you're out of your mind. I've known men like Leonidas. Once he gets you under a marriage contract, your life will be hell and you know it.'

'Perhaps, but as you've made clear on many occasions, this isn't your fight.'

'Sure it is,' I said. 'I liked the old man. I don't like Leonidas. I don't like the idea of him getting what he wants.'

'And what difference will it make if you are dead? For all his primping and posturing, Leonidas is a formidable warrior.'

'Leonidas is a bully,' I said. 'And I've been beaten up, hunted and jailed more times than I can count. I know bullies. I know how they think, and I know how to beat them.' I sounded more confident than I felt. Truth was, I doubted Leonidas was stupid enough to let me use magic in the duel, and it would be his right to refuse it. I had the same choices – I could deny

282

him the use of swords or knives, but then he'd just kill me with his bare hands. My confidence didn't improve when Reichis ran into the room.

'We've got trouble, Kellen. I just came from Leonidas's encampment. He's got a skinbag mage, Kellen. A proper one.'

That didn't make sense. Why would Leonidas have a Jan'Tep mage? The man was too arrogant to sit back and let someone else fight me. 'What else did you see?'

'Not much. But I don't think you want to fight this mage. He sent out men to find oraxian root.'

'What's he saying?' Mariadne asked.

'Nothing important, your ladyship. I don't suppose there's much oraxian root nearby is there?'

She laughed. 'Oraxian root? The hills around here are full of it. We could feed an army with it if it didn't taste so foul.'

Damn. 'I don't think they're planning to eat it. Some clans of Jan'Tep mages use it to augment shielding spells.'

Mariadne's expression turned fearful. 'Can you . . . I mean, with your spell, can you break through one of these shields?'

'I don't know. Is Leonidas particularly low on coin?'

She shook her head. 'Military officers aren't highly paid, but Leonidas always seems to have as much money as he needs.'

'Then no, I won't be able to break through his mage's shield.'

'Can you cast your own one of these mystical shields then? To protect yourself from Leonidas's sword?'

Reichis snorted. 'He can cast a shield all right, if what you want to be protected from is a light breeze.'

Mariadne's eyes went from the squirrel cat to mine. 'What?'

'I'm not very powerful as a mage, countess.' I held out my

right arm and rolled up my sleeve, showing her my tattooed bands. 'Most shields are formed using iron or ember magic, neither of which I can summon.' I pushed my will into the breath band and managed a faint blue glimmer from it. 'With breath magic, a bit of luck and a huge headache, I can cast a different kind of shield, but one far too weak to withstand a blade or a bolt of lightning.'

'And you believe this other Jan'Tep . . .'

I nodded. 'Whoever Leonidas has hired will be someone more than powerful enough to do the job. He'll get the mage to cast a shield around him during our fight. Not only will he kill me, but he'll also show off to his troops that he isn't afraid of magic. Hells, he'll probably *want* me to hit him with a powder blast just so he can look like one of those invulnerable demigods from the old Daroman epics. That mage of his will put a shield around him so strong I doubt even . . .'

Oh, ancestors. Is it even the tiniest bit possible that this can work? Because this plan is so stupid even Ferius Parfax would balk at it.

'Kellen?' Mariadne asked.

Screw it. Deception, trickery and foul magic. Always stick with your strong suits. 'Countess, you should go rest,' I said at last. 'I'll stay here with Erras until sunrise.'

Her eyes met mine. 'It's not too late to run. These concerns . . . my concerns, they are not yours. It was wrong of me to expect you to take them on. Leonidas is unmatched as a duellist and he has forty men at his back. There is no shame in—'

'I'm something of an expert in shame, countess. Now if you don't mind, I need to prepare.'

Her mouth moved as if she might say something more, but

then she just nodded. 'You must meditate, I understand.' She stood up on tiptoes and kissed me on the cheek and then turned and left. The simple gesture left me feeling strangely moved.

'Aw, ain't that just the sweetest thing?' Reichis chittered.

'You're pretty chipper considering I'm about to get killed and you're going to end up as Leonidas's pet weasel.'

'Maybe if we tell him just how sweet you are on the countess, he'll forgive you.'

I tried kicking the squirrel cat but he hopped out of the way. 'Get out of here,' I said. 'Go up into the hills and get us some oraxian root.'

Reichis scrunched up his face. 'Me? That stuff tastes awful and I'll have to carry it in my mouth.'

'Just go, Reichis. Until Leonidas puts a sword in my belly I'm still your business partner and this is part of our deal.'

'Fine,' he said, ambling over to the door of the crypt. 'What are you going to do?'

I took the note Erras had left for me and held it to the flame of one of the candles, letting it catch fire before dropping it to the ground. 'The old man and I have business.'

37

The Coward's Duel

We stood facing each other in the courtyard. Four blue slate walls, each roughly five feet high, surrounded us. The sun pierced the dull haze of a typical northern early morning. Twenty yards separated me from Leonidas, but the hatred between us was so palpable we might as well have been touching.

The major's troops had arrayed themselves behind him, along with the mage he'd brought. I couldn't tell from the man's clothes how skilled he might be. Some mages like to cut the sleeves on their coats short, believing the sight of the Jan'Tep bands will fill those around them with awe. Others – the smarter ones – don't. One thing I was positive about though was that Leonidas had no intention of following the rules set out by the marshals. Trust me: a cheat knows another cheat when he sees one.

On my side of the courtyard stood Mariadne and a few of her servants. The countess looked wan, as if it was only a matter of time before I got killed and she ended up married to this brute.

Thanks for the vote of confidence, lady.

Marshal Bracius, standing to the left of us, read out the

duelling agreement. The Daroman people do love their contracts. '. . . And should either party desire respite, they—'

'Cut that part,' Leonidas said.

'I'm sorry?'

'I said, cut that part out. I won't ask for respite, and I won't grant it either. He dies or I die. Nothing else.'

Bracius looked uncomfortable. 'I'm not sure that—'

'Oh, and when he's dead, I keep the animal. I'll use him to keep the rats out of my cellar. Or perhaps I'll just use him for target practice.'

Reichis started stalking towards Leonidas. I kicked him aside. 'Keep it together, partner.'

'Son of a bitch,' he growled.

Bracius was getting annoyed. 'You want me to put a clause in the duelling contract that gives you ownership of a felidus arborica?'

Leonidas smiled. Bracius looked at me helplessly. 'Agreed,' I said, ignoring Reichis's snarls. 'But if I win, the major's personal guard will be transferred to the command of Countess Mariadne.'

That got me a reaction.

'You would compare the life of your animal to the sword service of forty Daroman soldiers?'

'Well, your guys don't fight so good, but I don't see as you have anything else worth trading.'

Leonidas's guards looked ready to charge me, but he stopped them. 'Very well,' he said. 'Sergeant, come forward!'

One of the men took a step forward and saluted.

'Should all the gods abandon this world and that fool somehow kill me, do you swear on behalf of the men to follow the commands of Countess Mariadne?'

287

There wasn't an instant of questioning or hesitation. 'As you command, so I swear,' the sergeant said.

Leonidas nodded, and the other man stepped back.

I turned to Reichis. 'All right, partner, do you swear by the nine squirrel cat gods in the sky to hunt all the rats in that guy's cellar? Even the big ones?'

'You insult me!' Leonidas shouted. 'You insult my men and you insult the empire of Darome!'

I showed him a gesture with two fingers I'd learned in the borderlands. 'So kill me, you big, thick-brained ox. Come show me what you've got.'

Leonidas started towards me, but Bracius, bless her brave heart, stood in the way. 'We haven't agreed on the weapons,' she said, pointing to Leonidas's sword.

'He can keep it,' I said helpfully, flipping open my powder holsters.

Leonidas smiled.

'Major,' Bracius interrupted. 'With all due respect, you don't seem to have considered your opponent. I assume you want to forbid magic.'

Leonidas spat. 'Magic? No, marshal, I have no restrictions on magic.' Then he turned to his men and shouted, 'This dog thinks he can best a Daroman military man with his parlour tricks. Is he right?'

'No, major!' the men shouted.

'Is there any man or woman, mage or warrior, who can beat me in single combat?'

'No, major!'

'Does anyone talk this much before a fight?' I shouted, hoping someone might reflexively shout 'No, major!' Alas, they were too well trained.

288

Bracius glanced at both of us. 'I'm going to assume you're both ready and begin the count. So. Here we go. Seven . . .'

'Hey, you remember the last time we had to listen to a marshal count down from seven?' Reichis asked.

'Six!'

I looked down at him. 'Yeah, why?'

'You know what I call that time?'

'Five!'

The squirrel cat's tail twitched. 'The good old days.'

'Four!'

I chewed on the oraxian root, trying to ignore the bitter taste. 'Just remember your part.'

'Three!'

'What's my part again?' the squirrel cat asked. His sincerity was deeply disturbing.

'Don't screw with me, Reichis.'

'Two!'

'Kellen?' he asked.

'Yeah?'

'One!'

'I'm not guarding that guy's cellar even if you do lose,' he said.

'Fight!'

Leonidas bridged half the distance between us in a few steps. 'Come on, let's show them how fast you fall, *talam fezher*,' he said. That was cute. I didn't know Zhubanese hardly at all, but I was pretty sure he'd just called me 'weasel boy'. His men laughed at the jibe. I supposed they must all pick up a few words being this close to the border.

Okay, here we go. I tossed powder into the air, made the somatic shapes and quietly said the words. They don't need

289

to be spoken loudly, so I chose to keep them barely above a whisper. Twin red and black flames burned the air between Leonidas and me, striking him before he could move.

He laughed, and held up both his arms. 'You see? No magic can break the skin of a Daroman soldier!'

I pulled more powder and cast the spell again. Once again the fires licked at him. Once again he smiled. I looked over at his mage. The man was sweating as he poured energy into the shield. Projecting a shield is a lot harder than summoning one around yourself.

'Come on, spellslinger,' Leonidas jeered. 'I can barely hear your little magic trick. Give it one more proper try before I slit your belly!'

I pulled out a lot of powder this time, probably more than was safe, but I needed to be sure. The mage saw what I was doing and his concentration deepened.

'*Carath Toth*,' I said.

A burst of red and black death that would've knocked down a house shattered the air between us. The blast was fierce, full of rage and viciousnesss as it tore at the shield. But it wasn't enough. The air around Leonidas shimmered and shook, but the major himself was unharmed. He whooped the way a man does when his sweetheart first tells him she loves him.

'Right, Kellen Argos. Now I'll show you my magic!'

He stepped forward, but I held up a hand one final time. '*Leb'ethera dea'vetis*,' I said.

Nothing happened.

Well. Nothing visible anyway.

Leonidas looked at me, confused. 'That's it? That was your secret plan? To cast a shield upon yourself? Fool. You think

290

I walk into a duel without learning about my opponent first? I know everything about you, Kellen of the House of Ke. Exiled Jan'Tep. Wanderer. Spellslinger. I know you don't have enough magic in that breath band of yours to cast a shield that could stop a butterfly, never mind my sword.'

'True,' I admitted quietly, so that only Leonidas would hear, 'but I didn't cast the shield on myself, major. I cast it on you.'

'What? Why would . . . ? Why would you—' He started panting, struggling for breath.

'Shields are funny things,' I said, keeping my voice low so his mage wouldn't hear. 'They form a kind of barrier around you, protecting you from the outside world. They need to be awfully strong to withstand a powder blast. In fact, they need to be pretty darn impenetrable – otherwise the heat from the discharge could get through and the air could burn your lungs on the inside.'

'What's happening?' one of his men mumbled.

'Problem is,' I continued, 'you don't want it too thick or else it blocks everything – even the air you need to breathe. Your mage over there did all the hard work, piling shield on top of shield to withstand the blasts. Me? All I had to do was add a tiny breath shield on top. Like you said, it wouldn't even keep out a butterfly. But it is keeping out the air.'

Leonidas turned to the mage, who finally figured out what was happening. He tried to remove the spell, but that's the moment when Reichis went after his face.

'Too bad,' I said to Leonidas. 'He would've done great keeping your cellar clear of rats.'

Leonidas struggled towards me, falling to his knees as he clawed helplessly at the air around himself.

291

'Two things you should know,' I said. 'First, magic is complicated, and not something for amateurs to play with.'

I heard an anguished cry from the mage and a slight popping sound in the air as the shield disappeared. Leonidas sucked in air and struggled to his feet. 'And second, I have a message for you,' I said, pulling powder from my holsters and sending the grains spinning into the air. I intoned the words, different this time. '*Carath Erras.*'

The blast tore through Leonidas like a hurricane through a canyon. The major looked down at his stomach and saw the bleeding wreck of his insides threatening to come out. Instinctively his hands pressed against the wound, but it was far too big and far too deep to do any good. I knelt down next to him and whispered in his ear. 'The old man says goodbye.'

I'd like to believe that those were the last words Leonidas heard before he went to his ancestors. It would warm me on cold nights to think that he knew, right at that last moment, in the gate between this life and whatever comes next, that the red and black fires that had eaten through his belly and destroyed all his grand plans had come from the old man's tongue. Erras had won the final duel.

But by then Leonidas was probably already dead.

38

Gratitude

The death of Leonidas very nearly sparked my decapitation right then and there. When his men realised he had lost, they raised their weapons and came for me.

'Stop!' the sergeant shouted.

The men froze.

'Parade formation!' he shouted again.

The soldiers quickly stepped into four rows of ten behind their leader. He walked forward and knelt in front of Mariadne.

'Countess Mariadne,' he said. 'I am Sergeant Tarius. What is your command?'

I've never been a soldier. Maybe it's because of the shadow-black and all the old tales that say that one day a demon is going to take over my body and use it to commit atrocities, but I don't understand what makes one person willing to subvert his will to that of another. Then again, the way Tarius and all the soldiers with him were able to overcome their anger over their leader's death and their hatred for me in order to honour Leonidas's last command? You had to admire it.

Mariadne looked from him, to me, and over to Leonidas's body. A look of uncertainty quickly changed to resolve. 'Take him,' she said. 'Bury him with what military honours you see fit. Have the men set their camp outside the boundary of my home. You will join me tomorrow to discuss strategy for protecting Urbana Sarrix from further raids by the Zhuban.'

Tarius stood and saluted. 'Understood, countess.'

He turned and ordered six of his men to carry Leonidas out of the courtyard.

Mariadne knelt down before me and took my hand. 'Thank you,' she said. 'For me and for my poor old Erras. Thank you.'

'Get up, your ladyship. People will think you're sweet on me.'

Reichis rejoined us, blood covering his face and snout.

'You kill him?' I asked.

He shook his head, and I noticed a bit of something white and goopy coming out between his teeth that looked uncomfortably like part of an eyeball. 'Jush took shumthin' to remember him by,' Reichis mumbled.

Mariadne gave me an indulgent look. 'Still imagining your weasel talks to you?' she said, humour in her voice.

Reichis swallowed, then growled.

'Oh, please,' she said, looking down at him and wagging her finger. 'I know you understand what I'm saying, so I have to believe you can take a joke now and then.'

Reichis turned and walked away from us. 'I'd rather be huntin' cellar rats.'

As we entered Mariadne's home I fell to my knees and threw up on what looked like a very old rug.

'Kellen! Are you hurt?'

One of Mariadne's retainers stood by – a boy with a round face whose serious expression made me think of Erras. 'Countess,' he said, 'shall I fetch a physician from town?'

'I'm fine,' I said.

'But you—'

'It's nothing.' I pushed myself to my feet. 'Sorry about the rug.' I was shaking uncontrollably and already I could feel tears streaming down my cheeks. The boy offered me water, which I guzzled down until it rid me of the sour taste in my mouth.

Mariadne's eyes were wide, searching my face as if she didn't believe I was unhurt. 'Are you sure? Is it the magic you do? Are you in pain?'

'No,' I said. 'It's just the delayed terror catching up with me.'

'I can't believe that,' she said. 'The way you fought Leonidas . . . It was like watching a hero from one of the old sagas come to life.'

That made me laugh. 'I don't think any of the Daroman legends looked much like me,' I said, pointing to my left eye.

'Maybe they should have,' she said. She threw her arms around me and held me so tightly I had trouble drawing a breath. 'You're a hero to this house. You're a hero to me.'

She let me go but I still found it hard to catch my breath. 'I . . .'

She took my hand and interlaced her fingers into mine. 'Ask me, Kellen Argos. Ask me for anything and it is yours.'

Ask me for anything. Somehow the words took all the pleasure out of me, and I remembered who I was. A commoner. An outlaw. Sure, I'd done her a service and she was grateful. So grateful that she was eager to balance the scales, the way a good customer always pays their bills on time.

'I'm sorry,' she said, her hand still holding mine. 'That sounded awful, didn't it?' She took in a long, slow breath, and let it out just as slowly. 'For so long I've not been able to count on anyone except Tasia and Erras. Since Arafas died my life has been a series of proposals and threats, bribes and ultimatums. Every man who has come to this door has done so offering me something of value, but wanting something much more precious in return. And now you come along with your strange manner and your talking squirrel cat and your brave, brave soul.' She withdrew her left hand from mine and put it on my cheek. 'I meant no offence when I thanked you, Kellen.' She pulled me in close and kissed me on the lips.

I've been kissed before. Infrequently, true, but I did feel as if I had some points of comparison. Nephenia was the first, and the first time with her had been such a shock I couldn't really remember the sensation. Come to think of it, the second time she'd kissed me I'd thought she was some guy I'd helped save from Berabesq religious fanatics, so that had been pretty unexpected too. With Seneira, it had started as a way of helping her break the hold of the mystical torments that had been placed on her, and then become a kind of desperate relief from the pain. This was different.

Mariadne's kiss was warm and sweet and hungry. She was older than I was, more comfortable in her skin. She wasn't trying to make a grand statement or hold anything back. She knew what she wanted, and took from me as much as I took from her. I felt her hands slide up my arms, my neck, and finally her fingers wound their way into my hair, knocking my hat to the ground. My own hands were around her waist, pulling her in close, trying not to pull too hard.

I heard Reichis come to the door, sniff, grunt and then turn away. I ignored him. I ignored everything just to fall

296

into that kiss as long and as deep as I could. Mariadne's desire was palpable. It was real, and knowing. *She wants me*, I thought *Not out of love or expectation or gratitude. She just wants me as I am.* It wasn't something a shadowblack like me ever expects to feel.

A man shouldn't feel triumphant at a moment like this. That's what Ferius would've said. But I couldn't help it. My sister in all her arrogance had informed me that I'd be the death of Mariadne, but she was here, alive, in my arms. Leonidas, the man of violence – the knight of blades who Tasia had warned planned to destroy me – was dead. This, then, was what it felt like to be a hero. To not be reviled on sight, but admired. Desired, even. I knew it was petty of me, but I couldn't keep the thought out of my head: *I won.*

Mariadne pulled away unexpectedly, but stayed close, her head buried in my chest. 'We should . . .' She hesitated.

'Stop?' I asked.

Mariadne shook her head. Her hair tickled my nose. 'Go upstairs.'

I almost made a joke. I almost said that Reichis made me promise not to make hump-hump with the bitch countess. That's the kind of idiot I am on a daily basis. But not today. I took Mariadne's hand. 'Lead the way.'

She pulled me towards the stairs, but I heard someone running along the path towards the door. 'Wait,' I said, letting go of her hand and flipping open my powder holsters.

Marshal Bracius ran in through the door with Fen in tow. I took a pinch of the red and black powders. I had no reason to believe the marshals would have any interest in avenging Leonidas, but then I remembered what Tasia had said about the cards and the king of chariots. A man of secrets, she'd

297

said. If that man was Colfax, head of the marshals service, I might have a serious problem on my hands.

'Countess Mariadne,' Bracius said. She was breathing hard. 'We must speak. Now.'

Mariadne held up a hand. 'No, marshal. The duel was fairly fought. You put your name on the contract yourself. If there is a price to be paid for this, I'll pay it. But not now. Not today.'

'Yes, countess, but that's not it. My man Fen has arrived from the prison.'

I looked at Fen. His eyes weren't angry or determined or filled with anything I might've expected. They were sad. 'I'm sorry, but your maid, Tasia, I found her in her cell,' he said. 'She's . . .'

I don't know whether it was squeamishness, politeness, or fear of reprisal that kept him from finishing his sentence, but it didn't matter. The look in his eyes made it plain what word he'd left out.

39

The Rewards of Loyalty

I was grateful that they'd taken the time to take down Tasia's body before letting us in. Instead of seeing her companion hanging by a rope made from her own dress and tied to the bars of the small window near the ceiling, Mariadne's first sight was of Tasia covered by a sheet, lying peacefully on the sleeping pallet.

Fen handed me a deck of cards.

'She left these on the table. There weren't nothing else. No note, nothing. Reckon they belong to you, card player.'

I nodded, grateful for the small, simple gesture. The cards were in a bit of disarray – a few turned wrong ways up on the top of the deck. I stuffed the deck into my pocket and turned back to Mariadne.

'Damn the queen,' she said, her face full of tears. 'Damn her for this.'

Those words alone would have been enough to make Mariadne the new occupant of this cell, but Bracius was gentle when she said, 'My lady, I swear to you on my honour, it was Tasia herself who—'

'No!' Mariadne screamed. 'I don't care what you say. I don't care if she put the noose around her own neck. It was the queen who did this. She lied to me.'

'It was Leonidas who put Tasia in here,' I said.

'Leonidas is gone! You killed him, and now – now Tasia is dead? The queen must have ordered this. She—'

Bracius spun around and walked out of the room like it was on fire.

'Don't you walk away from me, you coward!' Mariadne shouted.

I put a hand on the countess's shoulder and she tried to pull away, but I kept a hard grip on her.

'She left the room for you,' I said. 'She left because if you keep spouting treason in her presence she'll have no choice but to arrest you.'

'I don't care,' she cried. 'I don't care about any of it any more. They took Arafas. They took Erras. Now Tasia . . . Kellen, they won't stop until I'm all alone.'

I wrapped my arms around her as tight as I could, and held her there as she cried into my shoulder and railed at the world. Eventually the fading light of the afternoon sun took the last of her energy with it, and she said softly into my ear, 'Take me back, Kellen. I want to go back.'

'I'll take you home,' I said.

'No. There's nothing for me there. Take me to the queen.'

'She's returned to the capital by now, Mariadne. You can't go to the palace like this. We need to—'

'Just help me to see the queen, Kellen. Please.'

'How? What are we going to do? Jump on a horse and ride for two days without food, water or clothing?'

She was silent, and for a moment I thought I might have persuaded her. 'The soldiers – Leonidas's men – they've sworn allegiance to me now. They'll take us to the Northern

Detachment and from there to the capital.'

'First of all, those aren't regular soldiers; they're Leonidas's personal guard. They don't get to order the Northern Detachment to do anything. Second, they have a word for suddenly turning up at the palace with forty private guards and a bad attitude. It's called an attempted coup.'

'Then help me, Kellen. Give me a better idea. But don't tell me to go home. Don't tell me to let this stand, because I can't. Tasia is dead, and someone must answer for it. I will take her body with me to the capital and lay her at the queen's feet until my beloved cousin explains to me why I should suffer my companion's death as meekly as I did my husband's.'

I wanted to tell her to let it go. Tasia was dead and nothing we could do would bring her back. Whether she had killed herself to protect the queen, or whether the queen had somehow arranged it to keep her silent, none of it mattered now.

Except, I guess it did.

'We need help,' I said finally. 'Someone with resources who can help us reach the capital safely and make sure we get in to see the queen.'

Mariadne looked up at me and wiped the tears from her eyes. 'Who?'

'Someone who's rather well respected but somewhat ignored,' I replied.

40

Fatherly Advice

'No, my dear,' Count Martius said, later that night as he waved us into his villa. 'An old fool I may be, but not a compete one.'

'How do you even know what we're here for?' I asked.

Reichis gave a snort. 'Because for a skinbag, he's a savvy bastard.' The squirrel cat ambled into the house. 'Probably knew about Tasia's death before we did.'

Martius motioned for us to sit on the divan before slumping heavily into his own chair. 'You just killed the commander of the Northern Detachment in a duel, tutor of cards,' he said. 'Word spreads fast when the world stands on its end.'

'We're not here about that,' Mariadne said. 'It's—'

'Tasia,' Martius interrupted. 'Forgive me, dear. That news has reached me too. It's not often a prisoner kills themselves only hours after receiving a reprieve from a death sentence.'

'Then you know it was murder,' Mariadne said.

'I know no such thing, countess.'

'Then how? Why?'

Martius shrugged. 'Who can say? Not I, certainly.' He pointed at her. 'And not you either.' He favoured her with something more akin to a father's smile than the acknowledgement of an equal. 'Tell me, countess, what good will any of this bring you? Will it make the moon set sooner or the sun rise any higher in the sky?'

'It will bring justice to Tasia, Count Martius. That is enough.'

'Justice. *Justice*. Young people love words like "justice" and "truth" and "love". Let me tell you something, both of you: Tasia has no need for your justice. It will not bring her one ounce of satisfaction. And it will weigh you down with a thousand pounds of sorrow, I promise you.'

Mariadne rose from the divan and hugged herself. It occurred to me that she had barely looked at me in the time since we'd left the jail. 'So what would you have me do, Martius? Go back to my keep? Sit there and wait each day until whoever caused Tasia's death decides that I too am an inconvenience that needs to disappear? Is it all my fault? Should I have married Leonidas and suffered him for a husband?'

Martius seemed to weigh his words carefully, but eventually he simply said, 'Yes.'

Mariadne spun around and I found myself on my feet. 'You can't be serious,' I said.

'Oh? And why not? Would it have made such a terrible match?' He ignored me and addressed Mariadne. 'Leonidas was on track to become the most respected and powerful man in Darome before our friend here put an end to him. You, countess, are beloved by many, and are of royal blood. You could have been the second most powerful woman in the country.'

'Or perhaps the first?' I asked quietly.

Martius looked to me. He nodded. 'Perhaps. There's no question that Leonidas had ambition without limits. The

303

nobility aren't happy with the fact that the queen is so young and seems determined to keep the peace, regardless of the danger Zhuban poses to our security.'

'Or to your pockets,' I said.

'Ah, true. Very true. Darome has always relied on conquest, and so has its nobility.'

'Then why don't they just assassinate her?' I asked.

'Have you met Colfax? The man keeps a hundred games going at once. Finds every possible threat to the queen and uses those marshals of his to snuff them out. No, a coup against the queen would take years of planning. And even if it was successful, they'd still need to get her to abdicate.'

'Abdicate? If they took the palace, why would they need her to abdicate?'

Mariadne turned to Martius. 'The throne. It's because of the throne, isn't it?'

'Yes, the grand Daroman royal throne. Just about the only remaining piece of magic left from the early days of the empire. They say it'll burn a man to cinders unless he holds the royal spirit. If the queen dies, who knows whom it'll pass to? Could be anyone in the imperial lineage. If she abdicates though, whoever she gives the throne to forges a new line of Daroman rulers.'

'You believe all this?' I asked. Even for someone who came from a culture of magic, it sounded superstitious.

Martius shrugged. 'Hardly matters if I accept the legend, does it? Only matters if everyone else does.'

'And what do you believe in, Count Martius?' Mariadne asked. 'Would you see us at war simply to sack the gold of another nation and grow fat on its wealth?'

'Me?' He gave a laugh and patted his belly. 'I am more than

304

rich enough and fat enough, countess. I am a plain-faced man, married to a plain-faced wife who loves him. I have a nice home in the capital, and one here for when I grow too old for the city. I couldn't care less about money or politics.'

'Then perhaps you can imagine how little interest I had in being the wife of a man who didn't love me, so that he could pursue war and personal power. Perhaps you can sympathise just a little with the fact that I have lived under siege since my husband died. Perhaps you can even forgive me for being angry when those I love best are taken from me.'

Martius rose from his chair and put his hands on Mariadne's arms. 'Ah, dear woman. That I can do. That I can do.'

He began to pull her into an avuncular hug but she put her hands on his chest and pushed just enough to keep her distance. 'Then perhaps you will even go so far as to understand that I can't go back to my home and wait out my days, never having tried to find justice for those who have died for their love of me, until one day someone decides that I, too, am in the way. And when they do? Tell me, what son or daughter of Darome will stand beside me?'

Martius nodded once, and made a small choked sound. I saw a tear in his eye. 'You shame me, my lady, and you are right to do so. I will give you what help a foolish old man has to offer. We will take my carriage and return to Sarrix for the body of your beloved Tasia. From there I will take you both to the capital and before the queen, that you may say your piece.'

41

Breaking Faith

All told, it took us three days to get back to the capital and the queen's court. None of us spoke much along the way. When we arrived, servants greeted us with a mix of confusion and deference, advising us strongly that we would benefit from a chance to rest and bathe before entering the throne room. In the end though, they got out of our way.

Except for Arex, the queen's social secretary.

'I'm telling you again – you don't go into the throne room angry.'

'Get out of the way, Arex,' I warned. It occurred to me that Arex was also the queen's cousin and knew, perhaps better than anyone else, how the strings of power and politics can be pulled.

'Sorry, kid – royal tutor or not, you don't go in there angry.'

'And me? Will you stand in my way too, "secretary"?' Mariadne asked, quiet fury in her voice.

Arex gave her a sympathetic look. 'Countess, you especially I plan to keep out of this room. You're both lucky that the queen returned early from the north, so there aren't many of your fellow nobles here to see you acting this way.'

'I'm asking you one last time, Arex. Step out of the way.'

I didn't want to fight him. Hells, I wasn't that sure I could take him. But Tasia was dead, and if someone in there hadn't ordered her death, they had certainly put the noose in her hand. Mariadne deserved answers.

'Don't do it, kid. It's not worth it.'

He was probably right, but I didn't care. I could feel Reichis tensing next to me. He always knows when the time for talk is over.

Martius sighed. 'You'd better let them in, Arex. Two more stubborn souls the world has never seen.'

Arex shook his head. 'With all due deference to your rank and relationship to the queen, my lord, this isn't your concern.'

Martius smiled. 'And with all due sympathy for your obligations and lack of rank, Arex, I'm afraid I'm making it my concern. Let them pass.'

Arex was visibly shaken, and seemed uncertain how to proceed. 'Do I take it that you are threatening me, Count Martius?'

'Oh, Arex, get off your high horse. You spend too much time in political intrigues. It's a wonder anyone ever manages to secure an audience with the queen. Just let these two in. Do you seriously think she'd refuse them?'

But Arex wasn't done. 'On your head then, Count Martius?'

'Yes, Arex. If it makes you feel better, it's on my head.'

Arex stood aside. 'All right, kid,' he said resignedly. 'Go ahead and see what happens when the countess here starts screaming at the world's most powerful eleven-year-old. I'll be sure to visit you in prison.'

Arex needn't have worried about Mariadne getting us in trouble with the queen. I managed that all by myself. It took all of two minutes for things to get out of hand.

307

'You will keep silent now, master of cards,' the queen said to me finally, holding up a hand in warning.

She whispered to one of the marshals standing next to the throne.

'The court will adjourn,' he declared, his voice reverberating through the room and the crowd itself.

Like a wind-up machine, every marshal in the room started moving people towards the exits. They executed their orders with a forcefulness that reminded you they were trained to kill anyone who threatened the queen. Within minutes the room was cleared.

Almost.

'You as well, cousin,' the queen told Mariadne.

'No,' she replied.

The queen turned to the remaining two marshals. 'Lirius, Ricard, you will escort Countess Mariadne from the throne room and accompany her to her rooms in the palace. If she finds those insufficient, you will provide her accommodation in the dungeon.'

'What about the animal?' Ricard asked, wary eyes on Reichis.

'He can stay.'

'My lady,' Lirius said, reaching a hand towards Mariadne.

'No,' Mariadne said.

'As you will it,' she replied. Then she and Ricard calmly lifted the countess off the ground and carried her out of the room.

'You didn't need to do that,' I said once they'd left. 'It was childish.'

The queen looked at me a long time before she spoke. 'If I acted as a child does, what would I do now?'

I thought about that for a moment. 'Yell at me, I guess. Hit me. Have me carted off to some dungeon somewhere.'

'Is that what you want me to do?' she asked.

'I suppose not.'

'Good, then stop behaving like a child yourself, and stop trying to goad me.'

I had to admire her composure. 'You visited Tasia in Sarrix before this all started,' I said.

She nodded.

'You told her to kill Leonidas.'

She shook her head. 'I'd hoped she would simply seduce him, embarrass him. Then Mariadne would have had a reprieve for a while.'

'But Tasia failed.'

'I made a foolish miscalculation. Leonidas, for all his faults, had somewhat more restraint than to sleep with the maid of the woman he intended to marry. Tasia should have left it alone.'

'So you didn't want her to kill him?'

The queen sat back heavily on the throne. 'We discussed it. Daroman women train in the combat arts from as young an age as men, and she considered herself up to the challenge. I thought it was a risk, but I told her that if it was safe, if she could catch him asleep, then it might be better for all of us.'

'But she failed.'

'She did what she thought was best. We all do. Sometimes we're wrong.'

'So you had her condemned.'

'There was no other way. Tasia was a good girl, but she would have broken eventually. Someone would have got to her. It was a stroke of luck that Leonidas, venal as he was, chose to demand her death, otherwise the magistrate might never have sanctioned her execution.'

309

'That's a cold way to see the situation,' I said.

'Look around you, Mister Kellen. I rule over a cold country.'

I considered her explanation, but then shook my head. 'I might have bought the necessity argument, Your Majesty. But when I convinced you to—'

'Forced me,' she said.

'Fine. When I forced you to stay the execution, you lied to me. You had Tasia killed anyway.'

'No,' she said.

'Then you sent her a message. You told her to take her own life.'

'I did send her a message,' she admitted.

'So you as good as killed her—'

'I told her to come with you back to the capital. I told her I would get her out of the country, that she didn't need to worry about betraying me. I told her she'd done enough.'

'Then why did she kill herself?'

Tears began to well in the queen's eyes. 'Because she didn't believe me. She didn't think I could keep her safe. She did what she thought was best.'

'She died for you.'

'For me, for Mariadne, for everyone.' The queen lowered her eyes. 'We all play our parts, Kellen.'

'And what is my part, Your Majesty? What role do I play in these grand schemes you navigate?'

'You?' she said, her eyes meeting mine, tears streaming down her face. Suddenly she leaped from the throne and wrapped her arms around me, her face buried in my stomach. 'You're supposed to be my friend, Kellen.'

She cried, like you'd expect an eleven-year-old to cry when she's realised the world really is against her. I looked down

310

at her, then at Reichis. He gave a little grunt. 'She's not faking, Kellen.'

The queen sniffed awkwardly. 'At least one of you believes me.'

It shocked me for a moment. With everything that had happened I'd forgotten that she could understand Reichis. That meant something. It had to. 'I'm sorry,' I said.

'I can't lose you, Kellen,' she cried. 'I've been alone such a long time now. Everyone else wants something from me. I have no . . .'

I felt something break in my chest. *Friends.* She was going to say she had no friends. An exile in her own palace. I'd lived as an exile for the past two years, but at least I had Reichis. Without him . . . I didn't want to think what that would be like. But who did the queen have?

'I'm sorry,' I said again.

'I need you to promise me, Kellen.'

'Promise what?'

'I need you to promise to stay with me. I can't do this alone, not now. I've been brave. For a long time now I've been brave, but I can't do it alone any more. I need you to promise to stay with me. Just give me two years. Just till I'm a little older. I need you to promise.'

I felt pulled in two directions. The queen had, at least in her own mind, given me a chance at life. She could have killed me when they'd first brought me here. Hells, she probably should have, for all the trouble I'd caused her. And yet she kept trusting in me, kept believing that I was looking out for her. But Mariadne needed me too. She was . . . I wasn't sure I could even make sense of what she was to me. Maybe Shalla was right and I craved love and acceptance so badly

311

that I'd take it wherever I could, no matter how unlikely it was to last.

The smart thing to do was to run, or at least to pick a side. Mariadne or the queen. Love or duty. How could two people who seemed to care about each other as much as those two be on opposite sides? Ever since this mess had started I'd felt myself pulled by conflicting loyalties. I was sick of it. I wasn't built for intrigue and politics. The biggest decision I'd ever had to make in life had been whether to have a squirrel cat for a business partner. So why should I let anyone force me to choose sides? I could protect the queen, couldn't I? I could protect Mariadne too. I just had to find out who was behind all of this and put them in the ground. I had plenty of experience with that lately. In fact, I'd just killed the man who had probably intended to make himself king. Killing more arseholes like him was definitely something I could do. I looked down at Reichis. He shrugged. 'This seems like just as good a place as any to make a stand.'

'All right, Your Majesty,' I said to the queen.

'You'll stay? You'll stay and help me?'

'Yes, Your Majesty.'

She shook her head. 'Ginevra,' she said.

'What?'

'My name. It's Ginevra. When we're alone, when they aren't here, call me Ginevra.'

'All right then, Ginevra. I promise.'

My acquiescence unleashed another flood of tears, so I held her like that for a little while longer, not knowing what else to say, or what else to do.

42

Scars

I found Mariadne locked in her room with the two marshals standing guard outside.

'You can go in, if you want,' Lirius said, the mild disinterest in her voice at odds with the way her gaze told me she was searching for an excuse to pummel me senseless. 'Our orders are to keep her in, not to keep you out.'

'You go,' Reichis said. 'I've had enough crying humans for one day. Just promise me you won't make hump-hump with the red-haired skinbag.'

I couldn't imagine a less likely outcome for this visit. 'Sure, Reichis. I promise.'

'Idjit,' he grumbled, and wandered off down the hall.

I nodded to the marshals and they let me in and closed the door after me. Mariadne was sitting by the window.

'I made a fool of myself,' she said. 'Again.'

I joined her and sat down on the bench next to her.

'Seems like we're all doing that these days,' I said.

She gave a small, unhappy laugh. 'What a circus of dunces we make. Every one of us bouncing around like a puppet on a string. Someone, somewhere, is laughing at us.'

'Of that I am sure, countess. But I plan to make them stop laughing very soon.'

She leaned into me, and pulled my arm around her before turning to look into my face.

'How old are you?' she asked.

'Now is that a polite question to ask a gentleman?'

'Come on. I want to know.'

I sighed. 'I had just turned eighteen years old when this nonsense began, a couple of weeks ago. I reckon I'm somewhere around fifty by now.'

'Eighteen,' she marvelled. 'Practically a baby. And here you are, acting like an old man already.'

'How old are you?'

'Oh no,' she said. 'That's definitely not a subject fit for conversation. Much too old for you, that's for sure.'

I found it funny that she hadn't considered I'd have thought about this already. 'Twenty-three,' I said. 'You're twenty-three years old.'

She pushed a finger into my chest. 'How could you know that?'

'Erras,' I said. 'That night at the inn. He told me you were seventeen when you got married.'

She shook her head. 'Poor old Erras. Never has a man so loyal been so unable to keep his mouth shut.' Mariadne leaned into me and started weeping again, and I couldn't help but hear Reichis complaining about humans crying all the time. Maybe that's all there was left. Tears and sorrow.

Then she looked up into my eyes. 'Not you too,' she said.

'What?'

She shook her head and then kissed me. After a while, she stood up from the bench and took my hand and guided me to the bed. 'Are you promised to anyone, Kellen?' she asked.

The question drew a bitter laugh from my lips. 'I'm an outlaw shadowblack, my lady.'

'That's not an answer.'

We stood there a moment while I searched for the right tale to tell. It shouldn't be hard. Deception had become second nature to me. Now though? The lies wouldn't come. Not when it came to Nephenia. 'There's a girl. We're not . . . promised. That's not the way she thinks.'

'But you love her, and she loves you.'

A stab of resentment took me unawares. 'She loves the man I ought to be.'

Mariadne's eyes caught mine, and she nodded as though what I'd said had made any kind of sense. 'Arafas, my husband, used to believe that if he just kept telling me how brave I was, how wise and true, eventually I would somehow live up to his ideals.' She shook her head. Angry tears slipped from her eyes. 'How is it love to demand we become something more than we are?'

Those words were like the keys to a thousand chains that had been holding me down my entire life. My parents. Ferius. Nephenia. Even Reichis. All of them expecting me to be something I wasn't, for my actions to prove them right. The weight of it . . . Ancestors. I couldn't bear it any more.

Neither could Mariadne.

The two of us stood there a moment, holding each other, not quite brave enough to lie down on the bed's soft coverings and deal with everything that would come next. Surging desire kept being tamped down by the awkwardness and uncertainty of our situation. I could practically hear Reichis

315

chittering at me, 'It's literally the one thing other than breathing, eating and shitting that skinbags do by instinct, you idjit. Just—'

'I'm sorry,' Mariadne said.

I took my hands away from her hips where they'd wandered. I nodded. 'It's all right. I understand.'

She put her hands on my chest and looked down at the floor.

'No,' she said. 'No, I take it back. It's not all right.'

'What?'

She shook her head and I felt her fingers playing at the buttons of my shirt. 'It's not all right,' she said, so softly I thought she might be talking to herself. 'When Arafas died, I felt completely alone in the world. I thought I knew what solitude was, but I was wrong. Tasia was there, and Erras. Now they're gone and I truly am alone, a woman with a title that matters only insofar as it inspires others to want it for themselves.'

I started to speak, but she put a finger against my lips for a moment and then went back to the buttons of my shirt. 'I'm tired of being desired by those I despise and not good enough for anyone else. I want to decide for myself what's right for me, Kellen. And what I want is to be free from politics, from strategy and, gods help me, free to act on my own desires, not my fear over what comes afterward. If you want to say no, say it because you don't want me, not because you're afraid for me. I'm sick of being afraid. I'm sick of not being good enough. I want to be someone else for a while.'

My shirt was now open to my waist, and she kissed my chest. Her lips made my skin come alive – like the near miss

316

of a lighting bolt shot at me by an enemy, an instant of fear quickly silenced by the rush of knowing you've beaten death one more time. I pulled at her dress and we sank awkwardly but unashamedly to the bed. Fumbling like country hicks in a barn in the hot afternoon we gradually got each other's clothes out of the way. Mariadne was five years older than me, but her skin was the even, sun-kissed tone of an artist's canvas. Mine was not.

'Those scars . . .' she said.

I said nothing, but held back the urgency I felt to touch her body in case my own had quashed her passion.

'Who did such things to you?' she asked, watching my expression.

'A lot of people,' I said. 'Starting with my own.'

She traced a finger along a scar on my shoulder. 'Your own people? The Jan'Tep?'

I nodded. 'I've been . . . something of a disappointment to them.'

She kissed the scar on my shoulder, then the one on my chest, then the one on my neck. She put her hands on either side of my face and looked at me.

'Because of this?' she said, her eyes on the unquenchable blackness around my left eye.

'Yes.'

'To hate one of your own, because of a simple deformity?'

'It's not—'

Mariadne leaned in, bringing her lips to the shadowblack. 'No—'

Her lips touched me for only for an instant before she pulled back in shock. 'It's cold! Is it always so cold?'

I nodded.

317

She looked at me for a moment as if deciding what to do, then she said, 'I like it.'

'You like it?'

Mariadne nodded. 'Everyone has a coldness to them, Kellen. But you keep yours where everyone can see it. Most everyone else keeps theirs inside and only lets it out when you get close to them. I like that I know where the cold part of you lies.'

I brought my hands to her sides, letting them glide gently up the softness of her skin, to her arms, then to her breasts.

'Are you trying to find the cold in me, card player? Or the heat?' Her smile was wicked.

I smiled back. I was tired of being afraid too. 'Both,' I said. 'But I think it'll require a lot more exploration.'

Mariadne leaned into me and brought her leg across my hips. 'Then let's begin.'

43

The Warning

It was first light when I headed back to my own room. I hadn't wanted to leave Mariadne, but I was in dire need of fresh clothes. I found Marshal Colfax waiting for me in the hallway.

'Seems like we had an arrangement, Mister Kellen,' he said.

'Not one I ever agreed to. Besides, things have changed.'

Colfax smiled. 'Change happens. Sometimes. Other times, though, we just think things have changed, when really everything's exactly as we left it.'

'Listen, marshal, the queen wants me here. She's asked me to stay and protect her from whichever bastards are trying to bring her down, and I aim to do just that.'

He gave a small nod of his head. 'Yep, reckoned what with all those Argosi ways I seen in you, you'd plan to do something like that. So tell me, Kellen, who's going to protect my queen from you?'

'Me? Marshal, I'm not the one she has to worry about.'

'No? Aren't you the one who went and humiliated her in front of the court up north? And then again right here, not a day ago?'

'That's . . . that's not what I intended.'

'Ah. Right. Not what you intended. Listen, kid –' Colfax tapped a finger on my chest – 'I do believe your heart's in the right place.' He moved his finger lower, just above my belly. 'But your soul ain't.'

'What's that supposed to mean?'

His finger drifted upwards until it was at eye level. My left eye. 'I've heard a hundred stories about the shadowblack, Kellen. Not one of them ends well.'

I went to bat his arm aside but he pulled it back before I could touch him. 'I would never have taken you for a superstitious man, marshal.'

'Oh, I'll heed all kinds of omens, portents and auguries when it comes to anything that might hurt the queen.'

I looked around to see if he'd brought back-up. 'Is this going somewhere?' I asked.

'Reckon it's not. I'll see you around, Mister Kellen,' he said, and walked away.

I went back to my room and pushed open the door, to be greeted by an unholy mess. Sheets were torn, scratch marks were everywhere.

Reichis was gone.

On the bed lay a note: *Thought you might want to join me at the Virtuous Maiden. It's a nice place to stop for a meal on your way out of town. Colfax.*

I looked around the room for blood, but I didn't see any, and prayed it meant that Reichis was all right. Either way, I was going to have to kill the head of the marshals service, and that was never a good idea.

44

The Binder

The little restaurant was crowded. A trio of serving staff – the boisterous middle-aged woman who owned the place, a stocky man who, thanks to his limited enthusiasm and effort, I presumed to be her husband, and a young woman probably in her late teens who might've been their daughter – roved back and forth between tables and the bar, serving drinks and cold food. I noticed they studiously avoided the table I shared with Marshal Colfax and the scrawny, wrinkled man in the filthy white robes beneath a dusty white coat and a close-shaven scrub of salt-and-pepper hair.

The marshal's own shoulder-length locks had long ago gone to grey, and his tanned, lined face belonged to a man who should've retired years ago. But wiry muscle showed through the open neck of his dark blue riding shirt, and when I met his eyes he looked back without a trace of concern.

'So . . .' I began.

The marshal put up a finger and waved for service. The younger of the serving maids came almost instantly. She had fewer years on her than I'd first thought. Definitely had to be the owners' daughter. She was petite, pretty and, though her tresses were blonde rather than black, they were styled just like the queen's. Maybe it was the fashion these days. She smiled at the marshal.

'Coffee,' he said pleasantly before she could ask.

'Water,' his companion muttered.

Colfax waved her away before I could order.

'So that's how it's going to be?' I asked.

He nodded. 'Tried the easy way, kid. Asked you nicely. Now, well, now I can't afford to be so polite.'

'Good. I prefer it that way.' I leaned back in the chair to let him see I'd left the flaps of my powder holsters open. 'What have you done with my business partner?'

The marshal raised an eyebrow. 'The squirrel cat? Don't worry about him. He's back in your room by now. Tough little bastard. Tore a strip out of my boys.'

The glib way he talked about having kidnapped Reichis – how it was all supposed to be fine now that he'd returned him to our rooms – made me want to wipe the smirk off his face. With a carving knife. 'You ever touch Reichis again and I'll do worse than that before I'm done with you.'

The marshal shook his head. 'Don't put this on me, Kellen. Like I said before, I asked you nicely.'

I considered a range of replies to that, but Colfax didn't strike me as the kind of guy who'd worry too much about idle threats from exiled spellslingers. Instead I waved for the server. She ignored me so I stood up and bellowed, 'Wine.'

She came back with all three drinks and gave me a slightly disgusted look that focused on the markings around my left eye. Guess the shadowblack isn't considered fashionable at this establishment.

'Don't take your anger out on the girl,' the marshal said, sipping his coffee. 'Ain't her fault you won't listen to reason.'

'It's a troubling medical condition I've had for a while now,' I said. 'Can't seem to take orders from craggy old bastards who confuse being a lawman with being the law.'

Colfax's companion gave a little sneering laugh that threatened to turn into full-blown chortling.

The marshal spared him a glance – a look of mild revulsion quickly replaced by a tolerant smile. 'The reason my acquaintance here is laughing is because you said something funny just then.'

I cocked my head at that one. 'Was it my smooth delivery?'

'Nope.' He took another sip of his coffee, then gave a questioning look at his friend and waited. The man drank his glass of water, then nodded.

'You recognise Sophistus here?' Colfax asked.

'Never seen him before in my life.'

'Right, well, not him exactly. But I reckoned you might've heard of his order. He's a kind of, well, I suppose you'd say he's a kind of spiritual hermit. From the old days.'

Sophistus smiled and reached a hand out towards me like he wanted me to shake it. I declined. Then I felt something crawl inside me.

'You probably know that we Daroman aren't exactly a religious people any more,' Colfax went on. 'It's not really that useful for a civilised people. But back in the day, hell, we were just as gods-fearin' as the next folk. We had lots of priests and holy women and all that claptrap. Cultures change over time though, and as we figured out more about how the world works and built more machines, we let go of a lot of our superstitions.' Colfax pressed his hands together in a mocking emulation of prayer. 'Did you know, Kellen, you can travel a hundred miles in any direction from this restaurant and not find a church or monastery these days? You certainly wouldn't meet a true believer.'

'Except for Sophistus,' I said, clenching and unclenching my fingers in case I'd have to make a fast move.

'Right, except for old Sophie here. He's what they call an Abjurist of Saint Daebolus. Well, that's not what most people call them. Most people just call them the white binders.'

I'd never heard of Saint Daebolus and until that moment I had no idea what an 'abjurist' was supposed to be. But the moment the creepy bastard in his colourless, filthy robes caught my gaze, his eyes went milky white and a subtle smile came to his face. In that instant I knew – I *knew* – what was about to happen to me. A *binder*, Colfax had called him. A white binder. A length of twisting pale rope to snare a shadowblack.

My mind sent a screaming command to my legs, demanding that they get me to my feet so I could run out of that place as fast as they could carry me. The order was ignored.

I knew Sophistus was smiling, not because I was watching his face, but because I could feel his expression mirrored on my own. 'That's it,' Colfax said, his voice gentle, as if he were coaxing a frightened pony. 'You just sit back down there and let it happen, Kellen. Best way to handle this now.'

I forced my gaze back to the binder. The withered, wrinkled forehead showed not the slightest sign of strain. My head turned of its own accord, bending effortlessly to his will. I could see the people at the tables around us, not one of them noticing what was happening to me. I couldn't even summon a look of terror.

'Show him the first part, Sophie,' Colfax said.

The tiniest crinkle appeared at the corner of the binder's

eyes, as if he were just about to laugh. My throat spasmed once, twice, a third time. I wasn't breathing.

'Remarkable, isn't it? You can't do much of anything right now unless Sophistus does it for you. Move, breathe – hell, you probably can't even blink unless he makes you.'

Dark spots appeared in my vision. Colfax nodded to Sophistus, and a moment later I sucked air deep into my lungs. Everything the marshal said was true. I couldn't use my arms or legs, couldn't tell my eyes to blink or my throat to swallow. I could barely make my eyes move.

'Don't bother trying to speak,' Colfax said. 'You can't.' He leaned back in his seat and let out the sigh of a man who's about to do something he doesn't want to do. 'That is, you can't speak unless Sophie wants you to.'

'Wench!' I shouted. The sound that came out of my mouth was strange to me. It was my voice, but deeper, more demanding. It reminded me of my father. I wished then that Ke'heops were here. He'd kill both these men without a second thought for what they'd done to me – for what they were *about* to do to me. For a long time now I'd thought my family was just about the worst thing to ever happen to this continent. I didn't feel that way now.

Father, please! If you can hear me. Mother . . . Bene'maat, if you're scrying for me, send Shalla. Do something before they make me—

'I'm out of wine, bitch,' I bellowed, my hand picking up my glass and pouring its contents on the floor. My voice was cold and full of menace to my own ears, but it was still my voice, even though Sophistus was choosing the words.

'I'm sorry, sir. I'll bring you more right away.'

'You'd better,' I said. 'Or I'll rip that half-witted head off

325

your shoulders and piss down your neck.' The last words came out in a pathetic squeak as the server left.

'Don't go having so much fun you forget to make him breathe now, Sophie,' Colfax warned.

Air filled my lungs again, my ragged breathing hoarse and painful. Tears came to my eyes. Those were mine at least.

'The world sure is full of wonders, ain't it?' the marshal asked. 'I have to tell you, Kellen, I never have believed things are as cut and dried as good and evil. I mean, I see a lot of trouble in my line of work. People do things, Kellen. They do them for good reasons or bad reasons. But to *be* evil? To lack any real . . . . Well, I guess you'd have to call it a soul. I thought all that nonsense was just some bill of goods sold by swindlers who made their living off superstition. But Sophistus here, he showed me different. See, ever since the days when there really was some fella called himself Saint Daebolus walking around, his followers been studyin' the ways of bindin' demons. All those wild shadowblacks from those Jan'Tep stories you must've heard as a kid? There's a reason they never made their way into the Daroman empire. Abjurists like Sophie here, they'd spend their whole lives in meditation, learning the ancient demon binding ways.' The marshal leaned forward, peering into my eyes as if he could see the darkness deep inside. 'That's what he's doing now, Kellen. He's got himself a lasso around the demon inside your soul.'

The waitress returned with another glass of wine. My hand swung out and knocked it to the floor. 'Stupid cow,' I shouted. 'I told you I wanted water! What's it gonna take to make you learn?'

'I'm sorry, sir,' she cried. 'I'll bring you water right away.' She practically ran into the arms of the older serving woman.

'Now, Kellen, was that really necessary?' the marshal asked, his voice loud enough to catch the notice of the other patrons. 'You did order wine, you know.'

I tried again to break free, but it was like grabbing hold of mist; there was nothing to grasp, nothing to fight against.

Colfax continued more quietly. 'Course it'd be great if Sophie could handle anyone who just happened to be mean, wouldn't it? Take a load off my plate, I can tell you. But being mean or nice, or right or wrong, those things aren't the same as evil. The shadowblack – now that's evil. And that's what you've got inside you, boy.'

Sophistus gave me a hungry smile, and Colfax patted him on the shoulder. 'The reason my friend here is lookin' so happy is that it's been ten years since anyone from his order caught himself a proper shadowblack. Usually people with the disease remember to stay away from normal folks, or get themselves killed when they forget. Poor old Sophie's one of the last of his order. Hasn't had any business for ages. But now you've come along, with the markings around your eye just as sure as a magistrate's verdict.' He reached across the table and took hold of my chin. 'Go on now, Kellen. Tell me I'm wrong. Tell me you're a free man inside that body of yours and I'll send Sophie on his way and you and me'll be square.'

I couldn't. He knew I couldn't, but he wanted to make me taste the bitter futility of trying. Instead I coughed, not because my body needed to, but because Sophistus forced me to.

'Right. Right you are, Kellen,' Colfax said. He looked towards the back door to the restaurant and the white binder turned my gaze there as well. The serving girl was taking a pail outside. 'Time to get to business, isn't it?' the marshal asked. 'You're a busy man. Lots to do.'

327

I stood up.

Sophistus closed his eyes, and I felt something change, just slightly, in the back of my head. I was still under his control, but now he was there inside me. When I looked again at the back door, I could tell the binder was in my head, watching through my eyes like they were windows.

'You got him, Sophistus?' Colfax asked.

I felt him nod. There was a strange excitement building up inside me. *It's him*, I realised, horrified. *He's excited by all this.*

Colfax looked up at me. 'Like I said before, Kellen, it's important to me that you remember that when we first had this talk, I asked you nicely.'

I felt my heart pounding as I struggled to gain control of myself, to shout or cry out or even fall to the ground.

'He's figured out what comes next,' Sophistus said. I heard his voice first in my mind and then echoing in my ears.

The marshal rose and put a hand on my shoulder. 'Sorry about this, Kellen. It's just how it has to be.' He leaned in close, his lips almost touching my ear as he whispered, 'You're gonna wanna tell yourself that this is all Sophie's doing, that you're just a vessel he's taken control of, but I don't believe that and I'll bet you don't either. Some part of you, something that was already rotten long before you ever met Sophie or me or even got those shadowblack marks, something deep inside you must want this to happen.'

Again I threw my will against the binder's. I had spent most of my life as a Jan'Tep initiate, learning to master my thoughts, to envision complex esoteric geometry without faltering, to bend the raw forces of magic to my dominion. None of that helped. '*You must want this to happen.*' The

328

binder repeated the marshal's words over and over inside my head.

I found myself swaggering towards the back of the restaurant. A few people looked up to see what I was doing. I gave them a smile and a wink. I heard a melody that I didn't recognise, and only then realised I was whistling. When I pushed through the back door of the restaurant, I saw an alleyway. The serving girl was kneeling there, washing wine glasses in a bucket of soapy water. She looked up, scared but not surprised, almost as if she'd been expecting me.

Run, I thought. *Please, just run!*

When she saw the look in my eyes, she rose up and retreated until her back was against the wall. The wine glass dropped from her hand, shattering on the hard ground.

Run, damn you! Don't stand there like a rabbit with its leg caught in a trap! Run!

I grabbed her roughly. She cried out, but didn't scream. 'Please, sir . . .' she said. 'Please don't. I'm sorry. Whatever I did wrong, I'm sorry.'

'Shut up and don't move,' I said.

Kick me, I pleaded silently with her. *Kick me in the groin and run. Drive the heel of your foot into my knee and break it. Scratch at my eyes. Scream! Do something! Don't let me . . .*

Unbidden, my hands reached out and took hold of the top of her dress. I could feel every thread of the fabric against my fingertips. The softness of cotton washed many times. The dampness of sweat from her labours suffused the neckline.

'Please don't,' she said, then once again, 'please.'

Don't do this, I begged the white binder. *You've made your point. It's over now, you hear me? It's over. You can stop!*

My grip tightened on the front of her dress. The material

bunched in my hands, loose threads catching on the calluses of my fingers.

The girl began to weep. 'Oh, no. Oh, no,' she moaned, as if it had already happened, as if it was all done now, and all that was left was to pick up the pieces of a broken life.

No! I screamed, but the white binder kept me mute. I hurled my will against him. *I am Argosi,* I said. *I walk the Way of Stone. You cannot make me bend. You cannot make me break.*

But he could.

Slowly, inexorably, my hands pulled at the fabric of the dress. I heard the crackling hiss of the stitches in the neckline begin to come apart. Every good thing I'd come to believe about myself since I'd first met Ferius Parfax was being proven wrong. *You've got to help me, Ferius,* I pleaded. *You said a piece of you is in me. Where is it? Where's the part that can't be chained? Show me the Way of Stone!*

The tear in the dress became a rip, exposing bare skin underneath. I tried to force my eyes closed, to escape the terror of this girl who had no idea why a stranger was doing this to her. *Stop!* I begged the white binder. *You've won. I'll leave town, I swear. I'll do anything you want, but please, don't make me do this!*

Nausea spread throughout my body, and I thought – I *hoped* – I might throw up. But the white binder did something to me and the queasiness went away. With my right hand still holding tight to the girl's dress, keeping her from getting away, the fingers of my left began to open the buckle of my belt. The white binder made me look down at myself.

I'll murder you, I swore silently to the binder. *If you make me do this, I'll find you. I'll get to you when you're asleep and*

330

I'll tear out your throat with my bare teeth. Colfax wouldn't go to all this trouble if he wanted me dead. That means I'll be alive, and you'll know I'm coming for you.

But Sophistus wasn't listening any more. He was too busy laughing.

Suddenly the back door of the restaurant burst open. The owners – husband and wife – came through, screaming a name I couldn't even make out through the echoes of the white binder's laughter. They carried knives in their hands and death in their eyes.

Colfax and Sophistus pushed past them before they could put me to the blade. Colfax grabbed me by the collar and slammed me against the back wall of the restaurant. 'What do we have here, Mister Kellen? You so damned black-hearted that you'd defile an innocent girl for no worse crime than she didn't serve you fast enough?'

I looked over at the girl, crying in her parents' arms.

'Next time,' my mouth said.

'Best quiet down now, Kellen,' Colfax said sagely. 'This here's a serious business.'

Sophistus took off his coat and covered the girl with it. She clung to his filthy white robes as if he were her saviour, crying into his shoulder as he patted her back, then stroked it. He smirked surreptitiously at me before passing the girl to her parents. I wondered why they didn't push the old man aside and gut me then and there. Maybe they figured the marshal was going to do it for them. If so, they were disappointed.

Colfax shook his head. 'Wish I knew what to do with you, Kellen. Technically speaking, what with your status in the court, I'm not even sure I have the power to arrest you.'

The parents started to protest and the mother took another run at me. Colfax held her fast. 'I'm sorry, Lavinia, truly I am. It's a horrible thing here. But there's nothing we can do. Kellen here is one of the queen's royal tutors. I couldn't hold him even if I wanted to. In fact, even if you went to the queen with this, she might not believe it. It's a damned shame, but he's in control here.'

'I'll kill you, you pig,' the father shouted.

The marshal nodded sympathetically, but kept a firm hand on him. 'You go back inside, take care of your girl. Heaven knows she's had a terrible ordeal and needs your love right now. I'll deal with Mister Kellen here – try to reason with him. Make him see the error of his ways.'

Still shaking with rage, their eyes on me the whole time, the couple took their daughter back inside. Colfax and Sophistus turned to me. 'So. Any questions about what you're going to do next, Kellen?'

All at once the binder was gone from inside me. I fell to the ground and threw up.

'Damn, Sophie – give me a warning before he's going to do that!'

Sophistus shrugged. Colfax knelt down and patted my head. 'Hard to come face to face with what you really are, isn't it?'

I threw up some more. Colfax put a comforting hand on my shoulder. 'There you go. Let it all out. It's a rough truth to come to.'

There was barely enough strength left in my arms to push myself up. The only energy keeping my body moving was a hatred so deep and so hot that I felt feverish.

'So I'll ask you again: any questions, tutor of cards?'

I shook my head. No questions.

332

'A bad business,' the marshal said. 'Nobody's got clean hands here. But my job is to keep the queen safe, Kellen, and if Sophistus could do this to you, well, then it stands to reason that there are other people, and other ways, to do it again. Imagine what might happen if they did it when you were alone with the queen. I can't take that chance, and if you care about her at all, you shouldn't want to either. Now, like I said, even I can't just kill a royal tutor in cold blood or drag your sorry arse out of town. So you're going to pick yourself up, go back to the palace and write your letter of resignation. Then I'd suggest leaving as fast as you can, before everyone figures out it's open season on you.'

As much as I hated Colfax, as much as I wanted to kill him and his damned white binder, he was right: I was a shadowblack. Over the last two years people who cared about me had tried to convince me it didn't mean my soul was forfeit. Turned out they were all wrong. The only thing left to do was to accept it – go back to the palace, grab Reichis and our belongings and leave as fast as I could. No retribution. No vengeance. Just running. Running for the rest of my life and hoping I never had to look into a mirror again for as long as I lived.

'One last thing,' I heard Colfax say as I felt his hand on the back of my head, twisting it around towards the alleyway. At first all I could see were feet clad in sandals, and just above them the hem of a woman's dress. It was red, deep red – for some, the colour of love. For others, the colour of grief.

'No,' I said, willing the image to disappear.

Colfax whispered in my ear, 'I had to, kid. Had to make sure you didn't get distracted on your way out of Darome, that you didn't get any ideas in your head about maybe

333

staying somewhere in the north where someone with a good heart but too much faith in humanity might convince you to come back.' The marshal gently but firmly forced my head up at an odd angle until I could see her fully, and her me. It was Mariadne, and the sight of her standing there, knowing she must have seen what I'd done, drained the last drop of hope from my body.

For a brief moment in my life there had been a woman, a smart, beautiful and blessedly damaged woman who had wanted me, who might even have come to love me one day. Mariadne had seen me lie, cheat, steal and kill a man without hating me. She'd touched the shadowblack around my left eye without running screaming away from me. '*I like it*,' she'd said, as if it were a birthmark or a tattoo. She knew different now. We both did.

Mariadne stayed in the alley looking down on me just long enough for me to witness the revulsion and betrayal on her face. I could see the disgust was so deep it wasn't even for me: she was disgusted with herself. She turned, and I heard the sound of her sandals clacking down the alley as she ran from me.

Colfax let go of my head and patted me gently on the shoulder. 'It's a tough road, kid.'

Sophistus, the White Binder, took control of me once more – just long enough to force my face down into the pool of my own vomit, before he too left.

45

The Alley

I lay there in the dust and dirt of the back alley, my cheek
half buried in my own puke, and listened to the sounds of
Colfax's boots and the binder's sandals as they walked away
from me. An honourable man, a brave man, the kind of man
who could have faced up to the truth of himself and what
he had to do next, would've remained there and waited.
Death would come, one way or another. Whether in the form
of a blow to the head delivered by one of the righteous souls
who would surely come running soon enough to seek retribution on the girl's behalf or a horse cart trampling blindly
through the alley in the dark. Maybe just by waiting for the
ground to slowly swallow me up. The part of me that was
too cowardly to lay down and die pushed me to my hands
and knees. My holsters had come open and most of my
powders had spilled onto the ground. It was a miracle they
hadn't come into contact and set me on fire. Of course, miracle
was the wrong word.

I scooped up what I could and replaced it carefully in the
holsters. By the time I'd gotten to my feet, I heard someone
coughing behind me. *Don't turn around*, I told myself. *Just
wait, and let them do what you haven't got the courage to do*

yourself. But the reflexes built up over two years of living as an outlaw betrayed me. I spun around, pulling a pinch of red and black powders without even meaning to, the spell I was so determined not to cast already on my lips.

'Perhaps you'd like to reconsider,' the tall one said, a crossbow aimed lazily at my chest. The other carried a short-hafted mace. Both wore the long grey coats and broad-brimmed hats of the queen's marshals service. Neither looked the least bit nervous.

'Why don't you come with us?' the shorter one said. He was stocky, with a carefully trimmed black beard that matched his eyes. There was something a little too refined about him – about both of them, in fact.

'Who are you?' I asked, the sound from my mouth so raw and gravelly it bore only the faintest resemblance to my own voice.

'Who do we look like?'

'You look like marshals,' I said.

The short one nodded. 'There you go. I'm Kaeus.' He jabbed a thumb at his partner. 'He's Jax. Happy now?'

'I said you look like marshals, but what I meant was that you dress like them.'

The smiles on the pair of them widened as their posture changed subtly, losing the hunched-shouldered, wide-legged stance of Daroman lawmen, and standing taller, less grounded, and infinitely more arrogant. 'Hello, brethren,' I said.

'You see, Kae'taius?' the tall one said to his colleague. 'Half the stories we've been hearing about Kellen of the House of Ke claim he's the shrewdest outlaw in Jan'Tep history. That he so quickly pierced our disguises suggests the tales are true.'

The shorter one pointed to the pool of puke on the ground

336

next to me. 'And yet, Jax'ered, the other half of the stories insist he is a fool, and his current situation indicates they have the right of it.'

'I'm a paradox all right.' I took in a slow breath and tried to loosen the muscles in my neck and shoulders in preparation for what would come next. Had it been anyone else who'd come to kill me, I probably would've let them. But Jan'Tep? No, I hadn't spent two years facing off against every hextracker and bounty mage in the territories just to get driven down the Grey Passage by this pair. Maybe if I did this just right I could get all three of us killed at the same time.

A bell ringing in the distance caught me by surprise. The sounds of shouts and people scattering were followed by the sight of men and women running down the street from the buildings on either side of the alley.

'Looks like it's begun,' Jax'ered said.

'Time to go, spellslinger,' Kae'taius added. 'She doesn't like to be kept waiting.'

I didn't budge. 'If you expect me to believe the queen of Darome sent a pair of—'

'Who said anything about the queen?' the Jax'ered asked, turning as if he expected me to follow.

'Besides,' Kae'taius said, chortling as he followed his colleague, 'from the sounds of things, I suspect Darome won't have a queen for much longer.'

337

46

Sympathy

The two Jan'Tep agents took me through back alleys and side roads until we reached one of the servants' entrances to the palace. The guards let us through without so much as a nod, which told me they were either on the take or someone had pulled a silk spell on them. Bribing or ensorcelling Daroman palace guards is a good way to either get yourself killed or set off a war, so even before we reached the diplomatic wing of the palace and the outlandishly decorated apartment – furnished to draw attention not only to its sole occupant's yellow-gold tresses, but with lines and shapes that complemented her slender figure – I knew who was responsible for bringing me back here.

'Sha'maat,' I said.

She was there, standing in the middle of the room as if she'd been waiting for me the whole time, the early dawn light from the large stained-glass windows refracting a prism of colours on her floor-length silver dress. 'Dearest brother,' she said with a sigh. 'You smell of . . . unseemliness.'

Even more than during our previous encounters, it struck me how much Shalla had changed – how much we'd *both* changed. Where before she'd covered what I'd always believed to be a decent, if a bit wayward, heart in an armour of petulance and smugness, now all that was wiped away by a presence equal parts commanding and unabashedly sultry. At only fifteen years of age, she was already an unstoppable force among our clan, and soon among the Daroman court as well. Of course, I was beyond caring about such things any more. 'Where's Reichis?' I asked.

'I imagine your pet nekhek is wherever you last left him.'

She ran a finger down her neckline. The sleeves of her dress ended in points at the wrist. The tattooed bands on her forearms gleamed with unnatural light, causing the thin silver of her dress to shimmer in six different colours. She was holding a hairbrush in one hand, as if she'd just finished styling her hair. Usually she wore it down, the long golden curls framing her face and neck. Now it was done up, arrayed in ringlets around her head – just like the queen. Just like the girl at the restaurant.

'When did our father turn you into such a heartless wretch, Shalla?'

She cocked her head. 'Is that how you greet your own sister? Who loves you. Who sent men at substantial expense and personal risk to protect you.'

My sister, I thought, *who says she loves me. Whom I swear I believe sometimes.* 'Your hair. You did that just to taunt me?'

She looked at me as if I'd wounded her terribly. 'How could you . . . I knew the memory of the girl would upset you. Now whenever you see this hairstyle you'll think of me and feel better.'

Her voice was utterly sincere.

'Was it you who did this to me, Sha'maat? Were you working with Colfax this whole time?'

339

She walked over to the mirror and started fiddling with her curls and the brush. 'Don't be silly. Could you really imagine me doing such a thing? And working with that frontier barbarian? No, brother, I discovered the presence of the white binder only a short while ago. I had my men follow you and used a scrying spell to see through their eyes.' She set down the brush on a shelf beneath the mirror. 'What they did to you . . . These people are monsters. I would have killed them all, but Colfax, fool that he is, has too much influence for me to openly challenge him. That's why my men had to wait until the marshal and his wretched old witch doctor had left before they could come to your aid.'

'Then I suppose I'm in your debt,' I said, my voice as cold and ironic as I could make it.

'You're welcome.'

I turned towards the door and prepared myself for whatever resistance her two lackeys would offer. They'd made a mistake waiting outside. At close distance, I'm faster on the draw than most Jan'Tep mages. 'Goodbye, Sha'maat,' I said.

'Oh, stop being so belligerent!' she called out to me before I'd gotten the door open. 'You've made a mess of things and I'm trying to help you clean them up. I'm trying to protect you!'

I felt her hand on my shoulder. I hadn't noticed her bridging the gap between us. When I turned around she surprised me by throwing her arms around me and putting her hand on the back of my head, pulling it towards her shoulder. I surprised myself by letting her.

'Dearest brother,' she said, then she repeated it, patting the back of my head over and over. 'Oh, my dearest brother.' I

340

wanted to pull away but I couldn't. I hated myself for it, for taking any comfort from her, but a man can only be brought so low before something inside him breaks and he'll cling to anyone who'll take him.

'I . . .'

'Shush,' she said, whispering in my ear. 'I know. I know what they did to you. That vile old man and his witch doctor, and the whore too. We'll make them all pay, brother.'

I tried to shake my head, but she was holding me tightly. She's half a head shorter than me and weighs as much as a summer breeze, but still she held me tight. I found myself crying. 'If you knew what they were doing, why didn't you stop them? Or warn me?'

She pulled my head back from her shoulder, and I saw tears in her eyes. I knew she was a liar and a manipulator. Even as a child she could switch those tears on and off for the price of a piece of candy. But part of me always believed her. 'I couldn't,' she said. 'I know it's hard to believe, but there's so much at stake here, more than you can know. I just couldn't.'

I started to say something, but she put a finger on my lips. 'No, brother, you need to listen now. The time for games and manoeuvring is almost past. You must do exactly as I say.' She paused as if she was waiting for me to protest. When I didn't, she continued. 'Events move quickly now. You will go back to your rooms and wait until I summon you to complete the next part of our mis—'

I shook my head. 'Sha'maat, I have to leave. Now. I can't take a chance that—'

'They'll kill you,' she said. 'Your enemies are waiting for you to resign your post so they can kill you.'

'Colfax wants me out of here. He's not going to waste time murdering me.'

'Colfax isn't the only one who has plans for you, brother.'

Anger and bile worked their way up my throat. 'Don't you get it? You stupid, conniving child. That's the whole point. Now that they can do this to me, if I stay here any longer they might use me on the queen. She—'

Sha'maat's voice was as calm and controlled as ever. 'The little queen has set her own course. She has no choice now but to follow where it leads. No, you must go to your rooms. Sit there with your pet and wait until I call for you. I've worked a set of warding spells on your chambers. No one will be able to get to you there, not even the white binder.' She put her palm on my cheek. 'If you love any part of your life, brother, do not leave that room, no matter who summons you.'

I tried to make sense of her veiled warnings and discern beneath them her true motivations. But there was nothing solid to hang on to. Why was it so important for me to stay out of the way? Did she want me to sit quietly while she and her lackeys . . . 'I won't let you kill the queen, Sha'maat. I won't betray her.'

Sha'maat's eyes narrowed and her mouth tightened. 'Why must you always be so naive? I know you're not stupid. Who is this Daroman queen to you? A silly girl with pretensions of grandeur.'

'Seems there's a lot of that going around these days.'

To my surprise, my sister slapped me. I don't think she's ever done that before. 'I am trying to look after you, brother. It's all I've ever tried to do, and yet still, even now, even after the mess you've gotten yourself into, still you treat me as if

342

I'm the child.' She grabbed my hands in hers and squeezed. 'Who is this Daroman queen to you? What can she possibly have promised that would make you so beholden to her?'

If Shalla's little tirade was meant to make me question my choices of late, then it worked. Why should I care about the queen of Darome? Because she'd saved my life? No – all that had done was allow her to put me in even worse situations. Because she'd offered to help me find a cure for the shadow-black? *Only there's no cure for a broken soul.* With that thought, the truth came crashing down on me. Sha'maat was right – the queen's promise of a cure was a bluff she'd played to keep me around.

'The queen isn't the one who can save you from the shadow-black,' Sha'maat said, as if she were reading my thoughts. Who knows? Maybe she was.

I pulled her hands from the side of my face. 'Don't play with me, Sha'maat. Not after—'

She grabbed at my arms. 'I'm not saying I can take away the shadowblack from you, brother. But I can keep you from being controlled by the binders.'

'How?'

'An artefact,' she said. 'It's old and it's expensive, but Father has secured one.'

Like a fool, like a dog who sniffs at food he'll never be allowed to eat, I looked around the room, concentrating on Sha'maat to see if she reacted to the places where I was looking.

'It's not here, brother.'

'Then where?'

She shook her head. 'No. Not yet.'

'Why not? If you have it, why not give it to me?'

'Because if I gave it to you now, you'd do something stupid. Better you stay fearful of what the binder might do to you. Better you do as you've been told and stay in your room until the business is completed. Then, after it's done, I'll come for you and give it to you.'

There was a knock at the door and a voice on the other side called out. 'Carreva, it's time.'

Sha'maat kissed me on the cheek. 'Go with Kae'taius and Jax'ered, brother. They'll see you safely to your rooms. Then you must keep everyone out until it's done.' I started to say something but she stopped me. 'If you can find no other reason to do as I say, then do it for this one: the white binder is here, in the palace.'

The cold fist that grabbed onto my heart felt so real I had to remind myself to breathe.

47

The Word

The two Jan'Tep agents escorted me back to my room and left me at the door.

'Kellen!' The squirrel cat barrelled into me as I entered the room and grabbed my leg in an oddly affectionate gesture.

'You all right, partner?' I asked, unsure how to deal with this uncharacteristic lack of him growling at me and blaming me for everything.

'Bastard marshals! They came in wearing chain mail from head to toe. I nearly wore my claws out trying to get at them.'

'I'm glad you didn't. We'll probably need your claws soon enough.'

'Damned straight. Fill up your holsters and let's go kill that rat bastard Colfax.'

'No.'

He looked up at me quizzically. 'You want to go to the queen with this?'

'No. We're done with the queen. We're done with all of it.'

Reichis's little nose twitched. He ran over to the window and hopped up on the sill. 'Kellen, something's going down in this skinbag hellhole. There are fires and riots in the city. When Colfax's men had me I heard one of his commanders sending most of the marshals out of the palace to try to help the city guard keep the peace.'

'Something bad's going down all right. That's precisely why we're going to stay here and keep the door shut until it's over.'

'What? What about the queen?'

'She'll have to find someone else to protect her.'

Reichis jumped down from the window and ambled back to where I stood. Then he bit me in the calf. Hard.

'What the hells is wrong with you?' I shouted, trying to kick him away.

'Me? You're the one who's running, again. Not twelve hours ago you promised that human runt you'd stay and protect her!'

'Since when do I ever keep my promises?' I asked, my voice thick in my throat.

'What happened, Kellen? What did Colfax do to you?'

'Nothing,' I said.

Reichis bit me again. I felt blood well up on my ankle. I lashed out with my foot, but he jumped aside and sprang back in to scratch a strip off my leg.

'Stop it!' I shouted.

The little bastard reared up on his hind legs. 'That's not how this works, Kellen. We have a deal. We're business partners. We tell each other everything. *Everything*. Now tell me what they did to you or I swear on the fur of every squirrel cat who ever lived, I'm gonna claw the skin off your bones!'

I believed him too. Reichis and me, well, I don't think I'll ever fully understand what our deal is. But he was right. He deserved to know.

'Colfax had a white binder with him,' I said, sitting down

346

heavily on the bed. 'A guy who can take use my shadowblack to control me any way he wants.'

'Did he . . . ? Was he able to . . . ?'

I nodded. 'He had me. Every part of me belonged to him.'

The squirrel cat's own shadowblack markings started to swirl as his outrage grew. 'We're gonna kill him, Kellen. You and me. Right now. We can't have no white binders or whatever you called him running around.'

'And just how am I supposed to kill him, Reichis? He can make me do anything he wants.'

'Did you fight back?'

I slammed my fist uselessly against the soft bedding. 'Of course I fought, you idiot! I fought with everything I had and it didn't make a difference. He didn't even crack a sweat. Can you understand that? I put everything I had into resisting him and he still used me like . . . like . . . ah, hells.'

I let my hands fall into my holsters. If I forced myself to scoop up the biggest handfuls of powder, I could drop them myself and end all this. But Reichis would never let that happen. He'd try to save me and the little fool would set himself on fire.

'What did he make you do, Kellen?'

I shook my head, unable to speak. As hard as it is to have a squirrel cat business partner who usually just snarls at you and steals your stuff, this – him trying to be caring towards me – it was worse. It reminded me that as worthless as my life was, I still had a responsibility, that there was one promise I'd made in my life that I was not going to break. Reichis's mother, Chitra, in her dying moments had told me how things would work between us. '*You must be his caution, as he will be your courage. You will teach him when to flee and*

347

he will teach you when to fight.' This was definitely the time for fleeing, which meant it was my job to get us out of here.

'We're going to wait until whatever damnation has come to the Daroman palace to do its work,' I told him. 'Then you and me are getting the hells out of here.' Once we were out of this city . . . once Reichis was safe . . . then I'd find a way to end myself before I could hurt anyone else.

'Tell me,' he growled. 'What did the binder make you do?'

Ignoring the question wouldn't do any good. Reichis doesn't care about propriety or privacy or even looking ridiculous by sitting there asking the same thing over and over again. Besides, he was right to keep asking, even if he didn't know why. My people have a word for those who do what I nearly did to that girl. I had to make myself say it now. Everything after this moment would be driven by cowardice and self-interest. Speaking the truth might be the only real act of freedom left to me. 'I'm a defiler, Reichis.'

48

The Plea

Either from exhaustion or the lingering effects of the binder's influence, the last threads that held me together finally snapped and I passed out on the bed. My dreams were full of helpless cries for help, of the girl at the restaurant and of the queen herself, begging for someone to save them. Save them from me.

I would wake for snatches at a time, gasping for air, terrified that the binder had forgotten to make me breathe. I would open my eyes and see Reichis sitting there, his face concerned and confused as he watched over me. Then I would lapse back into fevered sleep.

A few hours later though, awareness grabbed at my thoughts and forced me into wakefulness.

'Someone's knocking at the door,' Reichis said.

'What time is it?'

'Late. Nearly eleven.'

Groggy and nauseous, I hauled myself off the bed and walked to the door. 'Nobody's home,' I said.

'The queen wants to see you.' It was Arex.

I felt my heart stop in my chest. Did she already know? The queen of Darome surely had plenty of spies. Had one of them already gotten word to her?

'Open the gods-damned door, Kellen, or I'll kick it in.'

I turned the handle and then stood back and pulled powder. Arex opened it and looked at me with surprise. 'Is something the matter?' he asked. 'You look like hell.'

'I'm fine. No, wait. I'm not fine. I'm sick.'

'Well, let's go see what the queen wants with you, and then I can get you to a physician.'

I shook my head. 'No.'

'No? No . . . what?'

'No, I'm not going to see the queen.'

'Yesterday you were ready to square off with me just to get inside the throne room, and now she asks for you and you decline?'

'I'm an enigma, I guess.'

'What you are is out of your mind, Kellen! You don't refuse the queen! On your death bed, with a dozen Zhuban Elites holding you down, you don't refuse a royal summons.'

'Get out, Arex,' I said.

Arex glanced at the powders in my hands. 'Look, just see her for a minute. Things are tense, Kellen. There've been a dozen fires in the city, most of the nobles and their personal guards haven't returned from the northern border, and half of the rest didn't show up for court today. She needs a friend, Kellen.'

'Then you be a friend to her, Arex. You're related to her, aren't you? Leave me out of it.'

'She asked for you, not me.'

When I didn't reply, he just stood there and looked at me, probably wondering if he should just drag me there. Then he shook his head and said, 'I don't get you, kid. For all that nonsense outlaw spellslinger act of yours, I thought underneath it you . . . Oh to hell with you, card player. I'm done.' He turned and left, and I slammed the door and locked it after him.

'Time to start packing,' I told Reichis. 'As soon as all this is done, we leave.'

'And go where?' he asked.

'Anywhere. We don't owe these people anything. If the Daroman nobility wants to bring down their gods-damned monarchy, what the hells does it have to do with us?'

I heard Reichis chitter something, but I couldn't make out what it was.

'What?' I asked.

He wandered back over to the window and climbed up to the sill. 'Nothing,' he said, staring out at the fires in the distance.

I was interrupted twice more before things went to hells. The first one surprised me most of all. There wasn't even a knock at the door, just a woman's voice. 'Kellen, it's me.'

It was Mariadne. My hand reached for the door but I stopped myself. I remembered the look on her face in the alley. I started to say something and then realised there was no point.

'Kellen, please. Let me in. We need to talk.'

'You'll have to talk to someone else, your ladyship,' I said, the words sounding snide and vile to my ears.

'"*Your ladyship*"?' Her voice was full of confusion and anger. 'Is that who I am to you?'

'I'm sorry, Mariadne,' I said. 'Please, for your own good, just go away.'

'Kellen, let me in.'

I stood there quietly, my head slumped against the door that stood between us.

'Kellen, I need to see you. We need to talk about—'

My fist slammed against the door. 'How can you want to see me? How can you possibly want anything to do with me after what you saw me do? What the hells is wrong with you?'

There was silence on the other side of the door for a moment, and then she said, 'Kellen, I don't understand what I saw. I don't know why you would do what you did. The marshal, Colfax – one of his men made me come. There had to have been a reason. Did they threaten you?'

'I did it,' I said. 'That's what matters, isn't it?'

'I don't know,' she said. She was sobbing now. 'I don't understand what's happening, but I can't believe you would . . . I know that's not who you are. Kellen, I swear I'll listen . . . I'll believe you whatever you tell me, but just open the door and talk to me. Whatever this is between us, I know it's real. I know it's good. I just need to understand . . .'

I felt my hand on the lock of the door, ready to slide it aside. I wanted her then more than I've wanted anything in my entire life. The thought that she might listen, might let me explain, that she might believe me – when you've spent as much time in the desert as I have, you learn not to trust a mirage. 'Go away, Countess Mariadne,' I said. 'There's nothing in this world or the next that's going to make me let you in here with me.'

For a long time I heard her in the hallway. Sometimes she wept, or became angry and pounded on the door. Mostly she just repeated my name, over and over. I stood there through it all, forcing myself to feel a tiny fraction of the suffering I was causing her, as if it made any difference to the world. It was only later, after I finally heard her leave, that the last piece of what had once been my heart broke in half and I started sobbing like a child, because it turns out that even a man with nothing but black in his soul can feel pain.

49

Midnight

I was still standing at the door to my rooms as the clock struck midnight. Part of me wished Mariadne would return and give me another chance to let her in, to talk to her, to confess my every failure and hope that somehow she would accept me nonetheless. The other part, of course, knew that this was never going to happen. So when I heard the tentative knock, so quiet I thought I'd imagined it, I actually stumbled back a step. The second knock was a fraction louder. 'Kellen, let me in.' It was the queen. Her voice was barely a whisper through the thick door.

I reached out and put my hand on the doorknob. I swear I could feel the binder again – as if he was standing on the other side, his hand touching the same brass handle as mine, waiting for me to open the door and give myself to him again. When I closed my eyes I still saw the serving girl at the restaurant, her face full of terror as I . . . 'I'm sorry, Your Majesty,' I said. 'I'm indisposed.' I didn't know if the white binder was in the palace or not. Maybe Sha'maat had said that to give me an excuse to stay in my room, but the fear in my gut overpowered any self-loathing my soul could muster.

'Kellen, I need you to let me in.'

Why she didn't just have one of her marshals use their master key to open the door, or hells, just for effect, knock it down and see exactly how strong Sha'maat's spell was, I couldn't understand. Then I realised it was because the queen must've come alone. I looked at Reichis. The look he gave me back held little sympathy for me. 'No,' I said finally.

'Please, Kellen. You don't understand. I need you.'

Her voice was so plaintive I felt my hand start to turn the knob. But the memory of Colfax's last warning stopped me. *Imagine what they could make you do to her.*

'Go away, Your Majesty. I've resigned.'

'Kellen – please! You don't understand. Several of my guards have left their posts, there's something wrong—'

A terse whisper cut through the door to my room: 'Your Majesty, I need to get you out of here. There are men coming!' It was Arex's voice.

'Please,' the queen cried.

'We've got to go now,' Arex said.

'Kellen!' It sounded as if she was being pulled away, and I hoped that's exactly what was happening. Arex was in a far better position than me to keep her safe. Besides, he'd already proven he could beat me in a fair fight.

For a moment, silence. Then came the sound of heavy boot heels thundering through the hallway. 'Damn it,' Reichis said, his ears perking up.

'What's going on?'

'The nobles – Arex said most of them didn't show up at court today. And fires around the city, with the marshals being pulled from their posts. Kellen, this is a coup.'

I reached for the door and then stopped myself. Chances were, if I got involved, I'd end up dead. Worse, I might get

354

the queen killed in the process. Maybe it was better if I stayed out of it. *She's with Arex*, I told myself. *He'll keep her safe.* Unless of course he was part of the coup.

Reichis was growling at the door. Not chittering, not insulting me, not threatening me. Just growling. It's as if there's only so much of my crap he can handle before the bond between us starts to break. A braver man would've taken that as a sign and opened the door, but I was born a coward the way that some men are born with a club foot or cleft palate. In this life, you play the cards you're dealt.

Then I heard the scream.

The sound couldn't have been that loud, it just couldn't. Stone walls and an oak door? Not to mention the fact that she must've been at least thirty yards away. And yet it was as if the queen was standing right next to me. The fear, the raw, unchecked terror in her voice, was paired with a note of desperation, of need. For someone. For anyone. For me.

It was just a scream, that's all. It only lasted a second.

But it was enough.

Just enough.

For one brief instant there was no coward living inside me. There was no shadowblack around my eye. There was no white binder out there ready to creep inside my arms and my legs and every other part of me to use as he wanted. I couldn't even hear Ferius Parfax with her Argosi nonsense, cajoling me into seeing things a different way.

There was just that scream.

I heard another growl. I assumed it was Reichis, but it couldn't have been him because an instant later I heard him say, 'It's about damn time.'

I turned to look at him. His eyes were dark. His fur had

lost all its colour, becoming pure black. No stripes this time, no shades. There was nothing cute or funny or forgiving about him. He was a killer, waiting for the door to open so he could answer that scream with tooth and claw.

My hand reached for the door, but something inside me, or maybe it was Reichis, said, *No. Not that way. Our way.*

'*Carath Erras,*' I said, powder flying in the air, flames reaching out. The blast blew the heavy door clean off its hinges. Outside, the hallway was empty and silent.

Except for that scream, echoing over and over inside my head.

OUTLAW
OF
SHADOWS

For the reformed outlaw, it always comes down to this: you've got to bury the person you once were. No matter how hard you try to hang on to your dreams, your truths, your very soul . . . if there's one universal law to this business it's that, one way or another, the outlaw always dies in the end.

50

The Palace Coup

A few feet from where I stood, a trail of blood winding across the hallway floor like a snake led to Arex. Two men in Zhubanese leather armour were on him. One held him from behind as the other withdrew a sword from the social secretary's belly, the white fabric billowing out, following the blade, turning crimson with its passage.

I started to pull powder but realised that if by some chance Arex was still alive, I'd end up killing him along with the two assassins. I needed to get a hold of myself. *Think. Use your anger; don't let it use you.*

I slid my right hand into the leather pouch holding my steel throwing cards and sent a pair spinning at the face of the guy holding the sword. Reichis followed, unleashing a growl as he leaped on the assassin, climbing the man's body as if it were a tree until his claws were deep into the man's cheeks and eyes.

The Zhuban warrior stumbled back and his sword slipped from his fingers to clatter on the floor. I reached down and picked it up just as Arex, his face pale from advancing shock, managed to spin around, exposing his other attacker's back to me. Zhuban swords are curved but sharp at the point, so

361

as I thrust the blade into the assassin's back, I held out my arm to make sure he didn't fall back and have his weight push the blade all the way through to Arex. I pulled out the blade and turned to see the other assassin writhing on the floor, his arms flailing as Reichis hopped over them, back and forth, every time stealing more of the flesh from the man's face.

'Eat later,' I said.

Reichis growled and then grunted.

'Kellen, you've got to stop the others,' Arex said, leaning against the wall, his hand barely holding his guts from slipping out of his belly. 'They've got the queen. If they escape with her, it's going to be chaos.'

I supported him as he slowly slid down to the ground. 'Who took her?'

He nodded towards the men we'd killed. 'More of these guys. Zhuban warriors. Some of them are Elites, I think. They're wearing red masks.'

Red masks. The Zhuban wear such things not to hide their faces but to show that they are acting as agents of the universe itself. I wonder if it makes them feel any less guilty when they're slaughtering innocents. 'Where the hell are the guards? Where are the damned marshals?'

Arex coughed up blood. 'Everywhere but here. Something's going on in the city, and then someone tried to blow a hole in the south wall. The ones still here thought it was an attack – they went to stop it, but it must've been a distraction.'

'Where are the queen's personal attendants? Lirius, Ricard and the others.'

'Dead,' he said.

'Where's Colfax then?' I asked, even though I knew that wherever he was, the white binder would be too.

'In the city. The queen gave him a direct order to keep the peace . . . try to prevent loss of life. Kellen, go. You've got to save the queen. If they take her, there won't be a ransom. That's not what the Zhuban do. Ritual assassination is an . . . art form to them.'

I nodded.

'Take this,' I said, passing him my coat. 'I'll send someone for you. In the meantime, just keep pressure against the wound. The bleeding's not that bad.'

He looked at my face and gave a hoarse laugh. 'I should've played cards with you when I had the chance, kid. You're a lousy liar. Just go.'

We left him there to die, alone and in pain, and never knowing whether he had saved his queen. He'd deserved better.

Down two sets of hallways we found more dead Daroman guardsmen and the occasional Zhuban warrior. The score was not looking good for the queen's guards. The cries of the dying reached us from around a corner and Reichis and I raced down the east wing until we saw more blood. The palace was like a ghost town. Other than the occasional terrified servant, crouching in a corner, it was empty but for blood and bodies and the distant sounds of men and women meeting their ends.

How could this have happened so quickly? The timing was perfect – that I understood. The queen had just taken half the court north to the border. Then she'd ended up coming back early and many of them – probably her most loyal noble houses – had remained behind to monitor the border situation. But to line up the others . . . To bribe the guards and distract the marshals . . . It would take years to plan something this effective on such a scale. Had the Zhuban government done this on their own? Or were they working with Daroman nobles to bring down the queen? Or was it my own family, tipping the scales for one side or the other as I hid in my room?

I heard voices and followed them around a corner, tripping over a body on the ground. I recognised it as Cerreck, the retainer who announced visitors in the throne room. He wasn't dead, but he was nearly there, closer even than Arex had been. How many men had it taken to bring down the Daroman throne? How many had stood for the queen? One less than she'd needed, I realised coldly. One less because I'd cowered behind an oak door shielded by Jan'Tep spells as she called out my name.

'The queen,' Cerreck said weakly.

'I know. I'll find her.'

'Zhuban,' he said, trying to get to his feet. 'No gloves . . .'

'I know it's the damned Zhuban, Cerreck. How many?'

'The river. They're headed for the river entrance. In the palace cellars. It's supposed to be guarded at all times. They're not wearing gloves,' he wheezed finally, before slipping back to the floor.

I had no idea what he was talking about, and he couldn't answer my questions. Reichis and I ran along the hall towards the long staircase that led down to the cellars.

When we reached the bottom, I saw the butchered bodies of the guards who had been stationed there. The gate was held open by two long iron rods fitted with hooks at the end, jammed in to keep the heavy iron gate from coming down. The last few guards were fighting off six men in the leather-strapped armour of Zhuban Front Cavalry – the same types of warriors who had attacked us on the way north. Only these men weren't wearing steel caps. Instead, each of their faces was covered by a red mask.

'Carath Erras,' I said, tossing the red and black powders in front of me and sending them screaming into the back of one of the assassins. Fire ripped through him, but also caught the guard who was trying to fend him off. *Hells. They're all too damned close to each other.*

One of the five remaining Zhuban came for me, but Reichis had already scrabbled up a pillar and onto a shelf near the ceiling. He glided down onto the assassin and went straight for the back of his neck. The man brought his arms up to grab at Reichis, so I took one of the dead guard's spears and drove it into the assassin's belly. Then I saw that the last pair of Daroman guards were now dead, and the four remaining Zhuban had hold of the queen on the other side of the iron gate. The two on either side each pulled at the base of one of the iron hooks, and I watched as the gate came hurtling down, slamming into the hard stone floor with a deafening clang. Reichis ran for it, but the spaces between the bars were too small for even him to get through, and the Zhuban jammed their swords into the gaps, very nearly skewering him.

One of the men holding the queen looked at me, his head tilted slightly to the side. Beneath the thin red silk of his mask I could see that he was smiling. I pulled powder and was just about to flick it into the air when he grabbed the queen by her hair and held her out in front of him like some kind of prize fish. She screamed, her hands clutching

365

at the man's arm to keep her hair from being ripped out of her head.

'Let her go,' I said. 'Or I'll send you to whatever hell welcomes child killers.'

The queen kept writhing in his grasp, but the assassin put his other hand around her neck to keep her steady. The powder in my fingers was burning.

'Take the shot, Kellen,' Reichis chittered. 'If they get away with her, she's dead anyway.'

'You don't know that. Maybe we can track them to wherever th—'

'We're never going to find them, Kellen. Take the shot.'

The other assassins were pulling on a rope. A small boat was coming into view through the gate. 'Reichis, I'll kill her if I try.'

The man holding the queen shook her, as if he was daring me.

'Kellen, now!' Reichis shrieked.

The queen screamed again. Then she seemed to find a strange calm and she called to me, 'Kellen, don't let them take me, please. Shoot!'

The Zhuban didn't make a sound, but just smiled and mouthed a word: naghram. Then he began falling backwards, still clutching the queen in front of him.

Frustration tore through me. 'Carath Erras,' I screamed, flicking the powders in the air, the red and the black grains colliding, biting at each other, exploding in their rage as the spell drove their fire outwards, towards my enemy, towards my queen.

The blast passed right over them as they fell backwards into the arms of the Zhuban waiting in the boat. One of them threw something at me – a knife, I think. Reichis must have seen it first because he barrelled into the back of my knees, forcing me to drop down. The tip of the blade parted my hair as it flew by.

After that, the boat slipped away down the underground river, and she was gone.

51

Capture

I got back to my feet and started running, up the stairs and back along the hallways. I shouted for guards, but the only answers I got were the occasional moans and cries of the wounded and dying.

'Kellen!' Reichis said, racing to keep up with me.

'Come on,' I said. We were in one of the outer hallways, small, open-arched windows flicking by us as we ran. Flickering red and orange light caught my eye and I saw that outside those windows, in the city, fires were burning. Two . . . three . . . I couldn't keep track. There must have been at least a dozen, spreading chaos through the city – enough to keep the city guard, Colfax and whatever marshals he'd taken with him busy until this was all over.

'We've got to go,' Reichis said, panting.

'I know,' I said. 'We'll go round the long way and out the west exit.' From there we'd have to go around half the palace to get down to the river and start following it.

Reichis snapped at my calf. 'Damn it, Kellen, stop! There's no way we're going to catch them now.'

'There's no one else even looking for her, Reichis. We've got to follow them before—'

He growled. 'It's over, Kellen. It's over. We're never going to catch that boat. They've probably abandoned it by now and moved onto horses. Whoever else is involved with this is going to kill us if they see us, and whoever isn't is going to think we're a part of it. We're the ones who embarrassed the queen in public. She came back early from the north without her supporters, and people are going to blame us.'

I stopped, nearly falling over as a sudden weariness fused with my lack of breath. 'Reichis, this was my fault!'

'No, it wasn't, you idjit. But people will think it was, and they'll kill us for it. How're we supposed to rescue the queen if we're dead?'

I tried to calm my breathing, but I couldn't seem to slow it down. 'Then we've got to get out of here and get help.'

'Help from who?' Reichis asked. 'Most of the marshals are gone, and half the guards are dead. Nobody here trusts us.'

I thought about the cellar and the gate, the river and the boat, the carnage in the palace and the fires in the streets. 'Someone's been planning this for a long time, Reichis. This wasn't just a band of Zhuban assassins coming out of nowhere.'

'Maybe,' Reichis said, 'but we don't know who, or how many, or why, or how to stop them. And in the meantime, people here are going to content themselves with seeing our heads on the block.'

'So we just let the queen die,' I said. It wasn't a question.

'No. We let ourselves live. That's all that's left, Kellen.'

He was right, I realised. Whatever happened to the queen, I didn't have a way to save her. And no matter how half the nobles felt about her rule, people were going to want blood.

369

There's always a patsy in situations like this. And if I stuck around, well, it was going to be me.

We got to our room and I grabbed my saddlebags. It was a risk to stay around the palace, but the panniers contained the few items of value we had, as well as some of the ingredients for my powders. We'd need both to get out of Darome. We left the room and went back down the hall. The two assassins we'd killed were still there, but Arex's body was gone.

'You think there's a chance someone got him to a healer?' I asked.

Reichis snorted. 'I doubt it. He probably crawled off into one of the rooms to die in private.'

Only a squirrel cat would think of that one. I knelt down and pulled the mask off of one of the dead Zhuban – the one I'd killed. The one Reichis had done in wasn't in any shape to be examined.

'What are you doing?' Reichis chittered.

'His face,' I said.

'What about it?'

It's always hard to tell with a dead man. The skin tends to drain of colour pretty quickly. This one had black hair and his skin still held a hint of orange-brown. 'Do you think he's really Zhuban?'

Reichis stuck his snout in close to the dead man's face. 'He's got Zhubanese blood – that much I can tell.'

'So does a third of Darome.'

Reichis sniffed again. 'Hair could be coloured, I suppose. Of course, lots of Daroman have black hair. Skin might be wind-tanned or it could just be that way from living outdoors. Maybe a farmer?'

'Or a soldier,' I said.

'Sure,' Reichis said. 'Maybe.' Then he got up and started walking away, towards the stairs that led down and out of the palace.

'Where are you going?'

'You've wasted enough time satisfying your curiosity,' he said. 'I'm a squirrel cat, not some pet dog. This is the part where we leave.'

'You don't think it matters that these guys might not be Zhuban at all? Cerreck said they weren't wearing gloves. He was right too. None of these men has gloves on. Remember that Red Elite who attacked us back in the desert before all this started?'

'The one with the . . . mind thing?' Reichis had his paws up and circling inward as if he were trying to strangle a rat.

'The dehbru habat. He said that they could only touch the profane with special gloves.'

'The ones who took the queen . . .'

'No gloves, special or otherwise. There's no way they were real Red Elites or holy assassins or anything of the kind.'

'Fine. They're impostors.' Reichis waved his paws around the room. 'I think we've established that there's a conspiracy. Can we go now?'

'This could be important!'

'What are you going to do? Tell the marshals you've uncovered a vast conspiracy because the assassins aren't wearing gloves? This is your guilt talking, Kellen. It's going to get you killed. Worse, it's going to get me killed. You know what the difference is between the two of us in a fight, Kellen?'

'This again? How about because I pick fights when I have to, and you do it all the time?'

371

'No. The difference is you don't commit. You try to be clever and outwit everyone. Even when someone's trying to put a knife in your belly, you want them to see how smart you are. When a squirrel cat fights, he goes all in. He doesn't look for trouble, but when it comes, he doesn't hesitate. You hesitate, Kellen.'

'What's your point?'

'My point is it's time to choose. Either we get the hells out of here, or we take these skinbags down so hard they never get back up again. The queen's gone, so all that's left is revenge or escape. So what's it going to be?'

'I –'

Reichis sniffed the air. 'Someone's coming.'

I could hear footsteps. People running. 'It's probably just the marshals trying to re-establish order.'

'Unless someone already sent them after us. You know, like in a conspiracy?'

Perfect. 'Come on,' I said, grabbing my saddlebags. We ran into one of the open rooms and I barred the door behind us.

A few seconds later something slammed against the door and I opened my bags and tried to grab a few of the trinkets inside along with my powder ingredients. 'The window,' I said to Reichis.

The squirrel cat raced over and hopped up and out just as the door burst open. Four marshals with crossbows entered the room. 'Don't even try it,' one said as I started for the window. It was fifteen feet away. There was no way I could make it before he shot me.

As I dropped my bags and put my hands up, I saw Reichis starting to creep back in.

'Run, you idiot!' I shouted at him. 'If we're both caught, who the hell is going to get me out?'

I could see the squirrel cat battling his own desire to fight, but reason won out. He leaped from the window and disappeared into the night.

I breathed a sigh of relief. Not because I thought there was any way I could get out of this alive, but because at least I'd saved someone from dying on my account.

'Kellen of the Jan'Tep, royal tutor of cards, you are under arrest for treason against the throne,' one of the marshals said, just before they started beating me.

52

Repentance

They hung me from my wrists in a cell below the palace, every surface as grey as a marshal's coat, and with only the barest light seeping in from the lanterns that hung from hooks in the corridor outside. Sometimes one of the marshals would press one of those lanterns against the skin of my chest or my cheek until I screamed. They'd tell me that Marshal Colfax was coming, and whatever they'd done to me was nothing compared to what the old man had planned. One of them told me he hated to watch any man suffer the way I surely would. He asked if I wanted him to slit my throat. When I said yes, he laughed. I guess I should've seen that coming.

I didn't hold out any hope of escaping this place. Reichis was gone though, and I tried to focus on that. The best friend I'd ever had in this life was free, which meant that the last act I'd ever commit of my own volition had been one of self-sacrifice. That felt like a suitable insult to Colfax and his white binder and all the rest of them.

Unless Reichis screwed it all up and came back for me.

Please, you greedy, egotistical, unsympathetic, treacherous little monster, run as far and as fast as you can. Find yourself a proper business partner who'll help you steal and blackmail and murder your way to riches and happiness. While you're at it, find yourself a mate and make loads of little Reichises. Ancestors know the world needs more squirrel cats.

Lately Reichis had been talking about warm, tropical islands, even though I doubted he'd ever seen one. To his squirrel cat mind, a tropical island was like a softly padded stool in the middle of a giant warm bath. I could just imagine the tubby little bugger, lying on his back in some kind of hammock as servants dropped bits of butter biscuit into his gullet. The thought made me laugh out loud like an idiot. It also reminded me how hungry I was.

They hadn't fed me anything but sips of brackish water those first two days. I guess all those Daroman rules on the treatment of prisoners probably went out the window once the queen got dragged in her nightclothes into the darkness. I hadn't eaten the day before either. It's hard to imagine that you can hurt as much as I did and still be hungry, but even with my soul aching as badly as my body, I was famished. I should've felt ashamed about that.

Somewhere out there was a girl just eleven years old, taken by men with no conscience, and it was my fault. Somewhere out there was another girl, whose name I didn't know but whose body I had tried to defile, and that was my fault too. I thought about Mariadne. I wondered if the conspirators had killed her, or if they had simply captured her and would now use her the way Leonidas had planned. In the span of just a few days I had destroyed the lives of three women, and here in the darkness of my cell the feeling that clung to me hardest was simple hunger. I guess that's why I noticed the smell.

'Who's there?' I croaked. My voice was wrecked. One of the marshals had punched me in the throat.

The sound I heard was unexpected. A young woman's cry. Soft hands stroked the sides of my face, 'Oh, Kellen,' she whispered. 'What have they done to you?'

'Shalla?' I must've looked even worse than I thought if she was calling me Kellen.

I felt something warm press between my lips. It was some kind of meat. I chewed at it desperately, but nearly retched when I tried to swallow.

Her fingers flickered against my chest. '*Anekh amun*,' she intoned.

Warmth spread throughout my body. I felt my throat loosening, and the itching, burning feeling on my face and chest slowly disappeared, along with much of the pain the marshals had inflicted on my arms and back. I imagined I still had the bruises, but even those felt less sore. Sha'maat could have been a powerful healer if she hadn't turned her attentions to other arts. 'Thank you,' I said.

She put more food in my mouth and, after a few bites, water from a canteen that tasted as clear as open sky. After a few minutes I felt her arms around my torso. 'I would do more for you if I could, brother. I would kill each and every one of them.' Her voice was soft and pained, like the yellow-haired girl I remembered. Only she'd stopped being that person ever since she'd come here.

'Did Father send you?' I asked.

I wondered what possible good I might be to him at this point. I certainly wasn't in any position to advance whatever political machinations my family had dreamed up. Then I realised she hadn't answered me.

376

'Shalla? If Father didn't send you, why are you here?'

'I can't stay, brother. He is coming for you. The madman Colfax is on his way.'

'So they keep telling me.'

'He will try to break you, Kellen. You mustn't let him. You must trick him.'

A choked laugh escaped my lips. 'Trick him? I think the time for tricks has passed, don't you?'

'Listen to me, brother: You have to outwit the marshal. You have to outwit them all.' She came closer. 'I have brought you something,' she said carefully, as if she was afraid someone might be listening.

'If you're waiting for me to take it, I'm afraid my hands are otherwise occupied.'

'They've brought your things into this cell. Your saddlebags and your clothes.'

'My holsters?'

'No,' she said. 'Neither those or the silly . . . They kept your throwing cards as well.'

'Then there's nothing here that will help me.'

'They left one other thing in your room, brother. The maid's cards. I've put them in your saddlebags. I doubt they'll even notice. But when the time comes, remember them.'

'The deck I gave Tasia? What the hell am I supposed to do with that? If you were going to take such a risk, why not bring my powders?'

'Please, brother, listen to me: the powders would do you no good. They would never let you near them. It is the cards you must consider. You can still outfox them all.'

'Why?'

I felt her hesitate. 'No. I can go no further. Father will

377

know. He . . . sometimes he uses his scrying cards to watch us . . . to watch me. This you must do on your own.'

The knowledge that she'd disobeyed my father hit me as hard as any marshal's mace. In our entire lives I'd never known my sister to directly flout his commands – not even when he was nothing more than a lord magus and the head of our household. Now that he was mage sovereign of the Jan'Tep territories?

'Shalla, he'll punish you for disobeying him. Whatever promises he's made to you will disappear if he discovers you've gone against his wishes.'

For just a moment, the cell was filled by the sound of a single terrified sob. Then my sister hugged me once more and the next thing I heard was her footsteps as she left me there. But before she reached the door, she stopped. 'The girl – the one you . . . The one from the restaurant. She wasn't what she seemed.'

'Sha'maat, what have you done?'

'I sent one of my agents to her parents. With money. To make sure the girl would stay quiet. They asked if he would also like a turn with her. They asked if it was his birthday too, and did he want to play the same game?'

'I don't understand—'

'It was an act, Kellen. A piece of theatre, paid for by the marshals. All for your benefit. That girl beds men for money in a small room above the restaurant, and her "parents" solicit customers for her.'

I wanted to believe that. I wanted to believe it so badly I could almost forget every lie my sister had ever told me. Almost. 'Shalla, if Father ordered you not to come, then why are you here?'

It was pitch black in that cell, but when she spoke next I swear that I could see a yellow-haired girl of nine or ten, her eyes bright as she held her hand out to me. 'Because you are my brother, Kellen, and because I love you.'

53

The Man in Grey

'You hid,' Marshall Colfax said, pairing his words with a slap
to my face that nearly took my jaw away with it. The rugged
leather coat and broad-brimmed hat he wore were well matched
to the hard grey walls of my cell. The two guards who'd
accompanied him stood placidly a few feet away from us.

'You hid,' he repeated, this time using the back of his
hand. Something metal cut into my cheek on the return
swing and I realised old Marshal Colfax must be married.
Through the pain and nausea I wondered what kind of
woman had chosen to wed a man like him. I imagined her
pretty, though getting on in years. No doubt Colfax kept his
work away from home. Probably liked to garden during the
hot summer evenings, and listen to his wife read old Daroman
romances after supper. For some strange reason, I wanted to
know her name.

'I—'

He jammed his fist into my stomach. 'You hid in your
room as they took our queen.'

Our queen. The irony of that 'our' was clearly lost on him.

The cell went blurry, just for a moment. Then my vision
cleared and I focused on the things from my saddlebags, lying

in a pile on the floor. Not much to show: two shirts, an extra pair of trousers, a few underclothes, a canteen, a couple of shiny items I suspect Reichis had stolen from the palace and not told me about, and the cards Sha'maat had brought back from my room. The one showing on top was the king of arrows. If Tasia was here right now, she'd tell me it represented a strong man with a soft heart. Not the way I'd describe Marshal Colfax.

I wasn't angry with him though. After what he and his slithering old snake, the white binder, had done to me, you'd think I'd be spitting in his face, telling him all the dark and dirty things I planned to do to him if ever I got the chance. You'd think I'd be telling him it was all his fault, that if he hadn't done what he'd done to me I would've been able to protect the queen. But I didn't. There wasn't a trace of bile or resentment left in me.

Colfax had more than enough for the two of us.

In my relatively short life I'd seen men with murder in their eyes dozens of times. I'd seen bloodlust and I'd seen berserker rage. But I'd never seen any man as angry as Marshal Colfax.

'I thought this was supposed to be an interrogation,' I said, trying to get the words out as I alternated between coughing and retching.

He waited for me to stop vomiting before he put his hands around my neck and squeezed. 'You let those men take our queen,' he said. His voice was a furious whisper, but his next words filled my ears and echoed through the emptiness inside me. 'An eleven-year-old girl. And when they . . .' He looked as if he were choking on the words. 'She was in her nightclothes. An eleven-year-old girl dragged away in her nightclothes.'

For a moment it was as if he was trapped in that thought, paralysed by the pain it brought him. His grip on my neck slackened. His face looked older than it had before. After a minute though, his eyes cleared and stared into mine as his hand renewed its grip around my throat. 'But you were safe, weren't you? Hiding in the room she gave you. So tell me, what information could a lily-livered lying card player possibly offer?'

I was already lightheaded from my coughing fit, so the lack of air made me black out for just a second. The marshal squeezed again and I thought I might die, which would have been blissful at that point, except that, being a coward, I feared death even more than life. In that brief moment I remembered what Sha'maat had said: *You must outwit him, brother. You must outwit them all.*

'I can get her back,' I gasped when the marshal eased his grip.

That earned me a laugh. I listened intently. Was it genuine? No, I hadn't said anything all that funny. Was it the laugh that precedes a knife in the belly? Maybe. Probably. But there was something else there too. Confusion. Desperation. A shred of uncertainty that I needed to play as fast as I could, like a borrowed ace. 'They didn't take her far,' I said. 'She's still in the city.'

Colfax grabbed the hair on top of my head and shook me. 'How could you possibly know that, unless you were part of the conspiracy?'

'If I was working with the kidnappers, do you think I would've stayed behind to get my arse handed to me by you?'

The marshal reached behind his back and pulled something from his belt. An instant later, I felt the blade against my neck. 'You might, if taking the queen was just the first part of the plan, or if you stayed back to prevent anyone from following.'

Now it was my turn to laugh. The sound was hoarse, and weak, and filled with the discordant melody of my own self-loathing in a way that made me hope the marshal wasn't listening as closely as I had been. 'Have I done anything so far to make you think I'd be brave enough to stay behind and sacrifice myself so that a couple of Daroman nobles could make their bid for power over the throne?'

Colfax spat. 'No, you're too big a coward. On that score your credentials are well established, tutor of cards.' Then my words finally got through to him and he grabbed my jaw with his hand and yanked up. He was strong for an old man. 'Wait. What do you mean, "Daroman nobles"? The men who took the queen were Zhuban assassins.'

I tried shaking my head, but his grip was too strong, so instead I said, 'The men who took her were dressed like Zhuban assassins, sure, but that was just a ruse so you'd use up all your men to close the roads out of the city. They're working for a cabal of nobles right here in Darome.'

'How could you possibly know that?'

'Because they didn't kill her on sight,' I said.

The marshal tried his best to bore through my eyes with all the hatred and distrust he could muster. But behind it all I could tell he was hooked, if only a little bit, and had been asking himself the same questions.

'Listen,' I said as steadily and earnestly as I could. 'The Zhuban call themselves philosophers, but they're no different from any religious zealots. Their whole country is mad with devotion for their eight-spoked wheel of fate. They're obsessed with two things: destiny and purity. They won't even touch anything they deem contrary to the natural order.' I took a breath. Now we'd see if he'd buy this or not. I had to lead him along, but I wouldn't get him to buy the story if I fed it all to him myself. I needed him to write the last chapter. 'Can you imagine,' I asked, 'anything more contrary to their notion of the natural order than a heathen child queen who claims to embody a two-thousand-year-old spirit?'

The marshal's face was tight, his jaw clenching as he prepared to give me the knife. But then a light came on somewhere in that relentlessly dogged tracker's brain of his. 'They weren't wearing gloves,' he said at last.

I tried not to smile in relief. 'No gloves,' I echoed.

'So they weren't Zhuban . . .'

'If they'd been Zhuban they would have put an arrow in her mouth, slit their own throats and waited to stand upon the great wheel alongside the great astronomers and philosophers of their dead.'

'But then who . . . ?'

'Who else could have arranged all of this?' I asked as if the answer was obvious. 'Who had the ability to get these men into the queen's palace?'

Colfax shook his head. 'It couldn't be any of you Jan'Tep bastards,' he said. 'Too many magical wards in this place, and too many Jan'Tep mages bought and paid for by our royal treasury.'

I nodded just slightly, both because I didn't know for sure if that was true any more and because I didn't want to interrupt his train of thought by reminding him how much he hated me.

'So it was one of us. One of our own noble houses. Someone

384

who could put all the pieces in play, maybe even buy someone in the marshals service.'

He turned for a moment and locked eyes with his two men. Were they part of it? Could his own men be bought? I considered that all of a sudden I might no longer be the least trustworthy man in Darome. Colfax's eyes came back to me, searching for a shred of honesty in the treacherous landscape of my face, paying particular attention to the black swirling marks around my left eye, as if that might betray some secret to him. 'You think you can figure out who took her?' he asked.

I was so relieved that it was all I could do not to let all the stress and fear out of my body in one breath. I had to take a moment to steady my voice. 'No,' I said at last, 'not in a thousand years.'

The sudden rage in his expression was hot enough to burn a hole through leather. His left hand reached out and grabbed my throat again while his right pulled back to line the knife up for a killing blow.

'I don't have to,' I said quickly.

'What? Why?' Colfax demanded.

'Because they'll be looking for me.'

That stopped Colfax in his tracks. It was tempting to make him think about it for a while, but I decided not to press my luck this time. 'Look, why does anyone start a conspiracy in Darome?'

The marshal didn't hesitate. 'To increase their own influence or control.'

I nodded. 'So what do you do when you've got your hands on the queen herself? Kill her and take the throne?'

Colfax shook his head. 'That wouldn't work. It's never worked. The Daroman people would never let a regicide take the throne. The marshals service only works for the lawful ruler, and we'd never stop until we found the ones responsible and killed them. I'd find their friends, card player. And their families. Their lines would die out forever. Besides, if anyone who isn't the lawful ruler tries to even sit on the throne, the complex mystical forces inside it will judge them a tyrant and burn them to a crisp.'

'Right. So how is power ever transferred in Darome?'

'By inheritance. Usually the spirit passes to one of the monarch's children, but if she dies without an heir, the spirit will manifest elsewhere in the royal line. Problem is, nobody knows who's the lucky candidate until they show themselves at court and manage to sit the throne without bursting into flame.'

'So what would be the point of killing her? There'd be no way to guarantee . . .' An ugly thought came to mind. 'What if the queen is forced to abdicate?'

The marshal shook his head. 'That won't work either.'

'Because . . .'

'Because, believe it or not, the esoteric forces inside the throne won't allow it. Best we can tell there's a sort of . . . awareness that guides it. A decree of abdication can't be signed by the queen alone. It has to be endorsed by one of her trusted advisors as well. And the decree has no power unless the advisor is signing of their own will, true and free. The ruler can be forced to sign it – that's always been a necessary balance against royal power. But it won't apply unless a soul she trusts signs it as well. Without that, the new king or queen designated in the writ would just light up like a torch the instant their butt hit the throne. But there are only a handful of people the queen trusts.'

'She trusts you,' I said quietly. 'She trusts Arex.'

'I'd die before I ever did that. And Arex is the same; he'd cut his own hand off rather than betray that girl. There are only a few of us that the queen truly trusts, and not one of us would let her down like that, no matter what the cost.'

I waited for the last card to fall from the top of the deck. It didn't take long.

'You,' he said, the finger of his right hand pointed at me like a dagger. 'She trusts you. Her "tutor of cards". She's barely known you a fortnight, but that girl listens to you. If you countersigned the decree with her, the old wards that hold this place together would accept it. Then it would all be over.'

I let the apparent truth of it sink in. I say 'apparent' because I had no clue if any of this was true. It was just the only card I could think to play.

'You don't have to find them,' he said at last. 'They'll be coming to you, because they know that, although the queen trusts you with her life, you're utterly unworthy of her faith. They'll come for you, and through your weakness and ugliness they'll take the throne from her.'

It was hard not to feel hurt by those words. I had never been loved here by anyone except the queen herself. '*You have a kind face,*' she'd said to me once. It seemed like years ago. No one else would have ever said that about a man with the mark of the shadowblack around his left eye. But the queen trusted me. 'They'll come for me,' I said. *And I won't be here when they do.* I'd use the queen's love and trust one last time to get myself out of this situation and then I'd run again. The only difference was, this time I'd run further and faster. I'd hook up with Reichis outside of town and ride like the

387

wind. It's not that I didn't care about the queen. I did. It was simply that I couldn't beat the people who were out to get her, and there's nothing noble about dying for a noble cause. In this life, you play the cards you're dealt.

As if he could read my mind, Colfax put his hands around my throat again. But he wasn't squeezing. 'Then I guess the smart thing to do is kill you before they can use you, isn't it?'

No, that would be a stupid thing to do, I thought The odds that the conspirators didn't have a backup plan if they couldn't get her to abdicate were slim to none. If nothing else, they could always just set up a different Daroman court somewhere else, and put a new throne in it that wouldn't kill the usurper. I supposed if that were the case then it didn't matter whether Colfax executed me or not. 'Kill me and you won't find out who's behind this until it's too late,' I said.

'You already said you don't know who it is, Kellen, so killing you is the safest bet I've got right now.' He started to squeeze. I wondered if this was what it had felt like for Tasia, hanging in that cell, coming to the precise moment where there's no longer any turning back — no strength left to fight, and no voice to call for help. I thought about that king of arrows again, and all the other cards she'd left face up. Did she play a final hand of Bent Aces Solitaire? Not a good way to spend your last minutes. Maybe she had told her own fortune one last time? I felt oddly guilty that she'd taken the time to teach me the card meanings and I hadn't bothered to look at the ones she'd left. *Oh, hells, I really am thick*, I thought, finally understanding what Tasia had done and why Sha'maat had brought her cards to this cell. My vision began to blur. I had to get the marshal to stop choking me before the whole empire shattered into a thousand pieces.

388

I tried to kick Colfax but I couldn't get any weight behind it. On my second try I got my knee into his side. It wasn't strong enough to knock him away but he did briefly loosen his grip. I spent the tiny sip of air that bought me almost as fast as I took it. 'Cards,' I gasped.

Colfax glanced back at my things on the ground. 'What about them?'

I tried my best to suck in as much air as possible before answering. *Tasia, I sure hope to hell you knew a lot more than anyone gave you credit for.* I nodded towards my saddlebags, and the deck of cards sticking out from the opening. 'Give me those cards and I can tell you who's got the queen.'

He snorted. 'If you were any kind of fortune teller I imagine you'd have known not to come back here.'

I shook my head. 'The maid. Tasia. The one Leonidas tried to have killed. She knew who was behind all of this. She's left me a message in the cards.'

54

The Cards

'Take off the cuffs,' Colfax ordered his men.

As they let me go I fell to my knees and every ache in my body flared to life. The wounds that until now had been muted by my frantic efforts at self-preservation came right to the surface. Everything hurt. My face was swollen, my skin was red and raw, my stomach felt like I was bleeding on the inside. I wished Reichis was here. At the least the little squirrel cat bastard would say something funny. But maybe it was better that he wasn't. He'd despise me right now.

'Here,' Colfax said, handing me the deck of cards. 'You've got five minutes to tell me who has the queen or we put you down right here and now.'

I got my feet under me and took the cards before taking a seat. They felt different somehow. No longer did they represent the sad and hopeless final hours of a woman who planned to kill herself. Now they were a testament to what she'd died for. Tasia had been loyal, but a part of her had desperately wanted to tell me her story, to make me know why she would take her own life. And it was all here, in thirteen cards placed in order, face up on the top of the deck. I laid them out on the table in front of me.

The king of arrows.

The three of blades.

The ace of chariots.

The seven of arrows.

The golden outlaw.

The jack of blades.

The queen of chariots.

The knight of chariots.

The six of blades.

The ace of trebuchets.

The two of chariots.

The silver outlaw.

The ace of arrows.

'She said the face cards aways represent people,' I said, 'and the numbered cards can be people or actions.'

'What about the aces?' Colfax said, pointing at the third card.

'Emotions. The forces behind the actions.'

I picked up the king of arrows. What was it that Martius had said? A good king with a soft heart? 'The last king, Ginevra's father – what was he like?'

'Decent, as sovereigns go,' Colfax said. 'Tried to make peace where he could.'

I placed it back down. 'Three of blades. Blades stand for violence.'

'What about the three?'

'Peace. Did he have to fight for the throne?' I asked.

'No,' Colfax said. 'No brothers or sisters.' Colfax picked up the card. 'But three could mean the Treaty of Three Nations. The king signed a treaty between Darome, Jan'Tep and Zhuban just in time to prevent a war.'

'That explains the ace of chariots,' I said. 'Anger and change. I imagine a lot of the nobles probably didn't like the idea of peace in an empire that's made its fortunes on the back of taking over other countries.'

Colfax nodded. 'The seven of arrows is easy. Ginevra was seven years old when the king declared her the heir of the royal spirit. He used it as an excuse not to declare war or change any treaties. He wanted to wait until Ginevra was ready to rule.' Colfax pointed at the golden outlaw. 'So what does this mean? Never heard of fortune tellers using outlaws. Reckon she left it in there by mistake?'

I couldn't imagine Tasia being careless. 'Maybe it means something from outside the game – someone working behind the scenes.' *Arex*, I thought. It was Arex who made the comment to me about the outlaws on my third day at court. Could he have set this whole thing up, only to be betrayed at the last minute?

I put the golden outlaw aside for a moment.

'The jack of blades. A powerful warrior,' I said. I thought back to what started all of this, and who put Tasia in that cell in the first place. 'Leonidas.'

'Who you killed.'

'It was a duel, and not one I asked for,' I said. 'But leave that for now. The king signs a peace treaty that angers the nobles. They put pressure on him to break the treaty, but then he declares Ginevra as the next sovereign, so they'll have to wait a few years.'

'They'd have to wait a lot longer than that,' Colfax said. 'The queen wouldn't declare war just to please the nobles or fill their coffers.'

So how do they get their war? I thought back to Koresh

and his brutal treatment of the queen. Maybe it wasn't random meanness. Maybe he was pushing her to declare war against Zhuban? Or just waiting for the chance to kill her? Then what? 'Someone, maybe the golden outlaw, picks Leonidas to take over.'

'Leonidas would have declared war against his mother if he'd thought it would be to his political advantage,' Colfax said. 'So he goes after the queen of chariots. But if Ginevra was represented by the seven of arrows when she was a child, wouldn't she be the queen of arrows now?'

'I don't think it's that literal,' I said. 'The queen of chariots could just be any woman with royal blood – someone who could boost Leonidas's status enough to make him a credible candidate to rule.' Then it hit me. 'Mariadne. She's perfect – cousin to the queen, wealthy, well-liked –'

'But this must have been going on for years,' Colfax said. 'And she was married to Arafas.'

I pointed to the next card. 'The knight of chariots. But then look, the six of blades. Six for conspiracy, blades for violence. Leonidas had Arafas killed.' Not hard to do when you command the garrison that covers the northern border. Was that why there was so much fighting now? Had Leonidas provoked the Zhuban to launch ever more aggressive raids? It made the perfect cover if he wanted someone dead: dress his agents up like Zhuban warriors, and blame it on the enemy everyone knows is hungry for Daroman blood. Every time it happened, it would make it easier for the nobles to push for war. He had everything he needed to force Mariadne into marriage.

'But she wouldn't marry him,' Colfax said.

I agreed. 'The next card is the ace of trebuchets. Determination and self-interest. No, Mariadne would never marry him. And the queen won't give in to the calls for war.'

'But Leonidas, and whoever was pulling his strings, were using the military to circumvent her,' Colfax countered.

'Of course. So the queen gets creative. The two of chariots – the lowest number in the deck. She gets Tasia to seduce Leonidas and try to kill him.'

'Putting aside that you've just accused the queen of conspiracy to commit murder,' Colfax said, 'Tasia failed. Why kidnap the queen now instead of continuing with their plan?' The marshal stared at the cards, each in turn, probably trying to decide if I was making all this up or just out of my mind. Finally he picked up the silver outlaw and handed it to me. 'This is you, isn't it?' he said.

I took the card and traced its outline with my finger. Beneath the image of a masked character tricking a crowd of onlookers was its older name. 'The Outlaw of Ruses. The one that foils power. The one who messes things up. Me.' If I hadn't come on the scene and dug into Tasia's conviction, she would have been executed, Leonidas wouldn't have been embarrassed and Mariadne and the queen would've had more time to plan a more permanent solution. But I'd gone and embarrassed the queen, brought the verdict into question. If Leonidas hadn't been such an arrogant arsehole he probably would be halfway to the throne by now. But he was dead, and the queen weakened, and yet someone had decided they could still make the conspiracy work.

'That leaves just the ace of arrows,' Colfax said. 'You said aces were for emotions. So that would make this love, wouldn't—'

I picked up the golden outlaw and flipped it in my hand before he could finish. 'We need to know who this is – the

394

person behind Leonidas, behind everything. It's someone who's been around since the beginning. Someone powerful. But they didn't want the throne – not for themselves. So not a would-be king.' I threw the card back down on the table. 'A kingmaker.'

'A kingmaker who decided to be king after all,' Colfax said.

I nodded. A plot years in the making. A slow, gradual takeover that would restore Darome's martial imperative. The whole thing could have been nearly painless if I hadn't stuck my nose into it. Now, unless the queen abdicated, it was going to be a long and bloody process.

The marshal leaned towards me, showing every crack and crevice of his old face. 'Still plotting, tutor of cards?'

'What are you talking about?' I asked quickly.

He shook his head and smiled. 'You're a good actor, kid. Very convincing. I especially like how you're so careful to make sure I draw my own conclusions. Make it all feel like it's my idea, right?'

'I don't know—'

Colfax stood. 'Sure you do, Kellen. You're clever. Maybe the cleverest man in the whole damned empire. But you know what? I'm clever too.'

'You don't believe me?' I asked, and suddenly my insides were chilled by the possibility that this had all been a game to him – a way to make killing me just a little bit sweeter. I kept rubbing my arms, trying to work some life into them. I'm not the best hand-to-hand fighter. I rely on my powders for these situations. But I was a little bigger than he was, and even though I'd almost certainly get killed either by Colfax or one of his two men, I knew when to drop a three on the table in the faint hope the other guy draws a two.

395

He smiled a little wider and shook his head just a bit. 'Ah, relax, master of cards. I believe every word you said. Of course, by that I mean I don't believe a word out of your mouth, but that it turns out everything you said is true.' He drew an envelope from his coat pocket and handed it to me. 'You missed one of the cards, though.'

The envelope had already been slit open, but the wax seal was still on the back. It depicted an eagle with a bolt of lightning in one claw and a bleeding sword in the other. 'Wait,' I said. 'Isn't this . . .'

Colfax nodded. 'The Daroman Imperial seal. Not the queen's, of course. That one bears an olive branch rather than a sword.' He tapped on the blob of cracked red wax. 'Seal ain't had a lightning bolt on it for over a hundred years. It's from what some might call the good old days.'

Inside the envelope I found a simple handwritten card. It read: *Thought we might finally have that game of cards.*

'You know who sent this?' Colfax asked.

I could've held on to the name or tried to negotiate my release in exchange. But I knew none of that mattered. If the marshal wanted to, he could torture it out of me. My best shot was to give him a reason to trust me, if only a little. 'Martius,' I said. 'It's Count Martius.'

Colfax didn't respond. Instead he looked to the two guards still waiting at the door and then he reached into his pocket. He pulled out a clumsily rolled smoking reed and lit it, using one of the lanterns against the wall. 'Count Adrius Martius. Pays his taxes on time,' he said, accentuating the words with a puff of smoke. 'Sends his levies when called upon. Never participates in any grumbling or complaints against the crown.'

'Just one of Her Majesty's loyal noble subjects,' I said.

The marshal went and leaned against the wall.

I took the opportunity to stand up and test my legs. 'I'm guessing Martius has one hell of a claim to the throne.'

'Three generations back,' the marshal said quietly. 'His grandfather, Gallan, was elder brother to Eredus. But the royal spirit passed to Eredus, not Gallan. Both of them had children. The queen descends from Eredus, and Count Martius from Gallan. No one can predict for sure, but based on historical precedent, there's a reasonable chance that if she died the spirit could pass to him.'

'And the marshals service hasn't kept a very close eye on him because . . .'

Colfax dropped his half-finished cigarette to the floor and stepped on it heavily with his boot. A small self-punishment. 'Because he's always been a model citizen.'

I shook my head, trying to keep my mouth shut. But I failed. 'You dumb hicks,' I said, louder than I had intended. 'A guy has a claim to the throne, denied only by virtue of a so-called "royal spirit" that no one can see or touch, and you don't keep a watch on him because he's a model citizen? Being a model citizen when you have a valid claim to the throne is exactly what you do when you're planning a coup!'

The marshal's eyes flicked to his two guards again, then back to me. 'He might never have tried to make a move if you hadn't come along,' he said. 'Someone who the queen would take on as a trusted advisor, but who would sell her out to save his own skin.'

I had to laugh, just a little. 'Really? You honestly believe I'm the linchpin in his plans? You think if I'd never have come along, he would have spent his entire life as a loyal subject? Don't fool yourself, marshal. This guy's been planning this a long time. You can bet he's got a dozen scenarios ready to achieve his aims. I just happened to be the unlucky chump who triggered this one.'

Colfax took in a deep breath and let it out slowly. 'Reckon you're right,' he said.

'So now what? You want me to use the fact that he needs me to make her abdicate, so that I can what? Run in and rescue her?'

The marshal didn't even bother laughing at that idea. 'No,' he said. 'Even if I did trust you for a second, the odds aren't exactly in your favour.' The old man's face went dark. 'Getting her to abdicate isn't the only way he can control the throne,' he said.

'You mean he might kill her if I'm out of the picture.'

'No,' Colfax said. 'Not kill her. If he did that, we're back to the same spiritual roulette. Maybe Martius would get the spirit, but maybe it would be someone else in the royal line. You're a professional. Does Martius strike you as much of a gambler?'

He strikes me as somebody who's outwitted the entire Daroman court and its legendary marshal service for years. 'So then how does he get control?'

Colfax's expression became grim. 'He could do things to the queen. Torture her. Drug her. Use her to hold the empire hostage. Given time, he could probably even subvert and corrupt her will. She may have the wisdom of her ancestors, but she's still an eleven-year-old girl.'

The cold fury in his words infected my own thoughts, making it hard to focus. *Gettin' angry in a fight ain't no different than holdin' a sword by the wrong end,* Ferius's voice cajoled me. She was right too. I was missing something. Even with the queen under his control, Martius would need agents here at court to make sure whatever orders he forced her to issue were followed. I turned around and looked at the two guards, still standing like slightly bored statues a few feet away.

Colfax caught my look. 'Wait outside with the others, boys,' he said.

The two men hesitated for a moment but then turned, unlocked the door and walked out of the cell.

'Yeah,' the marshal said after they'd left. 'They're dirty.'

I looked back at him. 'Damn,' I said. 'You're pretty screwed, old man.'

Colfax shrugged. 'They won't do anything to me. If someone tries to get you out of here without my say-so, the whole place goes straight into lockdown. They need me to get you out of here.'

'And do what?'

Colfax reached into his long grey leather coat and took out my powder holsters. He handed them to me. 'You're going to go see Count Adrius Martius. You're going to sit down with him and the queen and their writ of abdication. You're going to look into that trusting eleven-year-old's face.' The marshal paused for a second. Then he looked me straight in the eye and said, 'And then you're going to kill her.'

55

The Cage

It took only a moment for shock to transform into so much rage that I nearly threw myself at the marshal. 'Son of a bitch! I thought you were supposed to protect her?'

Colfax had a strange look on his face. Maybe it was just exhaustion, or shame, but it looked a little different. Was it pity? 'I'm supposed to protect the crown,' he said. 'I can't let her be taken this way.'

'Why would they let me even get close to her, if that's a possibility?'

Colfax shrugged. 'A lot of reasons. They probably figure they can buy you. Or that you'll be too soft to do it. Or maybe it's because they know you don't care about the throne.'

I looked at him and shook my head. 'They're right. I won't do it. You send me out of here and the first thing I'm going to do is run.'

Colfax looked down at the crushed cigarette on the floor as if he might pick it up and try to fix it. 'I don't think so, Kellen.' He pointed at the door. 'I'm guessing the two guards behind that door are going to walk you all the way to wherever Martius is holding the queen. Knowing you, I don't doubt that you'll run. But I don't think those men will let you get far.'

'You've really thought this all out, haven't you?' I said, but deep down I knew he hadn't had to. Given the alternatives, why wouldn't I just go ahead and sign the damned writ of abdication as the queen's advisor and take whatever rewards might be forthcoming, rather than almost certainly getting myself killed?

'Yeah,' he said, a little sadly, 'I did.' He walked over to the door and pounded on it three times. 'Bring him in,' he called out.

The door to my cell opened up and two men I hadn't seen before entered. These were dressed the same as the other guards, but seemed a little, well, rougher. They looked at the marshal differently too, showing him a kind of subtle respect that I hadn't seen from the others. These were his men through and through. One was wearing long chain-mail gloves – the kind butchers sometimes use to keep from cutting their own fingers off. The other guard, coming in behind him, wore the same type of gloves, and was holding a cage.

'Reichis!' I called out.

The squirrel cat was throwing himself against the bars of the cage, chittering like a maniac.

'Get me the hells out of here, Kellen!' he said. 'Drop one of these skinbags and I'll take the other.'

'How long's he been like that?' the marshal asked.

'The little fella's been doing this pretty much all day,' said the guard holding the cage.

'What are you doing, Kellen?' Reichis screamed. 'Take that son of a bitch out and get me out of here.'

'I can't,' I said. 'There's no way I can take all of them. Why didn't you run? I told you to run!'

401

Colfax looked at me strangely. 'So it's true? You talk to him? And you can understand what he says?'

'Stick him, Kellen. Just get me out of this cage and I'll take 'em all down!'

'What's he saying?' the marshal asked, leaning closer to the cage but still out of the range of Reichis's claws.

I shrugged. 'He says it's all right to let him out of the cage. He respects your authority and promises to behave himself.'

That got me a brief smile. 'Yeah, listen, I don't know squirrel cat or whatever the hell it is this little monster speaks, but I'm pretty sure something got lost in your translation.'

'You'll be losing your ugly skinbag face in a minute,' Reichis chittered.

The man put the cage down on the room's only small table. They looked to the marshal expectantly. It took me a moment to figure out what this was, what was about to happen, and when I did, everything that had been done to me in that cell paled in the face of what Colfax planned to do next.

'No,' I pleaded. 'You don't have to do this. I'll do what you want.'

The marshal's eyes met mine, a trickle of sadness floating on the surface of an ocean of steel. 'I'm sorry, Kellen, but I know who you are. I know what you are and how you think. I need for you to know that I'm not fooling around here, that I won't hesitate.'

I begged him. 'I said I'd do it. I get that you're serious! Please don't do this!'

'It's too important. I need you to know for sure.' Colfax nodded at the two guards. One opened the top of the cage while the other reached in hard and fast with his metal-clad hands. He grabbed Reichis by the throat and lifted him out of the cage in a merciless grip that stifled any sound that the squirrel cat would have uttered. I saw Reichis's tongue loll from his mouth as he struggled for air. I lunged for the powder in my holsters, but the marshal slammed his fist into my stomach, causing me to double over. He grabbed the back of my hair and hauled me back up, so that I was facing towards the men holding Reichis. 'Do it,' he said.

Without an instant's delay the second guard took the squirrel cat's front paw between his two gloved hands. I heard a crack louder than it had any right to be, as he snapped Reichis's leg.

'You bastard!' I screamed.

The guard took hold of his other front leg and snapped that too.

'Stop! I'll do anything you want! Just stop!'

Reichis's head sagged, unconscious from the shock. The guard took one of his hind legs.

'That's enough,' Colfax said. 'For now.'

The guard immediately dropped Reichis back into the cage and sealed the top. The squirrel cat, usually full of fire and thunder, collapsed like a sack and lay still. I tried to reach for him, but Colfax had his arm around my throat and my arm behind my back.

'You lousy piece of shit,' I screamed. 'I'm going to kill you for this. I'll rip your throat out.'

'Maybe you will,' he acknowledged. 'But first you're going to go with those two traitors out there. They're going to take you to Count Martius, and then you're going to put our queen out of her misery. Because if you don't, I'm going to end your familiar.'

'He's not my familiar. He's my partner.' I don't know why I

403

bothered to say that. It's not like the marshal would have cared about the intricacies of an outlaw's relationship to a squirrel cat, or why I wasn't a powerful enough mage to have a true familiar, or why Reichis had agreed to be my business partner in the first place. But by that point I had tears trickling down my face and I couldn't think of anything clever to say, so I just said what should have been obvious. 'It's never going to work. You know that. They're going to know this might be the plan, and they won't let me near her unless they're absolutely sure they'll be able to control me. It's hopeless.'

Colfax reached down, picked up the mashed remains of his cigarette from the floor, and started smoothing it out. 'I know,' he said. 'But you ever hear that old gambler's adage? If the only card you've got is a three, you throw it down and hope the other guy's holding a two.'

56

The Kingmaker

The men charged with bringing me to Count Martius did their job admirably. I'd counted five marshals following us when we set out from the palace, but between the twists and turns and changing horses and a half-dozen other distractions enacted by whatever other operatives they had helping them, we'd lost them all within the hour.

There was nothing about the townhouse they brought me to that spoke of a vast conspiracy to steal the throne. The plain exterior with its four-column entrance and flat-topped roof was matched by an interior with only modest decorations and simple wooden furnishings. Everything was well made, well maintained, but nothing in the two-storey home stood out. This was especially true of its owners.

Adrius Martius was the same humble-faced, slightly overweight man of middle years and kindly face I'd thought had been helping me over the past few weeks. His wife was much the same as he was: brown-haired with streaks of grey and plain as a wooden bucket. She had a figure that might as easily have belonged to a farmer's wife, but for the lack of calluses on her hands, and the silver silk dress she wore.

'Mister Kellen,' she said warmly, taking one of my hands

in both of hers. 'Welcome, welcome. I have heard so much about you, but always second-hand. I wish I could have met you sooner and in our own home but, well, that wasn't really an option. How have your first weeks been in the royal palace?'

The words were those of someone playing a game with me, but the voice was so genuine I couldn't think of an appropriate response. 'Uneventful, madam,' I said at last, hoping I sounded clever.

'I see, yes. And oh my, are those markings around your eye what I think they are?' she said, pointing to the swirling black lines around my left eye.

I nodded. 'Shadowblack.'

'My, oh my,' she said, putting one hand to her mouth. 'Such an ugly name for something that's really quite beautiful.'

'Would that more people shared your perspective,' I said, and kissed her hand.

She nodded with a small giggle.

'Now then, Darlina, let's not keep the boy standing in the entryway,' Count Martius said, ambling towards us with a goblet in each hand.

'Wine,' he said, taking a small sip from one and offering me the other. 'From our little vineyard in Juven. I've warmed it over the fire and steamed in some caramel root. Care for a drink?'

I looked at the goblets and then back at Martius. 'I think you forgot something,' I said.

He looked down at the goblets. 'Well, that's certainly in keeping with my poor memory, but I can't think what I might have forgotten in the wine.'

'You forgot that you invaded the royal palace, kidnapped the queen, killed innocent people who were trying to protect

406

her and had me brought me here so you can bring down an empire for your own personal gratification. So no, I wouldn't care for a drink.'

Darlina made a face. It wasn't a mean face. More of a cross between hurt and sympathetic. 'Oh now, Master Kellen, I—'

'Now, now, Darlina. The boy's got a right to believe what he believes. It's no hurt against us that he's loyal to the girl.'

He set the goblets down on one of the shelves that lined the entryway. He motioned me into the parlour, reaching for my arm but pulling back when he saw my reaction. I thought about killing him right then, or grabbing his wife and threatening her life. But I knew it wouldn't get me anywhere, so I just followed him in and sat down in a high-backed red velvet chair near the fire.

'You're Jan'Tep, isn't that right?' he asked, easing himself back onto a long couch covered in the same fabric as my armchair.

'Not really, not any more. I'm what you might call "between nations" at the moment.'

Martius shook his head and sighed. 'All too common these days. People don't have cause to be patriotic any more, that's what I always say. Isn't that right, Darlina?'

His wife stood behind the couch and patted his shoulder in agreement. 'So many young folk these days have no sense of belonging.'

Martius went on. 'That's just it. People used to feel like they were part of their country, you know? That they shared something with the people that came before them. Now . . .' He leaned forward and extended a hand towards me. 'But you, I can see the Jan'Tep in you, Mister Kellen, no matter what you might say. I look in your eyes and I see that cleverness there:

407

the quick wit and the keen insight. Spotted it the first day I met you at court.' He shook his head as he leaned back heavily onto the couch. 'Not us Daroman though, eh, Darlina? We're not what you'd call a clever people. Want to hear a good Daroman joke, son?'

I just stared at him.

'Me too. Let me know if you ever hear one!' he laughed.

Darlina gave a little giggle again, and swatted her husband's head gently. 'Oh, he pulls that one out all the time. Thinks it gets funnier in the retelling.'

Martius cocked his head to the side. 'Well, you get my point. We're not a witty people, and we're not a curious people. But you know what we are? We're practical. That's it, in a nutshell. The Daroman people have always been practical.'

I let my hands slide down to my hips as casually as I could, letting them rest on my powder holsters.

'You're curious, right?' he asked. When I didn't answer he continued, 'You're wondering why we brought you here, why we're being nice to you instead of – well, I don't rightly know what people do in these situations. Beating you up and torturing you a bit for fun, I suppose.'

'Oh, Adie, don't even talk about such things,' Darlina said. 'Look at the poor boy. Those horrible marshals have already been at him.'

The count kept his eyes on me. 'Well, it's as I said, Mister Kellen, we're a practical people. And you know what isn't practical? Hurting people for no reason. That's not practical. Taking pleasure in the pain of others. Not practical at all. It's just self-indulgent. And we aren't a self-indulgent people. Colfax is a fool.'

'You mind if I ask an impractical question?' I asked.

Martius nodded to Darlina, who left the room. 'I reckon you wouldn't be Jan'Tep if you didn't,' he said with a soft smile. 'Go ahead, son. Speak your piece.'

I stood up and flipped the covers off my holsters. 'You're a would-be tyrant,' I said casually. 'You kidnapped an eleven-year-old girl in the middle of the night, caused the deaths of who knows how many people, and you're trying to steal the throne. So you're what we in my line of work call a real gods-damned villain. And now here you are, holding all the cards, and you're putting on this ma and pa farmer act for me. That tells me that you're either some kind of sick lunatic who finds all of this entertaining and probably likes pulling the wings off flies, or you're thick as wood and don't know any better. Now up until tonight you've played everything pretty smart, so I guess my question is, just how insane are you?'

Martius's eyes went wide, just for a second. Then he relaxed and shook his head. 'Well, son . . . Mister Kellen, I mean, I have to tell you I'm just a little bit disappointed.'

I started to speak but he cut me off.

'No, no. You've had your turn. I listened to all of it, and now you can listen to me.' He stood up and warmed his hands at the fire. 'I like to keep things polite, but I can tell that doesn't impress you in the least, so let me be plain. You don't need to figure me out. You might be clever back at the palace, but you haven't got the intellect to understand how everything I've been planning for the past ten years fits together. I could stand here all night long and talk about the Daroman civilisation, about its people and where we're going, about a childish superstition regarding a two-thousand-year-old royal spirit that's gotten so out of hand that

409

now they use it to put an infant on the throne and ask her what she thinks we should do about going to war. But I'm not going to bore you with any of that because I know a fella like you doesn't really care about such cold, hard truths, and frankly you wouldn't understand them.'

He stepped back from the fire and put his hands in his pockets. 'So let's keep it real simple now. I've got the girl. In a minute Darlina's going to bring her out and sit her at the table over there in the kitchen. We're going to put a pen in her hand and a writ of abdication in front of her. Then I'm going to hit her, real hard, until she signs the paper. She might want to hold out for a while, sure, but we've been working on her for a couple of days now, and I'm telling you she isn't in any state to put up a fight. Then I'm going to take that pen out of her little hand and I'm going to put it in yours, and you're going to sign that writ.'

'I won't—'

He put up a hand. 'I'm not done yet, son. Then the girl's going to die. I'm sorry about that. I don't take any pleasure in it. But I can't spend the next twenty years of my reign with a bunch of idealistic fools dreaming up ways of restoring her to the throne. Wouldn't be practical.'

'And you're a practical man.'

'Yes, sir, I am a practical man. We'll let you go, of course. I reckon you'll leave town pretty quickly, given everything we know about you – and make no mistake, we know a lot. Now I'm real sorry about your squirrel cat. Can't say I understand it, a man having an animal for a friend or familiar or whatever it is you people call it. But that's not my business. My boys tell me that Marshal Colfax said he's gonna kill him and, well, I honestly don't give a darn about that right now.

410

I'm telling you this because I'm trying to be straight with you here.'

Martius looked up at me and shook his head again. 'All you young people – you want everything to be happy, but when it can't be happy, you want it to be as awful as possible, just so you can feel righteous. Just like Leonidas. You know how much time I invested in that boy? I was this close, Mister Kellen –' he held up his thumb and the tip of his forefinger, nearly pinching them together – '*this* close to making him the king of this country. The countess was isolated and getting desperate. I would've gotten them married, and the nobles in line and the whole country would have risen up and demanded the queen abdicate. We would have had a real ruler on the throne again. We could have shaken the sleep and fat off this country and gone back to doing what we do best.'

'Conquering other countries?'

'Yes. We're an empire, Kellen. Conquering's what we do.' Martius pointed a finger at me and then pulled it back as if he'd realised he was being rude. 'But then you come along, with your little bits of magic and your overblown sense of heroics, and within a week you've got Leonidas in a duel. You know what would happen if I could bring that thick-headed boy back from the dead, Kellen? He'd get right up out of the ground and challenge you to another duel. "This time for sure," he'd reckon. Can't let go of his own sense of self-righteousness. Well, that's not how grown-ups think. You wanted to know why Darlina and I are being nice to you? It's because what we have here is a foregone conclusion. I've been at this for a long time, I've got it all worked out, and I'm not looking to create any more trouble than necessary.

411

My hope is we can do this dirty business – and I know it's dirty business, but, well, that's just what it is – anyway, we do this thing, and then we shake hands and say goodbye like civilised people. Well, I've said my piece now. What do you think?'

I looked into his eyes and saw something that made the muscles in my legs squirm like eels. No evil there, no meanness, no joy, no anger, nothing. He was just an ordinary, practical man doing what he thought made sense. I found it so terrifying I could barely speak. But then I remembered the queen and those screams as they took her away. And I thought about Reichis, lying in a ball in that cage, the bravest creature I'd ever known, with his limbs broken and bleeding. So when I could bring myself to reply, what I said was, 'You want to know what I think? I think that, even if for no other reason than you trying to make me swallow that load of nonsense, I'm going to blow your head off and make your wife cook it in a pot of stew, you lousy piece of dirt.'

As if on cue, a thunderous crash was followed by the front door of the house bursting open.

Two of Martius's men raced into the room, swords in hand. 'Leave it, boys,' the count said. 'We've got guests.'

Marshal Colfax entered, short-hafted Gitabrian fire lance in hand. Another man stood behind him in the darkness of the doorway. He stepped into the light and my heart froze. It was Sophistus, the white binder.

'Sorry, Kellen. I hope you'll understand that I had no choice in this,' the marshal said.

I tried to run, but with the slightest look the binder already had control of me.

Martius shook his head. 'You should've left well alone,

Colfax. But you boys in the marshals service never can do the smart thing, can you? You only ever see two paces in front of you, while the rest of us are thinking a hundred miles ahead.'

Colfax smiled. 'Your accomplices led us right to you, Count Martius. Your boys managed to lose some of mine, but not me.'

'So now what? You here to arrest me?' Martius said.

The marshal laughed. 'Arrest you? No, Count Martius, you've got too many friends at court for that.'

'So you're a murderer now.'

'Me? No, sir – the marshals service takes the law very seriously. But Kellen over there, well, he's a bit of a wild card, isn't he?'

Martius shrugged. 'Do what you came to do, marshal. I'm not running, and I'm not begging. Show me your hand.'

Colfax nodded to Sophistus, who smiled. He was all the way inside me now. 'Do it,' Colfax said.

I felt my hands flipping open my powder holsters. I looked briefly at Count Adrius Martius, and then my hands moved and my mouth spoke the incantation. '*Carath.*'

The blast was precise, and the twin fires struck their target with the all the fury of seven hells coming for their next occupant. A second later, Marshal Colfax fell to the floor.

57

The Queenslayer

Count Adrius Martius made no boasts over his victory, gave no eulogies for his defeated adversary. He just picked up his glass and took a sip of wine.

I wondered how and when he'd turned Sophistus to his cause. I doubted I'd ever learn.

Darlina came into the room. 'Time's up now, boys,' I heard her say. Out of the corner of my eye I could see her pulling the queen along by her hair. 'I think Her Majesty's ready to do the right thing.'

Martius nodded twice. 'Right, right you are. Here we are still chatting when there's important work to be done. Let's bring him into the kitchen, Sophistus.'

Sophistus started towards the kitchen when the marshal grabbed at the hem of his robe. 'Traitor,' he said, choking on his own blood.

The binder kicked Colfax's hand aside and forced me to come over to where he lay dying. I felt my hands reach down and wrap around the marshal's neck. I wasn't squeezing yet, just holding his life in my hands while Sophistus looked down on us both. 'It's okay, kid,' the marshal croaked. 'I know you can't help yourself.'

Sophistus reached inside me, and my hands started squeezing ever so slowly.

'The girl from the restaurant,' Colfax wheezed. 'Paid her. Just needed to get you away from the quee—'

I felt the binder push my hands to squeeze even harder, and, for just an instant, I was grateful to him. If I were free, I would have needed to put the queen's life ahead of my need to kill Colfax for what he'd done to me. If I were free, I would have had to let him have his last, half-hearted attempt at redemption. Marshal Colfax had broken me in a way that no one – not even my father – had been able to do. He had taken every story I'd heard, every fear I had about the shadow-black, and made them real. My hands squeezed so tightly around his throat that I could feel the muscles spasm. In a moment, he was gone.

'Oh, Sophie?' Darlina's voice chimed in. 'Have Mister Kellen bring old Colfax into the kitchen. I should get started on him too.'

I think I blacked out for a moment, because the next thing I knew I was in the kitchen, sitting at a round wooden table. The queen was across from me, with Martius and his wife on either side. The body of Marshal Colfax was laid out on the floor next to us. The binder stood off to one side, still keeping his eyes on me. Again I felt that lack of control that was so complete I found myself terrified that Sophistus might forget to make me breathe.

'Now, little lady,' Martius began, 'it's time for you to sign the writ so we can get this foolishness over with.'

The queen's eyes were full of tears, her face covered in cuts and bruises that I saw extended down beneath the nightshirt they had put on her. I felt a black, bloody rage

415

well up inside me, but I couldn't do anything about it. Darlina reached over and put a pen in the queen's hand and gently closed her fingers around it. 'Now I'll have no trouble from you, little miss. Adie has a soft heart but I'll take my sewing scissors and I'll cut pieces off you until you do the right thing and sign.'

The queen looked at me for a second. I couldn't even move my eyes to make any kind of expression of sympathy, and I realised I must look like I didn't care at all. She just smiled at me sadly and signed the paper. I wanted to scream at her, to give some kind of voice to the rage in my heart before it burst through my chest. Nothing came. Ginevra, who might have been a decent queen for her people had she not placed her trust in an outlaw shadowblack, signed away her throne, and with it her life.

'Well now,' Martius said, 'that was very nicely done, little miss. Very nicely done indeed.' He turned to Darlina. 'Dear, you've got such a way with children. Makes me wish we'd had our own when we were still young enough.' He turned to look at the queen for a moment. 'I almost wonder if . . . but, well, no, that just wouldn't be practical.'

'Oh, Adie,' Darlina said, patting his shoulder. 'You're such a soft heart. Now don't make me get all weepy. I need to work on old Colfax.'

She pulled down a box from one of the shelves and removed a long needle from it, the kind used for sewing leather. She held the needle between her lips as she sat down cross-legged on the floor, pulling Colfax's head onto her lap. 'Adie? I'm such a goose and forgot the thread. Be a dear and get it for me? The red one, please.'

Martius rose, pulled out a bobbin of red thread from the

box and handed it to her. 'Loves sewing, that woman,' he said as he sat down again. 'When I told her we had to hole up here, she tried to bring along half her sewing boxes.'

'Oh, don't exaggerate,' his wife chided. 'Besides, it's a good thing I thought to bring them, isn't it? How else would we go about taking care of old Colfax?' She threaded the needle and then pressed the point into the top of Colfax's right eyelid. She pulled it through, a little 'thwip' sound filling the air, and then pushed it through the bottom lid.

'Ugh,' Martius said. 'Don't think I want to watch once she gets to the ears.'

Darlina shook her head and kept running the needle between the dead marshal's eyelids. 'Spoken like a man who's never had to dress a turkey in his life.'

The queen gave a little sob and I realised what this senseless act must be doing to her. 'There, there, little miss,' Martius said. 'It's a bad business, I know, but Colfax is dead. He can't feel a thing.'

'Are you doing this for my benefit, Count Martius? Or simply for your own amusement?' the queen asked. Her voice was small, thin, but unwavering. It was the same voice I'd heard her use when the nobles in the court or her generals or anyone tried to get the best of her.

'Neither,' Martius said. 'It's those darned marshals of his. Even once you abdicate, some of them are likely to try to be heroes. Stupid really. Won't do anyone any good and, well, it'll be illegal once the proper ruler takes the throne.'

'You're desecrating him,' the queen said.

'Yes, little miss, we're desecrating him. Those marshals are just as superstitious as everyone else these days.' Martius turned to me. 'You see, Kellen, there's an ancient ritual we Daroman used to perform on traitors. You sew the eyes shut so the dead can't see. You sew their mouths shut so they can't speak. And you cut their ears off so they can't hear. Oh, that reminds me,' Martius said, turning to his wife, 'don't forget to cut his fingers off and put them in his mouth before you sew it shut.' He turned back to me. 'That's so their deeds in life will be forgotten. Foolish, isn't it? But I figure if it helps keep some young marshal from doing something unwise that'll just get him killed, well, it's worth it, now, isn't it?' The count picked up the writ and looked at it. 'Lovely handwriting, little miss. My compliments to whichever of your tutors taught you penmanship. Was it Koresh? Man always did have a fine hand for calligraphy.'

'This is meaningless, you know,' the queen said. 'I'll sit here all night and sign as many of those as you want me to, Count Martius, but none of it matters unless one of my trusted advisors signs it too. You'll never sit on the throne.'

Martius looked at her for a moment, amazed at her apparent calm, and then shook his head and said, 'But what do you suppose we have our friend Mister Kellen here for? And don't go trying to tell me he isn't one of your trusted advisors, little miss, because we all know you've got a soft spot for this one. Whole court knows it.'

The queen looked from Martius's eyes to mine, and then back again. 'It's true,' she said. 'He's my tutor of cards. He's my spellslinger. And yes, he is absolutely my trusted advisor. That's why he will never sign this document.'

Martius shook his head and sighed. 'Oh, little miss. This is why you don't put children on the throne. Mister Kellen here is very much going to sign the writ. Our friend Sophie here has him bound in ways you and I can barely imagine.

And if you're thinking that it won't count because it's under duress, well, that would be true of any other kind of spell, I suppose. But this here's different. Sophistus isn't forcing Mister Kellen to sign it. No, he's binding the evil in the boy's soul to make him sign it. Kellen's got all the free will in the world right now. It's the shadowblack inside him that's doing the dirty deed, no different than if Kellen himself had sold you out. We spent a good deal of time and no small expense checking this out, and we're assured that this'll get around the so-called royal spirit and all the magical nonsense in the palace and the throne.'

Darlina gently took the pen from the queen's hand and placed it in mine. I dropped it. 'Sophie, get your act together here,' she said, her gentle tone softening the words.

The binder nodded. 'It takes more concentration for finer muscle movements.'

Darlina put it back in my hand and this time my fingers wrapped around it.

'Now, will you be able to get a good signature out of the boy?' Martius asked. 'I don't want my first royal writ to be all smudged. The historians would be carping about it for ages.'

Sophistus nodded again, and I felt my arm start to move, ever so slowly.

'Kellen,' the queen said softly to me.

I wanted to yell or scream, *You stupid girl!* Hurt as she already was, I wanted to shout at her, *This was your plan? This? A child's fantasy that . . . that what? That I can break free from something I can't even understand?* Everything was going to go to seven hells, and all because this foolish little girl had thought I had a kind face and somehow that could make everything okay.

'Kellen,' she said, so softly I thought for a moment it was just inside my head. But I could see her across from me and see her mouth moving. 'What makes a person evil?'

'Get on with it, Sophistus,' I heard the count saying. He sounded very far away for some reason.

'In a moment,' the binder answered back. I felt myself starting to laugh and realised it was him. 'This is amusing.'

The queen ignored him. 'Kellen, how could you be born evil? How can a thing be evil without the freedom to make that choice?'

Move, I told myself. *Just move.* I tried. I tried as hard as I could just to move, to twitch a finger or open my mouth or anything that would feel like I was me, that I was in control; that I was a person, not an instrument for someone else to play. I tried to think of a spell. But my magic was weak. It had always been so weak. Just like everything else about me. And even if I were a better mage, what spell can you cast without your own will?

'Kellen, you know it's true, deep down. Under all that hatred and loathing you feel, under all that fear, you know you're not evil.'

Right. Because of my kind face, I thought.

My right arm was now perpendicular to the line on the writ where my signature would appear below the queen's.

'Kellen, I know you don't believe that you're a good man. That's okay. Maybe you don't have to be good on the inside. Maybe I can be good for you.'

Stupid, I thought. The words of a child overwhelming whatever wisdom was supposed to come along with being the two-thousand-year-old spirit of her royal line. How could one person be good for another? The shadowblack was inside

420

me – a pure, toxic evil. So what if I didn't feel evil? Does anyone? Doesn't the murderer believe at some level that he's righteous? Doesn't the defiler think he deserves what he takes?

'For goodness sake, Sophie, I need to get the supper on,' Darlina said.

'A moment . . .' the binder said.

I could see him in my field of vision too. Something was different. The muscles in his face were clenched, and he was struggling. Then my hand started moving and I made the first letter of my name. It sat there like an indictment as the pen continued to move.

'Kellen, maybe there is something inside you that you can't change. Perhaps the shadowblack truly is evil. But maybe it takes more than that. Maybe evil is only evil when it's what we can't change combined with what we choose not to.'

Maybe it's what we can't change combined with what we choose not to. I thought about the things I'd done in my life. I thought about Reichis and how many times he'd kept me from running. I was a coward, but his courage had sometimes been enough to make me stand and fight. I was weak and foolish, but Ferius's wisdom had sometimes been enough to make me clever. I was a liar by instinct, but Nephenia's fearless honesty had taught me to be truthful, sometimes even to myself. Maybe that's how it was with the queen. I was broken inside, but what if I didn't need to be good? What if I could just . . . *do* good? Could I still be a coward and do the brave thing? Could I still be evil and do the *right* thing? Wouldn't that be one hell of a spell?

My hand slowed down. It was barely moving.

'Sophistus, don't make me come over there and reprimand you,' Martius said.

421

The binder was sweating now, and, I realised, so was I. What was happening here? Could it really be this simple? Was the cure for evil nothing more than . . . what? Believing you could be good? No. It wasn't that. It was something else. Ever since I'd run from my people, I'd been fighting to be free, to make my own decisions, to not let anyone control me. I'd always believed that if I ever committed myself to anyone or anything, if I ever served someone else, I'd be a slave. So I'd become an outlaw. A slave to nothing, to solitude, to myself.

I felt the binder's invisible hands clench around my soul. Funny thing that: until I met him, I'd never really believed I had a soul. Now he was putting everything into binding it and that made it real to me.

In that instant I gave whatever soul I had left to the queen – not forever, because having a soul isn't the same as living in a prison, but for now. For right now. *I can be good for you*, I swore silently.

I heard a voice start to say something. It sounded like my name.

'Sophie,' Martius said, 'why's he talking?'

'I—'

Then I heard the voice again, stronger this time, and realised it was coming from me.

'My name is Kellen Argos, you withered old bastard. I'm the Path of Endless Stars. The queen's spellslinger. And my shadowblack soul may be rotten to the core, but I'm still more than good enough to kick your arse.' I saw Sophistus's expression change as he felt the last part of me slip from his grasp. Yet there still must have been some small connection, because I could tell he knew my next words even before they passed my lips. 'Carath Erras.'

422

The explosion took away my hearing for a few seconds. I felt myself choking, but not on smoke. I wasn't breathing. At first I couldn't remember how – couldn't command the muscles between my ribs to fill my lungs with air. Then, all in a rush, I was breathing again, so much and so fast that I became lightheaded. When I calmed down enough to make sense of the world again, I saw that I was on my feet with my hands out in front of me. The white binder was doubled over and folding to the floor, a small, round blast mark on the wall behind him. My fingertips stung from the sloppily fired spell, but I revelled in the pain. I was myself again.

No, I thought, my chest releasing its tightness, knowing I was now bound to this strange little girl for as long as she needed me. *I'm better.*

58

The Reckoning

The sound of the blast brought Martius's other men into the room, but freed from the white binder I blasted them out before they could get through the door. Three bodies now littered the floor, the life draining out of them. Count Adrius Martius, the would-be ruler of the Daroman empire, gazed down upon the death of his servants and his dreams with an equanimity that only a truly practical sort of madman could muster. 'Well,' he said, leaning his elbows on the kitchen table, 'that's that, I suppose.'

I let my hands drift back to the holsters at my sides.

'You won't need those,' he said. 'There's no one else here but us and the boys. Had to be that way. Couldn't take a chance on anyone getting greedy and talking.'

'So that's it? I take out one old monk and a few thugs, and your whole conspiracy falls apart?'

Martius gave a weary little smile. 'You ever plan a palace coup, son?'

'Can't say I have.'

'Well, first lesson is, no matter how well you plan it, no matter how careful you are, you go into it knowing if it fails you're done for. That's just how it is.'

424

'You don't seem scared,' I said.

He shrugged. 'Wouldn't make a difference. Fear is just a lot of trouble that won't change the outcome one bit.'

'A careful, practical man like you? You expect me to believe you didn't make any contingency plans?'

He gave a laugh. 'Contingency plans? Kellen, what do you think this was? Leonidas was supposed to take the throne, not me. But you're right, I suppose. I've done other things. There are other plans still in motion. But nothing I can change and nothing I'll live to see. Come here, darling,' he said to his wife. She walked past the queen and knelt down to kiss Martius on the cheek and give him a rough hug.

I pulled my hands out, pinching just enough powder to take them both out, flexing my fingers to make sure I had the dexterity to aim precisely and not let anything hit the queen. She rose up and put her small hand on my arm. 'No,' she said.

I looked down at her. 'You can't mean it.'

She shook her head. 'You killed those others because you had to. There was no other way. But I don't want you to put any stains on your soul for me. I need you to be good for me.'

I thought about ignoring her and just doing what needed to be done, but I was afraid of what it would do to her, to her faith in me.

'There're plenty of knives in the drawer, little miss, if you want to do the deed yourself,' Count Martius said.

The queen looked over at the man who had engineered so much misery in such a short time. I couldn't imagine the anger inside her right then, but her hand felt hot against my skin.

425

'No, thank you for your courtesy, Count Martius. But the first thing a queen learns is the cost of every royal act upon her soul. Feeding my desire for revenge would not be –' she gave a weary little smile – 'practical.'

Martius didn't respond, didn't nod, didn't show any sign that he understood.

'You won't be troubled by us any more,' Darlina said, rising to her feet. 'I'll cook something up that'll send us to the long sleep. No sense waiting around for the marshals service or our own allies to do us in, once they figure out we failed.'

I thought about that, and about what Martius had said about other plans being in motion. I looked down at Colfax's body. 'Give me one of those knives,' I said to Darlina.

We left them there and walked out of the kitchen, past the parlour and into the entrance hall. I took a cloak from a hook on the wall and used it to cover the queen against the cold. I wasn't sure where we were, or how to make our way back to the palace, but there were horses outside and all I needed right now was to get away from that place as fast as possible.

'Kellen,' the queen said softly as I bent down and wrapped the cloak around her shoulders.

'Yes, Your Majesty?'

'I've been very brave,' she said.

I nodded. 'Yes, Your Majesty, you have.'

She took a very small breath and let it out again. 'Is it all right if I'm scared for a while? I think . . . Is it all right if I'm not brave, just for now?'

I picked her up in my arms and pushed the front door open with my foot.

426

'It's okay,' I said softly. 'I'll be brave for both of us, just for a little while.'

'I knew you would save me,' she said in my ear.

Looking down at her small body, the bruises and cuts bearing mute testimony to a hundred violations, seeing the tears of relief and something a little like love in her eyes, and worst of all feeling the tight, sudden clench of her arms around my neck as she held on for warmth and reassurance, I hated myself for the myriad ways I'd failed her. I had betrayed her once at the palace when they came for her, a second time when I'd used her kidnapping as a way to escape punishment for my failure. And even now I was betraying her, by letting her think I'd saved her when, in fact, she had saved me.

As we stepped out into the cold night air, I reminded myself that I was born a coward, the way that other men are born with a club foot or cleft palate. In this life, you play the hand you're dealt.

But if I had to, for her, I would be brave for just a little while longer.

59

The Broken City

It took us several hours to find our way back to the palace even on the sure-footed horse we rode. I still wasn't familiar with the capital city, and the queen, her body resting back against my chest, fell in and out of a kind of fugue state as we travelled.

Two-thousand-year-old soul or not, her mind and body had suffered more than anyone should. She'd held up a long time under whatever tortures Martius and Darlina had devised for her in their cold, practical hearts. But eventually we all pay the barman for what we drink, even when all he serves us is pain and sorrow.

What slowed us down the most though was steering around the flames and chaos that filled the streets. Buildings were on fire in several districts we rode through. In others, looters were taking apart the very bricks and using them to enact further destruction.

Martius had been right about one thing: the Daroman people weren't nearly as strong as they needed to be to keep an old and decaying culture alive. How many confederates had aided in his plans? It would take years to track them all down. I shuddered to think what vengeance the marshals service would mete out once they regained control. Part of me wanted to help them do it.

'We're almost there,' the queen said softly, opening her eyes and looking straight up at the night sky as if she could navigate our position from the stars.

'Almost home,' I said.

She gave a sad little laugh. '*Home.*' Then she looked at me and said, 'I thought I heard . . . Did you kill a man back there?'

I nodded. One of the looters had come for us. Most were smart enough to stay out of the way of a warhorse, and the queen in my arms just looked like any little girl. Sometimes one would throw a brick at me as we rode past, hoping to knock me from the horse, but few men had the aim or strength of arm to make that work. This one though had found himself a good long spear and seemed to know how to use it. I had blasted him from existence without even slowing the horse. I'd had to stop after that as my black powder had run low. I didn't know how many more times I could do the spell. My body was bone-tired, and my fingers had no feeling left. But if I did need the spell, I couldn't rely on old Erras any more. So I'd stopped off in an alleyway and done some dark business with the bloody souvenir I'd brought with us from Martius's hideout. I hoped the queen understood why I was doing such a foul thing. In any case, she made no comment about it.

'I appreciate your protection, Kellen,' she said as we rode, 'but once this is over I would ask you not to kill my subjects if you can at all avoid it.'

I smiled. 'I'll try to limit the number of murders I commit.'

She nodded and her eyes flittered shut once again. 'That's

429

good.' Her hand squeezed my arm. 'You're not an outlaw any more, you know.'

An hour later we reached the palace gates and I saw what awaited us, and realised I was going to have to break my promise sooner than I'd expected.

60

The Price of Promises

Forty men stood between us and the palace entrance. Forty Daroman soldiers who had no good reason to be outside the gates with three dead guards at their feet.

If I'd been smart I would've put the queen in the hands of a marshal as quickly as I could find one after we'd left Martius's hideout. But I hadn't. I was tired, and angry, and I'd been beaten half to death by the damned marshals service. I had wanted to bring the queen in myself, sneak her inside the palace and then jam my thumb in the face of the first marshal I found and told him to fetch me some coffee and my damned squirrel cat. It would've been a good moment. But in this world, things don't work that way. In this world, you come through hell only to find forty soldiers with their shiny steel helmets standing between you and freedom. Forty soldiers I'd met before, when they served under Leonidas.

'Get off the horse,' one of them commanded. He was the one I'd met back in Sarrix. Sergeant Tarius.

I knew we wouldn't get ten feet before they caught us, so I dismounted.

'She comes down too,' he said, pointing to the queen.

'Who?' I asked.

'You know who. Get her down or I will.'

'Say her name,' I said.

The sergeant took a step closer. I flipped open the flaps of my holsters and dug my hands inside. His men readied their weapons. Tarius looked at me, weighed what he saw in my eyes. 'You can't take us all,' he said evenly.

'I surely can,' I said. 'I've got enough powder in my holsters to send every one of you on a short ride to the seven hells.' I pulled my hands out, each one filled with powder, their endless hatred for each other even now making them burn in my palms. 'I just have to be willing to make the journey with you.'

'Kellen, don't . . .' the queen said.

'She'll die too, spellslinger,' the soldier said. 'Did you think of that?'

'Say her name,' I repeated.

'Ginevra,' a voice said, softly. Beautifully. Painfully. 'Ruler of Darome, daughter of a line of great kings and queens. My beloved cousin.'

The soldiers parted as Mariadne walked between them.

'Cousin, will you not greet me?' she asked.

The queen dismounted from the horse. 'Countess Mariadne,' she said, curtsying. 'Beloved cousin.'

Mariadne stepped towards me, with plenty of sorrow in her eyes, but no fear. 'It's over, Kellen. The queen comes with me now.'

I shook my head slowly, never taking my gaze from the countess.

She smiled. 'So fierce. Just like you were when you fought for me. Was it only a few days ago? Hard to believe, isn't it?'

432

'Perhaps it was just a dream, your ladyship. I've never been known for my heroics.'

She came closer and placed her hands on mine. 'Unfortunately that's not true, Kellen.' Ever so gently, she turned my wrists. I let the powders fall to the ground, far enough apart to keep them inert. 'Good,' she whispered. 'That's good. We can make this work, you and I.'

'Really?' I said. 'How exactly?'

Mariadne put her hands on the sides of my face, a gesture uncomfortably reminiscent of my sister's. 'I didn't betray the queen, Kellen. I had no knowledge of Martius's plans. I never knew he planned on using me to take the throne.'

'I know,' I said. As gently as I could, I forced her hands away. 'But then Leonidas died.'

She nodded. 'He died. You killed him. To save me.' She leaned in and kissed my neck before whispering in my ear, 'And I love you for it.'

Again I pushed her away.

She sighed. 'It's your fault, you know.'

'It almost always is,' I agreed. 'But perhaps you can tell me how I'm to blame for this particular act of treason.'

My jibe had no discernible effect on her. 'After I saw you in the alley with the serving girl I didn't know what to do. I was confused, angry. Hurt. I sought out Martius in the palace, since he'd always seemed to be friendly towards you. I hoped he could restore my faith somehow.'

'I guess that's one thing we'll always have in common, your ladyship; we're both terrible judges of character.'

'Martius didn't speak ill of you, you know. He said that Colfax had found a way to control you, and that you'd had no choice in the matter.'

433

'But he gave you a choice,' I said.

Her jaw set, as though this was the real conversation she'd been building up to. 'Yes, he did. He told me what he'd planned, and more importantly, he told me what would happen to the country if I didn't take the throne.'

She turned and opened her arms to the palace. 'Look at the mighty fortress of the Daroman empire, Kellen. Look how tall it stands, how fierce its armies, how unassailable its traditions. And yet here we are, with a queen rendered helpless by a mere forty soldiers. The ruler of the empire without her fortress, without her armies. All that's left is tradition.'

'You don't think much of tradition, I suppose,' I said.

She laughed. 'Tradition? No, I suppose I don't. Tradition didn't help me when my husband died. It didn't help me when Leonidas was ready to force me into a marriage that would've been an endless series of rapes followed by a swift death the first time I defied him.'

'And now?'

Mariadne turned back to me. 'She can't hold the throne, Kellen. Don't you understand? She'll be dead within the year. You think Martius was the only one with a plan? Even with him gone, there will be others. Who will fight them? You? You think you can kill them all?'

'Just the first thousand. Then I'll give the others a chance to reconsider.'

'It doesn't have to be this way, Kellen,' she said, pleading with me. 'Come with me. We'll take Ginevra away from here. You'll sign the abdication and I will take power. With you at my side and Ginevra under my control I can keep the empire safe. I can keep her safe too. She can lead a normal life, be a normal girl, joyful and free.'

434

The queen spoke up. 'It is a lovely dream, cousin,' she said. 'But you forget – I am not a child. I embody the memories of two thousand years of Daroman rule. My destiny is to safeguard this nation. I was not born to play with dolls.'

'Don't listen to her, Kellen. She's been raised her entire young life to believe in that foolishness. Once she's with me – once she's with *us* – she'll soon learn to be a normal girl again. We can make her happy.' Mariadne leaned into me. 'I can make you happy, Kellen.'

'Countess, I've recently come to learn that searching for happiness by trying to fulfil one's own desires doesn't actually work nearly as well as one might expect.'

She looked into my eyes, challenging me. 'Ask me, Kellen Argos. Ask me for anything and it's yours.'

For an instant I was back in her home, Leonidas's blood still on me, the rush of having survived – of having won – filling me with pride. And then Mariadne, her gaze so full of wonder . . . . as if she were gazing upon one of the heroes of legend: '*Ask me, Kellen Argos. Ask me for anything and it is yours.*'

'Take your men, countess. Take them and return to Sarrix.'

She came close, wrapping her arms around me. 'And would that make you happy, Kellen? Truly?'

I leaned into that embrace, feeling the warmth of her body against mine, letting the scent of her hair fill my senses so completely that the world around us began to disappear. 'No,' I whispered into her ear. 'But do it anyway.'

I felt, rather than heard, the heavy sigh that came from somewhere deep inside her. Then she hugged me one last time and stepped back.

435

In her hands she held my holsters. I had to admire her technique. If nothing else.

'I'm sorry, Kellen,' she said.

The soldiers took a step forward and raised their weapons again.

'I have a confession to make,' I said.

'What?' Mariadne asked.

'Forgive me, your ladyship, but I wasn't talking to you.'

The queen, Ginevra, looked up at me with that impossibly trusting gaze of hers. Seemingly so young and naive, yet wise beyond anything I knew. She nodded as if giving me leave to continue.

'When we first met, that day in court when I was to be executed . . . ?'

She nodded again.

'I was going to murder you.'

Mariadne's eyes widened. The queen's didn't.

'I figured that if I could kill you before you passed sentence, I might be able to negotiate with whoever would take over. The thing about death is, someone always benefits. You just have to figure out who, and then cut a deal.'

'Yes,' the queen said drily. 'It's a wonder no one ever thought of that before.'

I smiled at that. She reminded me of Reichis sometimes. 'Stupid, I know. I mean, how could I ever hope to kill you when you had all those guards around you? There must have been a dozen marshals in that room. And me? Hells, I didn't have a sword or a knife. I didn't even have my holsters. All I had were dirty fingers. See, they'd taken away my powders, but never bothered making me wash my hands.' I held them up in the air. 'See? Positively covered in the stuff.'

436

Mariadne's expression changed from surprise to a kind of disappointment. 'Still a boy,' she said. 'Despite the scars and the shadowblack and everything you've seen and done, Kellen, you still dream of being the hero – not because it's what you want for yourself, but because you hear the voices of others whispering to you that you're not good enough as you are. Your mentor, the Argosi. That girl Nephenia . . .'

'Best you not mention Nephenia,' I said, my fingers already forming the somatic shapes. 'Thinking about her just reminds me of the man I'm supposed to be.'

Mariadne held her arms out wide. 'Go on then. Try your magic. I've made a number of inquiries about that spell of yours. The mages here explained how you use Jan'Tep breath magic to make that blast spell of yours work. When I asked why you mixed a dead man's tongue in one of the powders, the mages had a theory about that as well. But Erras loved me, Kellen. Loved me for who I am, not who I ought to be. Loved me so completely that he would never bring me harm, not in this life or any other.'

'Even if he knew what you had become?'

She smiled sadly. 'Even if he knew that, Kellen.'

'I guess you're probably right. The old man adored you. His spirit would never let the powders do their work against you.'

I brought my hands up and made the somatic form with each hand: bottom two fingers pressed into the palm, for restraint; fore and middle fingers pointed straight out, the sign of flight; and thumb pointing to the heavens. 'But I ran out of that powder earlier tonight, and had to brew a replacement.'

There was barely enough time for Mariadne's eyes to widen

437

before I flicked the powders from my fingertips into the air betwen us. '*Carath Colfax*,' I whispered, the invocation coming out colder than the north wind. It blew a hole through her chest just big enough to let the breeze pass through.

61

Mercy

Sergeant Tarius and the rest of his soldiers stared at Mariadne's corpse, momentarily paralysed with shock. Then the sergeant brought his sword up high in preparation to cleave my head from my shoulders. 'And then what?' I asked, as calmly as I could manage.

He froze. *Smart man*, I thought.

'You kill us and it's over for everyone,' I explained. 'No Martius to take power. No Leonidas to command the armies.' I looked down at Mariadne's body. 'No countess to protect you.'

The soldiers were looking to their leader, and at each other.

'Do you want to know what I see?' I asked. 'I see forty dead men running across the country looking for a place to hide. Forty corpses wondering what happens when one of them decides to sell his comrades to the marshals for a pardon. You all remember the marshals service, right? "Trajedam necri sodastium frigida." *The trail never runs cold.* With no Mariadne on the throne, who's going to stop them from coming for you? You've got no deals left to make. Whoever takes the throne is going to want to reassure the country that they're safe, that their queen has been avenged and, most of all, that

439

the men who killed her have suffered like no one else in Daroman history.'

Sergeant Tarius took a step back from us. 'If we stand down . . . ?' he asked.

The queen stepped forward. 'No deals. I will not pardon you. There is no punishment save death for men who betray their country.'

'Then . . .'

Tarius looked to me as if I might give him some consolation, so I did. 'You'll have to run,' I said. 'Get your families, if you have any, and go. Get out of the country. I've heard Tristia is nice in the autumn, if you can find a ship.'

'But the marshals—'

'They'll be busy, for a while,' I said. 'The queen plans to order them to find every noble involved in the conspiracy. Every *noble*,' I repeated for emphasis.

The sergeant looked at the queen. She looked at me, one eyebrow raised. 'Still boxing me into corners, master card player?'

'That's right, Your Majesty. Perhaps next time you'll think twice about hiring a convicted felon.'

She looked back to the leader of the soldiers and nodded once. 'Very well. I will instruct the marshals service to focus on bringing every noble involved in the conspiracy to justice. This should take some time, I imagine.'

Almost in unison the soldiers breathed a sigh of relief. I wondered how long that would last. I'd spent two years as an outlaw and that had been two years too long. I suspected a lifetime of it wouldn't agree with these men. One of the soldiers, a young man probably no older than I was, called out. 'We were only following orders,' he said. 'It all made sense. The queen being too young, the need for strength – for stability? What happens to the country if everything they told us is true? We didn't know what the right thing to do was.'

'You almost never do,' I said. Then I took the queen's little hand in mine, stepped over the dead guardsmen and walked her into the palace.

62

A Shadowblack Mark

Three weeks later, Reichis and I stood in the throne room before the queen. The squirrel cat's legs had mended nicely, thanks to the army of healers and a fortune's worth of aquae sulfex the marshals service had graciously paid for. It's funny how things turn around sometimes.

'Would you like to sit in my lap, master squirrel cat?' the queen asked. She looked much as she had the first day I met her – a full dress of embroidered gold with rose-coloured trim covering her body from the top of her neck to the bottom of her ankles. Martius and his wife had not been kind to her.

Reichis looked up at me. 'Ah, what the hell,' he said. He ambled over and climbed up her leg to her lap, causing her to giggle. She motioned to one of her guards, who produced a small wooden box, opened the lid and held it out for her. The queen reached inside and took out a butter biscuit, which she offered to Reichis. Within moments a fairly efficient routine of biscuit feeding was in place and the squirrel cat was making reasonably disgusting and self-satisfied moans of pleasure. In short order he finished them off and fell into a doze.

'You're going soft,' I said to him. I couldn't help but notice there were no butter biscuits for me.

The queen turned to the two guards standing behind her throne and nodded to them. They left us alone in the room. 'The servants tell me you've packed your bags.'

If she was trying to make me feel guilty, it was working. I'd as much as sworn to stay by her side, to let her be the goodness that seemed to be missing from me. But on that ride back to the palace I'd had to kill for her, and when we'd arrived, I'd as good as murdered a woman who, for a very brief moment, had let me feel what it would be like to love someone who could love me back as I was, not as I should've been. None of that had been the queen's fault of course. Such things never are. 'Reichis is doing better,' I said. 'I've recovered – mostly. The marshals seem to have things under control and now it's just a matter of parading nobles through court and up the gallows. It's time for me to go.'

The queen looked at me with those mysteriously wise eyes of hers. 'You blame me,' she said. It wasn't a question.

I couldn't deny it. Despite my own failures, despite everything, I did blame her, at least a little. 'This place has been nothing but pain and guilt, enemies and obligations,' I said. 'There's nothing here for me.'

'And what is it you want?' she asked.

'I think you know,' I said.

'The shadowblack. The white binder.'

I nodded. Even now, weeks after it happened, the feeling of being so completely under another man's control haunted me. I woke up at night struggling for air, dreaming that the binder had forgotten to make me breathe. The thought that

443

there were others, that it could happen again, was too much for me.

'What if I told you . . . ?' the queen began hesitantly. 'What if I promised that I would help you? Stay with me, work with me, and I will devote the resources of the empire to finding a way to cure the shadowblack. There are passages in books here in the library telling of men who could remove it.'

'With all due respect, Your Majesty, you used that line on me once already. I don't believe you would devote all your resources to curing one itinerant card player of the shadowblack. You've got an empire to run. You might want to keep your promise, but eventually expediency would outweigh optimism. I'd rather get a head start while I have the chance.'

'Why do you think I chose you, Kellen, that day when they brought you to me for execution?'

I smiled. 'You said I had a kind face.'

The queen smiled back at me. 'Yes, there was that. Did you really believe that was enough to make me trust my life to you? That I had no other choices?'

I'd wondered precisely that every day since I'd arrived. In the end, I'd had to conclude that she was simply desperate for someone who had no connections to the Daroman system of nobility and patronage and had gambled on me.

The queen gently picked up Reichis and set him down on the arm of her throne. She stood up and took a step towards me. She lifted one arm and reached around with her other hand to pull at the clasps of her dress.

Horrified, I spun away from her. 'What are you—'

'Do you know the Daroman ritual enacted when a ruler turns thirteen years of age, as I will in two years' time?'

444

I heard the faint click of another clasp coming apart. 'No, and I don't want to know, Your Majesty.' I couldn't imagine what she was thinking. I started to walk to the door.

'Stop,' she commanded.

'Whatever you think you're doing, I beg you, don't,' I said.

The click of another clasp opening echoed eerily across the marble chamber. 'When a Daroman ruler comes of age, there is a celebration in the capital. The people feast while dignitaries and diplomats of other nations come to witness the ceremony.'

Another clasp.

'It's a peculiar tradition, you see. The king or queen, in a show of profound humility, must stand before the Daroman people without their crown, without their royal vestments, without any clothes at all.'

'Your Majesty . . .'

'Naked,' she said.

I heard the light *swoosh* of fabric from the top of her dress slipping away.

'In two years, the people of Darome – the nobility, friend and foe alike, and even rulers of other nations – will see me as you are about to.'

'I will not,' I said.

'Turn around, Kellen,' she said.

I shook my head and prepared to walk away.

'Unholy squirrel cat gods, Kellen!' I heard Reichis chitter. 'She's—'

'No, master squirrel cat. Let him see for himself. Turn, Kellen Argos,' she repeated. Her command was so clear, so final, my head turned of its own accord.

The queen was standing with the top of her dress hanging

445

down like a drunken barmaid prompted by a patron's largess. She held her arms across her chest, covering herself but revealing the bare skin of her left side. There, just below her shoulder, was a winding blackness. Too detailed and fine to be a bruise, too familiar to be anything but what it was.

'Shadowblack,' I whispered.

She nodded. 'In two years time, Kellen, I will stand naked before the world, and they will see me. They will see this.'

Suddenly it all made sense. The tutors, their power – their utter lack of fear that she would turn on them. They knew, and kept that knowledge to themselves as leverage so they would have free rein to hurt her anytime they wanted to. That was why the queen had picked me. Not because I was a spellslinger, not because I was an Argosi and certainly not because I had a 'kind face'. She'd picked me for the same reason that no one else in the world would have. I was shadowblack. Like her.

Martius must have known. He'd had her under his control for days. Why not use Sophistus to force her to do his bidding? *Because he couldn't,* I realised then. *She's devoted her soul to her people.* Still, Martius could've made her shadowblack public. And yet he'd said nothing of it. Maybe it was true, what he'd sworn so passionately – that despite everything, he was a patriot. If his plan failed, he didn't want to launch the empire into chaos.

And chaos it would have been.

Even in a place like Darome, a queen with the shadowblack could never sit on the throne. A shadowblack is always an exile, always potential prey for those who think they can benefit. That's why a shadowblack is alone. Always.

And if another white binder came along?

446

I made my decision without even a thought. 'We should start right away,' I said, my voice barely audible to my own ears.

The queen said nothing, but simply nodded once before carefully doing up the clasps of her dress – the thin thread holding them her only protection from a world of enemies who believed they could take her down when the time came.

I would disabuse them of that notion.

63

The Dutiful Son

A few minutes later Reichis and I walked back to our rooms. The palace hallways still felt strangely empty – the combination of betrayals and reprisals having reduced both the palace guard and the nobility by substantial numbers. It was just Reichis and myself and the occasional potted plant lining the hallway. In an odd way, it made me feel safe.

'This place is giving me the creeps,' Reichis said.

'Really? The only people here are the ones the marshals trust the most. What are you afraid of? Ghosts?' I imagined him standing in front of some ghostly apparition, growling and cussing at it. 'No ghost defeats a squirrel cat,' he'd say. I snickered at my own joke until I realised he hadn't said anything back. 'Reichis?'

He was crouching near one of the plants, silently, like a dog who'd peed on the floor and was waiting for a beating from his master.

Crap. I flipped open my holsters. She had given me comfort in my darkest hour. She'd more than likely saved my life at great cost to herself. And yet I knew, even then, that whatever moment had taken place between us, no matter how much she loved me deep down, the yellow-haired girl was gone and the manipulative Jan'Tep diplomat was back. 'You can come out, Sha'maat,' I said.

'Whatever do you mean, dear brother?'

I spun around. She was close enough to touch me. 'How did you sneak up on me?' I asked.

She smiled and kissed me on the cheek. 'Daringly,' she said. 'Using dark and devious conjurations.'

I tried to think of what spell might have allowed her to do it, and how only my sister would be so vain as to risk her soul just to make an entrance.

She saw my expression and laughed before pointing down to her feet. They were bare. 'Dark magic indeed, dear brother.'

'I'm glad to see you haven't lost your taste for pointless games,' I said. 'But I'm surprised you'd show your face in the palace.'

'Oh? But why not? We were completely loyal to the queen during these events. Not one Jan'Tep sided with the conspirators.'

'Not that anyone can prove anyway.'

'More than that,' she said. 'My men and my spells helped kill the soldiers Martius left behind to hold the palace. Even now, the Jan'Tep are helping the queen to seek out Martius's accomplices.'

'And deciding which ones will be caught and which ones won't?'

She pouted. 'Oh, now don't be cross with me. I've come with a reward. Father is pleased with you.'

'Somehow I doubt that.'

'He gave me a message,' she said. She hugged me and whispered in my ear. 'You have honoured your family, Ke'helios.'

For a long time I just stood there. *Ke'helios.* My father had given me a mage's name. Why in the world would he do that? What had I done to . . . *Ancestors.* The day Sha'maat first appeared at court, she'd delivered his commands: *'You'll learn the queen's secrets for us and, when the time is right, you'll kill the countess.'*

I'd done precisely what Ke'heops had ordered me to do. Mariadne was dead and the queen had just revealed her deepest secret to me. Had Sha'maat and my father tricked me into doing their bidding? That day, in the cell beneath the palace – had my sister truly been defying Ke'heops to help me, or had it all been another one of her manipulations?

I remained there like a burnt tree stump until she was gone. Reichis growled and got to his feet and we started walking towards our room. 'You know something, Kellen?'

'What?'

'I know she's your sister and all . . .'

'Yeah?'

'But twice now that bitch has used her skinbag magic to put me to sleep. She's starting to bug me.'

I chewed on that for a moment. 'Me too, partner.'

Reichis paused in the hallway beside a potted plant and pissed against it. 'I might need to kill her one of these days, Kellen.'

'I suppose that might be inevitable,' I said.

He started ambling down the hall. There was a little spring in his step. 'Come to think of it, we should probably kill all of them, just to be safe.'

'My whole family?'

'Well, yeah, as a start. But think bigger.'

'What? No Jan'Tep at all?' I asked.

'Nope.'

450

'What about the Zhuban?'

He stopped for a second and scratched his snout. 'Nutjobs. We should probably kill them too.'

'Daroman?'

'Yep.'

'Gitabrians?'

'You mean those poncy contraptioneers who nearly sucked my soul out so they could stick it inside some stupid metal dragon? Let's murder them first.'

'So,' I said, 'just you and me then.'

The little squirrel cat looked up at me and grinned. 'On an island?'

'We can let some of the islanders live though, right?'

'Sure. We'll need someone to pour our drinks.'

It was my turn to smile. 'And feed you butter biscuits?'

'Oooh, butter biscuits,' Reichis said, as if I'd just invented the wheel. 'Hey, do you think they restocked the ones in the baths yet?'

'Only one way to find out, partner.'

We turned on our heels and started back the other way, towards the baths. Reichis gave a grunt. 'If there's another stinkin' langzier in there, you get to throw yourself in front of it this time.'

I stopped and watched my strange, furry little business partner saunter down the hall as if he owned the place. I would too, I realised. If something or someone came after Reichis, I'd throw myself in front of them.

That thought made me strangely happy.

Acknowledgements

The Band of Outlaws

Writing can be lonely out there on the long roads, and turning the first spark of an idea into the finished book you're holding in your hands sometimes feels as risky as trying to steal magic from the gods. Putting together a book is a lot like pulling off a bank heist: it helps if you've got the right bunch of rogues helping to crack the safe.

THE BRAINS

'I got a plan, see? A real good one. Gonna make a big score right under the noses of them flat-footed coppers.'

The earliest version of *Queenslayer* was written before the first four books in the series, back in that more innocent, bygone era of summer 2011. My good friend Eric Torin and I had planned on writing a book together and thus spent countless dinners tossing ideas back and forth, pitching characters and settings, debating who Kellen should be and who he could become. Eric ultimately decided the project wasn't right for him, but never stopped helping me, listening, reading, and always pressing me to give the stories and characters more depth. One day you're going to read a book by Eric Torin. You'll be amazed.

When I look back at 2011, before I had a book deal or an agent, and realise that it was one of a hundred novel concepts I'd made my wife Christina listen to, I'm reminded of just how valuable it is to have someone in your life who treats your idiotic ideas as if each one might be a diamond in the rough. I hope you have someone like that in your life, because I honestly don't think I'd have become a writer without Christina in mine.

LOOKOUTS

'Gotta keep a close watch, see? One tiny mistake and this whole operation is blown to hell.'

I'm pretty sure I'd make the world's worst bank robber. I'm terrible with details, leap ahead without looking and, so far as I can recall, I've never come up with a decent backup plan in my life. You can succeed that way sometimes, but only if you're lucky enough to have the right people watching your back.

My fellow writers Kim Tough (kimtough.com), Brad Dehnert (bradleydehnert.com), Wil Arndt (wfgordon.com), Claire Ryan (claireryanauthor.com), and Jim Hull from Narrative First (narrativefirst.com) made me fix all the boring bits so you wouldn't have to read them.

Kathryn Zeller beta-read the original version of the book, spotting one of the most glaring story problems and prompting me to fix it in a way that made it all so much better. Simone Hay, official arbiter of all things squirrel cat, once again lent her careful eye to the story to make sure Reichis got his due. Nazia Khatun, an *actual* squirrel cat, helped me make sure that when I smoothed some of the rougher edges in the story I nonetheless kept the dramatic intention behind them.

Felicity Alexander, my kind and eternally patient editor at Hot Key Books, helped me work through some of the most challenging scenes in the book and helped me make sure it fitted properly within the overall series. Talya Baker, as always, caught my endless bits of repetition, endless bits of repetition (hah – didn't catch *that* one, did you, Talya?) and brought sparkle and flow to any number of passages in the text where I'd gotten myself lost in mediocrity. Melissa Hyder proofread the novel, and caught every single one of my spleling mistakes.

MASTERS OF DISGUISE

'Quick, put these on. Gotta look the part or we'll get nabbed for sure!'

How many great books don't get a chance to find readers just because the covers aren't right? The answer, in my particular case, is none. That's because Art Director Extraordinaire Nick Stearn steers the design process, leading artists like Sam Hadley on the covers and Sally Taylor on those gorgeous Daroman outlaw cards inside the book itself. Jamie Taylor then takes all those pictures and text and carefully crafts them into the book you're holding in your hands.

SAFECRACKERS

'You wanna bust in there? That place is locked up tighter than Fort Knox! Nobody can crack that safe. Nobody!'

Well, actually, *somebody* can. In the case of *Spellslinger* it was my wonderful agents (aka blackmailers) Heather Adams and Mike Bryan, whose reputation for the putting the right book in the hands of the right publisher meant that Mark Smith, then CEO of Bonnier Zaffre, and Jane Harris, Director of Hot Key Books, not only bought the series but gave it the kind of support authors dream about.

GETAWAY DRIVERS

'Pedal to the metal, everybody! We gots ta get the diamonds outta here before the coppers arrive!'

Scoring the perfect heist isn't worth a thing unless you can get the goods into the right hands. The inexhaustible Bonnier Zaffre sales team keep on convincing bookstores to carry the series. If you're reading this book in a language other than English, it's because the indefatigable Ruth Logan and Ilaria Tarasconi found the perfect publishers for it in your country. Those publishers, in turn, selected the amazing translators who transmute all my idioms and stylistic quirks into your language.

The scariest thing about being an author? You can do all that – have all those amazing people helping bring your book to life – and still have it fall flat. That's because books only thrive when the folks working in bookstores happen to read them and recommend them to their customers, when journalists and bloggers take what precious little time they have and devote some of it to your book and, most of all, when readers discover something they love and share it with friends, family and colleagues. So thank you, each and every one. You're a damned fine bunch of outlaws!

THE NEXT HEIST . . .

As I write these rather lengthy acknowledgements, I'm also busily preparing *Crownbreaker*, the sixth and final book in Kellen's journey. Crafting a six-book fantasy series in which each story has to be complete in itself and yet inextricably part of a greater whole, and set in a world filled with different peoples, cultures, magic systems and no end of intrigues, is exactly as hard as it sounds. Only two things keep me going: the first is the ineffable delight of making something that, if I do my job well, is both entertaining and meaningful. The second is my anticipation of putting that final book in your hands in hopes that you enjoy it as much as I do.

In the meantime, you can reach me at www.decastell.com and @decastell on Twitter. I'll always be happy to hear from you.

Sebastien de Castell
January 2019
Vancouver, Canada

Thank you for choosing a Hot Key book.

If you want to know more about our authors
and what we publish, you can find us online.

You can start at our website

www.hotkeybooks.com

And you can also find us on:

We hope to see you soon!